NATALIE COLBURN

A Call For Blood

THE CROWNING GAMES

Praise For
A Call For Blood

"Love the complex characters and dynamic world building; the suspense kept me on the edge of my seat... beautifully written!"
~ *Berlyn Hayes, author of Heirs of Secrets*

"Secret plots, lovable characters, a fight against a corrupt government, and plots bigger than the main characters know... A Call For Blood has that and more!"
~ *Tommie Michele, author of the Drafted series*

"For readers of the Hunger Games and Red Queen, welcome to your next highly enjoyable read!"
~ *Kayla Ann, author of Well of Dreams*

A Call For Blood

Book Cover by Natalie Colburn

Limited Edition Covers by Susanna Fullerton

Developmental Edits by Kelly at SkyBoundEditing

Line Edits by Danielle Harrington

To David, thanks for being an awesome big little brother.

CHAPTER ONE

Keith

AS I STEP THROUGH the doorway, a blast of frigid air stings my bare face. Goosebumps travel over my arms, covered by a sweater and a thick wool overcoat. For a brief second, I hover on the doorstep of our house and debate whether or not I want to run back in and grab a third layer. Or maybe I'm just trying to postpone today.

Camille makes the decision for me.

My sister links her arm with mine, pulling me outside. Her natural warmth seeps through my clothing, and I move closer to her. Her slight smile is contagious, and soon I'm smiling instead of wincing.

"It's not too cold for you, is it?" Her teasing voice is light and happy.

I attempt to keep mine the same. "Definitely not." My body involuntarily shivers.

Camille laughs, shaking her head. "Oh, definitely not."

1

I make an effort to join in her laughter, even throwing in a wink.

I know she sees through my façade. She knows me too well not to, but instead of calling me out, she gives me an understanding smile.

Her focus shifts to the sky, and I follow her gaze. There's a gray blanket of what appears to be snow clouds that's made its home above our small town, Salcoast of the Gulf. The sun is barely peeking over the horizon, as if it also doesn't want to face today.

Camille lets her jade green eyes close, and she looks surprisingly at peace. Her only protection from the wicked breeze is a simple, light, deep green cloak. Her hood remains down, revealing her rich black hair, which falls over her shoulders in waves. I don't know how she manages to appear as relaxed as she does. A part of me wants to pull her back inside and hide her from today.

My father soon follows us out of our house. His brown eyes, similar in shade to mine, lack their usual warmth, and it isn't just due to the cold. I give him a hint of a smile, and his eyes soften slightly. His medium-length, dark hair lies uncombed. He's dressed more similarly to me—in layers of clothing—versus Camille who wears only a cloak. It helps to reassure me that I'm not overexaggerating the cold.

"Are the two of you ready?" My father's voice is rough, as if he's having a hard time speaking.

At his words, Camille's eyes flick open.

"Ready as I'll ever be," I say.

Camille gives me a sideways grin, detecting my sarcasm.

My father leads us down our front yard and onto the streets. From Camille's tight grip on my arm, I can tell she's more nervous than she's letting on. I try to give her a reassuring look, but it falls flat.

The streets have been decorated well for today's occasion. Silver and black banners hang from almost every shop's eaves, and their walls are adorned in matching streamers and twine. Certain people have even dressed up, evident in their different shades of silver, gray, and black clothing. Hollow-faced children run through the streets, weaving in and out of the crowd, their anxious parents calling after them. Some, especially the younger children, have genuine smiles on their faces, while others, like my father, don't try to hide their displeasure. A deep scowl is etched on his face as we integrate into the crowd, our feet joining the hundreds of others that hit the cobbled road.

Officers, dressed head to toe in perfectly groomed uniforms, stand out as tall, looming figures. Their masked faces survey the crowd, ready to restrain any insurgents with deep purple cuffs made of Nightrock hanging from their belts. I've never witnessed an officer use the cuffs on someone with a gift, but my father warned me about them. It would remove an individual's ability to access their gift, blocking the flow of power.

Those under the age of fifteen will be dropped off in the building just outside the arena. At least Central has the decency to hide the activities of today from the youngest children. The crowd all moves in the same direction, as we have for our entire lives.

Today is Combatant Day.

It is a reminder of the iron fist the king holds over the country. As law-abiding citizens, we won't have to fear for our lives. We'll be allowed to watch from the safety of our seats while those who've been detained in prison this year are forced into the arena to fight whatever beast or champion Central decides to throw at them.

There will be rounds, of course, and champions are hand-selected by the king himself, each picked because of their unique gifts and skills. They'll be put up against prisoners who've been beaten and starved due to their time spent in a local cell or one of the prisons in the Shadows. I haven't missed a Combatant Day since turning fifteen, as decreed by law. Being seventeen, I've gone two years, and both times the arena has reminded me of a slaughterhouse. Prey animals, penned up with no way of escaping, while the butchers lead them to their fate. The only difference between the two is that at least the animals die with purpose. In the arena, people are dying simply for breaking the law. Oftentimes their only crime is petty thievery to steal food for the many hungry mouths at home. That's why a real smile is hard to spot amongst the older faces as we all move to watch people be brutally murdered.

However, Camille's face bursts into a true grin as she spots Michael and Lizzy waiting for us further down the street. Michael notices us and begins walking against the crowd. My father and I trail behind Camille as she rushes to greet Lizzy with a warm hug and Michael with a shy smile. We've known them both for as long as I can remember, and our families have always been extremely close. Even my father has regained some warmth in his expression at the sight of the two friendly faces.

"How are you kids doing?" My father manages to almost sound like his normal self as he ruffles Michael's hair.

Michael tries for a smile. "I know I'm supposed to say good, but it doesn't feel right."

I understand what he means. It's only been a little over a year since Michael and Lizzy's father had been arrested. It hadn't been a surprise to hear that he'd been stealing during one of the seasonal markets, but the realization that we would have to witness his death in the arena was much worse.

Last year had been Lizzy's first Combatant Day, and she had to watch as her father's blood was spilled within the very arena that looms ominously in the distance. It's something I know Michael finds unforgivable, and quite honestly, I agree. Add it to the list of deplorable and inexcusable acts of King Edward of Myria.

"Hopefully it will be over quickly this year," I say quietly enough so that the closest officer won't overhear. Camille still shoots me a dark look like she always does whenever any of us do or say something even remotely rebellious.

"I couldn't agree more." Lizzy exhales deeply. "Let's get to it shall we?"

She gently pushes me forward, leaving Michael to walk with Camille behind us and our father to bring up the rear. Lizzy and I share a smile. I know exactly what she's doing. It's been pretty obvious that Michael and Camille have a thing for each other, but neither of us really know when it started. I like Michael, but I still glance behind me as we walk.

He better never harm her.

As we near the arena, the crowd and the decorations adorning the shops begin to thicken. The walls have come into clear view now, and the smooth brick has been covered by larger-than-life-size posters of the king's competitors. Each one depicts a clear picture of his or her face as well as the champion's name and gift. The one facing us is a girl with long, medium-length brown hair, tied back into double Dutch braids. In her hand, she threateningly brandishes a long knife with a sword still strapped to her waist. But the most unnerving part is her eyes—malicious and bent on causing harm, with golden specks thrown onto her dark green irises.

The elegant text displayed says her name is Sabrina Pelos and that she's a metal wielder. I've always found it funny the way our country decides to group our gifts, which are all varied in skill and talent. Being a "metal wielder" could mean anything from being able to control any metal object to being an extremely skilled black-smith. Considering that she's competing in the arena, I'm positive it's something deadly.

After twenty minutes of small talk and walking, the five of us finally reach the entrance to the arena, where the population of officers seems to quadruple in size. They line the entire wall of the arena and the entrance hallway. I exchange a look with Lizzy and even glance back to confirm with my father. The arena has always been well guarded, but I can't remember there ever being *this* many officers.

The crowd begins to split off, each picking their respective entrance. Guards line the walkway, but there are only two guards positioned directly in front of our door. I've always been bad at remembering faces, but these two are very distinct. The man has a tattoo running down his face, even visible beneath his helmet. I can't quite make out what it is, but the ink paired with his electric blue eyes makes him memorable. He's a lie detector, gifted with the ability to know if someone else is lying. Of course, I don't know if that's the official name for it, but I think my title is descriptive enough.

The woman is tall, even taller than me. She has bright pink hair that spills out from underneath her helmet. As the couple in front of us moves to pass through the doors, she places a hand on each of their shoulders. Her eyes flutter shut before they spring back open, and she gestures them through. From past years, I figure she's searching us for weapons—something like a human metal detector.

As the grand oak doors are held open for the couple, the sounds of cheering, yelling, and talking float through the air.

Lizzy steps forward, and I step out of the way so Michael can join her.

Tattoo smiles. "What are your names?"

"Elizabeth Lanzo."

"Michael Lanzo."

The interrogation contains only a few more questions, simple and easy to answer if someone has nothing to hide. The two of them are let in through the doors without hesitation from either of the officers. Then it's our turn.

The questions, again, are simple enough. What are our names, what region of the Gulf are we from, and have we attended before? The final question isn't as easy as it should have been.

"Do any of you want to cause problems in the arena today?" Tattoo's smile fades, which honestly, I find less threatening than his false look of friendliness.

Camille and I both repeat the same line.

"No, sir."

My father's words sound choked as he struggles to spit the words out. "No, sir."

Camille and I immediately tense. I take a step toward my sister because even without a gift, I recognize the lie in my father's words.

Tattoo's frown only deepens, and through the slits in his helmet, I watch a single eyebrow raise. But instead of calling to the other officers stationed at the wall, he only waves a hand forward. The oak doors are already propped open for us, leading into the main arena, which overflows with people making their way to their assigned seats. Camille and I follow silently behind our father, both clenching each other's hand.

It doesn't help ease the tension flowing throughout my whole body when Camille gently nudges my side with her elbow.

"The woman didn't touch us."

CHAPTER TWO

Keith

IT DOESN'T TAKE LONG to find our seats. Our father is an honored instructor at one of the nearby schools, lumping us with the other respected members of the Southern Gulf and granting us floor-level seats. Our seats are directly to the right of a slightly elevated booth, which is strictly reserved for if the king and his family decide to visit our arena this year.

Lizzy and Micheal's family used to have seats right next to us, but when their father died a criminal and their mother fell incredibly sick—terminally ill the doctors labeled it—they were demoted and given seats further up, farther away from the arena floor. Our seats are perfectly positioned to give us a spectacular view of all the killing.

Lucky us.

The arena itself is huge, and the amount of seats placed in rings on top of rings fill the entire building—stopping only where the edges of the roof start to curve inward.

There is a gaping hole directly above the center of the arena, letting in a pool of light to brighten the whole stadium. Directly to our left is the slightly raised booth reserved for the royal family. Every year, they appear at one of the Combatant Day arenas, each strategically placed in the unique sectors of Myria. The Shadows, the sector where the worst criminals are held, and Central, where the king and the royal family reside, are the only two sectors without an arena. The Shadows, because all its citizens are usually the ones spirited off to compete and die in the arena, and Central, because it's too bloody of a scene for the esteemed citizens most loyal to the king.

From what I learned during my years at school, there are three arenas constructed in the Gulf. As the largest sector, both land and population-wise, the Gulf requires more arenas than the other sectors to ensure everyone can attend. It's also the only sector that directly borders the Myradian Sea, and therefore, provides the rest of Myria with its portion of ocean delicacies, which we never receive ourselves. It's all shipped off to Central in crates, and in return, we get minimal, rough meat, the product of large stock from somewhere I honestly don't know. My father always reassures Camille and me that eating the meat is better than starving to death like those in the Lates—the laboring sector—often do.

I am not sure how he knows stuff like that, and I've never asked. My father's tone is always so shut off when he speaks about it. I know some things about the other sectors. For instance, the Gust is the favored sector in Myria. It's full of the rich and people with talented gifts. But how different could the Lates be from the Gulf? Either way, Camille and I learned never to complain about the quality or amount of food on our plates.

As I take my place between my father and my sister, I try to calm my nerves. My father hasn't spoken since the incident at the entrance, and Camille has been just as silent. The peace she held this morning has faded under the tension dancing around our father's straight back. Her fingernails have been chewed to the quick, almost drawing blood. I gently reach out and grab for her hand as I see her attempt to continue chewing.

"Don't bite your fingers off."

Camille manages a smile and rolls her eyes. "I won't." Still, she proceeds to chew on her bottom lip. "I just hope *he* doesn't do anything crazy. With as much security that's here, the three of us would be dead in an instant." Her voice is barely above a murmur as she jerks her head in our father's direction.

I give her hand a reassuring squeeze. "I know. I'm sure it'll all be alright."

Camille gives me the side-eye. "I hope you're right. I'd prefer to live through the day."

Before I can respond, the horns blast through the arena, and a heavy silence fills the stadium. An empty moment passes as we wait in dreadful anticipation for the first combatants to enter the arena, but no one ever comes. Instead, a new horn sound fills the air, this one louder and more powerful than the first. From the gap in the ceiling, cameras zoom in, some surveying the crowd and the others focusing on the booth directly to our left.

I stifle a groan of despair as the King and Queen of Myria walk through the curtains, arm in arm. Behind them enter their two children, Prince Jacob and Princess Amaia.

Prince Jacob appears relaxed, with a smug grin on his face as he looks down upon the crowd. Princess Amaia, on the other hand, stands with her back straight and her head carefully surveying the stadium. Their presence explains the ridiculous amount of security. Even as they walk through, more guards flank each member of the royal family, providing a protective circle around the royal booth. The silver lining in their uniforms distinguishes these personal guards from the rest of the city officers.

The silence is broken as the majority of the crowd gains their composure and begins to cheer for the royal family. I clap as I know I should, and Camille follows my lead. My father remains still and unmoving, the only sign of his pleasure being the wide smile that breaks his otherwise stoic face. It's almost more unnerving than his previous silence. As everyone stands and cheers—us included—Camille shoots me a worried look, and I return it.

As long as I can remember, the king has never decided to visit our side of the Gulf. Of course it would be today out of all days—the day that my father lied to the officer.

"Please, just relax Dad," I mutter under my breath.

He glances down at me and takes a deep breath.

"Listen, they're right there. They'll know if you do anything or act off," I say.

His shoulders relax, but he still doesn't clap or cheer.

"Dad, please." My voice is louder now, more desperate. "Camille and I are worried for you. For us."

This makes him look down at me again, and this time, his eyes are softer. He nods and brings his hands together once, just in time for the king to raise his hands, signaling us to take a seat. I slump down into my chair and release a deep breath. I only hope my dad can hold it together.

"Thank you all for joining us on this very lovely morning!" The king's voice is amplified throughout the whole arena, and from the lack of a microphone, it must be the product of someone's magical gift. "My family and I are pleased to be here as we all watch those who have committed crimes against us, the lawbreakers and the wrongdoers who were not content with abiding by my instructions! As they will soon see, they are far outnumbered by citizens who are loyal to me and my crown. They are outnumbered by you!" He pauses, giving the crowd a chance to cheer. We follow his lead, clapping and cheering. My father concedes a few claps, which is better than nothing. Still, Camille shoots him a frustrated look.

His speech goes on, and I stop paying attention, only watching to know when to cheer. Instead, I focus on the two royal children, each positioned next to their respective parent. Prince Jacob shadows the king, and Princess Amaia stands behind the queen. As the king speaks, the prince seems to grow even more relaxed, even occasionally raising his fist along with the crowd. The princess, on the other hand, remains passive, boredom sliding onto her face. Her fingers play lazily with a loose thread on her throne's cushion as if she's heard this speech a thousand times.

I suppose that might very well be the case.

Despite her blatant lack of interest, her sharp blue eyes still search the crowd as if she's looking for someone or something. And yet, her eyes don't move in our direction once.

When the king finishes his speech, Camille gently elbows my side, getting my attention. As the royal family sits in their plush thrones, another horn blasts, and the first combatant enters the arena.

She's a small, willowy girl, not older than seven, with dark shadows underneath her eyes. Pain is written clearly across her haggard face. Poking out from beneath the thin rag that clings to her body are her prominent hip bones, visibly displaying her starvation. She may have once had bright green eyes and lively brown hair, but they have since faded, both dull and lifeless. Deep purple Nightrock cuffs hug her wrists, draining energy away from her to suppress a gift she likely hasn't developed yet. Despite everything, she still holds onto a small dagger with a grip so tight I'm shocked the weak wooden handle hasn't snapped.

I fight back the tears that threaten to spill down my face, and Camille's eyes widen in horror. I wish I could whisk my sister away and hide her from the scene.

My previous fake smile slips, and I refuse to join in the crowd's jeering. It takes everything in me to hold back the vomit rising in my throat. I risk a glance at my father, and his face is nothing but stone. Suddenly, I no longer feel upset with my father's visible anger. Camille clutches my arm, a spark of heat stinging me through my jacket. Her jaw is clenched in anticipation, finally witnessing the true brutality of today.

From across the arena, a wide grate creaks open. The whole arena hears the harsh growl even before the fuming lion emerges. The animal looks just as starved as the little girl, its ribcage jutting out beneath its yellow-orange hide. Its fur itself looks mangy, like maybe it has some affliction that is causing it to fall out. With one glance, I already know this is not going to be a pretty sight.

Instead of watching the starving beast tear into the little girl, I fix my gaze on the royal family. More specifically, the princess. One glance at the king and his son, with their looks of pure glee, and I know if I look at them any longer, I'd be the one launching myself across our seats instead of my father.

Princess Amaia's mouth is set in a hard, disapproving line. Her arms are folded across her chest, and she sits half slumped in her chair as if she can't bring herself to sit straight up and observe the arena. Her eyes are locked on the bright blue sky peeking through the roof. Her mother rests a comforting hand on her daughter's knee. As if sensing my stare, the princess glances down at me and then immediately looks back into the sky.

After the haggard little girl—who barely manages to scar the lion with her dagger—is shredded to pieces and devoured, the next round continues without pause. As the rounds go by, and the king's weapons of choice against the prisoners are revealed, Camille focuses her gaze on her folded hands, fixating on her fingers. I grit my teeth in frustration that my little sister has to sit through this.

My father only grows more and more tense, his body stiff as a board and his eyes locked on a spot across the arena. My mind keeps itself distracted, counting the chairs in the upper levels.

The last round doesn't come fast enough, signaled by the final horn melody. This time, it's a group of five grown men against one of the king's champions. Her face is familiar, and I realize she's the girl who was displayed on the poster outside.

Sabrina Pelos.

Even though the men are armed to the teeth and out-number her, it isn't even close to a fair fight. True to the poster, Pelos can control the metal weapons the men try to brandish against her. She spends the majority of the fight toying with them, torturing them by allowing them to believe they have a fighting chance. But still, all five of them end dead in the dirt.

As the arena is cleared, the king rises again, and the crowd, as if under his control, begins their deafening cheers. Camille and I reluctantly bring our hands together, obeying the king's wishes. Our father doesn't, but I can't bring myself to plead with him this time—not with the first little girl's face still etched into my brain. The nearest officer, standing at attention, notices my father's refusal. Reaching for the gun at his belt, the officer begins to walk toward us.

"This concludes this year's Combatant Day." King Edward speaks directly into the camera now focused on his face. "Until next year."

Before I can react, before the cameras have fully flickered off, and before Camille can exclaim a word of warning, my father has already moved. A knife that was stored deep in his thick coat flies through the air. I watch as it soars in an elegant arc directly toward the king's head.

Instead of making contact, the king's head swivels, and the knife hits the throne with an echoing thud. The entire arena goes silent. Camille whimpers in fear while my mouth falls open.

My father tried to assassinate King Edward.

And failed.

Camille

EXACTLY SEVEN YEARS AGO. That was the last time I saw my mother.

It had been an eerie morning to begin with. When I'd woken up and looked out of my window, the streets were silent. Even on December mornings, I could always count on a handful of wild children making their way to the schoolhouse—or maybe some older folks on a relaxing stroll. But no, that morning, it was absolutely silent.

Keith and Mom were already awake when I dragged myself to the kitchen. Keith was warming up the last of our eggs, and Mom was rinsing off the plates from our dinner last night. They both had their running shoes laced on and were shedding grains of sand from their daily run on the beach.

As soon as I walked in, I could tell something was wrong. They weren't talking or bantering like normal. Mom didn't have her signature warm smile, and Keith didn't give his normal "Good morning, Cam" that I had become so used to. My father wasn't far behind me, emerging from his bedroom with a frown and furrowed eyebrows.

His footsteps were louder than mine, and Mom looked up.

"Good morning, my love." Her smile was back.

My father wrapped her up in a warm hug, and I could almost see him using his gift to share his emotions of love with his wife. "Good morning." He pressed a kiss on the top of her head.

Then he reached and ruffled Keith's hair with a wink. "Good morning kiddos."

Keith brushed our father's hand off of his shoulder. I thought that maybe Keith and Mom had gotten into an argument, and that was why he was in such a sour mood.

How very wrong I was.

The officers came right after breakfast. The harsh knock shook our little shack, and the door looked like it was going to come clean off its hinges. My father was out of his seat in seconds. Mom caught his arm and gave him a tight smile. Keith reached for my hand and gripped it so tight I thought it was going to fall off.

I hadn't known it at the time, but Mom had already told Keith about what was happening on their walk that morning.

The tension in the air clung to me like a second skin. I could feel my body rising in temperature as my heart began to race faster than normal. I must have instinctively reached out to my mom because she shot me a hard glare.

"Camille. Stay in control."

I blushed and focused on keeping my gift to myself, like Mom had instructed me to. That was the one thing she got on me for, always insisting that no one could know I already developed my gift—not even Keith.

The officers didn't wait. They burst through the door, their guns raised high. Five of them entered, and a crash sounded, signaling another five coming through the back door.

Keith's eyes started pooling tears, and I pulled him into a hug. We sat like that, our dining chairs positioned close, holding each other as two officers pinned our father's hands behind his back, and the rest moved to circle Mom.

Almost in a panic, she looked over at me and placed her hands on my shoulders. "Stay in control," she repeated. "Stay alive."

And then they ripped her arms away. Keith jumped up as if to fight back. I tightened my little arms around his waist, willing him to remain next to me. He yelled, screaming at the officers as they clasped the Nightrock cuffs on Mom's wrists and dragged her out of the house. She bit her lip, holding back tears. Still, her watery green eyes never left mine, and I knew what she was trying to communicate.

Don't fight. Stay alive. Don't lose control. It'll all be okay.

The officers left as quickly as they had come. My father stood perfectly still, watching the door as if willing Mom to come back. Keith and I broke into tears, and I was probably burning up or freezing cold. Keith must have blamed it on the emotions or a sickness, because he never mentioned it to me again.

That process is protocol for those who aged past thirty and still have not developed a gift. They are considered a waste of King Edward's resources—not that I understood that seven years ago.

The level of terror that eight-year-old me felt then was nothing compared to what I am feeling now as I watch the king rip the knife out from his throne.

I'm almost positive no one in the arena has drawn breath.

I know I certainly haven't.

Instead, I'm gripping Keith's hand like a lifeline while he stands in shock. A million scenarios run through my head—the first being me standing up and finishing off the king. With a single thought I could burn him from the inside out. Or give him a physically frozen heart. The idea is tempting.

I look at my dad, his eyes blazing in anger. He would probably encourage it.

But my mom's words come back to me. "Stay in control. Stay alive."

If I were to lash out at the king, that would be signing my death wish. *That is, if I'm not dead already.* In an arena full of officers, I don't stand a chance of making it out. And neither does Keith. Even though my father seems to have disregarded our safety, I can't put Keith and myself in even more danger. So I push my emotions outward, letting them float away in the form of my gift, creating an insignificant increase in the temperature of the air.

Officers flood to our seats, barking orders, and it breaks the crowd out of their frozen silence. Some people are screaming, and those sitting closest to us scramble to get as far away from our father as possible. I don't blame them. He likely just got us all sentenced to death—and he didn't even succeed in his assassination attempt.

My only response is to cling to Keith as he moves to block me from view. We both jump as a piercing scream cuts through the air. King Edward is kneeling on the floor, visible tears streaming down his face. I suck in my breath as I recognize my father's look of concentration.

He's using his gift, worming his way into the king's head to fill it with every single emotion of pain and devastation he is feeling. I've never seen my father use his gift so brutally, and it's terrifying. But his victory is short-lived as officers clamp Nightrock cuffs on his wrists and drag him into the arena. All the cameras have now gone out.

The queen kneels beside her husband, keeping a hand on his back. King Edward slowly rises to his feet, rage boiling in his dark blue eyes.

"Silence." It's only a single word, but the entire crowd goes quiet, sinking back into their seats with the help of the officers fighting to keep them under control. His voice is deathly calm as he continues. "Who is this man?"

The officers share looks of matched confusion, and my father saves them the trouble of answering.

"My name is Andrew Atwood, sir. And we are tired of living under—" His voice breaks off as an officer socks him in the jaw. I can hear the crack echo around the arena.

The king smiles pleasantly at our father, his gaze not moving as he points a finger. "Grab the children."

My father flinches and wrestles with the officers, but I don't understand his attempt at defending us. Did he think they would let us go?

Keith pushes me farther back behind him, but I know it's futile. They have us pinned in seconds, and it's pointless to fight.

The Nightrock cuffs pinch against my wrists, and I almost cry out as I feel the immediate draining effects. Instinctively, I reach for my gift, but it's gone. I can't remember a time it hasn't been there for me to rely on. My body shivers against the sudden blast of harsh, cold air.

"Don't touch her!" Keith snarls.

I want to shake my head at him, but I can't even make the effort to raise my head. He's struggling against the three officers who effortlessly restrain him. I'm not shocked that the Nightrock has no effect on him.

King Edward's laugh pounds through my head. "Oh? Do we have another fighter? Like father, like son?"

His joking tone hits me the hardest. This is it. I'm going to die.

Keith curls a lip and elbows an officer in the stomach. He grunts in pain. In return, another officer knocks him over the head with the butt of his gun. Keith crumples to the ground, and that's when I find my will to fight. I try to scratch at the officer restraining me, but from his deep laugh, I know I look pathetic.

The officers drag us to stand next to our father. Well, to say we're standing would be generous. I'm placing all of my weight on the officer who is restraining me, and Keith is lying in a heap on the floor.

"Citizens of the Gulf!" The king's booming voice is seriously worsening my headache. "Let the Atwood family be an example for you. Despite Mr. Andrew's most excellent attempt at ending my life, he failed. Miserably." The last word is drawn out.

Through half-lidded eyes, I glance up at the royal family. Only the king seems to be taking such pleasure in the show. Prince Jacob is studying the floor, his eyebrows furrowed. Princess Amaia is sitting straight in her chair, looking like she wants to tackle her father. Even his wife, the queen, looks uneasy.

"And for that, Mr. Andrew will most certainly die." My father doesn't even flinch. "But not today. Sadly, the cameras have missed this spectacular twist of events, and I would hate for the rest of Myria to miss out on the opportunity to witness his brutal death. Yet, Combatant Day has officially ended, and waiting until next year seems much too tiresome. There will be a public execution just for Andrew Atwood so all attention may be on him, since that is clearly what he desires." He flicks a finger, and the officers begin to drag my father away.

My father, on the other hand, has other plans.

He plants his feet in the dirt and shoulders one of the officers to the ground. They skirmish, but my father can't fight against a seemingly never-ending supply of captors. King Edward smiles.

With a bleeding mouth and a nasty gash on his forehead, my father still forces himself to face the king. "What about my children?" His voice cracks, and I realize he either really believed he would succeed or severely underestimated the king's bloodthirst. It doesn't make me feel any better.

King Edward's smile grows, splitting across his entire face. "You will never know." My father viciously shakes his head, his eyes wide with panic. "Now remove this man from my presence."

My father still struggles, but he's dragged out of the arena in the direction all the other prisoners entered to face their death. Now the king's rage has nowhere to focus except on me.

Well, me and an unconscious Keith.

The king's cruel grin is unnerving. "Now the real fun begins."

CHAPTER FOUR
Keith

I WAKE WITH A pounding headache. I put a hand to my left temple and, sure enough, I have a massive bump that throbs as soon as my fingers brush it. I throw myself back down onto my pillow. Except there is no pillow.

Stars flood my vision as the back of my head thuds against concrete. I groan and force my eyes to open. It's much darker than my own room and the air is stickier. It smells like a mixture of marinated body odor and old abandoned vomit. Panic rises in my throat.

"Wow." The laughter is clear in my sister's voice. "They weren't able to knock the stupid out of you? Bummer."

I pretend to throw something in the direction of Camille's voice. I can perfectly imagine her eye roll as she lets out a light chuckle. At least she's here with me.

Carefully, I force myself to sit up and fully observe where I've woken up. It's a small cell, with three walls of bars and one of concrete. I'm lying in the farthest corner from the door on nothing but the cold, hard ground. The rest of the cell is empty, besides Camille, who sits criss-crossed on the floor across from me. I can see through into the neighboring cells. They appear empty, but farther down the dimly lit corridor, there are other people being held captive.

"Where are we? What happened?" I'm not sure I want to know the answer.

"I think we're in the cells underneath the arena." Camille shrugs. "At least that's where the king told the officers to take us. They blindfolded me on the way, so I can't be sure."

I blink and shake my head, trying to recall what happened. "The last thing I remember is Dad, and then the knife, and then the officers, and then you, and..."

Camille raises an eyebrow. "Well, you didn't miss much. Our father is just going to be publicly executed someday in the future. The king didn't say specifically. Then he was dragged off to some place." Reading my mind, she shoots me a look. "And I have no idea where, so don't ask. After they took him away, the king ordered the officers to take us to a nearby cell where we would await our sentence."

For a moment, I'm speechless. That was the last time I would see my father. I wish I could have told him I loved him.

"He didn't say what he's going to do to us?"

"No, Keith, he didn't. He's sadistic. I think he enjoys torturing us by keeping us uninformed."

I sit up a little more and rest my head against the concrete wall, shutting my eyes to block out the light drifting from the lamps in the hall. From Camille's tone, I can tell she's done with today. It might not even be the same day, considering I'm not really sure how much time has passed since I was knocked unconscious. Even with the gap in my memory, I know I'm done with today too. I'm in desperate need of a soft pillow and a nap. An actual nap, not the unconscious sleep I just had.

"Why do you think he did it?"

It takes a moment for my brain to realize Camille's talking about our dad. To me, the answer is obvious. He's always made it clear he disagrees with how Myria is run—and rightfully so. What did he think would happen after the king was killed? Who would replace the man? Prince Jacob doesn't seem any better.

"Why do you think he threw that knife?" She scowls, staring at the floor.

I frown, wondering how much I should say. Are there cameras in here? "It was all too much. It's the anniversary of Mom getting taken away, and you know how he gets. Seeing the king was the icing on the cake."

Camille pushes herself off the floor and begins to pace. "That's a stupid excuse. It's not like we all weren't feeling the pain and the hurt and the anger. Imagine being Micheal and Lizzy!" She throws her hands up in frustration, and her voice rises in volume. I glance behind her into the hallway and through the other cells, but nobody is paying her any attention. "They had to see their own father die in the same arena! You don't see *them* jeopardizing their entire family without a second thought. And—"

"Camille," I interrupt from my spot on the floor. "Don't you see what he was trying to do? He was trying to free Myria from the king."

"No, he was trying to create an impossible level of chaos in which there was never a world where we escaped." She sighs in resignation. "And now we're going to die."

"I wouldn't say that." A girl's voice, light but powerful, speaks from outside the cell.

Camille turns to face the hallway, and I jump to my feet. Too quickly. I sway unsteadily and use the bars for support as my head spins.

"I also wouldn't do that." Her lips curve upward and she takes a step forward, her full face becoming visible in the light. Princess Amaia. Flanking behind her are two other figures, both wearing matching uniforms. The silver designs designate them as higher-ranking officers, like the ones that flanked the royal family in the arena.

I wonder how much she heard…

"Why are you here?" I ask, surprising myself with the boldness of the question.

Camille shoots me a "what are you doing" look, but Amaia smiles, her blue eyes flashing. "Well, I'm not going to kill you, if that's what you mean."

The boy to her left laughs. His messy black hair falls in curls around his face, and his dark eyes dance playfully.

"I'm going to take you out of here, and Miles and Lydia will get you both fresh clothes and warm food."

At the mention of food, my stomach grumbles. "How long have we been down here?"

Amaia cocks her head. "Not long, it's still the evening of Combatant Day."

Camille frowns at the princess. "Why are you taking care of us? I thought the king would have us killed."

The boy, Miles, responds instead, amusement in his voice. "Would you prefer death instead?"

Camille closes her mouth and scowls at the boy with messy black hair.

The princess shoots Miles a look, but it appears more playful than reprimanding. "Excuse Miles's sense of humor. He likes to joke." She shifts on her feet. "After much deliberation, the king and his court have decided to grant you the opportunity of a lifetime. You will both be entering the Crowning Games as competitors. The first six Games will test your ability to survive, and the final six will demonstrate your ability to rule."

Despite her best attempts at keeping her expression blank, Camille's face lights up. My frown deepens, and my eyebrows scrunch together on my forehead.

The Crowning Games. I've heard mention of them beginning soon, with Prince Jacob getting older, but Camille and Lizzy's excitement never held mine nor Micheal's attention. Still, my father had explained the Games to the four of us a couple of months ago.

When the Crown Prince reaches nineteen, twenty-four individuals are selected to compete. They are chosen from each of the six sectors, with the majority of them coming from Central or the Gust. Those would be the more important ones. Everyone from the other sectors, like the Lates or the Gulf were added to create the illusion of inclusivity.

All of the participants compete in twelve different Games over the span of a year, each one varying in degrees of lethality. At the end of all the Games, the winner is decided based on a popular vote amongst the king's court and the citizens of Myria. The king's court, however, naturally has a significantly larger say in the matter, considering being the victor meant marrying the Crown Prince—in this case, Prince Jacob. The current Queen of Myria had been chosen in the same fashion. She had competed to marry the Crown Prince, now King Edward.

I don't see how both Camille and I could compete. I'm certainly not interested in marrying Prince Jacob.

As if sensing my confusion, Amaia laughs. Her laugh is shockingly light and happy. If I squint my eyes just right, I can pretend her father isn't King Edward. "I'm not sure if the news has reached this part of the Gulf yet, but this year, there will be two Crowning Games. One for my brother and one for me."

Oh, that makes more sense. Except it really doesn't. I'm competing to become the Prince of Myria? With the combination of this realization, the pounding headache, and the stench in the cell, I am overcome by the urge to vomit.

Amaia unlocks and swings open the door, gesturing for us to follow her down the corridor. Camille hesitantly obeys, and I curse myself for my own slow, unsure steps as my head continues to pound. Her guards wait for us to exit, taking up the rear to herd us past the other cells. Each of the criminals eyes us suspiciously, but no one says a word. They all are bruised and bleeding, from young to old.

King Edward is responsible for the torture of these poor people who have likely only been caught for something small and insignificant. And here I am, following that same monster's daughter, getting prepared to play a series of deadly Games designed as a publicity stunt.

I am grateful the princess keeps a quick pace. It makes my head throb, but at least I'm getting out of the dark and morbid line of cells—although my heart still hurts for those who are forced to remain. She leads us up a level of stairs, exiting the cell area and emerging onto the now-empty Combatant Day arena. Seeing the stadium unoccupied is haunting.

Amaia and her guards walk us through a side door. Then we're finally outside and the lingering smell of death from the arena is replaced by salty, fresh air.

The sun is low, barely hovering above where the ocean meets the sky. From here, we have the perfect view of

Salcoast, our region of the Gulf. The Myradian Sea is a handful of miles away, its waters glinting with light from the setting sun. The houses are in varied states of disarray—some on the verge of collapsing, while others barely stand tall.

If I focus enough, I can make out our house, which is one of the closest to the sea. The back door leads straight out onto the beach where Mom and I used to run every morning before it became just me. I wonder if I will ever see it again.

The male guard whistles, and with a jolt, I realize the others, including Camille, have already made it into a beautifully painted white and silver closed carriage. Two powerful black horses stand at the front, heads held high in anticipation of their next orders. The other guard, Lydia, sits at the reins.

For a brief second, I consider running. Even with my concussed head, I figure I might stand a chance of escaping. Most certainly, I know the area better than the princess and her guards. I could make it to the main town and then disappear. From there I don't know where I would go. Maybe to the forest just outside the border of Myria where my Mom always talked about going someday. And for that brief second, I seriously consider bolting. But Camille is already in the carriage, and I can't leave her.

So instead, I hurry to the door, which Miles patiently holds open for me, and step inside.

Chapter Five

Camille

A ROUGH KNOCK ON the door interrupts the best sleep I've had in a while.

The Cascading Inn's bed had been so much more preferable to the concrete floors of the cell. I couldn't tell how long we had ridden in the carriage, but when we arrived, the sun had completely disappeared from the sky.

The boy had led Keith away to his room, and the girl had taken me to mine. I didn't know where Princess Amaia went, and honestly, I didn't care. As soon as I saw the soft bed, I absentmindedly nodded along with Lydia's instructions, and as soon as she left, my head hit the soft pillow...

Before I even have a chance to roll out of bed, a tall, red-haired girl throws open the door.

"Listen, she's going to kill me for letting you sleep in." The girl charges through the room without even looking at me. She sweeps my discarded clothes from yesterday into her arms and places a new set on the edge of my bed. They look like they're identical to the clothes she's wearing—a pair of stretchy black pants and a loose-fitted, gray, zip-up jacket. "Quit staring and get up!"

The girl flings off my covers, and I jump out of bed.

"Sorry," I mumble.

She waves her hand in dismissal. "No need, I just really don't want my head chewed off because you're late." She takes a deep breath and smiles, pushing a long, dark red curl from her face. "My name is Aubrey Hedbauren. Princess Amaia put me in charge of making sure you know what's going on."

I can't help but laugh. "I don't mean to be rude, but I have no clue what I'm supposed to be doing. I know we're competing in the Games now, but I'm clueless about everything else."

Aubrey frowns. "Okay, well, here." She gestures toward the clothes she's placed on my bed. "Put these on and I'll wait for you outside the door. We'll walk and talk at the same time."

She's gone almost as quickly as she entered. A genuine smile slides onto my face. The girl reminds me of Lizzy—sweet but all over the place. I quickly slide into the clothes Aubrey left for me. The pants are comfortable. They're tight but stretchy. And the jacket is made of some soft material that I'm unfamiliar with. The quality of the clothes is a clear reminder that I'm no longer dealing with the Gulf. I'm dealing with Central now.

I catch a look at myself in a small mirror hanging on the wall, and I clap a hand over my mouth, but laughter still escapes me. My raven hair is a tangled mess atop my head, resembling a bird's nest.

Quickly, I search the room for a hairbrush, finding one in the nightstand drawer by the bed along with some simple black hair ties. I untangle the knots and bring my hair up into a ponytail, securing the thick strands with one of the hair ties. Looking at myself one final time in the mirror, I note that I look stronger in these clothes somehow. Or maybe it's the stony look in my green eyes that makes me seem older than fifteen.

Thoughts of my father flicker across my mind. Where has he been placed to await his death? Is he beaten in a corner somewhere? The idea makes me uncomfortable, so I push it away.

As I exit the room, I'm not sure what to expect from Aubrey. She's leaning casually against the wall next to my door. In one hand, she's holding an untouched vanilla cream doughnut, and in the other, she has a second doughnut, which she takes a bite of.

"Want one?" she asks through a full mouth.

I blink at her kindness. "Sure. Thank you. I'm actually very hungry," I say as my stomach growls at the sweet smell drifting in the air. She hands me the treat and looks me over from head to toe.

"Good, now let's go."

In between bites of my doughnut, I ask, "So can you tell me what's going on?" I don't know why I find it so easy to be around her.

"Well, you know you're competing in the Crowning Games. What else do you want to know?" She asks the question so nonchalantly it takes me off guard.

"Why am I still alive? Wouldn't it be easier to have us killed?"

"Eager are we?" Aubrey takes another bite of her doughnut. "Well, the king wanted to kill you, but Amaia gave him a different idea. She suggested that placing you two in the Crowning Games would be killing two birds with one stone: win over the crowd by making the king seem slightly more human while still likely killing you off."

Both her casual use of the princess's name and the mention that I'm still going to die catches me off guard. "Excuse me?"

Aubrey eyes me carefully. "He announced it on live television yesterday. Gave some speech about how he's giving you and your brother a second chance to prove yourself. If you can win, you deserve to live."

The rest of the sentence hangs in the air.

And if Keith and I don't win, we'll die anyway.

So the only way for us to live will be for Keith and I to win the Games and not die in the process. And if what Princess Amaia said yesterday was true, the first six Games would be the most deadly because they are meant to test our ability to survive.

Suddenly my doughnut doesn't taste so good. "Where are you taking me?"

"Just downstairs for a moment," she says, taking the hint to change the subject. "Then we'll be arriving in Central."

I frown, trying to calculate the distance in my head. Even if we had traveled all night in the carriage, it would still be impossible to make it to Central today. "How far did we travel yesterday? Aren't we too far to make it there today?"

Aubrey smirks, her icy blue eyes dancing mischievously. "You know you live in Myria where everyone has some kind of magic, right?"

Her reminder makes me flinch. My own "magic," as she calls it, has disappeared. I've never gone this long without being able to feel my gift lingering in the back of my mind, ready to control the temperature of any object with a single thought. I observe my hands, looking at the bracelets which encase both of my wrists. The effects of the Nightrock cuffs don't hurt as much as they did when the officers first put them on. However, it's still a constant ache—tolerable but permanent.

"What's your gift?" I ask.

"I don't know if I should tell you. Typically it makes people not trust me."

I raise an eyebrow. "Try me." I'm not sure what makes me so curious, but now I really want to know.

"I can control your mind. I can make you do whatever I want you to do."

"Oh." I pause. "Yeah, I could see why people might mistrust you. But I would know if you were in my head, right? Or could you even be in my head while I'm wearing these?" I hold up my cuffed hands.

She hesitates. "It depends. Nightrock works in weird ways. And honestly, we don't even fully understand it yet. Some people are more reactive to it than others." She pauses for a moment. "And yes, you would know if I was in your head. At least, the people I practice with say they can feel it, so I would assume you would too."

I fully digest her words. It's hard for me to imagine people my age actively practicing their gifts instead of hiding them like my mom always told me to do. She said officers would take me away if anyone ever discovered the amount of power I have. I trusted her words, deciding that it wasn't worth the risk to test if it was true. Even when she was taken, I never told anyone. Keith still doesn't know about it.

Aubrey and I speak at the same time.

"What's your gift?"

"Where's Keith?"

There's an awkward silence as neither of us answers.

"It's your turn to answer a question," Aubrey insists.

I bite the inside of my lip, considering what I should say. "What do you mean?"

Aubrey raises an eyebrow. "What's your gift?" She gestures to the cuffs on my wrists. "You obviously have one. Keith got his pair taken off last night. So, what is it?"

Following my gut, I decide to be truthful. "I can manipulate the temperature of just about anything. Even people. I've never really been bothered by winters or summers because I can regulate my own body temperature."

Aubrey gives me a look of… Is that respect? Admiration?

"I'm shocked you managed to keep it hidden for so long."

Eager to change the subject, I ask, "Where's Keith?"

Aubrey waves a hand in dismissal. "Don't worry, we're actually about to meet him and Miles in just a moment."

She stops at the end of the hallway where a set of stairs lead down into the inn's lobby.

"You ready?"

I nod, unsure of why I wouldn't be.

Aubrey swings open the door, and I get my first good look at the common area. Last night, I had been too focused on sleeping to notice anything I had walked past.

The room is spacious, with bright, red brick walls and snug wool carpets. On the far wall, there's a small bar where the grumpy innkeeper sneers at us. Or maybe he's not grumpy and just doesn't like Central—or, more importantly, the king. Aubrey clearly isn't from the Gulf, and in these clothes, I look just like her. Like I'm from Central. There are tables and chairs near the bright fireplace, which floods with room with warmth.

Forgetting Aubrey, I run toward the fireplace. Not because of its heat, but because of who is standing by it. Keith and I wrap each other up in a long hug. After a minute, I take a step away, holding onto his shoulders to survey him. He wears black pants of a similar stretchy material nowhere near as tight as mine. His silver jacket is partially unzipped, revealing a simple black shirt, and his usual wild brown hair is neatly combed to the side.

"Are you okay?" I ask.

He nods. "Are you? They didn't hurt you at all did they?"

I give him a smile. "I'm okay."

His hands brush over my wrists, touching the Nightrock that still encases them. "Why didn't they remove yours?"

I look down, aware of Aubrey watching me. "I'm not sure."

Keith frowns down at the cuffs, but before he can say anything else about them, a boy's voice interrupts.

"I really do hate to break up the reunion, but Aubrey's already made us late." The messy-haired guard from yesterday, Miles, says.

Aubrey rolls her eyes as she shifts her gaze to Miles. "Whatever. Save the scolding for later. Amaia's already going to have my head."

Miles gives her a playful grin. "Are you all ready for Central?"

Ready? Again, do I really have a choice to be anything else?

Chapter Six

Keith

TELEPORTATION IS NOT GOOD for people whose heads have just been bashed in. My head only stopped pounding this morning, and now it's started all over again.

It all happens so quickly. Miles reaches for our hands while Aubrey reaches for his shoulder, and then we're gone. It feels like my limbs are being twisted in every direction, and my mind screams as my vision blurs. When my feet finally find solid ground, I carefully open my eyes. Miles releases his grip on my hand, and I sway on my feet. Aubrey places a gentle hand on my shoulder, steadying me. Even Camille looks a little queasy, her face tinged green.

I look around at the most impressive room I've ever been in. The walls are lined with elegant arcades, each arch rising far above my head. Stylish windows decorate the room, letting in bright sunlight. The rounded ceiling is a magnificent shade of royal blue with splatters of white and silver, as if the painter had added them as an afterthought. There must be well over a hundred people talking amongst each other, but the room still manages to feel spacious, like we aren't surrounded by people.

I notice quite a few individuals are wearing the same black pants and gray jackets that Camille, Miles, Aubrey, and I are.

"Where are we?" Camille murmurs, her voice awestruck as she takes in the splendor of the room.

Miles grins. "Welcome to Central."

"Well, clearly we're in Central. I mean, what is this room for?" Camille sounds annoyed, but her tone is also laced with genuine curiosity.

Aubrey answers instead of Miles. "We're in a borrowed room on Lord Prancis's estate. He kindly offered up his home for our use until we make our way to the palace itself. The competitors and their families have been making themselves at home for weeks now in anticipation for today."

"I feel like I'm missing something," I interrupt. "What's happening today? And are you both competitors too?" The thought curls in my stomach. I haven't talked much to Aubrey, but Miles seems like a nice guy. Under different circumstances, he would be someone who I could see myself being friends with. The thought of having to fight him for a chance at surviving the Crowning Games puts a nasty taste in my mouth.

Aubrey gives me a look of understanding. "Yeah, Miles and I are both competing. We both kind of have to. My father's important and Miles is the representative from the princess's unit." From my confused look, she adds, "The royals' personal guards are called their unit."

"I'll have you know, I'm very much here by choice," Miles says.

Aubrey rolls her eyes. "Yeah, sure. It was either you or Hunterson. Amaia didn't have much choice there."

"Hey!" Miles playfully shoves Aubrey's shoulder. "Be nice to Hunt, he's my bestie." His voice rises an octave for the last part, making him sound girly.

Aubrey laughs and turns back to Camille and me, but not before my sister and I share a bewildered glance. Neither of us knows how to respond to their friendly banter. Still, Camille has a light smile on her face, which I take as a good sign.

"Anyway, ignoring him," Aubrey says with a pointed look in Miles's direction. He grins. "Today is the day where the public first gets to see all of us. Each of us has been assigned a horse from Lord Prancis's stable, and we'll parade through the streets of Central and end at the palace. There'll be cameras as well, so everyone in Myria can watch our debut."

This time, she gives me a pointed look.

"What?" I can't help but put my hands up innocently.

"That means," her voice drops to a whisper, "you have to behave. The king is looking for an excuse to be rid of you both, and you can't give him a reason to deal with you prematurely. Do you understand?"

My eyebrows furrow. "Then why bother keeping us alive in the first place?" My voice matches her hushed whisper, although I don't think anyone is close enough to overhear us.

Miles and Aubrey both narrow their eyes but are saved from answering by a new voice.

"Right on time, you four. Couldn't have been cutting it any closer."

I swivel around and find myself face to face with Princess Amaia. Her blonde hair falls over her shoulders in perfect waves as her blue eyes search mine. She's smiling and looking past me at Aubrey who gives her a half-smile and a shrug.

"On time though."

"Barely," Miles mumbles under his breath, and Aubrey sticks her tongue out at him.

Amaia refocuses her gaze on Camille and me. "How are you two doing?"

"Well taken care of," Camille says in a perfectly poised voice. It seems like she's taking Aubrey's comment to heart.

Amaia turns to look directly at me. My heart begins to race a little faster and a mix of emotions surge through me—too many to pick out any individual feeling.

After a moment, I finally manage to speak. "Fine."

"Well, I'm happy to hear that Miles and Aubrey have taken good care of you two. I'm sure they've informed you of what you will be doing today?"

Camille nods, and that's enough of a response for the princess.

"Good," she says. "Because the doors should be opening any second now. Aubrey, you may go find your family."

Aubrey dips her head, almost lowering herself into a curtsy. Then she's gone, lost in the crowd.

"Keith, follow Miles. He'll make sure you don't get lost. Camille, I'll personally escort you to your awaiting horse."

The princess walks away, and I notice the dress she is wearing. It's jet black with silver vines that wrap around her body. The bodice snugly hugs her torso, and the skirt streams down in many layers, brushing the floor. I also notice a single silver dagger hanging from her waist, its hilt decorated with black flowers.

"Keith." Camille faces me with a raised eyebrow, and I shake myself out of my stare. "Are you going to be okay with him?" She jerks her head at Miles, and he scoffs, putting a hand on his heart.

"Wow, no need to talk about me like that while I'm right here."

Camille ignores him. "Keith?"

I take a deep breath, steadying myself for what I'm sure is going to be a long day. "I'll be okay. Watch out for yourself, alright? I'll make sure I find you when we get to the palace."

Camille gives a quick nod and then follows after the princess, her brown ponytail swinging behind her.

As Princess Amaia predicted, the set of massive doors on the other end of the room opens, and the crowd squeals in excitement. Miles remains in place, leaning against the wall, letting everyone else exit first. I'm grateful because the majority of the others look like they're fighting to be seen by the public first. People are crying and hugging their parents in what could be a final goodbye. Some competitors are more like me—by themselves.

A small, wiry boy is dressed the same way I am, and yet, the clothes look so much bigger on him. The boy can't be more than thirteen. Tears pool in his eyes as he watches the sunlight beaming through the open door. There's nobody around him, so I drift toward the boy. Miles follows right behind me.

"Hey." I give the boy the warmest smile I can. "What's your name?"

The boy looks up at me with soft brown eyes, and something in my heart breaks for the poor kid.

"Oliver," he sniffles.

Miles crouches down and gently ruffles the kid's hair. "You're going to be alright, okay Oliver?"

Oliver nods his head vigorously. "I know." His little voice cracks, and I wrap him in a hug, just the way I would with Camille when she was younger.

"It's time to go, kid." Miles's voice is gentle but firm.

Oliver nods again and takes off for the door, ready for it all to be over.

I turn to Miles. "He's so young. What happens if he wins? Certainly the princess is far too old to marry a thirteen-year-old."

Miles's lips tighten, the only outward sign of his displeasure. "He's not supposed to win."

The gravity of his words hit me like a truck. Oliver's place in the Games is nothing more than an inevitable fatality. An extra life to dispose of in order to add more intensity.

The idea disgusts me, and my lip curls upward. "How is anybody okay with this? He's just a kid."

Miles looks at me, his eyes hard. "Honestly, Keith, we're kids too. What are you? Seventeen?" I incline my head, and he continues. "And I'm eighteen. The truth is that you have to grow up fast around here if you want to survive."

I run a hand through my hair, loosening the neatened strands. It feels too perfect to exist in a place so far from it.

"We should probably head out now," Miles says carefully. "We don't want to be late. Again."

He adds the last part in an attempt to lighten the mood—and it works, at least a little bit—until another girl walks past us, sneering. Her brown hair, weaved into intricate braids, isn't anything special. Her eyes, on the other hand, are surprisingly familiar. Dark green with gold flecks. Her name comes back to me as I picture her face on the poster that hung outside the arena yesterday morning. Sabrina Pelos, one of the king's hand-picked champions.

She passes by without a second glance, and I can tell from the anger flashing in Miles's eyes, he doesn't like her either.

We follow behind Sabrina. Most of the room has cleared out by now, so it isn't hard. As we step out, we're greeted by the bright glare of the sun and the screams of thousands of people who have all gathered to watch us make our way through Central.

The amount of green everywhere takes me by surprise. Tall, healthy trees tower over the streets and long fields of grass stretch farther than I can see. The building we exit is the largest house I've ever seen—a grand mansion. Hedges line the ground where a beautiful river flows through Lord Prancis's property, acting as a moat.

Dark horses have been lined up for the competitors, each saddled with matching silver riding equipment. In pairs, they occupy the road leading to shops and other stunning houses. From what I can tell, all the female competitors have been led to the front while the boys have been pushed to the back. Not that I mind. Hopefully, I'm less visible from the back. Although, from the sheer amount of people surrounding the streets, I doubt I will manage to go unnoticed.

Sure enough, we aren't even halfway down the path to the horses when a small boy reaches out to grab my leg.

Miles reaches for his waistband, which I'm sure hides a hidden weapon, but I shake my head at him. One look at the little boy, and I'm positive he couldn't hurt me if he tried.

"I think you're really brave." The boy's little voice comes out strong, and my eyes widen in disbelief. An older girl—maybe not much younger than me—rushes out from the crowd and grabs his hand.

"I'm so sorry, Mr. Atwood. My brother, he just likes to get himself into trouble."

I don't know what I'm supposed to say. I'm shocked that she knows my name. I feel the presence of the cameras, zooming in closer to observe, and I remember Aubrey's warning.

"It's alright. No worries." I smile at both of them.

"See, Emmie, he's nice," the little boy says proudly. "I told you so."

Emmie, his sister, places a hand over the little boy's mouth. "Excuse me again. Tommy doesn't know what he's saying." She eyes the cameras, which are getting closer by the second. "Although, I agree, you are incredibly brave."

Before I can react, she and her brother are gone. Folded back into the crowd like they had never existed. Miles urges me forward, his mouth pressed into a hard line as if thinking something over.

"Careful." He hisses.

I follow behind him silently, willing myself to keep my head down. It appears that King Edward doesn't have an iron grip over the entire country, not even in Central. The thought makes me smile, and it gives me hope.

CHAPTER SEVEN

Camille

THE PARADE THROUGH CENTRAL isn't as bad as I'd been initially expecting. I'd imagined a jeering crowd with scorn for anyone who wasn't one of them. Someone who didn't belong in Central, like myself. Instead, the crowd could not be more ecstatic as we pass, with certain competitors receiving louder cheers than others, making it clear who the public already favors. Aubrey is in front of me, farther up the line, her bright hair shining, and the shouts she gets are among the loudest.

Her words about the Games come back to me. If Keith and I don't win, we die. And the public's opinion is supposed to have a significant impact on the final result. I wonder if the cheers for Aubrey mean she already has an advantage. The thought makes me grind my teeth. Her life isn't on the line. At least, not in the same way mine is. She can lose the Games and still survive. I sit higher in my saddle. If there's already competitors with high popularity, I will have to make up for it.

Next to me rides a willowy girl, who looks like the smallest breeze could knock her right out of the saddle. Although, for now, she's safe. Despite it being the beginning of winter, there isn't a cloud in the sky or a breeze in the air. Only the sun shines, just bright enough to warm the air.

As if also basking in the perfect weather, the crowd's cheering never relents. I wave back at everyone, matching their smiling faces. I can hear the distant buzz of cameras, but they don't bother me. Looking ahead at Aubrey and the other girls, who are waving and blowing kisses, I'm not doing anything out of the ordinary. In fact, hopefully I'm helping my case.

My energy is returning, beginning to flow through me as soon as Princess Amaia removed the pair of Nightrock cuffs when I had mounted my horse. Even though the weather is already perfect, there's comfort in knowing my gift is back and ready to be used at a moment's notice.

My excitement only increases as part of the crowd holds posters displaying my name. My name! Maybe I'm not at such a disadvantage as I thought. Although Aubrey's is definitely more present than mine, alongside a handful of other girl's names—like Sabrina Pelos and Prill Prancis.

Frequently, my name is written next to Keith's, but there are even a handful that have my name by itself. A part of me wonders about the crowd's reasoning, but the other part of me basks in their support. My grin only grows as we make the final turn through the streets, and the palace peeks into view.

It sits higher than the rest of the city, perched on a grassy hill that cascades down in rolls of grass. Ponds are sprinkled throughout the lawn, surrounded by half walls of elegant gray stone. The paved path leading to the front gate is decorated with towering trees, which blanket the area with shade.

The palace takes up almost my entire view. There are tall, pointed towers at each corner and shorter ones that stick out of the middle of the walls, each one covered with a jet-black, pointed roof. With its white brick laced in silver and black trim, and its perfectly placed crystal windows, the entire structure reeks of royalty.

The horses' hooves clomp against the pavement as wide silver gates are held open for us to pass through. With the cheering crowd left behind, I turn around in my saddle and wave, shooting a wide smile in their direction. A lot of them wave viciously back, and another thought occurs to me. I find the nearest flying camera and focus on its lens. I'm not sure how they plan on getting this footage out to the rest of Myria, but it feels important to include them. I wave and smile at the camera, and it lingers on my face before turning to capture the rest of the competitors.

I face forward again, and the footman guiding my horse leads me to the wide-open doors of the palace. He helps me slide from my horse, and the willowy girl and I walk through the doors together. The inside is even more wonderful, with vaulted ceilings higher than any roof I've seen—with the exception of the Combatant Day arena. There are levels of stairs leading off in different directions, and I want to explore where each one leads. Before I can reach out and touch a very realistic statue of a stallion, the willowy girl clears her throat, and I follow her to where the other girls wait at the foot of the largest staircase. I stand by Aubrey, who is the only friendly face I recognize.

"Sorry, you missed the briefing beforehand." Aubrey winces. "That's my fault. Either way, some servants will come to get us in a few moments and show us to our rooms, where we'll stay until breakfast tomorrow."

I smile despite the fact that Aubrey might be my biggest competition.

"How was the parade?"

I shrug, trying to contain my actual excitement. "I know this might be backward, but I'm starting to feel good about being here."

Aubrey gives me an understanding look. "I know. It's all messed up but look on the bright side. You still have a chance to survive. I think it's okay to feel pretty good about that."

Servants flood the entry hall as soon as the last pair of girls enter the room. The pair look around with matching sneers on both of their faces, as if everyone is beneath them. One girl looks vaguely familiar, but I can't place where I recognize her from. The other girl's face is cruel as she stares daggers at me. I wince at the harshness of her gaze and look around the rest of the room, trying to find Keith, but the boys have not arrived yet.

Aubrey catches my look. "He's fine. They just keep the boys and girls separate upon entering the palace. You'll see him at breakfast in the morning."

I don't acknowledge her. Instead, I survey the girls—all of whom will likely be trying to kill me in the next couple of weeks. Lovely.

The servants are quick to usher all twenty-four of us up a staircase pushed to the side of the room. We all follow in almost complete silence. Now and then, there are mutters of "ooh" and "ahh," but other than that, we stay quiet.

I try to focus on memorizing the route we take, but with all the twists and turns, and walking up and down stairs, I quickly lose track and instead play with my hands, heating and then cooling them. It's always been a way to pass time. And I'm not exactly sure how much time goes by before we reach our rooms, but it feels like too long.

A servant steps forward, her voice cool and commanding. "This hallway is where your rooms are located. You are not permitted to enter another competitor's living space without their direct permission, including the boys. They will be staying a couple of halls down. Tonight, no one will be permitted outside of their room, but in the morning for breakfast, one of us," —She gestures to the other servants around her—"will come to show you the way. From there, you are granted access to the rest of the palace, unless otherwise instructed by anyone working for the royal family or the royal family themselves. Is that understood?"

We all murmur our agreement.

"Good. Now for room assignments." She starts down the hallway, reciting names as she reaches each girl's designated door. My room is snuggled in between Garden Burrow's, one of the snobby girls who came in last, and Nicole Idomet's, a girl I don't recognize. But by her golden tan skin, I assume she's from the Gulf.

As I follow an older woman inside, I audibly gasp. My jaw drops as I take in the gorgeous room. For starters, it's so spacious that I'm sure it could fit our entire house. Giant bay windows, lined by a cushioned seat with pillows so large I could easily fall asleep on one, overlook one of the ponds and a flower garden. The rug covers almost the entire floor, and I can't help but reach down and feel the soft fabric. Dark, polished wood bedside tables hug both sides of the bed. The bed itself could comfortably fit me three times over. Tapestries hang down from the frame, but they don't completely cover the mattress from sight.

The old woman chuckles. "Stunning, isn't it dear?"

I nod in amazement.

She chuckles again. "Well, the bathrooms are just through that door, and that side room over there is your closet. Help yourself to whatever you'd like. If you need me, just push the button over there." She points to a small gray button right above one of the bedside tables. "And I'll be over here as fast as I can." She smiles at me, and for a second she reminds me so much of my mom it hurts. Not in appearance, but in the way she speaks and carries herself.

"Thank you so much," I say as I perch myself on the edge of my bed. "I'll press the button if I need you."

She inclines her head and then leaves me alone.

The first thing I do is explore the closet. It's practically its own room, with everything from outfits identical to what I'm wearing now to stunning formal dresses. I wonder when I will be needing those? For now, I grab a simple, silk black shirt and matching pajama shorts and walk into the bathroom.

The amount of bath scrubs and soap scents on the shelves is overwhelming. I grab the first bottle—labeled cinnamon nutmeg—and start the bath water. Baths have always been preferable over showers for me. Not only are they relaxing, but they also provide my gift an easy release as it expends its efforts to keep my bath water at the perfect temperature.

I sink to the bottom and comfortably rest my head on the alabaster. The fancy levers and buttons intrigue me, but I'm too content to get up. My gift flows through the water, effortlessly warming it to my taste. I could fall asleep like this.

My mother always loved warm baths, and I was always willing to remain in the bathroom to keep the water temperature perfect. Those nights my mother and I would laugh and talk and cry together. I wonder what we would talk about tonight if she were here...

Before I get too lost in thought, I quickly scrub my hair and my body, and bubbles quickly fill up the tub. I experiment on the bubbles with my gift. Heating them is tricky, and I mainly pop them. But freezing them with a single thought produces crystal-looking spheres resembling snow globes.

Eventually tiring of my game and acknowledging that it probably isn't a good idea to fall asleep in the bathtub, I drag myself out and wrap myself in thick, soft towels.

It isn't long before I'm completely dry and in my pajamas with my hair piled on my head. I flop down on my mattress, and my eyes don't take long to drift shut once I hit the soft pillows.

CHAPTER EIGHT

Camille

THE NEXT MORNING, THE servant is back, removing the covers and shaking me awake.

"Time for breakfast, Miss."

I groan and roll over, pressing my face against the pillow. "Do I have to?"

The old lady only laughs and shakes her head.

I get myself out of bed, glancing at the sun rising over the grassy hills. Its light reflects off the pond, and birds flutter by.

With the servant lady watching me carefully, I head into the closet and survey the clothes. From the bedroom, the old lady answers my unspoken question. "You can pick whatever you would like to wear. Just leave the silver jackets alone; those are only to be worn during the Games."

I grab a pair of stretchy pants, similar to the ones I wore yesterday, and a loose blue shirt. I change in the bathroom quickly and follow the woman out into the hallway. Aubrey leans against the wall across from my door and winks at me as I walk out.

"Don't worry, Shiloh, I'll show her from here."

The servant, Shiloh, wordlessly drops into a low curtsy and hurries away down the hallway.

I turn to Aubrey. "What's so special about you?"

Aubrey raises an eyebrow.

"She didn't curtsy to me."

Aubrey bursts out laughing. "That would be because you have no title." Her deep blue eyes sparkle. "My father is Lord Hedbauren, one of the five Lords of Central. You already know about Lord Prancis. His kids are not as friendly by the way."

"Oh." I remember her mentioning that yesterday, and it makes sense considering the way she holds herself and her apparent closeness with Princess Amaia. "Does that mean I'm supposed to curtsy to you as well?" My question is genuine. I want to make sure I don't mess anything up, but the look Aubrey gives me is incredulous.

"Please do not. That would honestly just be embarrassing. For me and for you, believe me."

My face heats up. "Oh, okay. I just wanted to make sure."

Aubrey smiles and gives me a gentle nudge. "I'm just messing with you. Sorry, I hang out around Miles and my brother too much."

"Your brother?" She gives me an odd look at my sudden interest. "Is he our age?"

"Yeah," Aubrey shrugs. "Why?"

"Does that mean he's competing?"

Aubrey nods. "There's a lot of sibling pairs competing in the Crowning Games. Typically, there's only a set of girls competing for the Prince's hand. However, this time around the addition of the princess's Game opens up more potential for siblings."

"Why would they add the princess's Game?" It's been a question that's been nagging me since Princess Amaia brought it up.

Aubrey eyes me curiously. "I'm not really sure. I think it was Amaia's idea. My brother would know more about it since he sits in council meetings sometimes with my father."

I'm not buying her response, but before I can ask another question, Aubrey comes to a halt.

"This is the breakfast room." I silently scold myself for not paying more attention to how we got here. "We'll eat here every morning, but people will come and go as they please. Dinner is more formal, and we'll all sit together to eat."

She pushes open the door, and the room is already full. I don't pay much attention to the space itself. Instead, my gaze fixes itself on the back of Keith's head. As if sensing my intentions, Aubrey leads me in his direction, and as soon as I reach him, I wrap him in a hug. He turns in surprise, quickly returning the hug.

"How did you sleep?"

"The best I've ever slept to be perfectly honest."

Keith smiles in agreement.

"Is this your sister?" a boy I haven't seen before asks Keith.

With one glance, I figure he must be Aubrey's brother. His matching red hair falls in gentle locks around his face, and dimples show when he smiles. He carries himself tall, with the same sort of confidence Aubrey does. His eyes are different though. Instead of bright blue, they're a deep, forest green—darker than mine.

Keith nods. "Yeah, Camille, meet Ryden."

"Also known as my least favorite person," Aubrey adds, sticking her tongue out at Ryden.

He rolls his eyes and reaches a hand out to me. "Nice to meet you." He brings my hand to his mouth and presses a light kiss against my skin.

Unsure of how else to respond, I choke out a soft, "Thank you," and look anywhere but his eyes.

"Always such a lady's man." Miles jumps on Ryden from behind, appearing out of thin air. "Save some for me." His voice is layered with teasing sarcasm, and I frown at him.

Aubrey smacks them both, and they pretend to rub their arms in pain. "Ignore them. They're a bunch of idiots."

Miles begins to defend himself, and he and Aubrey bicker. I take the chance to examine the room. There are groups of tables scattered around, and the majority of them are taken up by other competitors. Along the far wall is a long table full of delicious-smelling food, which grabs my attention, and my stomach starts to growl.

Keith takes a step closer to me. "Do you want to get something to eat? I'll come with you."

It isn't much of a question, and Keith and I walk to the table, leaving the others behind.

"How do you feel about this place?" I ask, taking advantage of our privacy.

Keith gives a deep sigh and frowns. "Honestly, I don't know. So far Miles and Ryden seem alright, but still, it's weird considering we're about to be competing against each other. For something I don't want." The last part he says quietly, as if he hadn't meant to say it out loud.

"Keith." I grab his shoulder so he has to look directly at me. "Forget about the whole prince and princess thing. You're trying to win so you don't get killed in one of the Games, alright? You're fighting to survive."

Keith nods, but his brown eyes still look wary. "I know, Cam. I just don't understand why the king didn't kill us and be done with it."

I let a moment of silence hang in the air. A million responses rush through my head.

It'll be more impactful when we die in the competition.

According to Aubrey, he's only keeping us alive to die later, unless we somehow win the whole thing.

I settle for, "It doesn't matter. Okay, all that does is..."

"Hello," a girl's voice drawls. "Aren't you two cute?"

Keith and I both swivel to look at the newcomer. Her dark eyes narrow at us, and she grins, but not in a cheerful way. More of an I-will-eat-you-alive grin. Behind her towers a huge boy, who looks like the definition of all brawn and no brains. As if sensing trouble, another boy slides up next to me, his cold blue eyes meeting mine.

"Is there a problem, Prill?" the boy asks, cocking his head to the side.

The girl, Prill, sneers. "I don't see one."

The boy grins. "Good, we wouldn't want the poor kids to die of terror, now would we?" His smile shifts, and I realize he isn't here to defend us.

"Sorry, we're just trying to get food." Keith tries to take a step past Prill and the massive block of flesh, but Prill places a hand on his arm, stopping him.

"I'm sure you are." Her voice is like ice. "Poor kids didn't have a good enough daddy to keep them fed, I'm sure." Keith's jaw clenches, and I grab his hand trying to drag him away before this confrontation escalates.

"What do you think, Carter? Asher? Am I right here?"

The block of muscle laughs while the other boy smirks.

"I'm sure that's true Prill. But you can't expect much else. They're from the Gulf." The second boy sneers as he says it. "And from what I hear, their poor father is set to die, isn't he?"

Keith has had enough. "Shut up!" he snarls.

"Oh? He's got a bark, but does he have a bite?" The boy's chin juts up, and he turns to me. "Something tells me this one is who we should really worry about." He reaches a hand towards me, but I turn the air around me scalding hot, and he's quick to snatch his hand back.

But not quick enough to avoid Keith's rage. He pulls his arm out of my grip and leaps at the boy. Flames spark in the boy's hand as he dances backward. "I wouldn't try that here, Atwood."

I worriedly look around the room and see that everyone is looking at us now. Aubrey and Miles are already walking toward us, but someone else beats them to it.

"Asher, knock it off." Princess Amaia's voice is crystal clear—sharp and commanding. "You know better. Take your sparks somewhere else." She can't be much older than Asher, but she speaks to him like he's a scolded child. Asher glares but doesn't dare challenge her as he stalks out of the room, the door slamming shut behind him.

"Prill, Carter, why don't you follow him? The three of you clearly do not understand the expectations we have of you while you are in our home." Her voice drips with disappointment, and Prill drops into a low curtsy. Without another word, she follows Asher and Carter.

Then the princess turns to Keith and me. "Are you two alright?" Her voice is softer now, almost gentle. And I hate the way she acts as though we're children.

"Fine, thank you," I retort.

Amaia raises an eyebrow at my tone.

I grab Keith and drag him toward the food table, but not before he whispers a small "Thank you." Amaia smiles and nods at him.

As we walk away, I mutter, "What is she even doing in here? Isn't this only for the competitors?"

Keith faces me. "Stop sounding so hateful. She defended us there. Plus, Miles says the royals can come and go as they please. Don't read too much into it." He gives me a sharp look, and I ignore it.

"She acts so full of it. Just because she has power over us doesn't mean she has to wield it every second she gets."

Recognizing the uselessness in his argument and my own stubbornness, Keith shakes his head and gives an exasperated sigh. "Fine, Cam."

Even though he's shut it down, I want to say more. Every time she intercedes on our behalf, it doesn't feel like someone is caring for us. It feels more like she's rubbing my face in the control I don't have.

By the time we reach the food table, everyone has gone back to their normal chatter and stopped blatantly staring at us. I begin to pile a little bit of everything onto my plate but hesitate when Keith doesn't grab anything.

"I already ate with Ryden and Miles before you got in." He chews on his lip. "Doesn't it seem wrong how much food there is here?"

I smile, eager to leave the tension from earlier behind. "More for me."

But Keith's eyebrows stay furrowed. "That's not what I mean." He walks away, back toward Miles and Aubrey. I frown but decide to leave him be. When Keith gets this heated, it's always best for me to give him space. So much for easing the tension...

"You two are quite the interesting pair," Ryden interjects.

"Thank you?" I respond, unsure of when he snuck up behind me.

"You're very welcome," he says, winking at me. I curve my lips upward. "Better than being boring."

"Is it?" Now I'm sure I've blown it. All he does is stare at me. His deep green eyes skim me over, taking me in. After a moment of brief silence where I continue to load my plate, he speaks again.

"Do you really like omelets?" His voice is full of judgment, and I give him a look of confusion.

"I have no idea what that means."

He laughs lightly, and there's a smile on his face. I can tell he's enjoying this as his expression sparkles in entertainment. He points to the yellow half-circle I just put on my plate. "That is an omelet. And they're disgusting and not worth eating."

I simply shrug. "I won't know until I try it."

"Fair enough."

He watches me pile more food onto my plate.

"How much are you going to take?" I scowl at him but put down the final serving spoon. My plate is starting to overflow. He laughs again.

"Why don't I show you to one of the training rooms so you can start practicing for the first Game? It'd be terrible if you died in the first round."

There's a sense of comfort in his words, like he has an actual interest in whether I live or die.

"Sure." I take a bite of my omelet. "And I hate to inform you, but these are absolutely delicious." I point to the omelet.

Ryden shakes his head and leads me from the room, my plate of food still in my hand.

CHAPTER NINE
Keith

THE DAYS FLY BY as I get into a routine. Wake up. Breakfast. Training. Lunch in Miles's room. More training. Dinner. Sleep.

The training room is an open space with every weapon imaginable hanging from the walls. Swords, daggers, bladed staffs, and even guns. I'm still not sure why guns are available. Miles explained that in the arena they wouldn't be allowed. They ruin the entertainment value by providing quick and easy deaths.

On one side of the room, there are targets where competitors practice blade throwing and archery. I haven't felt the need to touch that corner. Miles said those skills wouldn't likely come into play in the first Game—which, I've been informed, is a free-for-all fight between the competitors.

I will be given one weapon of my choosing and released into an arena with twenty-three other boys, each bent on winning for themselves. Sounds like the time of my life. Especially since no matter how hard Miles pushes me, my sword skills remain abysmal. I can't brandish a knife properly, and I also can't throw a spear in the right direction. Aubrey even spent an entire day trying to teach me to use a double-bladed staff that she favors, but to no avail. Even without Miles or Aubrey using their gifts, I haven't come close to beating either one of them. This poses a whole other problem.

There aren't many rules to the first Game, meaning everyone can use their gift. Which I am still sorely lacking. Miles tried explaining how his teleportation works and how he can only transport a certain amount of people—and only to a certain distance. It all depends on his concentration and energy levels. Transporting us from the Cascading Inn in the Gulf to Central had been pushing his limits, and he'd passed out as soon as he got to his room.

Aubrey even tried using her gift on me, which was the oddest experience I've had. It was like I was a passenger in my own body watching my arms and legs act outside of my control. She thought maybe direct contact with a gift would help me find my own...

None of it has worked so far, and I'm starting to believe it won't ever work. Maybe I don't have one. When I voice this fear to Miles, he brushes it off.

"Listen," he says. "Everyone is born with a gift inside them. It's just a matter of bringing it to the surface."

"That can't be true," I argue.

"And why is that?"

"My mother didn't have a gift. If she had the ability to show one to the officers when they took her, she would have."

Miles gives me a look, as if torn between staying quiet or saying something.

Either way, it's the day before the first Game, and I haven't made any progress.

"Come on, Keith. Pick up the sword and let's go again!" Aubrey barks at me. Her face isn't even flushed, and her hair is tied back without a strand out of place. Unlike myself. My hair is a mess, and I'm sure my face is red and sweaty.

I close my eyes in frustration, grit my teeth, and reach for the fallen sword. I stand and face Aubrey again, who's already waiting for me. Before I can swing, Miles calls out, "Spread your feet out a little more."

I adjust my stance, fighting my irritation. Today, Miles, Aubrey, Ryden, and Camille have all come to watch and practice themselves. Everyone is trying to get as much training in before tomorrow morning as possible, so the room is more crowded than normal. For the time being, Aubrey and I face off, while Ryden and Camille circle each other in the square next to ours. Camille, it turns out, is a natural. She's learned to wield a sword and a set of daggers, surprising me by actually pinning Ryden once. The bow and arrow targets have been one of her favorite places to be. The ease with which she's picked everything up is disconcerting, especially compared to my utter lack of skill.

And no one has mentioned the revelation of her gift. Even *that* came naturally. Her ability to manipulate temperature suddenly revealed itself in a fight against Miles when she turned his sword's hilt flaming hot. In a way, it's comforting. At least she will be able to protect herself if anyone comes at her. I only hope it'll be enough.

Once my feet are planted correctly, Aubrey attacks. Her movements are fluid and graceful as her sword arcs downward. I block her attack just before she slices my arm off, and our swords ring upon contact. Pushing against her blade, I slide my sword to the left, slashing at her leg, but she's too quick. She dances backward, skirting my blade.

Then she moves even quicker, leaping to the side and striking the back of my knees with the flat edge of her weapon. The metal thuds, and my legs fall forward. I lose my grip on the sword, and it careens across the floor. I try to get up but stop as I feel the point of Aubrey's sword pushing into my back. I meet Miles's gaze from across the arena. He's raising his eyebrows at me, expecting me to do something.

I swing my legs out, catching Aubrey's ankles and causing her to stumble. It gives me just enough time to roll out and spring up. But I'm still without a sword. Aubrey grins approvingly before launching herself at me again. She moves like a snake—quick and deadly. I don't have time to react before she's wrapping her free hand around my arm and pulling it backward, all while sliding her sword against my throat.

"Better." Aubrey releases me, and I snarl in frustration.

"It's not good enough," I almost shout. "I only managed to escape the first time because you didn't immediately stab me straight through."

Aubrey's face hardens, and she doesn't say anything else.

"Try again," Princess Amaia's voice demands from the edge of the ring.

I don't know when she got there, but my face burns with the knowledge that she's been watching. She stands next to Miles, and even Ryden and Camille drift over to watch. Camille shoots me an encouraging smile, but her eyes are full of concern. Miles gives me the thumbs-up.

I glare at the princess. She's wearing clothes similar to Aubrey and Camille's—stretchy pants and a loose t-shirt. It's much different from the formal dresses I've seen her wear. The more casual clothes suit her better.

"Let's go again." Aubrey draws my attention back to her. "You're starting to get the hang of it, you just need a little more practice."

I shake my head. "I need a break."

Aubrey frowns but lets me walk off. I reach Camille, and she hands me a bottle of water and offers a reassuring pat on my shoulder.

"Why are you pausing?" Amaia's eyes swirl with emotion. I stare at her, deliberately taking another sip of my water. Neither of us look away.

Miles clears his throat. "Ryden, ready to get a beating?"

Ryden smiles. "I'm pretty sure you mean the other way around, Jumpy."

They grin at each other. Miles unsheathes his sword, and Ryden slides out his pair of daggers. The two of them are well matched, and I know their fight will go on for some time.

I break my staring contest with the princess to turn to Camille.

"You're really starting to get the hang of this," I say, repeating Aubrey's words.

She can't contain her proud smile. "I guess I am."

The princess interrupts. "Keith, you can't go into the Game tomorrow fighting like this. You have to keep practicing."

"I'm trying," I mumble.

Her lips curve downward in a small frown. "I know you are," she says quietly. "But your footwork is flimsy, and you're not properly gripping your sword. That's why you keep losing it."

"Hey!" Camille steps in between us. "Back off. He's trying." Her voice cracks a little. Probably because she knows I'm likely going to die tomorrow.

"And I'm trying to help." Amaia's voice is tinged with annoyance.

"Working him to the point of exhaustion isn't helping!" Camille snarls, jabbing a finger at the princess.

"Stop it, both of you," I say. "We'll just have to see how tomorrow goes."

Amaia gives me a withering look. "Absolutely not." She tosses me a sword and jerks her head toward one of the rings. She draws her own sword from her waist.

Realizing what she wants me to do, I gape at her incredulously. "You want me to fight *you*?"

Amaia grins. "Yes, that's what the sword is for." She brandishes hers expertly in the air, stepping backward as she goes. "You know," she teases. "To fight with."

I'm not sure why, but I'm grinning too, filled with a new surge of energy. Aubrey's not paying us any attention, focused on Miles and Ryden instead, but Camille glances at me worriedly. I roll my shoulders. "It can't hurt, can it?"

Aubrey glances over at us, amused. "Oh, it most certainly can. Good luck, Keith."

I roll my eyes, my playfulness returning. "Believe me, I'm gonna need it."

I walk to meet Amaia, who patiently waits for me in the center of a ring. Her blonde hair is loose, but she doesn't attempt to put it up. A smile dances on her face, and her eyes sparkle. I wince as my bravado fades away. This is probably going to be a quick fight. Everything about her screams predator. And I'm her prey.

As soon as I'm close enough to her, she drawls, "Are you ready, Atwood?"

Something about how she says my last name doesn't enrage me the way it does when Asher says it. I set my feet the way Miles showed me and shift the sword in my grip.

"Using a sword has less to do with the sword and more to do with you. Relax your body, starting with your hands. You're holding onto your weapon for dear life. Instead," —She demonstrates with her own hand— "keep your palm relaxed but still secure."

I mimic her hold, and she nods in approval.

"Better. Now let your body relax. If you keep yourself stiff, you'll never be able to properly move, much less attack effectively."

I take a deep breath, and as I exhale, I let my shoulders roll back, trying to match Amaia's posture. She smiles this time, encouraging me.

"Good. Now, let's begin."

The princess moves with a whole new level of inhuman speed—and I thought Aubrey moved quickly. Could it be her gift? I had forgotten to ask what it was before we started. She strikes with her sword quickly, and the force of it sends my sword flying from my hand. Then she knocks me to the ground. With a thud, I hit the floor, and Amaia leans over me, her face close to mine and her sword at my neck. "Again."

And again. And again. It feels like hours of Amaia knocking me over or pinning me. This time, I hit the floor face first, and my head rings at the impact. Distantly, I hear my sword clatter to the ground, and I growl in frustration. I throw myself back up before she can pin me. Rolling out of her way, I leap up and face her, still unarmed.

"Trust your instincts," she says as she jumps over my head. She must be using her gift because I can feel the sparkle of energy radiating off of her. It's different from Miles or Aubrey's gift, which both act in silence. Amaia's is loud and sharpens my awareness, lighting through me like fireworks.

Taking her advice and acting on instinct, I dart for my blade, ducking underneath Amaia's sword as I go. In one motion, I collect my sword and bring it up, matching her attack. She's grinning again, and so am I. Energy crackles and sparks off of her as she darts again, moving with the elegance of a white tiger. Her movements get more aggressive as she pushes me backward, but I manage to match her hit for hit. Until she disappears for the briefest moment and then a sharp blade is piercing my back.

"Got you." Her voice tickles my ear.

Just like that, the energy is gone. My arms feel heavy, and my sword droops toward the floor. My body slumps, and Amaia gently grabs my arm to hold me upright. I shut my eyes. "I still didn't win. I would've died there."

Amaia holds me at a distance, her eyes gentle now instead of harsh. "You're almost there though. That time I actually had to try."

I know she means it to be comforting, but it's not.

"I have no sword skills. I can't hold a dagger properly. For goodness' sake, I don't even have a gift to balance it all out!" My voice is rising in volume, but I don't care. This has all been pointless. Tomorrow, I'm going to die, and there's nothing I can do about it.

"You'll get there," she says patiently. "Let's go again."

I shake my head and hand her my sword. "No more for today."

"No more?" She quirks an eyebrow at me.

"You said it yourself. I can't go out there and fight."

"Fine." Amaia's eyes are daggers as they stare back at me in a challenge. "Then don't."

Ignoring the crowd of people who have gathered to watch, including Prince Jacob, I walk out.

Chapter Ten
Camille

THE ROOM IS SILENT after Keith leaves. Everyone stares at the princess, who is still breathing heavily and covered in sweat. She glances at the floor, her brow furrowed in concentration. Chatter only returns when Prince Jacob loudly clears his throat.

"Aren't you all supposed to be practicing?" he drawls. His features are even more cruel up close. His sharp jawline combined with the upturned corners of his lips and cold blue eyes only add to his daunting air.

Princess Amaia moves out of the ring, and Aubrey and Miles immediately swarm her. Their lips are moving, but Amaia still doesn't respond. Instead, she makes her way out of the training room, and Aubrey and Miles quickly follow on her heels. Prince Jacob studies them as they leave, and I wonder what might be racing through his mind.

"Do you want to practice with your bow some more?" Ryden is still next to me, his voice loud in my ear despite his quiet tone.

"Why don't you go with them?" I gesture to where Aubrey, Miles, and the princess had just disappeared.

"I don't want to." Ryden says matter-of-factly.

I frown, lost in my own thoughts. I'm still caught up on the way Keith's body seemed to become something of its own during his spar with the princess. He moved with such precision and speed. It was quite the opposite of his unnatural and jerky movements beforehand. It was like something in him shifted, requiring the princess to concentrate and focus on every swing of her sword.

Ryden waves a hand in front of my face. "Camille? Are you in there?"

I shake my head to clear it. "Yeah."

He gives me a look of disbelief.

"Yeah," I repeat. "We can go shoot some targets."

He grins at me, and I grin back. Ryden has been extremely helpful in keeping me busy and focused on learning how to defend myself, leaving no room to think about how quickly my life has been flipped around. The first few days in the arena, I had stuck by Keith, mainly sparring with Aubrey. But Ryden showed me the bow and arrow, and I fell in love with the weapon. He's been happy to accompany me to the targets almost every day because his talent is knife throwing.

"Actually, I was wondering if she could come with me," Prince Jacob says. His voice is light and warm compared to his cold eyes.

Ryden and I turn to see Prince Jacob standing behind us, staring me down. I want to shrink inside myself at his gaze, but Ryden throws his arm around my shoulder, forcing me to stand tall.

"Hello, Your Highness." Ryden bows his head.

"Hedbauren," Jacob nods in return, then turns to me. "Would you come with me? I have," —He pauses, drawing out his syllables— "something for you to see."

I don't know if it's the slight breeze in the room or the ominous way he speaks, but chills slide down my back. Ryden must sense my unease—or maybe he agrees that it's a bad idea for me to go off with the prince alone. "Do you mind if I tag along, Your Highness?"

Jacob's sharp gaze focuses on him. "And why would you do that?"

Ryden shrugs. "It sounds interesting."

I bite the inside of my cheek to contain my grin.

Jacob looks back at me. "Do you trust him?"

Paired with his sinister tone and his slanted eyebrows, it's a curious question. I think about it for a second. There is a huge part of me that knows trusting anyone here is a bad idea. Everyone is connected to the royal family, and more importantly, King Edward. It's almost easy to forget that he doesn't exist and that this is all only some fun competition. I think that's why a small part of me whispers that, yes, I do trust Ryden. At least more than anyone else here—with the exception of Keith.

"I trust him enough." Both Ryden and Jacob grin at me, but I don't smile back. "Now, what do you want to show me?"

The prince waves a hand. "Follow me."

So Ryden and I follow him through a thread of hallways I haven't been down before. Or at least, I don't think I have. To me, they all look identical, which is why Aubrey still takes me to breakfast every morning and walks back with me to my room after dinner. I get lost without her.

As we turn down a hallway lined with officers, I recognize that we've entered a different part of the palace. Instinctively, I squeeze closer to Ryden, my heart racing a little faster. For all I know, Prince Jacob could easily be leading me to my death. But Ryden gives me a reassuring smile, and I take a handful of deep breaths. I want to ask where we're going, but I don't want to break the silence.

Jacob stops at a small gray door and nods at both of the officers standing on either side. Their hands shoot up in matching salutes, and the prince walks through. Ryden and I follow close behind him, leaving the officers in the hall.

The room whirs with the sound of technology, and screens line almost every square foot of the wall. At the center of the room is a control board. Each screen flashes through different pictures of the palace, but when one of them contains moving people, I realize they must be recordings.

Prince Jacob watches me as I survey the room, still unsure of why he brought us in here. "What is this place?"

Jacob holds up a finger and moves toward the control panel.

Ryden answers instead. "It's active security footage of the whole palace. See there." He points to a screen displaying the kitchens and servants hurriedly scurrying about. "That's them preparing tonight's dinner."

"Wait, so it's all happening right now?"

"Yes," Ryden smirks. "That's what 'active' means."

I blush in embarrassment. "Well, how was I supposed to know? It's not like we have this stuff in the Gulf."

"That's true." It might be my imagination, but Ryden's eyes seem to grow sad.

"If you two are finished discussing the concept of a camera over there, I have something to show you. Remember?" Jacob's voice tinges with annoyance. Afraid to see him truly frustrated, I scurry over to him with Ryden behind me. He clicks a button, and the largest screen directly in front of us changes. I can't contain my gasp as my father's limp body is displayed. The camera is situated in the corner of a nasty prison cell. The ground is cracked and stained with blood. From what I can see of the room, there's no windows or doors. My father is lying on the floor, beaten and bloody, and it makes my stomach sick. How many of those blood stains are his?

Ryden reaches for me, but I move away from his touch, and Prince Jacob watches me, gauging my reaction. But I stare impassively at the screen, waiting for him to shift or move.

"He's alive." The prince's voice rings out, shooting through the static running in my head. "I thought you'd like to see him."

"Why would you assume that?" Even to me, my voice sounds cold. Ryden looks slightly concerned, but Jacob smiles. I resist the urge to smack the look right off his face.

"He is your father, after all, is he not?"

"Only by blood." A father doesn't abandon his children like he did.

Jacob's smile only widens while Ryden's face softens.

"So, I was right about you. You are different from the rest of them." I'm not sure what he means by that, so I remain nonchalant. "First, you don't fight back on Combatant Day, even though we both know you could have lit that whole place on fire." My face goes slightly red because he's probably right. "Then, you stand up to my sister. Which by the way, I've never seen anyone dare to talk back to her. And now, here you are, denying attachment to your father." The look he gives me is awed.

"That girl is used to everyone lying down at her feet, but she can't talk to my brother like that." I don't know where this coldness is coming from, but I realize I've been holding in a lot of pent-up frustration and anger. "Even if she is a princess."

Jacob's malicious grin doesn't unnerve me as much as it did before.

"Well, this is my gift to you. You can come in and see this man whenever you'd like. He'll be alive for quite some time since we've realized he holds some very precious information." Jacob's voice holds too much enjoyment. "You can even bring your brother in here if you like. I've already cleared it with the officers on watch. Enjoy." Moving to leave, he hesitates. "Just remember you owe me one."

Prince Jacob winks at me. Then he struts out of the room, leaving Ryden and I staring at the screen.

Hesitantly, Ryden reaches a hand out and places it on my shoulder. "Are you okay?"

I snap. "Yeah, I'm perfectly fine, Ryden. Why wouldn't I be?" I laugh without feeling. "I mean, who else gets to watch their father linger on the brink of death because he's being tortured for information? So yeah, I'm doing lovely. Thank you for asking." Tears spring to my eyes before I can stop them. Angrily, I move to swipe them away, but Ryden grabs my wrists for a moment before he moves to brush the tears away with his thumb.

"I don't know what kind of people you hang out with, but no, I haven't met someone who gets torn from her home after watching her father be sentenced to death. And then, she's expected to fight to the death against twenty-three other blood thirsty girls all while her father is lying on a filthy prison floor because he tried to kill the king." Ryden pauses, pretending to think. "Well, other than you, of course."

I must really be going insane because now I'm chuckling while the tears continue to roll down my face.

His face, however, is serious. Ryden looks intently into my eyes. Green meeting green. "You know it's okay to not be okay right?"

I don't answer, and he sighs. "Listen, I've spent a lot of time with you over the past couple days, and I know you're tough. You're handling all this like a pro, but it's okay to break down every now and again." He wraps me in a quick hug, and I let him.

"I can't show Keith." The words spill out. "He'll do something stupid. He'll try to save him."

Ryden nods, sadly, but in agreement.

The tears flow faster, and I bury my head in Ryden's shoulder, grateful for the comfort. We sit like that until my tears clear, and then a thought occurs to me.

"I have to win, don't I?" Ryden freezes. "That's the only option. Otherwise, they'll kill me because there isn't a world where King Edward lets us live."

It's not exactly a question, but his silence is answer enough.

CHAPTER ELEVEN
Camille

MY BREATH SHAKES AS I step out into the roaring crowd. Ryden and Aubrey are directly ahead of me, walking side by side. They even pause to raise their intertwined hands in a sign of unison. Watching them makes me briefly wish I'd taken the time to track Keith down and enter with him. But I haven't seen him since he stormed out of the training room yesterday, and it's not like he sought me out either. Plus, I don't know how to keep our father from him. It wouldn't be the first secret I've kept from him, but this one feels different. More selfish.

So I walk out of the palace hall without him and into the largest room I've ever seen. That is, if it can even be considered a room. Its layout is similar to the Combatant Day arena back home, but three times the size. The seats appear to be packed, and while the arena in the Gulf had been full of false cheering and forced smiles, this crowd seems genuinely excited. Almost everyone is standing from their seats to stomp, clap, and cheer for the competitors as they exit the palace gates.

Aubrey, Ryden, and I walk out directly into the middle of the arena floor, which is covered with obstacles and different terrain to make the first Game even more entertaining. A screen displayed on the far wall lights up with live footage of the event as well as a large timer which will signify the end of the Game. Cameras spin around in the air, focusing on not only us but the crowd and the royal family, who sit perched in a tall booth overlooking the arena. The queen and both her children are all waves and smiles, although from what I can see from my spot on the ground, Princess Amaia's smile looks more like a grimace. The king's lips, however, are pressed into a thin line, and his eyes are trained directly on mine. His stare is scrutinizing as he slowly cocks his head.

I incline my head, and his lips curve upward into an amused smile. Unnerved, I look away and focus on following Aubrey and Ryden across the arena. Directly underneath the royal family are two sets of stairs: one leading to the left of the booth and one to the right. Aubrey and I head to the right while Ryden walks off to the left, giving me a quick wink as he goes. I smile back at him, grateful for his support.

Halfway up the stairs, the crowd bursts into a thunderous roar, and I pause to look back at the entrance. Sabrina and Asher have entered, with Garden right behind them. Sabrina's hair is threaded into a crown on her head, with glints of metal weaved through it. Asher holds his sword out of its scabbard, dangling it by his side. It's completely lit up by a fire trailing from his fingertips to the very edge of his blade.

Garden only has a sword strapped to her back, but she doesn't need anything else to be intimidating. Her gift is creating powerful illusions, and although I've never seen her use it, Ryden warned me to stay away from her in the arena. Not being able to trust my senses is a definitive way to get myself killed.

Asher thrusts his fiery blade up into the air, pausing to look around at the crowd and basking in their praise. I smirk and pull on my gift, which has been begging to be released since I woke up this morning. Reaching out with a sharp, ice-cold blast, I freeze his blade and the air surrounding it. Asher's flames flicker and begin to dim as his wild grin turns into a confused frown. I feel his flaming gift pushing back against mine but, gritting my teeth, I push the temperature down even more, snuffing out his fire.

It's only for a moment before I let go, and Asher regains control of the flame, but it's long enough that his face is bright red in frustration and embarrassment. Aubrey, who has paused next to me on the stairs, laughs and turns to me. "Nice one."

"Thanks, he deserves it."

"Won't argue with you on that one."

Aubrey and I climb the rest of the way to our seats, which are each labeled with a silver nameplate. Aubrey is on the edge of the row, but my seat is farther down, tucked between a girl with rich tanned skin matching my own. There's also an empty seat labeled 'Sabrina Pelos.' Lovely.

The girl on my left is sitting with a sword lying across her bouncing lap with her dirty blonde hair pulled back from her face in a simple ponytail. I recognize her as Nicole Idomet. Aubrey had pointed her out one morning at breakfast. She's the only other girl competing from the Gulf. I wonder what part of the sector she's from? But from her closed-off expression, I don't risk asking her.

Sabrina doesn't have the same courtesy as she gracefully sits down next to me.

"I hope you said your final goodbyes this morning." She sneers in my direction. My first impression of her had been spot on. "I wouldn't want you to die down there without your family knowing." She fakes a concerned hand to her chest. "Oh wait, you couldn't say goodbye to your parents even if you wanted to."

I keep my gaze focused on the entry gate, refusing to reply to her taunts.

"At least you've still got your brother," she drawls. I grit my teeth. "Although, let's be honest. We've all seen him in the practice room. Even if you have a chance of surviving today, he certainly doesn't."

"Shut up." I clamp my mouth closed before I say anything else. My gift rears in response, eager to reach a burning hand to her throat and see what insults she wants to throw out then.

Of course, she continues, this time leaning toward me as if sharing a secret. "In fact, I heard that Asher and Carter both personally would like to be the ones to do it."

Before I can reach over to claw her eyes out, Nicole cuts in. "She told you to shut up, and if I were you, I'd listen." Her voice is steady as her dark brown eyes pierce through Sabrina's.

"What is she going to do? Kill me?" Sabrina's voice is filled with laughter, and I grind my teeth together so hard it hurts.

Nicole shrugs. "I wouldn't be surprised."

Either unsure of how to respond or losing interest, Sabrina remains quiet and turns her head away. Either way, I'm grateful for her silence, especially as Keith and Miles enter the arena. They both have swords attached to their waists just like the one on mine. Keith keeps his eyes bent on the floor and his brows furrowed in concentration. It seems like Miles is trying to shake him out of it, but I know there's no hope in trying to reach him. My brother is the most stubborn person I know, and if he doesn't want to do something, there's no hope of making it happen.

I don't have much time to hope Keith focuses enough to survive today because as soon as Miles and Keith have taken their seats, loud horns echo throughout the arena. Sure enough, as I glance down both rows of competitors, Miles and Keith are the last ones to arrive.

The king's voice bounds across the room with the help of someone's gift, and I shift in my seat to face the royal booth.

"Welcome my beloved citizens!"

Nicole snorts into the back of her hand.

"I am so grateful for all of you joining us here today to watch as twenty-four lovely ladies and twenty-four young men compete for the place of your future princess and prince as well as the future match for both of my children!" The crowd's cheers are almost deafening, and I have to fight the urge to cover my ears.

"Today's Game, the first of the Crowning Games, is quite simple. All forty-eight of the competitors, from their respective groups, have chosen a single weapon. They will then have the chance to fight it out in the arena. All of them have been dutifully training in my palace in anticipation for today. Of course, as citizens of Central, you all will have a final say in your future royalty, but we use these Games as a way of weeding out the weak and highlighting the strong. Keep a watchful eye on the competitors—not only in today's Game, but throughout the year, because we want the winners to be worthy of the crowns they will wear!"

The crowd cheers again.

"The rules are simple. Only one weapon is allowed along with the ability to use their unique gifts. With the assistance of some of my officers and their gifts, everything will be contained to protect you all from any magical outbursts. The competitors have two choices to exit the ring. Tap their head twice as a request for removal. At this point, the competitor is safe from harm and will be escorted back to their seat. The second choice is to leave as the victor of the first Crowning Game."

He pauses for a brief moment.

"I suppose there is a third. Considering that fighting until the end is a true mark of bravery, tapping out is the coward's way out. If one wishes to be a true warrior, worthy of leading this kingdom, they will die rather than give up. So naturally, death is encouraged," King Edward snarls, and disgustingly, the crowd cheers even louder at the prospect of blood being spilt.

Taking cue from the officers, the boys' row stands up and follows the lead officer down the stairs. A little boy catches my eye. His whole body is shivering, and he clutches a small black dagger in his hand, hanging on to it for dear life. I remember Keith telling me about him. His name is Oliver, and he can't be older than thirteen—maybe even twelve. Keith follows right behind him, his brown eyes focused on the shaking boy.

As the final boy's shoes hit the arena floor, a small shock rebounds through the air. Whatever gift or gifts the king is having people use to protect the public must have just gone into place. There are twenty-four officers, each of whom escorts a boy to their spot against the wall.

"Begin." The king's voice echoes in my head, and I lean forward.

My only hope is that what little skill Keith has will be enough.

Chapter Twelve
Keith

My head pounds as the king's voice is amplified throughout the arena.

"Begin."

Immediately, the other boys charge off the walls, drawing their weapons as they go. Miles and Ryden are across the arena as they stand back-to-back, paired against Giler, the one with impregnable skin, and Silas, whose gift of breathing underwater is useless in this Game. I'm grateful they can handle themselves. My own sword hangs at my waist untouched as my heart beats rapidly against my chest.

I spent all of last night twisting and turning in my bed, afraid to close my eyes because of the nightmares that were sure to come. The image that tormented me was Asher drawing his face into a sneer, charging toward me and holding a bright red blade dancing with flames.

The fear of nightmares wasn't the only thing that had kept me awake. The princess's challenge played on repeat in my mind. Telling me not to fight is something easy for her to say. It's not her life on the line. Yet, a strong part of me realizes that she's right.

The truth is, I can't fight, and even if I could, there's nothing I could do to save myself. I can't wield a sword—or any other weapon—and my gift hasn't shown up. I don't stand a chance against Asher, who hasn't reached me yet only because another boy, Hunter, has intercepted his path.

Even if I could fight, what could I do?

Kill one of the other boys?

Fight until I reach the point of death?

Instinctively, I glance up toward the royal booth.

The king and the prince are eagerly focused on the action occurring elsewhere in the arena, and the queen looks down with an almost bored facial expression. Princess Amaia, however, is looking at me curiously. A small smile dances across her lips as if she knows the conclusion I've come to even before stepping into the arena.

I bring my hand up and deliberately tap the top of my head twice. Princess Amaia's smile grows as do howls of disapproval from the crowd. The king's gaze shifts to me, and the dark look in his eyes makes me want to run in the other direction. A part of me rejoices that I could do something to enrage the man. Apparently, he doesn't like the idea of someone ruining the fun of his Game.

Two officers are quick to grab my arms and forcefully drag me back to the stairs that lead to my original seat. I catch a glimpse of Oliver watching me with wide eyes. He had been trembling the entire walk down, but now determination is etched on his face, and he readjusts the hold on his dagger.

The little boy gives me a strong nod and turns away before I can react.

Adrenaline still courses through my body as the officers lead me back up the stairs. I can't help but glance over at the royal booth as I pass. The queen's face remains indifferent, staring down at the arena like the whole crowd is beneath her. The king appears to have moved his attention back to the boys below. However, a glint still lingers in his eyes. His son is unfazed and still eagerly watching the Game. But Princess Amaia's bright blue eyes are still fixated on me. She gives me a small, curious smile and a light shake of her head. I stare her down, unwavering. Her smile only grows.

The whole crowd gasps, and both of us look back to the arena. I locate Miles first. He and Ryden are still fighting against the two other boys, and while neither of them have the obvious upper hand, they aren't losing. I search the rest of the arena for the source of their surprise.

A water pool erupts, and I find my answer. Hunter is still fighting against Asher. As their blades move, clanging with each hit, they simultaneously use their gifts to thwart the other. Small concentrated fires are bursting at Hunter's feet, but because of Hunter's gift, the flames don't last long. Every time a fire starts, Hunter calls on the nearest pool of water to drench not only the flame but also himself, helping to prevent the fire from latching onto his body.

But while the crowd's attention is fixated on their fight, another figure catches my eye. Oliver has moved from his original position and is now creeping closer to Asher. Dread pools in my stomach as I realize his goal. He carefully dodges any loose rock or obstacle that might give his presence away. His little knife looks so big clenched in his tiny fist. All it would take is one small misstep, and Asher would burn the boy to a crisp. Not to mention, Asher is wearing Hunter out with more power and stamina behind his gift. It won't be long before their fight is over and Asher notices Oliver.

I want to scream out and launch myself from my seat to tear him away, but I've already given up my ability to help him. With a quick glance at my sister, I see that Camille is just as on edge as I am. She's leaning forward in her chair, ignoring whatever words are coming from Sabrina's mouth. Her and the girl next to her are both holding their breath. Desperately, I look back toward Miles and Ryden, who are too preoccupied in their own fight—now against four other boys instead of two—to notice Oliver's advancement.

The world slows down as Asher switches tactics and sends a rope of flame swinging through the air. As it whips around, it strikes Oliver right in his little chest. His high-pitched scream can be heard from every seat, and my heart drops as he falls to the ground. The crowd's own cries echo throughout the arena. I want to curl my lip in disgust at their sudden sadness. It's hypocritical of them to grieve for Oliver when just moments before they were cheering and excited for the entertainment.

Cameras circle the boy's smoldering shirt and lifeless brown eyes, displaying the image of Oliver's dead body on the large screens posted in the corners of the arena. His little dagger is still clenched in his hands.

Searching far down to my left, looking past the royal booth, I find Camille again. She isn't looking at me, her gaze fixed on the arena. Her normally bright green eyes have faded to dull and emotionless. Her face is a blank canvas, wiped clean as she simply stares at the battles ensuing on the floor.

I look back to see how Miles and Ryden are faring, but my eyes keep lingering back to Oliver's broken figure. Asher and Hunter are still fighting, not at all bothered by the dead little boy at their feet. All of Hunter's energy is focused on combating Asher's flames and sword swipes. It only takes a small mistake, and Asher's sword strikes flesh.

It tears open a flowing wound on Hunter's sword arm, but taking King Edward's words to heart, he doesn't tap his head like he should. He puts a final burst of energy into crashing a huge wave down on Asher, drenching the flame wielder. Instead of being put off, this only encourages Asher as he strikes a blow to Hunter's chest. Hunter collapses to the floor, and Asher moves on to his next target as if he didn't just end two lives.

I shut my eyes even as a small tear squeezes past my eyelid. I don't make an effort to wipe it away. Anger takes root as images of Oliver, both alive and dead, flash through my mind.

Would I have been able to save him if I had stayed?

Certainly my presence alone couldn't have done any-thing. Could it have?

Overcome by bitterness, my eyes spring open, and I fixate them on the King of Myria, whose face is overcome with glee. Even the crowd is back to cheering now, forgetting Oliver and Hunter. Instead, their focus is on Miles, who jumps around the arena, avoiding the now enormous Carter, whose gift is making himself the size of a giant. It's disgusting the amount of people sitting in this arena who have already moved past Oliver's death.

The king doesn't glance my way again, but Princess Amaia does. Her face remains passive as if nothing bothers her either. But the fire dancing in her eyes says otherwise. Anger and an overwhelming sadness consume us both as we break eye contact. I don't understand how or why she has the self-control to remain in her seat. If our roles were reversed, I would have already stabbed the king through the eye by now.

More people begin to join me in the row of seats, and I can't help feeling relieved as more and more competitors decide their own lives are more important than this stupid Game. Miles is one of the last people to find his way back to his seat, and I breathe a sigh of relief as he plops down a few seats down from me. This morning, when he had found me to ensure I didn't walk in alone, I was shocked at his kindness. I'm grateful that his body isn't lying next to Hunter and Oliver.

Ryden, not to my surprise, is the last one left standing and announced the winner of the first Game. It's hard to get the best of someone who can read your mind.

Now, as Camille rises along with the other girls, I can only hope she makes it out alive.

Chapter Thirteen
Camille

WITH HIS CLOTHES STILL smoldering, Oliver is removed from the arena as we make our way down the stairs. Officers carelessly drag his body out as if he is simply a sack of flour. The sight threatens to bring more tears to my eyes, but I swallow hard and urge them away.

I follow behind Nicole, purposefully placing my feet on each step, determined not to stumble or fall. My face burns in embarrassment at the thought of me tumbling down the stairs in front of the crowd. I try to put on a confident look for their benefit, but I know it falls short. A part of me wants to glance back up at Keith, but the thought turns my gut to stone.

I wish I could sock him upside the face for deliberately placing last and going out without a fight. Yes, his skills were abysmal, but if he didn't even try, he wouldn't stand a chance at surviving the Games, much less winning them.

As my feet hit the arena floor, I push the thought of Keith from my mind. If he doesn't want to put in effort, I'll have to hope that my performance is good enough for the both of us. At least I don't have to worry about him dying today.

Officers lead each of us to our spot against the arena wall, and the girls on either side of me already have hands on their sword hilts. The girl to my left is from the Lates. I recognize her. She has tangled brown hair pulled back into a ponytail, and her long arms hang awkwardly at her sides.

As the king declares for the Game to begin, I make her my first target. Simultaneously, I pull out my sword and charge toward her. Her eyes widen at my sudden movement, but she brings her sword up to catch mine. Her slow reaction speed makes me grin. I might stand a chance.

However, my grin is quick to disappear as the girl lights her entire body on fire. Flames flick out toward me as extensions of her arms. The rest of the arena fades away—even the dull roar from the crowd. I put every bit of my focus on matching her sword strikes while keeping my distance from the flames. Sparks fly from both of our blades as they clash against each other. Recalling the advice Miles gave during practice one day, I keep my sword moving, sharp and quick. I can feel my arm tiring, but from the Lates girl's movements, I can tell she's equally exhausted.

She's expelling more energy because she's using her gift. The thought gives me an idea. I think back to how I snuffed out the flame, however briefly, from Asher's sword.

Taking a handful of swift steps backward, I shift my energy to my gift. It responds eagerly, rising with the adrenaline that pulses through my body. I outstretch my hands, and in one moment, I snuff out the flame from the girl's body.

With a shocked gasp, the girl crumples to the floor. The sudden removal of her gift immediately leaves the Lates girl drained. For a split second, I consider moving on to let her lie there and recuperate.

But then I remember Keith's abysmal performance, Aubrey's hidden warning, and Ryden's silence when I asked him if I have to win.

The girl looks at me with fear in her eyes as I raise my sword. Her cheeks are flushed and a cut across her arm is bleeding through her jacket. I must have made contact and not realized it. Before I can bring my blade down, the girl quickly reaches to tap her head twice.

A sigh of relief passes through me as officers come forward to take the girl away. Before I can take a moment to catch my breath, I'm tackled to the floor. My blade slips from my fingers and clatters away from me. Snarling, I push against the other girl, rolling so I am positioned on top of her. As I look down, I recognize her from the first breakfast we had. Prill Prancis.

She's been in the practice rooms, always accompanied by Asher and her brother, Carter. They liked to show off, taking the center practice ring and exhibiting their gifts. Prill can shrink herself to the size of a bug, making her nearly impossible to see unless you know to look for her. That's how I assume she snuck up on me. She must have shrunk herself to an unnoticeable size and waited until the fight with the Lates girl was over before catching me by surprise.

Prill snarls back at me and kicks up, sending me sprawling across the floor. Dirt scratches against my cheeks, stinging my skin. I scramble to my feet as fast as I can, aware of the fact that she's armed, and I am not. My sword is still lying on the floor a handful of yards to my right. Prill is crouched, with her sword in hand, grinning maliciously.

I don't let her get a moment's rest before I reach out with a strand of fiery heat. She clenches her teeth in pain, stumbling as she steps toward me. I rush for my sword, but Prill anticipates that. Pushing through the heat, she swings her sword for my neck. Instinctively, I duck and roll, grabbing a handful of dirt from the arena floor. As I launch myself back to my feet, I'm face to face with her. Without hesitation, I blow the handful of dirt in her face, and Prill shouts in frustration at her sudden blindness. I use the momentary distraction to scoop up my sword and turn to face her.

Her dark eyes are filled with rage as she matches my stance. We both grip our swords, ready for the other to initiate. Aubrey shifts to her left, and I mimic her movement, so we begin circling each other. With every step, I take a deep breath and let my gift simmer. It reacts to the blood pounding through my chest, aching for a way out.

"I'm shocked, you know." Prill's voice cuts through the air like daggers.

I play along to give myself more time to gather my strength. "What do you mean?"

"That you managed to take Kimberly out."

I figure that's the name of the girl I fought. I shrug. "And?"

"I guess it doesn't matter." Prill shrugs back. "I'm going to beat you."

She leaps across the circle and attacks. I barely ward off the blow in time. If I had been a second later, my head would've been severed from my neck. The crowd cheers, but I don't know if there's another fight happening or if everyone is glued to me and Prill.

I respond by putting my full strength into each blow. Somehow, even though she's eagerly matching my strikes, she manages to taunt me. Words about my father and my uselessness flow from her mouth. My moves become progressively more and more aggressive, the only outward sign of the impact her words have on me. Inside, however, my gift rears in anger. The pressure builds in my chest, begging to be released. Heat curls at my fingertips, and I clench my jaw.

Distracted by the attempt to keep my gift under control, I'm too slow to block Prill's sword. Instead, I shift my body so the blade misses my heart and tears into my side. The blow knocks me to the floor, and once again, my sword clatters out of my hand.

Spitting out a mouthful of dirt, I glare up at Prill.

"You poor thing." Her eyes gleam with victory. "You tried so hard, and yet, you weren't any more useful than your brother."

I try to push myself to my feet, but my side screams in pain. My silver jacket is already stained a bright red.

Prill laughs at my attempt. "You know, I thought your brother would've stuck around to fight during his round. That little boy, Oliver, spoke so highly of Keith whenever we were all practicing together. I know Carter will be disappointed he didn't get to shut the kid up himself."

Between ragged breaths, I spit in her direction. Prill's smile widens. Her voice drops. "Keith left him alone. Because of your brother, Oliver had to die by himself. If you ask me, I'd say he deserved it."

Her final words send me over the edge. While there's some truth in her words, the image of the little boy's smoldering body fills my mind with rage. No child deserves what happened to him.

With one look at me, Prill's face goes sheet white as she realizes she went too far. My gift rushes out of me in waves, reaching for Prill. It surrounds her in fiery heat and goes even further, targeting her from the inside. Prill screeches in pain.

The entire crowd goes silent as the cry pierces through the sky. Her sword slips through her fingers as my gift doesn't relent. In my peripheral vision, I see the other competitors pause to watch. To my left, Sabrina and Garden watch, pausing their fight against Aubrey, whose face is drained of all color.

Prill, in a desperate attempt to surrender, tries to reach for the top of her head. But I don't feel like letting her tap out. Between her and Oliver, she's the one who doesn't deserve to live.

Before my gift can finish burning her from the inside out, I glance up at the crowd. My brother's face is the first thing I see. His eyes are full of fear and even disgust. He looks repulsed by me. Of course, he can't hear what Prill said. He doesn't understand that if our roles were reversed, Prill would kill me without a second thought.

Still, I find myself easing up, recalling my gift back to me. As soon as the pain is more bearable, Prill's hand falls twice on her head and officers hurry her out. I find myself immediately regretting my decision to show her mercy. From the look of pure hatred on her face, I have made a very serious enemy. Great, just what I need. Hopefully I at least score well for forcing her into submission.

Once I turn around, I don't look back at her or my brother. Instead, I pick up my sword and advance towards Sabrina and Garden. It shakes everyone out of their stupor, and the crowd begins cheering again at its loudest volume yet.

Chapter Fourteen
Keith

EATING DINNER WITH ALL the Crowning Game competitors is more formal than breakfast. Breakfast is more of a come-as-you-please-and-leave-when-you-want type of deal. Dinner has a set time for when we all sit and eat. Although sometimes awkward, most evenings aren't too bad. I sit with Ryden and Miles at the designated boys' table, and we usually discuss my abysmal day of practice. Typically, other boys will chime into our conversation, most often Oliver.

His absence is what contributes to the silence that hangs over both tables at tonight's dinner. Even Asher, who so casually killed two other boys today, eats his mashed potatoes quietly. Every once and a while some hushed whispers or quiet conversations would penetrate tonight's silence, but they don't last long. I keep my head down, still unable to get the image of Oliver's scorched body or the sound of Prill's screeches out of my head.

Even Miles, normally the most talkative between the three of us, is silently picking at his piece of meat. He hasn't taken a bite of his food and keeps eyeing the spot Oliver usually sits in.

Another boy, Axel, sits directly across from Asher. He's gripping his fork so hard I'm surprised the metal hasn't bent. With Axel's hateful stare, and a potential weapon in hand, it's a wonder he hasn't driven it through Asher's heart. The royal family's presence must be what stops him.

King Edward and Prince Jacob look as gleeful as ever. The queen is absent from her normal chair, but Princess Amaia still sits in her seat, leaving a space between her and her father. She absentmindedly twirls her noodles around with her fork, clearly deep in thought.

I risk a glance up at Camille, who I still haven't talked to all day. Stubbornly staying in my room until dinner, I had successfully avoided talking to anyone about anything.

Camille is taking small bites off of her plate, but her eyes are downcast and focused. Prill is at the other end of the table, eyes furiously focused on her pasta. Naturally, I worry for my sister, despite Ryden assuring me that she would be alright. My concern is only heightened because Carter hasn't touched his food all night. He's only sitting with a dining knife clenched in his hand and staring a hole through my sister's head, much like Axel is with Asher. At least Prill doesn't seem fixated on immediate revenge.

We all jump a little when Sabrina's voice drawls out loud enough for the whole room to hear her. "Well, tonight's dinner was just delightful. But I do think I'm about to head off to bed. It's been quite an eventful day." She leans her head back and yawns.

Ignoring most of the room's glares, she stands, gesturing for Garden to follow. Garden stands and exits the room right on Sabrina's heels, which I find interesting. Garden had won today's Game after Sabrina and Aubrey fought it out, resulting in Aubrey getting second place and Sabrina receiving third place. It seemed odd that Garden would choose to follow Sabrina instead of the other way around. Their exit seems to encourage everyone else to get up and leave, and the majority of the room is quick to clear out.

When Carter stands, his chair screeching against the tile, my head perks up. I eye him as he slowly walks past the girls' table. He comes to a steady stop right behind Camille, and I'm up and out of my seat in the blink of an eye.

Before I can reach him and tell him to shove off, he sneers, "I hope you know what's coming for you, stupid girl."

I freeze as I watch Camille slowly turn in her chair, her eyes calculating. "You should be more concerned with yourself." Her voice is cold. She glances down the table at Prill, who has also risen from her chair. "Both of you should."

Carter snickers. "You can't touch me. Not without getting yourself killed. But guess what?" He points a grubby finger in my direction. "He's fair game once we're in the arena." He leans closer to Camille's face. "And I will not hesitate to make him suffer."

Unfiltered rage flickers in Camille's eyes, and as she moves to get out of her seat, I reach Carter, stepping between him and my sister. "Back up, Prancis."

He smiles at me and holds his hands up in mock innocence. "Yes, sir." Prill strides up behind him, her lips curled upward at me. Without another word, they walk out of the room, leaving everyone staring at Camille and me. Even Ryden and Miles are looking at us a little warily.

King Edward hasn't looked up from his plate, while his son's face sparks with excitement. Prince Jacob is leaning forward, eagerly watching the spectacle. Princess Amaia observes us with careful eyes. I meet her gaze, and her lips press together in warning. I turn away from her. If she has something to say, she can say it out loud.

Camille finishes getting up and moves to follow Carter and Prill, not speaking a word to me or even sparing me a second glance. I follow her out into the hallway, waiting to speak to her until we don't have an audience.

"Cam."

She stops and turns to look at me. "What do you want?" Her question is dripping with exhaustion. I simply wrap my arms around her in a tight hug. She allows me a moment before gently extracting herself.

"You know I can handle myself, right?" She sounds accusatory, and I take a step back, confused.

"Sure, I do. After today, I know you can. But that doesn't mean I can't stand up for you."

Her face sours. "Really Keith? And how do you plan on standing up for me? Especially when you can't even stand up for yourself?" Her words hit me like bricks, and I almost stumble backward.

"What do you mean?"

"What I mean is that you didn't even try to fight today!" Her voice echoes through the empty hallway. "You gave up! Just like that. You took last place without even try-ing."

"Why should it matter?" My voice gets louder. "I'm not here to win some stupid crown."

"Then what do you think is going to happen? That you're just going to refuse to play in any of the Games and at the end of it all be sent back home and life returns to normal?" Camille snarls, her eyes flashing.

"No, of course not. I'm not naive. But I'm certainly not going to lose myself in the process."

"Oh, so you fancy yourself a martyr, then? Like dad?" This sentiment strikes deep.

"What has gotten into you?" I demand.

"I'm trying to survive here, Keith!" She throws up her hands in frustration. "And you should be too."

I shake my head. "Not if it means becoming a killer."

She goes silent, the fire in her eyes rescinding. "So that's what this is about. You're upset because of what I did in the arena."

"How could I not be? I've never seen your eyes go so cold." I shudder as I recall the look that crossed her face. "I don't want them to turn you into a monster."

"She said Oliver deserved to die," she says barely above a whisper.

I don't know what to add to that, so I simply stand there. Blinking. Taking the information in. Finally, I know what to say. "That doesn't give you the right to torture her the way you did."

Abruptly, I turn and leave. I don't know if I run or walk, but I know I make it to my room. When I get there, however, I immediately see that I'm not alone.

Amaia stands outside my door, pacing back and forth. She's lightly chewing on her bottom lip before she spots me. She appears as shocked to see me as I am to see her.

"Hello?" I speak first.

"Oh." She stumbles over her words, and I frown. When does the Princess of Myria stumble? "Hey. I just wanted to see if you were alright after today. And then with dinner. And I don't know—maybe see if you needed someone to talk to? I mean, if not, I can leave. I totally understand." She's talking so fast that I'm barely keeping pace with her.

"Um, can you start from the beginning?" I'm still confused as to why she's here. In front of my door.

She stops pacing and looks at me. Her lips curve into an embarrassed smile that has me feeling a little warm inside. "Yeah, you're right. I'm sorry." She lightly shakes her head and stands a little straighter.

"I just wanted to say I think you did a really good job today."

"By not fighting?" I clarify, raising an eyebrow.

She shrugs. "Everyone fights in their own little ways, and I liked the way you did."

"Well thank you, I suppose." After a moment of silence with us just looking at each other, I clear my throat. "Was that all you were out here for?"

Amaia's eyes are thoughtful as she surveys me. "Are you okay?"

I don't have a feigned answer. The honest response is what ends up pouring out. "I don't know."

She nods and gives me a sad smile, but before she can say anything else, more honesty spills out of my mouth.

"I mean, you seem to think what I did was a good thing, but was it? My sister seems to think it was the wrong decision. If I had stayed in that arena, Asher would have come after me instead, and Oliver wouldn't have died." I crease my brow in distress. "Who knows what the king's punishment will be? I didn't technically break a rule, but I must have embarrassed him by not playing along. I'm sure there's going to be repercussions."

"Don't worry about my father. I'll handle it."

"How?"

"Don't worry about it." Anger flashes in Amaia's voice as she dismisses my concern with a wave of her hand. Then her eyes soften. "I can see where you're getting the rest from, I suppose." She sighs. "But you're alive. Why don't you focus on that?"

"Because I'm alive and Oliver isn't!" I shout in frustration.

"Yes, that's true, and now you have to figure out what you're going to do with that."

She's suddenly calm, and it aggravates me.

"Isn't that the problem? Alive, I'm useless. I don't even have a stupid gift yet."

Amaia gives a small frown. "It's in there somewhere, Keith." She taps a finger on my chest. "Seems like it's very well hidden, but believe me, it *is* in there."

She says this with such conviction that it stuns me.

"Okay."

CHAPTER FIFTEEN

Camille

OF COURSE I GET lost in the hallways...

One would think I'd at least know the way to and from my room by now, but apparently not. Thankfully, I haven't run into any officer-infested hallways, so I know I'm not anywhere I'm not supposed to be.

When I hit a dead end that I had been certain would open up to my room's hall, I growl in frustration. It's all too much. Keith is angry at me now, Prill looks like she wants to rip my head off, and it all doesn't matter anyway because my chances of dying this year are extremely high.

Folding my head into my hands, I lean against the wall to try and take some deep breaths. I can feel my gift pulling at me, begging me to let it free as if that could release the tension building in my chest. My heart races, and I let myself fall to the floor, keeping my head in my

134

hands. The pounding in my temples won't go away, so I close my eyes and focus on breathing.

In and out.

In and out.

In.

Out.

IN.

OUT.

I have no idea how long it's been before someone's heavy footsteps echo through the hallway. Heat rushing to my face, I peek through my fingers, but all I can see are black pants and shiny shoes. I don't know whether I should feel better or worse that it's not an officer who's caught me breaking down.

"Are you lost?"

My head jerks upward. Ryden is looking down at me with a light smile on his face, but his eyes flash with concern.

A laugh chokes through me. I sound deranged. "Not at all. I'm perfectly fine, thank you very much."

Ryden doesn't run away like he should—especially as I feel my gift building like a storm. I'm afraid it wouldn't consider him anything more than collateral damage if I unleashed it. Instead, he plops himself on the floor next to me.

"I wasn't really asking." He smirks at me. "It was more of a statement. Something along the lines of, 'you're los t.'" His playful eyes and light grin make me smile back at him.

"Okay, you got me." I toss up my hands and look down the hallway. "I have no idea where I am."

He doesn't laugh at me, which I'm grateful for. In fact, he studies me with his thoughtful green eyes, and suddenly I feel rather self-conscious. I can still feel the flush on my cheeks from my heavy breathing and slight embarrassment. I anxiously rake my fingers through my hair, which I'm sure is now in brown tangles. Thank goodness I didn't start crying or there would be marks from the tears. I catch myself.

Why do I even care? I don't care about anyone's opinion of me—except maybe Keith's. And after our argument after dinner, it's clear that his opinion of me isn't good right now anyway. So why do I find myself unconsciously brushing at my messy hair and hoping my bright red face fades?

Ryden stands up, offering out a hand. "Would you like to see something?"

I pause, my gaze flickering between his outreached hand and the mischievous glint in his eyes.

"Come on, you know you can trust me."

This should probably send off some kind of warning bell in my head, but it doesn't.

I grab his hand, and his eyes light up as his face breaks out into the goofiest grin. I laugh and use his arm to pull myself up.

"I take this as a yes?" Ryden quirks an eyebrow.

"I guess so," I say, rolling my eyes.

"So, you do trust me." He sounds proud.

I shrug. "Apparently." A thought occurs to me. "Although, how did you know where to find me?"

I might be imagining it, but Ryden's pale face is tinged pink as he refuses to make eye contact with me.

"Umm, well…" He chews on his bottom lip, and I stare him down. "It's just… Your thoughts were very loud."

I take a quick step back from him and rethink the whole "trusting him" thing. I can't help the mix of anger and disgust that plays across my face, and Ryden is quick to reach his hands out to my shoulders. I don't know why I let him, but I do.

"No, no, no!" Ryden viciously shakes his head. "I wasn't reading your thoughts, I promise. I would never do that." There's something genuine to his voice that makes me believe him.

"Okay." That's all I say because, well, that's all there is to be said.

Ryden's worried frown only deepens. "Listen, it's like radio static. Everyone's thoughts are always talking and whispering and shouting, and well, it drives me up a wall. So, from an early age, I learned to tune some of it out and make it all background noise. None of it makes any sense unless I want it to, so I promise, I wasn't listening in on your thoughts."

I ponder his explanation. "I suppose that makes sense."

I start down the hallway at a quick pace, pulling myself from Ryden's gentle touch.

He hurries to catch up with me. "Are you mad at me now?"

I chew on the inside of my lip, thinking it over. "I don't think so. I mean, I believe you. Plus, I'm sure I'd be able to know if you were in my brain, like with Aubrey. It's just an odd thought that you would be able to hear my... what did you call it?" I pause. "Static?"

Ryden nods. "I think the more attached to someone I am, the louder their... static is."

My grin is back. "Oh, so you're attached to me?"

This time his face definitely turns a bright shade of pink. "I mean, yes? No? I don't know. What am I supposed to say to that?"

"I'm just playing with you." I give him a light bump on the shoulder. His sweet smile has something inside my stomach pleasantly twisting. I'm grateful for the distraction he provides. I've almost forgotten everything that's happened today. "Now, what were you gonna show me?"

"Oh right!" Ryden reaches for my hand and leads the way down the hall. "This way."

I don't know what's more charming about him—his goofy smile or his sense of direction. He doesn't pause at any turn and easily guides to a hallway I recognize as the one with our rooms.

"I mean, thank you for taking me back to my room, but I hate to break it to you, I've already seen this hallway."

Ryden's eyebrows dance. "Are you so sure?"

I laugh lightly. "Yes."

He heads down the hall, shaking his head in amusement. I follow behind him, curious. It's only when I get a better look at all of the individual doors that I realize I was mistaken. The nameplate closest to me reads, "Miles Repsport." We aren't in the hallway to my room. Instead, although the ceiling arches and the wall patterns are identical, we are in the hallway leading to Ryden's room.

He opens his door, and I hesitate outside the entrance.

"Is this even allowed?"

Ryden grins. "Sure, it is. Now come on, hurry, before it's gone!"

"Before what's gone?"

He tugs me into the room, which looks practically identical to mine. There are slight differences in the layout, but the most noticeable one is the balcony. It opens up to a gorgeous field of green grass and has a perfect view of the now-setting sun. Ryden's amusement only grows as he takes in my reaction. I walk out onto the balcony and take a deep breath of fresh air. The most stunning sunset I've ever seen is slowly fading beneath the horizon. Pinks, oranges, and blues all mesh together, shooting across the sky in a perfect display of art.

Ryden is standing next to me now, gazing up at the sky.

"It's gorgeous."

Ryden nods. "It most certainly is."

A small blush forms on my cheeks. I raise an eyebrow at him before turning back to the view. "Thank you for this."

"Of course." Ryden shrugs. "Does it make you feel any better?"

I stare up at the shifting colors in the sky and ponder my response. "Yeah, it does. I can almost forget about today. Almost."

Hearing the sadness in my voice, Ryden takes my hand and lightly squeezes it. "For what it's worth, I think you were pretty awesome today."

I snort. "Seriously?"

"One hundred percent."

I stare at him, trying to decipher if he's being serious. "Why?"

"You're not afraid to do what you have to do. Prill would have killed you if the roles were reversed, and even if you let her tap out today, what's to say she won't kill you in the next Game? And I find the amount of control you have over your power awe-inspiring."

I bark out a laugh. "Sometimes I think my gift controls me more than I control it." As if hearing the conversation, heat begins to tickle my fingertips and the bars of the balcony become ice cold to the touch.

Ryden shakes his head at me, his expression serious. "Our gifts aren't their own living things. It's not like it can act on its own, so I disagree. You have complete control over it, and it's not your fault you want to use it."

As he says this, the truth of it rings through me. My gift reacts to me, and I would like nothing more than to burn down this palace if I could. Maybe that's why I constantly feel the need for release.

Interrupting my thoughts, Ryden asks, "You're coming with us tomorrow, right?"

"Tomorrow?"

"Yeah, Miles is treating us all to a surprise."

"I wasn't invited," I say.

"Well, I'm inviting you now. Aubrey's dragging me along, and I'll do the same to you if I have to."

"Fine." I decide to ask him a question that's been bugging me. "Why are you being nice to me?"

He tilts his head in response. "What do you mean? Is my kindness a bad thing?"

"Actually, yeah," I say. "It's a little unnerving. I didn't expect anyone from Central to be kind to me or Keith. But you, Miles, and Aubrey have been. And it's... unsettling."

I'm only half teasing because a large part of me feels wary of their immediate attraction to my brother and me. When Ryden's smile slowly fades, I lean even closer to him, curious as to what he'll say.

Running a hand through his red locks, he sighs. "Honestly? Amaia told us to keep an eye on you two. Help you guys adapt to living here and help you through the Games."

I recoil. "The princess asked you to be friends with us?"

Something in my voice must concern him because he takes a step closer to me, grabbing both of my hands. "Yes, she did, but before you say anything else, I've actually come to enjoy your company. I can't speak for Miles and my sister, but I promise you, I'm not faking anything with you."

His words are so deep and emotional, and all my built-up questions almost float away. His green eyes are filled with something I can't describe.

"Did she tell you why?" I ask, deciding to ignore his last confession.

Ryden furrows his brow. "Yes, she did."

"And the reason would be...?" I look at him incredulously.

"I can't tell you."

I pull my hands from his. "Why not?"

He growls in frustration, walking into his room. I follow behind him, determined to get an answer.

"I can't tell you why. Not yet at least."

"Not yet?" I demand.

He begins to pace around his room. "Eventually, I should be able to, but I'm telling you I can't say anything else about it." He fidgets with his hands. This is the most riled up I've seen him. "Trust me, I would tell you if I could."

"Okay." There's that word again. Trust. "If you say so."

He gives me a pained look. But that's not helpful to me. Not when King Edward's daughter has such an interest in my brother and me.

"I'll just have to figure it out for myself." I walk away, catching the relieved look on Ryden's face before I'm out the door.

CHAPTER SIXTEEN
Keith

THE KNOCK ON MY door is too early considering that the sunlight behind my curtains has barely peeked into the room. I turn over, bringing a pillow over my head, hoping to block out the noise. More knocks echo issue through the door, but I keep my eyes pressed shut, refusing to get up. Last night, after Amaia left, I decided I would skip breakfast and simply stay in bed. I sigh in relief when the knocks finally cease, and it appears like my visitor has let me be.

At least until a loud voice booms in my ear. "Wake up!"

I jump up, shouting in shock. The pillow I had been holding over my head is now clutched in both my hands, ready to hit whoever is in my room.

Miles's laughter is deep as he takes in my response. I look over at him. He's leaning over, clutching his stomach. In between breaths of laughter, he manages to choke out, "What are you... Going to hit... With a pillow... Oh, this is great!"

I chuck the pillow at his face, but he catches it, laughing even harder. "Goodness, I can't wait to tell Amaia about this one!"

I frown at him. "Excuse me?"

Miles straightens up, his face still mirthful and his eyes glinting with amusement. "She'll love to hear about your newfound fighting ability. Maybe they'll even let you take a pillow into the arena."

I scowl at him. "Oh, shut up."

"Only if you get up. We've got places to be and things to see. Let's go."

"Where are we going?" I glance back at my bed. "And why did you feel the need to come zipping into my room this early in the morning?"

"It's a surprise." Miles walks to the door but pauses before leaving. "Hurry and get changed into something light. We'll be waiting for you at the end of the hallway."

He slips out, not even bothering to open the door. He simply teleports himself from the room.

Show-off.

I quickly change and brush my teeth, leaving my hair uncombed. It looks fine enough. I exit my room. Waiting for me at the end of the hallway, as promised, is Miles, along with Ryden and Camille. I give Camille a small, apologetic wave. I said a lot of hurtful things to her yesterday, and yes, I was angry, but it doesn't excuse how I treated her. She gives me a sheepish look in return before turning back to focus on whatever Ryden is saying.

"Aw, there's Pillow Man." Miles teases me, his amusement is still fresh.

"Yeah, yeah, yeah." I roll my eyes. "Now can someone please tell me where we're going?"

Ryden cocks an eyebrow at me. "Miles didn't tell you?"

Camille's eyes brighten, and she shoots me a grin. "Don't tell him. It'll be a surprise." I want to argue, but Camille seems happy, so I let her have her victory.

"What's going to be a surprise?" Aubrey asks from farther down the hall as she walks toward us. "And who are we keeping it from?"

"Keith doesn't know where we're going yet," Ryden answers.

"Oh, imagine being out of the loop," Aubrey teases.

"Imagine being on time for once in your life," Miles snarks from his position in the front. He's already leading us away from the rooms, eager to get moving. Aubrey walks closer to him to throw back another insult, and Ryden and Camille fall into place behind them. I awkwardly trail behind the group, unsure of how to join either conversation. Camille saves me by slowing her pace to match mine and leaving Ryden to move closer to Aubrey and Miles.

"How are you doing?" Camille asks a little timidly, as if unsure she wants to hear a response.

"Better," I say. "And I'm sorry, Cam. I didn't mean to snap at you yesterday. It's just with everything happening, from you almost dying to not even knowing what's happening to Dad... I don't want to lose the only family I have left."

Camille casts her eyes downward, looking anywhere but at my face. "I don't want to lose you either. I just think we have very different ways of showing it."

"Very. Are we cool then?"

She nods. "We're cool." Then she gives me a playful shove on the shoulder. "Also, about time! You never apologize for anything!"

I gasp in fake hurt. "Says you."

She rolls her eyes and loops her arm through mine, hurrying our pace to catch up with the others. Miles leads us all out to the stables where five pure white horses have been saddled and left waiting for us. When he instructs us all to get on, I don't hesitate. Something about the relaxed and powerful animal strikes a chord in me, and I easily situate myself into the saddle, mimicking Aubrey as she elegantly slides herself onto her horse. Camille struggles initially, but Ryden offers his hands as a step stool, and she uses his help to pull herself up.

A pair of officers watch us carefully from their positions at the door of the stable. One of them steps forward as Miles urges his horse toward the exit.

"Where are you all heading, Mr. Repsport?"

Miles flashes his signature grin. "Just out for a ride. We'll be back before dinner. And don't worry about the Atwoods. They're with us."

The officer gives me and Camille a hard look before grumbling, "Fine, go on. But don't be a minute late."

Miles nods his gratitude and then leads us all out of the stable.

There's something freeing about riding unleashed through green fields and away from the palace grounds. Instead of going directly into the heart of Central, Miles leads us toward a grove of tall pine trees located on the opposite side of the palace's main gate. Once we hit the safety net of the trees, Miles slows our pace, and I can't help but appreciate my surroundings. The scent of pine is overwhelming but in a good way. The trees come together to create a canopy of shade, the morning sun filtering through.

For a brief moment, the idea of escape flashes through my mind. It would be easy. Leaving Miles, Aubrey, and Ryden behind. Urging Camille to follow me as we ride away from the stupid palace.

Aubrey must catch my wistful glance because she pulls up beside me with a sad smile. "You wouldn't make it."

"Who says I was thinking about making it?" I challenge.

Her smile slips. "Nobody said anything. Your desire for freedom is written all over your face."

Heat rises to my ears. "Is there anything wrong with that?"

Aubrey shakes her head. "No, absolutely not. Just... the patrol of officers that surround the palace and are constantly combing through Central. Oh, and tack on the fact that the whole country knows you're a competitor, so your face is definitely recognizable. Yeah, absolutely nothing wrong with that."

"Thanks for reminding me."

"Anytime," Aubrey fires back.

My gaze lands back on Miles who is leading his horse off to a tree and dismounting. Instructing us to do the same, he loops his horse's reins to a thick branch and then walks deeper into the forest. There is a wide gap between a pair of large trees, which opens up to a peaceful circle of soft grass. One glance at Camille and I can tell she's breathing it all in just the way I am. I wonder if it also reminds her of the woods which I used to run by in the mornings with our mom.

"It's gorgeous!" Aubrey exclaims.

Ryden lightly whistles in awe. "How did you find this place?"

Miles's cheeks turn a light shade of pink as he shrugs. "Just somewhere I go to think. I thought we could all use the refresh." His eyes briefly glance over to Camille and so do mine.

She had a look of awe on her face, and I'm grateful for Miles, even though he woke me up early. Camille certainly needs a moment outside of the palace, and if I'm being honest with myself, so do I.

Aubrey looks at Miles with a smirk before plopping herself onto the ground. The grass around her springs down to accommodate her.

Ryden follows suit, stretching his hands out behind him as Camille sits beside him. I sit next to Camille and Miles sits across from me until we've formed a circle. For minutes, we all sit in silence. I watch Camille lie down on her back, closing her eyes and basking in the sunlight. There's a part of me that wants to reach out and make sure she's doing alright. Yes, I understand why she did it, but it doesn't change the fact that she used her gift to almost burn Prill to death. I'm positive that does something to a person...

Miles is the first to break the silence, jumping to his feet, and exclaiming, "I almost forgot!"

And then he's gone.

I peer around the grove, trying to see where he went. A decent amount of time seems to go by, but neither Ryden nor Aubrey seem concerned, so neither am I. At least until Miles shocks us all by reappearing directly behind Aubrey. She lets out a yelp before slapping at his legs.

"Seriously? Was that really necessary?" Aubrey glowers up at him, but the rest of us are rolling in laughter. Even Camille is giggling a little bit.

Miles chuckles. "I would say so."

He sets two baskets down on the ground, which I hadn't noticed before. I assume that's what he disappeared to grab. He opens up the lids, and we all lean over to look inside. The amount of food in both baskets is definitely too much for the five of us. But we all reach in and grab something. I snatch a vine of grapes from underneath Aubrey, who scowls at me but settles for a ham sandwich.

"Go ahead, dig in! No need to thank me or anything." Alone, the words might sound annoyed, but Miles wears a proud smile.

"Thanks, man. This food is good."

Miles shrugs it off. "It's nothing. Just trying to brighten up the mood. I mean, we all deserve a celebration!" A broad grin splits his face. "We survived yesterday, only eleven more Games to go!"

Halfheartedly, I smile along. It's another reminder that I'm alive and Oliver isn't.

"Hear, hear!" Aubrey raises a hand and nods in agreement. "We all needed a break from those stuffy walls and the stupid Games."

We all laugh for a brief moment, except for Camille, who stares at Aubrey intently. "How long have you two known each other?"

At first, Aubrey and Miles both seem taken aback by the question, however, Ryden observes my sister with an amused look on his face. Miles is the first one to recover. "Since I was about eight years old, I think. So, like, ten years."

Camille nods, engrossed in the conversation. I don't blame her. I don't know much about any of them, except their expertise with seemingly every weapon they've shown me. It's nice to hear something personal.

"That makes sense." Camille looks back and forth between Aubrey and Miles. "You two seem close." She's saying it in a suggestive tone, emphasizing the word "close."

Aubrey laughs. "We are, but in the same way Ryden and I are close. Miles is like our annoying younger brother."

"Hey!" Miles reaches to flick Aubrey in the nose. "Rude. Plus, I'm older than all of you."

"You never let us forget it." Ryden rolls his eyes. "It's your favorite comeback whenever Amaia tells you to do something."

A look passes between him and Camille, and I eye my sister curiously. She blinks in innocent confusion. I roll my eyes—it's my way of telling her we'll talk about it later.

"It's true. I'm older than her. I should have superiority." Miles grins, proving he's only joking, but Camille takes it seriously.

"Well, then why does she?"

Miles gives her a strange look. "Really? The title 'Princess Amaia' doesn't give it away?"

"I mean it. You're a part of her personal guard, right?" Camille pushes.

"Her unit," Miles corrects.

"How did that happen? You seem way too chaotic to purposefully choose to follow orders."

Aubrey laughs, drawing the attention off of Miles. "That he most certainly is."

"So, what's the story then?" Camille asks.

Miles twiddles his fingers, looking up at her. "Not much of one. When the Princess of Myria, daughter of King Edward, asks you to do something, that means you do it. That's kind of how it works." He glances up at the sky. "And, on that note, I think it's probably time we head back to the real world."

"You mean the one where we're all fighting each other for a stupid crown?" I say sarcastically.

"That's the one," Aubrey sighs.

"Don't forget to include the part where Miss Atwood over here is now fully integrated into the true ways of Myria." Miles winks at Camille, and I pause to gauge her reaction.

She just chuckles. "Guess so."

Miles stands up and holds a hand out to Camille. "Need a hand, Miss Deadly Princess?"

"I won't say no." Camille grabs his hand, and he pulls her to her feet. At least she seems to be taking the whole situation better than yesterday.

All five of us begin our trek back to the horses, back to the palace, and back to the world I'd prefer to run away from and leave behind.

CHAPTER SEVENTEEN

Camille

AUBREY AND I WALK into the training room, and I already want to leave. Seventh place. That's the designation next to my name on the newly installed giant scoreboard.

For the past week, I've spent almost every minute possible in this room ever since I saw that pesky number seven. It's not the number one spot it needs to be. That place is occupied by Garden, who had shocked me the first morning the scores had been displayed. Unusually alone, Garden had come up to me and congratulated me on my placement. She even complimented my skill and dedication in the arena. Even though Ryden, Keith, Miles, and Aubrey had all been trying, nothing had improved my mood better than what Garden had said.

"You were awesome out there, by the way. Not a lot of the girls here would have had the nerve to do what you did. Prill's a bully and had it coming. You showed the

Kingdom of Myria what it means to be a girl from the Gulf."

Her words sounded genuine, not harsh and sarcastic like I've come to expect from her attached counterpart. Also, they were nice to hear. Finally, someone who understood that it hadn't been me aiming to kill for fun...

Plus, if I have any chance of surviving this thing, I have to win.

I've gone to see my father too, always bringing Ryden with me. There, we discuss ways of ensuring King Edward doesn't kill me and Keith after the Games are over, even if we somehow survive. We must win. That's why the big number seven drives my determination to train. I must turn myself into just as much of a threat as Aubrey, Garden, and Sabrina.

Gratefully, Prill and Carter are nowhere to be found today. Their presence always ratchets up the tension in the room, making it nearly impossible for me to focus.

Keith and Miles are already in an arena sparring with wooden staffs. Lately, this has been the new method of training Miles has been attempting. Aubrey and Ryden had explained to me that using something nonlethal might encourage Keith to stop holding back. Watching him roll on the floor to avoid Miles's strike makes me think that maybe this will help Keith's skills improve.

His gift, however, is an entirely different matter. No one can come up with an idea to bring it out. I'm not sure how to help, and despite everyone's constant reassurance that he must has a gift, Keith and I share the same concern: he could be like our mother, whose gift refused to surface before she turned thirty. Keith can't afford to wait that long. We still haven't been told what the second Game will be, but I have a feeling it will be as deadly as the first—if not more so.

"Swords or something different?" Aubrey asks, in an oddly cheerful mood.

"Let's try the axes." I propose.

Aubrey wrinkles her nose. They aren't my favorite either, but at least the weapon is something unique, and it will force me to build more strength in my arms. It's also something Aubrey and I are equally poor at, so it gives me a higher chance of having the upper hand.

Before we reach the axes hung up on the wall, the room goes silent as every fight pauses. Even Sabrina stops throwing knives against the wall and goes still. Aubrey tenses and draws in a deep breath before we both turn to see what has caused the interruption. Princess Amaia and Prince Jacob have entered the room.

Instead of their normal comfortable training clothes, they're both dressed in the nicest outfits I've seen them in, including what they wore on Combatant Day. Prince Jacob's dirty blond hair is perfectly groomed with not a strand out of place. He wears a pressed black jacket buttoned up to his throat. The shoulders and sleeves are lined with silver embellishments, matching the sash across his chest. Silver and gold medals decorate his jacket. Princess Amaia has her hair pulled back in a crown of braids with loose strands curling down her face. Her black dress hangs off her shoulders and falls in gentle waves to the floor. Her long sleeves are tight until they reach her elbows, where they begin to hang off her arms. Intricate silver designs follow the neckline, mimicking the belt along her waist, which dangles to the floor. A stunning silver necklace occupies the hollow of her neck. Directly behind each of them is a set of officers. Except their uniforms are different, inverting the colors of black and silver.

I stiffen as another two figures enter behind them. King Edward and Queen Eliza are right behind their children, in matching regality. They're arm in arm as they make their way to the far wall of the training room, where I now notice a board of knives has been removed and replaced with a row of elaborate seats—not quite thrones, but close enough.

The royal family sits down, Jacob to the left of the king and Amaia to the right of the queen. On either side of them, there are five empty seats. The unfamiliar officers, which are most likely members of each royal's respective unit, take their places behind Jacob and Amaia, standing on either side of their shoulders.

"Please continue. We are simply here to observe today. The Lords of Central and the Lords of each sector will be joining us shortly." King Edward's voice is cheerful, and even his eyes seem to sparkle with joy. It's unnerving, and neither Aubrey or I move. Sabrina is the first one to break the silence. Her knife strikes right in the center of the target, thudding against the board. Slowly everyone returns to what they were doing, except for Keith, who is staring at the royal family. I can't tell if his eyes are glued to the king or the princess. Miles shakes him out of it with a whack to the shoulder.

"What's all of this about? Did you know they were coming?" I hiss at Aubrey. Her face pales, and she looks a little nauseous.

"No," she whispers. "Although I guess I should have known. Ryden said he had something important to do today, so I should have assumed that meant my father was in the palace." Her voice is laced with bitterness—either at her father's presence or Ryden's withdrawal of information. "Let's work with swords today."

I nod in agreement. If the king himself is watching, it's more important to be working with something I'm decent at. Switching directions, Aubrey and I walk toward the sword display.

"Miss Atwood," the king summons.

Aubrey tenses by my side but doesn't say anything. Knowing I don't have much of a choice, I lower my head and walk toward the seats against the wall.

Glancing up at Amaia, her eyes unreadable, I lower myself into an awkward curtsy. Laughing, the king shakes his head. "No need for that, child. I only wanted to see how you and your brother are getting along here."

I don't know what to say, and this time I find myself flicking my gaze up at Jacob. He appears to be as curious to hear my response as his father is.

"We've been doing excellent, Your Majesty." I incline my head even deeper. "Only thanks to your generosity, of course."

"Hmm." King Edward gives a vile smile. "I am quite generous, aren't I? I would say it has worked out quite well. My children seem fascinated by you and your brother, even before you managed to easily overtake my own advisor's daughter in the Games."

I swallow hard, trying to hide my wince. I had forgotten Prill was the daughter of Lord Prancis, and her father would likely be entering the room shortly.

"I wouldn't say easily, Your Majesty."

The king's smile only widens. "I would argue otherwise, but I suppose it's okay if you would prefer to appear modest." He waves a hand. "Mr. Atwood." I turn to find Keith, but he's already looking in our direction and doesn't miss the king's words. Miles and Aubrey both linger behind him, their faces entirely passive. Keith walks up to all of us, his gaze firmly fixed on the king. To my surprise, there isn't any anger flashing in his eyes. Only collected calm.

"Yes?"

The lack of formality makes me wince. Amaia does too. It's the first break in her composure. The king's grin turns into something malicious.

"I'd like to see how far you and your sister have come since your father's terrible mistake."

Keith's eyes remain empty of emotion.

"I understand why my children have such a severe interest in your sister. She demonstrated potential in the first Game. But I haven't seen much from you, Mr. Atwood. I would like to more clearly understand my daughter's obsession with keeping you here."

The word "here" could easily be replaced with "alive."

The king's eyes slide over to meet Princess Amaia's. That's when I realize this isn't a punishment for us. She must have done or said something to her father that he didn't like. The tension in her face and her refusal to even glance in my brother's direction only confirms my suspicions. Is this because of Keith's stunt in the arena?

Keith's brow furrows as he moves his gaze to the floor.

"What would you like to see from us, Your Majesty?" I say, pulling the attention away from him.

"I'd like to see the two of you at each other's throats." He says this casually, leaning back in his chair.

I don't know what to say, and this seems to deepen the king's pleasure.

"Oh," I murmur. It's all I can get out.

He turns to Jacob, and the man now sitting beside the prince. I recognize the man immediately as Ryden's father. Scanning briefly around the room, I lock eyes with Ryden, who's standing next to his sister with his arms folded. His attention is glued to me, and he gives me a curt nod. I breathe a sigh of relief as I know he has my back.

"Clear the middle of the room," the king instructs.

Keith and I wait in silence as everyone in the training room goes eerily quiet. They're all watching us now.

Some, like Nicole, look as nervous as I feel, while others, like Sabrina, look entertained. The rest of the Lords file into the room. The only other one I recognize is Lord Prancis. Pure hatred is etched onto his face as he looks down at me. More and more competitors walk in, confused by the air of suspense in the room. Jacob and Ryden's father is quick to clear the space as everyone gathers to watch.

Keith grips his sword tentatively, and I try to give him an encouraging smile, but it comes out as more of a grimace.

"Start whenever you're ready." The king lounges comfortably in his chair, the complete opposite of Amaia. She's sitting perfectly straight, and her eyes are trained on Keith's back, as if staring at him hard enough will communicate something. I recognize the terror flickering in her eyes. Something is going on here. There must be something at stake. From the king's gleeful smile to Amaia's concentrated stare, I have a feeling my life and Keith's life might really be on the line.

Unsure of how to begin, I start to circle Keith.

"Seriously? We're actually doing this?" Keith grumbles. "We already know you're going to win."

"Maybe," I say loudly, trying to make sure the king catches every one of my words. "Maybe not."

From a brief glance at Ryden, who gives me another nod, I know I must be doing something right. Ignoring Miles and Aubrey's matching looks of fear, I lunge for Keith.

Slowly and sloppily, he deflects my blade. I strike again, this time faster, jabbing the hilt of my blade into his side. He grunts in pain and confusion.

"What are you doing?" he hisses at me.

I dance backward. "Come on now, brother, don't hold back. I can take it."

Something finally seems to click in his head, either from my words or the sharp look in my eyes. He sets his feet properly. Then he lunges at me, attacking swiftly. I dodge with a roll and bounce back up to my feet. It's not enough because Amaia's still staring daggers at Keith, and Ryden is now biting his lip. I understand. I'm only fascinating because of what I did to Prill. With my gift. Keith doesn't even have one. As far as I know, he's the only competitor whose power is dormant.

I grit my teeth, and this time, I come at him with full force. Aubrey once explained that sometimes gifts only show themselves out of desperation. So, I'll have to make Keith desperate. His eyes widen in shock as he barely blocks my blade from slashing into his arm.

"Come on!" I mutter.

I press even harder with my blade, and Keith barely blocks each hit. His face is bright red with exertion, and he looks like he's about to throw his blade down in submission. Princess Amaia must know it too because now she's leaning forward, her gaze boring into my brother. Her eyes grow heavy with exhaustion with every hit Keith blocks, and a theory starts to form in my head. I drop back and retreat to my gift. With half a thought, I reach out to brush the princess with a wave of smoldering heat. She tenses and whips her eyes to me in a snarl. I ignore her and go for an attack.

Sure enough, he stumbles slightly, and Amaia's concentration refocuses. This time, I place a blanket of scalding heat on the princess's skin. As if sensing her discomfort, Keith glances at her, catching her wince.

Keith looks back at me with wild eyes, enraged. "What are you doing? You could kill her." He whispers the words as if he doesn't quite believe it.

I glare at him. "It'll take the attention off of you failing, won't it?"

He gasps in disbelief. Then I tackle him, discarding my sword. We hit the floor with a thud, and I remember how we used to wrestle as kids. So much has changed since then. He's never fought me with such hatred before.

Still, I have the advantage of surprise, so I pin him, reaching for his sword which he had discarded also. I bring it to his throat.

"If you don't stop me, I'll do it."

I tighten my blanket of heat around Amaia, and with a brief look at her, I note the sparkling tears in her blue eyes. For a moment, I delight in knowing that despite being the Princess of Myria, I can cause her pain. But the distress in my brother's eyes fills my consciousness with guilt. He looks torn between punching some sense into my head or wrapping me in a hug. I'm sure my own green eyes are wild, and I press the blade even closer, shoving the guilt aside.

Keith's gaze hardens and then shifts in concentration. Suddenly, I'm thrown off of him.

I scramble to my feet, still grasping Keith's sword. But when I find my footing, I'm not staring at Keith anymore. I'm face to face with a giant black wolf. Its teeth are pulled back in a snarl, and it's standing defensively over Keith, who rolls into a sitting position. Keith's look of surprise matches the look of shock plastered on everyone's face. Even King Edward carries a sneer of surprise.

He did it...

I wince at the force I used with him, but I know it had to happen. Keith's gift is active now. I just hope it's enough to temper the king's grudge against us.

Keith

"WHAT IS GOING ON with you?" I demand.

"What do you mean?" Camille looks briefly shocked to see me outside her door before her face goes blank.

"You've been ignoring me all week."

She raises an eyebrow. "And?"

I throw my arms up, exasperated. "And that's not cool."

She grins at me, but it doesn't quite reach her eyes. "That's all you can come up with?"

I frown and fold my arms, blocking her way down the hallway as she moves to escape this conversation—the same way she has ever since our fight in front of the king.

"No, you aren't getting out of this. You're acting differently, and you know it."

Camille crosses her arms too. "Oh, is that so? If you're talking about the whole thing in the training room, I will not apologize for it."

"How far were you willing to go?" I ask, anger in my tone.

"As far as it was going to take!" Camille loses all sense of false calm, her face curling into a sneer. "Your life could have been on the line. And you know what, it worked out just fine for you, so quit acting like the high and mighty perfect brother! You found your gift now, so maybe, just maybe, you won't die in whatever stupid Game the king has planned for tomorrow. And listen, I didn't kill her, did I? Doesn't that count for something?"

Camille's eyes don't hold a hint of remorse, only anger and hurt. I gape at her. I don't understand how she doesn't see what's right in front of her. I'm not trying to say I'm perfect, but her outburst is proof enough that something's wrong.

"Would you have killed Amaia?" My voice comes out as a whisper.

The fact that she takes a moment to cock her head and think is all the answer I need. I start to shake my head and move out of her way, in complete and utter disbelief.

She doesn't move though. Instead, she reaches out to touch my shoulder. "Keith, I would have done whatever I thought I needed to do in order to save you."

With that, she walks away, leaving me to watch her fading figure. I hope she's meeting with Aubrey or Ryden so she doesn't end up wandering the halls for hours on end trying to make her way to breakfast.

Watching her turn the corner, I groan in frustration and stare at the ceiling.

"Trouble in paradise? Sibling edition?" Miles shows up in front of me, and I roll my eyes.

"Were you eavesdropping?"

Miles holds up his hands. "No, I don't want to get involved with that." He gestures toward the corner where Camille disappeared. "But I did happen to notice your sister storming through the halls and then found you sulking. It doesn't take much to connect the dots."

"How can I help her?" I ask, more hypothetically than anything else. "I think this place is turning her into a monster."

Miles shrugs. "Honestly, I have no idea. My closest sibling is my little brother, and I haven't seen him for a handful of years. Sorry. My experience with handling sibling temper tantrums is close to zero."

I raise an eyebrow at him. "You have a brother?"

"Yeah, but he doesn't live in Central—and thank goodness for that. Although he is missing out on the amazing food which is currently waiting for us." Effectively changing the subject, I realize.

I don't push though, instead nodding. "I *am* starving."

Miles and I both walk to the breakfast room. I wonder if it's obnoxious for him to walk everywhere with me when he normally would teleport himself around the palace. He hasn't ever complained about it, but I'm certain it can't be very convenient for him.

When we enter the breakfast room, I search for Camille, but she isn't here. Either she ate quickly and then left or she's lost again. Aubrey is in our claimed corner, patiently twirling a dagger in her fingers. Her face lights up as we approach the table.

"About time you two. What kept you so long?" Her tone is playful, but after meeting my eyes, her brow scrunches in concern. "Is everything okay?"

Thankfully, I'm saved from answering by Miles. "Sibling drama." He waves a hand dismissively.

Aubrey still looks worriedly at me but nods in understanding. "Camille was in here a few minutes ago. She grabbed some bacon and then left. She seemed upset, so Ryden followed her. He'll make sure she doesn't get into too much trouble." I know she means to be comforting, but honestly, I don't know how to feel about Ryden. He's been spending an awful amount of time with my sister, and they seem to be getting close. Yet, I barely know anything about the guy—other than the mind-reading powers.

"Thanks," I murmur and head to the food tables, grabbing a couple slices of toast and leaving it at that. I feel like eating anything more might result in it spilling out of my mouth. I sit between Aubrey and Miles and nibble on my food as they argue pointlessly. As soon as I finish my final piece of toast, I stand up and both of their gazes snap to me.

"I'm going to the training room. I'll see you guys later."

Miles rises out of his chair. "I'll come with you."

Before I can shake him off, a voice drawls behind me, "Actually, I was going to see if you wanted to come with me today."

I don't know if it's because I'm already on edge or because it's the princess's voice, but instinctively, I draw on my newfound gift. A huge, beautiful golden eagle rests on my shoulder, its sharp eyes focused on Amaia.

"Should I feel threatened?" She tilts her head, her face dancing with amusement.

"Maybe," I grumble.

"Well, I didn't mean to frighten you. I was just wondering if you would be willing to come with me today. I think I might know how to help you improve your gift before the Game tomorrow." Amaia's voice is light, and for a moment almost vulnerable, as if she genuinely wants me to come with her. I glance at Miles, but for once he's silent and has his gaze fixed on the table.

"Okay, I'll come." My excuse is that I do need to practice with my gift. It's so different than Miles's and Aubrey's, and they've been struggling to help me gain control over it. So far, I haven't been able to consciously draw on it and form the animal I want. Even now, I hadn't meant to create a giant eagle, it just sort of happened.

But in reality, I'm curious about her. She seems so different from her father and her brother. She holds herself with the same confidence and pride, but there's something deeper—an actual beating heart that the rest of her family seems to lack.

Amaia's smile has me mirroring her expression, the tension from my argument with Camille releasing from my shoulders. She steps backward to give me room to fully get out of my chair.

I wave to Aubrey and Miles. "See you guys later."

Aubrey wishes us luck. Miles, on the other hand, looks between me and the princess, an odd expression on his face. Glancing over at Amaia, I notice she gives Miles a sharp shake of her head, and her lips quirk up.

He rolls his eyes before waving at both of us. "Have fun."

Chapter Nineteen
Keith

AMAIA LEADS ME TO the same stables Miles showed us a few weeks ago. This time there's only one horse saddled, and she clearly wants me to get on. Following her instructions, I mount the gorgeous mare but glance down at Amaia.

I hadn't noticed it in the breakfast room, but today she is dressed more casually than I've ever seen her. She's wearing a deep green sweater paired with a set of thick black leggings. Dark brown boots are laced up over her pants, reaching just below her knees. Her hair is tied back in a loose ponytail, with a handful of strands falling free to frame her face. A light breeze brushes across her face, making her eyes bright and alive.

She's grinning at me, and I realize I'm staring.

"Are we going to go or are you going to keep studying me?" Her voice is light and playful.

Heat surfaces in my cheeks.

"Um, yeah, I, we can, we can go," I stammer. "But where's your horse? I mean, you'll have to lead the way, since I don't know where we're going. So, yeah, you lead the way." I clear my throat, ignoring the fact that nothing I just said made sense. The wicked smile playing across her lips proves she has an idea of why I'm so flustered.

"I don't need a horse." She winks at me, and I avert my eyes. "Try to see if you can keep up."

She sprints down the grassy hill, and I'm frozen, watching her run gracefully to the bottom. She stops, giving me a hard look, but something tells me she's not annoyed. She's more amused.

"You coming?" she calls, and I shake myself out of my stupor and use my heels to urge my horse forward. The two officers from last time aren't around.

Beneath me, my mare eagerly accepts my request to pick up speed. She begins to gallop, as if she's been waiting to run all day. I quickly adapt my position in the saddle to match her energy, leaning forward and acting on instinct. She only runs faster, galloping straight past Amaia, whose smile has tripled in size. I glance back, expecting to see her behind us, but she's keeping pace with the horse, and it looks like she's doing it without even breaking a sweat.

"How are you doing that?" I call to her.

She shakes her head, laughing. "You have to earn that answer. Now come on!" Almost impossibly, she pulls ahead of the mare, and I use the reins to encourage the horse to follow.

Very quickly, I recognize the patch of trees Amaia is leading us to. It's only been a couple of weeks since Miles led all of us to the same circle of trees with a wide clearing in the middle. Amaia slows to a stop, so I pull lightly on the reins, and sure enough, the mare beneath me obeys.

Amaia pats the horse's neck. "Good girl, Sparrow."

"Her name's Sparrow?"

"Yes," Amaia says. "She's my horse."

She says the words casually, but underneath them is a pool of emotion. I want to know more about Sparrow, but Amaia shifts away from her horse and changes the subject.

"What's your gift, Keith?"

Her question confuses me, since she was there when I first used it—and again when I used it this morning.

"I can make animals form, I suppose."

"Any kind you want?"

I frown, considering her question. "Honestly, I'm not sure. I've made a wolf and then an eagle. And a bunny," I add. "I was practicing in my room."

Laughter dances in her deep eyes, and I sense the tease before it comes. "A bunny?"

My face burns. "It's just what came up."

Amaia eyes me curiously, her face still bright. There's a quiet moment, but it's not awkward. She looks up at the sky. Her face is relaxed, basking in the sunlight.

I break the silence. "What's *your* gift, Amaia?"

Her answer is swift, like she's been expecting the question. "I already told you, you have to earn it." She winks at me again.

It's my turn to change the subject. "So, how are you going to help me with my gift? Or are we just traipsing through the woods for fun?"

Amaia cocks an eyebrow at my tone but doesn't respond. Instead, she just gestures for me to follow her to the center of the clearing. She sits on the ground, crossing her legs. Unsure of what else to do, I copy her.

"I come here to think. I thought it might help you clear your head."

The thing is, she's right. Even the last time I was here, the gentle whisper of the wind and the melodious birds chirping made the rest of the world fade away. Already, I'd forgotten that Camille and I are at odds again, and that tomorrow is another day in which I'm likely to die.

"How is that going to help me? As peaceful as it is out here, I don't feel a sudden clarity about my gift."

Amaia leans back on her hands, gazing up at the sky. "Our gifts are naturally tied closely to who we are. Our personality, our thoughts, and even our emotions determine their strength. This tends to make them most powerful when we feel incredibly sad or upset or even happy. However, it also makes them the most volatile and more difficult to control. So, it's important to find a balance—a way to not let our emotions control us. And as a result, not letting our gift get away from us."

Something clicks in my head. "So that's why..."

Amaia cuts me off. "Your sister has a lot of pain and hurt. It only encourages her powers to be released, especially if she doesn't bother trying to keep them under control." She pauses, biting her upper lip. "You take it differently than her. It's obvious you're hurting, but it doesn't consume you the way it does her."

Immediately, I snap to her defense. "She's been through a lot."

"So have you." Amaia's voice is tinged with genuine sadness, but her mention of my sister brings up another question.

"Why did your father have Cam and I fight? I don't understand it."

Amaia pauses, chewing on the inside of her lip. "My father wasn't happy about you backing out before the Game could even get started. It didn't occur to him that anyone would be bold enough to refuse to fight."

"So, I made your dad mad?"

"You could say that." Amaia chuckles dryly. "He wanted to have you killed."

"Oh." I blink.

"Yeah, he would have framed it as an accident either in a Game or in the training room. He wouldn't do it outright because then it would make him look weak and indecisive for going back on his word when he's already announced he would be letting you and your sister compete."

What Amaia says makes sense I suppose, however, I'm still curious. "So, why am I not dead?"

Amaia squints. "I stepped in. Told him that you'd be more beneficial as entertainment, you just needed your gift first. And so, that was his ultimatum. If you could use your gift, you could live."

I don't know what to say to that. Amaia saved my life. And so did Camille. I grimace as I remember how I yelled at her this morning.

She clears her throat. "Anyway, back to your gift."

I nod, trying to ignore the emotion in her eyes as she stares at me.

"Close your eyes."

I don't hesitate to obey, but as I do, I feel her shift closer to me. Her breath tickles my face as she speaks. "Relax and act on instinct. You already know it's in there. You can form any animal you want. All it takes is a controlled thought."

I don't say anything, but it's hard to control any of my thoughts with her face hovering so close to mine. I wouldn't be surprised if our noses are only centimeters apart.

"Don't let it build and grow in your anger. You have to let it stem directly from you." She places a hand on my knee. As soon as her fingers brush against me, I feel a deep sensation in my chest. It growls, eager to jump out. It happens so quickly that I fight to catch my breath. Camille, my father, and my mother all flash through my head, followed by Miles and Aubrey. It ends with King Edward's gleeful smile, and an uncontrollable rage consumes me. If Amaia's hand wasn't on my knee anchoring me, I would have let it all go. Instead, recalling Amaia's warning about regulating emotions, I take deep breaths, in and out, and my gift relaxes. This morning, when I unintentionally used my gift, as soon as it appeared, it left.

Now, I can feel its permanence. And instead of the growling snarl that normally accompanies it, it rests with a soft purr.

I open my eyes.

Sure enough, Amaia's face is centimeters from mine, and she's grinning right back at me. She moves backward but keeps her hand resting on my knee, which I'm not going to argue against. Through her touch, I can feel her warmth and her support.

Taking a deep and concentrated breath, I release my gift. The black wolf shimmers into existence on my left. I let go of the strict control over the animal, and of its own accord, it snuggles into Amaia's lap. She laughs pleasantly.

"How does the whole personality and emotions thing work with other gifts?" I ask. "Like, at home, there's an old lady who runs a bakery. Her gift is her inhuman ability to make extraordinary cookies, and exactly how you want them, without even having to order. What does it mean if she chooses to let herself go a little more?"

Amaia laughs a little bit, even rolling her eyes. She leans away from me, taking her hand with her as she goes. "I'm sure that her personality is actually what makes her gift work so well. But her gift is harmless." Her voice darkens, barely detectable, but I catch it. "Ours aren't Keith. If she puts a little too much of her sadness into her cookies, nothing happens. If you put too much of your own sadness into your wolf, it becomes a lot more dangerous."

I nod in understanding. "You said, 'ours aren't.' Can I know what yours is?"

She shoots me an elusive grin. "Not yet."

I consider her super speed today and her incredible acrobatic skills when we sparred. "Are you some kind of superhuman?"

This time a sad smile flickers on her face. "Aren't we all?"

There's something in the way she says this that makes me go quiet. The only sounds in the clearing are those from the woods and a soft content whining from the wolf, who rests his head in Amaia's lap.

Suddenly, Amaia breaks the silence. "Keith." I look up to meet her gaze in concern. Her eyes are tight, and her voice raw. The wolf buries himself deeper in her lap. "Do me a favor and don't die tomorrow."

Chapter Twenty
Camille

"WHEN DO YOU THINK they'll kill him?" I ask Ryden. I'm surprised that the question doesn't bring me any feelings of pain or sadness. Just resignation.

He doesn't look at me, his dark eyes fixed on the screen displaying my dad. The room is empty besides Ryden and I, just like it was the last time we were in here. As far as I know, the closest person is an officer standing outside the door. There is something peaceful about this room, about watching my father sit in the corner of his cell alone in his thoughts.

This time his entire face is purple and bruised, and his lip is bleeding. Nothing looks broken, so I figure a healer must have visited him to prepare him for another round of torture. Again, it should disgust me, but I don't feel anything but icy-cold indifference toward the man who left Keith and me to fend for ourselves in these stupid Games.

"I'm honestly not sure," Ryden finally answers.

"Do you know how long the king normally keeps his prisoners?"

Ryden frowns. "Camille, I hate to break it to you, but it's not like a one-case-fits-all deal. There have been people who have lived their entire lives and then died in the Shadows, and then there are those who are executed within a few weeks." He pauses, gauging my reaction. My face remains passive and collected, so he continues. "It's all about when His Majesty decides they no longer serve a purpose."

I nod and lean against the control board. There are chairs that we could sit in, but neither of us ever takes them. I prefer the freedom to easily begin pacing rather than sit and do nothing. Either Ryden feels the same or he would feel bad sitting while I stand, because he always remains by my side.

"How are you doing?"

I sigh, unsure of how to answer. In truth, I don't know how I'm doing. Nightmares of Prill screaming and Keith dying have kept me awake nearly every night this month. The argument with my brother from earlier doesn't help anything either. Not to mention, I still haven't told him about our father.

"That complicated?"

"Keith and I got into a fight this morning."

Ryden makes a gentle sound in his throat, encouraging me to continue, without directly asking.

"I don't understand why he can't even have a dash of gratitude!" I exclaim, passion in my voice. "Does he not realize that I might have saved his life? Why does he care so much if *Princess Amaia*," —I say her name with a sneer— "gets hurt if it means he lives. She's King Edward's daughter! Certainly, that means she can't be trusted."

I glance at Ryden who's eyeing me warily. The fight drains out of me as soon as it starts. "Sorry," I mumble. I'm still not confident about Ryden's connections to Amaia. "You're just easy to talk to."

Ryden shakes his head and takes a step toward me, grabbing one of my hands and wrapping it in both of his. "No, you're fine. You just were swinging your arms around, and I didn't want to get slapped in the face."

I gasp and playfully slap his shoulder. "Hey!"

Ryden tries to smother his grin. "Not to mention the temperature in the room was definitely rising a couple of degrees, and while you may be immune to your own gift, I most certainly am not."

Internally, I wince. "Sorry, I keep doing that."

Ryden gives me a little shrug and raises both of his hands. "You're getting better with it. And it's not like I was breaking a sweat or anything."

I smile at him appreciatively. At least he knows how to brighten my mood. Still, I have questions that I want answered, but I know he either won't or can't.

Sensing my distress, he moves behind me and wraps his arms around me. I lean my head back against his chest, grateful for his support. He rests his chin on top of my head.

"I'm sorry," Ryden says softly. "I can't tell you anything you want to hear. I would if I could."

"I know."

It's become my instinctual response at this point. I know he would tell me what's really going on between the royal family—more specifically, Princess Amaia and my brother—if he could. But he can't, so I refocus my gaze on the screen as we stand in silence.

A screech echoes through the room, startling both of us. Ryden's embrace ends, and his shoulders tense. My eyes survey the room, trying to find the source of the sound, and it takes a moment for both of us to realize that it's coming from my father's cell.

Ryden stands taller as his own father walks into the cell, flanked by two officers. My father doesn't even look up at them.

"You really do look terrible." Lord Hedbauren's voice is as icy as I expected.

Again, my father doesn't even acknowledge him.

With a nod from Ryden's father, the two officers move forward to force my father to stand.

Finally, my father looks up at the finely dressed man. My father's eyes are unwavering, staring a murderous hole through Lord Hedbauren's head. If looks could kill, Ryden's father would have fallen over.

Hedbauren sneers. "I take it you haven't been faring well."

My father glares at him, unblinking.

"You know this could all end, don't you?" Hedbauren begins to pace back and forth in what little space the cell offers. "All you have to do is tell me where they are."

My father's lip curls in disgust, but still, he says nothing.

"Really?" Hedbauren rolls his eyes. He looks so much like Ryden that it's off-putting. The same red hair. The same green eyes. But they lack the kindness that Ryden's have. Where Ryden is all warmth, his dad is all cold. "I would have thought the idea of reuniting with your children would have made you think twice. You could be back home with both of them already."

I'm biting my lip so hard that the metallic taste of blood fills my mouth. I've chewed my bottom lip to pieces. I move away from the control board, getting closer to the screen. Ryden's quiet footsteps follow right behind me. An eerie silence fills the cell, leaking through the screen and into the security room. Sensing my unease, Ryden grabs my hand and gives it a small squeeze.

I wait for my father to accept—to tell Lord Hedbauren whatever he needs to know—and when my father opens his mouth to speak, I begin to hope.

"Your promises mean nothing to me." He spits blood straight into Hedbauren's face.

The hope dies in my chest...

With a swipe of a finger, Hedbauren brushes the blood off of his cheek, flicking it to the floor. "You value the people who failed you, who have left you to die here, over the lives of your children?"

I hold my breath to wait for his answer, even though a part of me already knows what it's going to be.

"Some things are worth the sacrifice."

The words shoot a bullet straight through my chest. I stumble backward, and Ryden gently grabs one of my elbows, keeping me upright.

"Take him away," Hedbauren says harshly, and two officers drag my father out of the cell. Ryden's father follows, slamming the door shut behind him.

A silence settles in the room, and I can feel myself struggling to breathe. Tears prick at my eyes, but they never fall. Ryden keeps his hand on my elbow, supporting me as I take in the fact that my father chose something else over me. I shouldn't be surprised. Still, betrayal digs at me.

"What was your father talking about?" I ask.

I turn to look at Ryden, and for the first time, his eyes are blank and completely closed off from me.

"I'm not sure." He hesitates though, which tells me he's not being completely honest.

I remove myself from his grasp and turn to directly face him, placing my hands on my hips.

"You're lying."

He winces but doesn't say anything.

"Why don't you just tell me your best guess?"

Ryden looks at me with such an odd expression that I wonder if I'm wrong about him. Maybe he is only working with whatever Amaia and her crew are involved in.

But then he surprises me, the look fading from his face as his eyes light back up. "Well, my father's been trying to track down a group of rebels for a long time."

"Rebels? There are rebels in Myria?" I ask incredulously.

Ryden raises an eyebrow. "Of course there are. Do you blame them?"

"So that's why they're keeping him alive. They think my father is part of the rebellion?" I ask in disbelief. "Wouldn't his attack have been more coordinated?" Even as I say it, a nagging feeling presses against my brain. I think back to the lady who didn't touch us, and the lie detector who let us go.

I probably shouldn't be surprised that it hadn't been a one-person thing. The fact that it could have been somebody else is what stings the most. Instead, our father decided to jeopardize himself and his whole family for something doomed to fail.

Ryden presses his lips together in a hard line. From the look on his face, he isn't surprised at all. He probably already assumed or even knew that this was the case before today.

Ryden wraps me in an embrace, his warm arms comforting me. Even as his words do the opposite. "At this point, I don't think it's much of a question, Camille."

My breath shudders. He's right.

"Knowing my father, he won't stop until he eliminates the entire population of rebels, and it sounds like your father might have the information he and King Edward need to do just that."

Chapter Twenty-One
Keith

THE CROWD SEEMS MUCH larger and louder than last month's Game—and that's saying a lot considering that this Game isn't in a closed arena. We're all in a field located on the palace grounds. But instead of being the open and flat land it typically is, massive hedges have been grown overnight.

Amaia hadn't been pulling my leg when she explained the second Game to me yesterday on the way back to the palace. It really is a giant hedge maze. According to her, it's simple enough: get to the end. But as I walk onto the field with Aubrey and Miles, I can't help but feel extremely overwhelmed. Even Miles whistles in surprise.

From where I stand, I can't even see where the hedges stop as they roll in a seemingly endless pattern across the field. Large metal bleachers are placed the entire way around the maze, and the ones on the opposite end—marked with flags—must signify the end.

"Gosh, this is going to be so stupid," Miles groans, and I silently agree. But to be fair, I can think of a stronger word than stupid.

Aubrey nods, her tight ponytail loosening as she does. "Hopefully it won't be as dangerous." With both Miles and my raised eyebrows, Aubrey adds, "Maybe. Hopefully."

As we get closer to the starting line, I search the crowd. I tell myself I'm only looking to see where the royal family is seated, but I know I'm really seeking out Amaia. She had been with Miles outside my door this morning. Her entire body had been coiled with tension, and she hadn't said very much to either of us as we made our way to breakfast. She had left us with a simple "good luck," and gave me a sharp look before walking away.

Aubrey leads us to the seats that are set up on the ground specifically for the competitors. She leaves us as we sit down with the rest of the boys and heads to her own seat. I scan the rows of chairs, trying to find Camille. I saw her at dinner last night. She had been in deep conversation with one of the girls. She hadn't even looked up in my direction once, so I figured it would be safer to leave her be.

I don't know how to feel about Ryden's matching absence, but at least she'd have someone to make sure she got here. My mind lingers on our fight. I would just have to apologize to her later.

I go back to searching for the royal family, and finally, I find them. They're perched higher than the rest of the bleachers, right in the middle, with a perfect view of both the start and finish line. I don't know how I missed them. Amaia's already looking at me, her eyes full of concern. Her hair, usually so perfectly kept, is frizzy, and she is brushing her blonde curls away from her face as the wind forces them to fly around.

A deep laugh interrupts my focus. Asher sits down right next to me. "Fancy yourself a princess, do you, Atwood?" His voice matches the sneer on his face. "Too bad you'll probably be dead by the end of today. What a tragic love story."

I can feel heat rise to my cheeks, along with a mix of embarrassment and anger. My face twitches as I keep my gift on a tight leash, even as it starts to grow restless. "It's just a maze."

My confidence surprises me.

"Sure, but it's going to be filled with everyone else vying for the hand of the same princess you are." Asher's sneer only grows, and I'm overcome with the desire to push him out of his chair.

"I'm not vying for anything." But the words sound false, even to my own ears. If I don't win the Games, Amaia will marry another victor. The idea of her exchanging vows with one of the other competitors makes me uncomfortable. Would she enjoy being married to someone like Asher?

Certainly not, I tell myself.

Asher laughs cruelly. "Sure you aren't. Just like I'm not going to win the title of prince. If, for whatever reason, there's a world where you survive, with the power I'll have, I'll make you wish you hadn't."

Miles snorts from next to me. He's eyeing Asher sharply, but the rest of his body language is relaxed. He appears almost bored. "Dramatic much?"

Asher turns to snarl at him. "You think you have a chance? Just because you're in her unit doesn't make you an automatic win. Especially because it's *you*."

Miles flinches at the last part but then rolls his eyes. "You talk a big game, Asher."

Asher smirks, facing forward in his seat again.

"Do you think you'll win?" I ask under my breath.

At first, I regret my question because Miles's face reddens for a second. But then he grins, playing it off.

"I don't think so. Something tells me Amaia wouldn't want to marry me."

Miles's trace of sarcasm confuses me. "So why exactly are you competing?"

"Like Aubrey explained earlier, a member from both Amaia and Jacob's unit has to compete. Amaia asked me to do it, so I said yes. The other guy on our team, Hunt, wouldn't have done well with all the publicity." He spreads his hands wide. "I, on the other hand, thrive under the attention."

Something in his tone still sounds off, like there must be more to the story, but before I can ask, King Edward rises from his seat. I survey the competitors and realize I missed Camille's entrance while Asher was talking to me. Her hair is pulled back in two tight braids, and she balances a knife on her leg.

"Were we supposed to bring weapons?" I mutter to Miles.

He shrugs. "I think it's a personal preference. Personally, I think they just slow me down."

I bite down a complaint at not being told that I had the option. Although, to be fair, I probably wouldn't have chosen to take any. I'm lousy with a sword, and like Miles pointed out, it would only slow me down. Instead, I ask, "Why don't you just teleport to the end?"

Miles grins. "I wish I could, but that's not the way it works. I have to be able to envision where I end up. That's why jumping around a room is easy but trying to zip myself to the end would probably do more harm than good. I'd most likely end up somewhere else in the maze, and then I'd be disorientated."

"That makes sense, I guess."

Miles nods and then glances at the king, who is explaining the Game. It's what Amaia told me yesterday. As soon as it starts, all of us will be sent to different starting positions inside the maze, and from there it's a simple race to the end. However, every competitor will have their gift and be allowed a weapon of their choice. Again, would have been nice to know. According to the king's words, attacking another competitor during the race is highly encouraged. The more death, the better.

Like in the first Game, the boys will be going first, and the king dismisses us to the starting line. Miles stays next to me, but Asher drifts down the line to stand next to Giler Rose, son of Lord Rose, which doesn't upset me in the slightest.

"Good luck, Keith." Miles gives me a thumbs up. "This is going to be fun."

"We have very different definitions of fun," I mumble back.

He laughs, and then he's gone.

In the blink of an eye, I am too.

We've been thrown into the Game, each teleported to a different spot in the maze. The hedges are almost twice my height, and there is no hope of seeing over them. Instinctively, I reach for my gift. The giant black wolf appears at my side, his sharp teeth glinting. Looking around, I see that I've been placed in a corner with only one path forward. The wolf walks in front of me, his head sunk low and his shoulders raised.

Carefully, I follow him, trusting his instincts to get me out. Meanwhile, I take in everything I can, noticing that I can still make out the edges of the elevated royal family's booth. They're farther ahead of me, and that tells me there's still a fair amount of space between me and the halfway point. I hear the crowd quiet down, but I can't see them. I wonder if they can see us, but as soon as the thought occurs, the crowd screams out in alarm. I swivel on my feet, but there's nothing there. It must be somebody else located somewhere else in the maze.

I take a deep breath and steady myself, following carefully behind the wolf, who makes a sharp left at a crossroads. His ears are on high alert, and from his nose sweeping through the air, I figure he knows how to get to the end better than I do.

But when he freezes and starts to growl, raising his hackles in warning, I tense. Footsteps pound on the ground, and my heart starts to race. I turn around, trusting the wolf to guard my back. He growls even louder, and his bushy tail flicks back and forth. I glance back at him and find a boy staring at me. I wrack my brain to remember his name. I know he's from the Lates sector. That much I remember. It would be more helpful if I could remember what his gift is.

He drags his bleeding leg behind him with a grimace on his face. He doesn't move, gripping a short sword in his hand. The determination on his face distinctly reminds me of poor little Oliver.

I hope the boy doesn't decide to fight me. Even with his injury, I am at a disadvantage without a weapon. Holding up both of my hands, I take a step forward. The wolf whines in anticipation.

"Do you need help?" I ask.

The boy—Landon, I finally remember—curls his lip, but he doesn't attack me. "Why would you help me?"

"Why wouldn't I?"

Landon seems to consider my question. Then he scoffs and drags himself down a different row to the left.

The wolf looks at me, asking if we should follow him. I gently shake my head, and the wolf dips his majestic head. At least I tried.

"Hurry," I mutter.

The encounter makes me eager to escape this maze. The wolf swings his head back at me, and I swear he rolls his eyes. But he picks up speed, his black paws thudding against the ground at a more rapid pace. I have to jog to keep up.

Shouts from the other side of the hedge make me pause for a second, but the wolf isn't slowing. So, I press forward, trying to block out the other boy's screams. It isn't long before they stop, and I don't want to think about what that could mean.

Instead, I breathe out a deep sigh of relief as the wolf makes another right, leading me out to the final stretch. There's a red mark signifying the finish line.

But before I can take another step, something tackles me from the side. In my surprise, I release the wolf, leaving myself completely defenseless. Asher grabs me by the ear and slams my head to the ground. Hard. My vision blurs, and I struggle to keep my eyes open. I try to escape his grip, but he is a lot stronger than I am, and he also has years of experience fighting.

Trying to focus my thoughts, I reach for my gift. This time, a gorgeous hunting leopard leaps on top of Asher, tearing into his arm. Asher shouts in pain but rolls over, bouncing back to his feet. Using his uninjured arm, he swipes at my leopard with a flashing dagger. Trying to use the distraction, I force myself to get up and stumble toward the finish line.

However, even while wrestling with the leopard, Asher reaches out and sets my arm on fire. The pain is blinding, and I scream. The crowd's roars start to dim, and I distinctly hear a girl scream right along with me.

I fall to the floor again, and the leopard flashes out of existence. Asher smugly crosses the finish line, leaving me for dead.

I can feel the life swiftly draining out of me.

As I prepare to die, a voice echoes through my head.

Get across the line. Get across the line.

The voice says it with such force that I listen, trying to crawl toward the line.

Get across the line. Get across the line. Get across the line!

The voice chants powerfully through my head. With my vision still blurred, my head pounding, and my skin screaming, I drag myself across the line, signifying the end of the Game. Then all I see is black.

Chapter Twenty-Two
Camille

I PACE OUTSIDE MY brother's door while Ryden leans against the wall, his arms folded and his eyes carefully focused on me. Aubrey sits on the floor, her head buried in her knees. I wouldn't be surprised if she's fallen asleep. I've lost track of how long the healers have made us stay out of Keith's bedroom. Immediately after breakfast, I asked Ryden to take me to my brother's room, and Aubrey came with us. A couple of hours ago, Miles had stopped by with a sandwich for each of us, apologizing that he couldn't stay. Apparently, he had been summoned elsewhere.

Which only angers me. It seems as though the only one who summons Miles anywhere is Princess Amaia, so she's the one keeping him from waiting to see if my brother is okay. Yesterday, after the Game, the healers didn't let us stay outside his door at all, insisting that it would only make things worse.

So, here we are.

"What are you thinking?"

I stop pacing, and Ryden peers at me intently.

I hesitate, glancing at Aubrey. I have a lot of questions, but I'm not sure if I should ask them in front of her. She's clearly in the princess's pocket, and the majority of my questions are about the princess. Starting with the fact that I didn't miss Amaia's piercing cry of pain as Asher lit up Keith's arm. She had also been the first person down at the finish line, ushering Keith into the arms of the nearest healer. Then she had disappeared and not returned to watch our Game. I also remember the unhappiness on King Edward's face as he watched his daughter exit with my dying brother.

A part of me is grateful for the princess, but an equally suspicious part of me doesn't trust her. On its own, the fact that she's King Edward's daughter is enough to make me wary of her. Add on the secrecy surrounding her, Aubrey, Miles, and even Ryden? I don't trust the princess. That's the short of it.

"I'm just thinking." I shrug, ready to stop there, but Ryden's eyes encourage me to go on. "Where's Princess Amaia? She seemed so concerned with Keith after the Game, but now she's nowhere to be seen."

Ryden frowns, but Aubrey is the one who responds. She lifts her head up to look at me, her eyes thoughtful.

"She's the Princess of Myria. She has things to do." Aubrey's voice is stiffer than normal, and now it's my turn to frown.

"What things?" I jump on the opportunity to learn more about the princess.

Aubrey's eyes narrow, but she doesn't look angry, just tired. "Her father uses her for diplomatic missions on occasion. He usually reserves those for Jacob though. She's mainly in charge of..." She pauses, searching for the word. "Less diplomatic missions."

"That doesn't explain why she screamed as if she was the one dying on that field while Asher torched my brother. Or why the king was content to let her walk off with him. Or why she hasn't even bothered to check up on him." I'm pacing again, studying Aubrey for a response.

She looks at me with sadness in her eyes. "Camille, listen," She releases a deep sigh, and I can tell she's just as exhausted as I am. "I get it, I really do. You have every reason to doubt all of us and try to figure out who you can and can't trust." Her voice turns into something harder, and her tone shifts to scolding. "But what I'm telling you now is true. Amaia is on your side. We're on your side. You can trust us."

I clench my teeth together and focus my gaze on Keith's door—until she mumbles something under her breath. I swivel back to her.

"Excuse me?" I snarl. Ryden is at my side in an instant, placing a hand carefully on my arm.

Aubrey stands up, snarling right back at me. "Keith gets it. He understands that we aren't here to hurt you two! All we've done is help you, and you don't have an ounce of appreciation."

I laugh sarcastically. "Yeah, you've really been helping us!" I jab a finger toward my brother's door. "My brother is lying practically dead in that room right now because of what Amaia's father has done to us."

Aubrey gets into my face, and Ryden tries to play the mediator. His hand is still resting on my arm while he uses the other one to push Aubrey back.

"That's her father," Aubrey retorts. "You don't get to pick the people who give birth to you, so instead of judging her, maybe you should take a moment to realize how lucky you are to have the parents you do."

Ryden tenses and gives me a warning look, but it's too late. She chose the wrong thing to go after.

"Seriously?" I screech. "You think I should consider myself lucky to have the parents I do? The first one was taken from me because she didn't have enough strength to fight off the officers." Aubrey looks like she wants to interrupt, but I don't let her. "Then, my father—the only family I have left—decides to throw us all to the curb for some stupid act of revenge. So yeah, you're right, I should be *beyond* grateful for both of my parents!"

I push her chest with force, and she jumps backward, hissing at the heat pulsing through my palms.

"Camille!" Ryden's voice is harsh. "Stop."

I don't touch her again, but my eyes don't leave Aubrey's. She looks at me incredulously. I would feel better if she appeared angry, but she appears even more exhausted. "Look, I get it, your life hasn't been perfect, and it certainly isn't right now. But I'm telling you, you'll want to trust us." She gestures to Ryden, who looks torn between both of us. "I know you trust my brother, so why don't you trust the rest of us?"

"I know he's hiding things. At least he doesn't pretend like he's not."

Ryden looks at me pleasantly surprised, and Aubrey opens her mouth to say something else, but at that moment, Keith's door opens, and our argument is forgotten.

"You can come in now. Just please keep the volume down." The tall, dark-haired nurse sweeps us into his room, giving me a pointed look, which I ignore. My attention is all on Keith.

He's lying on the bed, watching us all come in. Minus a few minor scratches on his face, he seems perfectly normal. Beside him is a steaming dinner plate full of loose corn and green beans sitting underneath two perfectly cooked chicken pieces. I smile. At least someone got him his favorite meal from home.

Keith looks at me a little warily, and I know he's still nervous about me. So, I try to break the tension.

"You know, just because we're upset with each other doesn't mean you have to go and nearly die."

Keith grins.

"Yeah, sorry, that's my bad." Keith glances at Aubrey and Ryden, who both watch him with concern, but from a distance. Considering my interaction with Aubrey just now, I'm grateful she's allowing us some space.

"Do you remember anything?" I ask.

He grimaces. "Just Asher and my skin burning off my arm. I know I made it across. How did you do?" He sits up, eyeing me carefully. "Are you okay?"

I wince, thinking about how I did in the maze. I was too worried about where Keith was, and if he was still alive to be able to put my full effort into the Game. "Well, thankfully, I avoided Prill, Sabrina, and Garden. I did get into a fight with the Workensire sisters, but I escaped relatively unscathed. Especially compared to you. I placed tenth, which isn't bad."

It's not good enough to win, I repeat to myself.

"What about you guys?" Keith nods up at Aubrey and Ryden.

They both answer at the same time. "Alright."

Aubrey comes up to the other side of Keith's bed, sitting down by his legs.

"But don't stress about anything. You've got a week of rest ahead of you." Keith starts to protest but Aubrey cuts him off. "Amaia's orders."

Keith rolls his eyes in annoyance, and I can't help my sudden spark of anger. Watching me carefully, Ryden notices my face twitch, and with a wordless exchange, he understands what I need.

"Well, I'm glad you're doing well, Keith. We wanted to make sure you were doing okay, but Camille and I are going to get some practice in before dinner."

I smile apologetically at my brother, and he returns it tentatively.

"See you guys later."

Ryden and I walk in silence the rest of the way to the training room. Maybe punching something will help me get some of my anger out. But when we walk in, I see something even better. Sabrina is snapping at Garden, while perfectly arching more of her knives at the targets in the corner of the room. My frustration at Aubrey and embarrassment from yesterday's Game needs a target. Seeing my sinister smile, Ryden laughs under his breath, but doesn't try to stop me.

Ignoring the crowd of other competitors already practicing, I stride to the center of the room. Ryden slips me my favorite sword before letting me stand by myself.

"Pelos!" I call from the middle of one of the arenas, sword in hand. My gift immediately jumps to the surface, ready to prove itself. Ryden leans up against the rope, amused.

Sabrina immediately swivels toward me, picking up on the challenge. Gleefully, she unsheathes two daggers from her hips, smiling menacingly.

"Wonderful." She glances to the side of the room, where Prince Jacob is watching the two of us carefully from his throne. It doesn't bother me though. He gets to watch the show.

"I'll finally get to spill some Atwood blood."

I give her a smug smile. "You wish."

Chapter Twenty-Three
Camille

I'M SURPRISED WHEN PRINCE Jacob clears his throat and stands from his lounged position in his royal chair, which still hasn't been moved since my fight with Keith. Jacob is not alone either. The ten Lords—five from Central and the other five each from their respective sectors—are seated next to the prince. I can't help but give Lord Prancis a quick wink in return for his stone gaze. Prill stands behind him with a smirk on her face as if she thinks I'm about to be pulverized. Another Central Lord is watching me, but his hazel eyes are solemn instead of angry. It looks like he's in mourning. His daughter, Carlena Escotos, died in yesterday's Game.

"Isn't this going to be fun to watch?" The prince's voice is dripping in amusement.

Sabrina inclines her head. "Of course it will be." She turns back to me and bares her teeth.

"May I offer a little wager?" Jacob asks.

Sabrina raises an eyebrow in anticipation. "What kind of wager, Your Highness?" The formality with which she speaks shocks me. Yes, she's a member of Prince Jacob's unit, but I would have expected the two of them to be more relaxed—like how Amaia and Miles are with each other. Although, Prince Jacob does seem like the type to hold a tighter grip on his unit.

"I think the winner should get some kind of advantage in the next Game." The Lords all look at Jacob and then at each other. Acting before thinking must run in the family.

"What kind of advantage, Your Majesty?" This time the hesitant voice comes from an older man dressed in a deep blue robe. His sea-green eyes seem concerned, but I can't tell who it's for.

"Well, Lord Miller," Jacob says snidely. "I think they should get an early practice run of the course before-hand."

Although his offer sparks my curiosity, I don't look up at him, even as I feel his eyes on the back of my head. I keep my gaze pinned on Sabrina, who is still sauntering her way over to me.

"That sounds fair." Sabrina's eyes lock onto mine.

"Camille, what do you think?" the prince asks.

I consider the question before answering. "I think I don't need any extra incentive to beat her to a pulp." Sabrina's foot crosses the arena line, and I pounce on her.

She's ready for me though. She quickly sidesteps and brings one of her knives arching towards my neck. Anticipating the move, my sword meets her blade. She grins in surprise and shifts backward. The movement is slight, but it gives me enough of an advantage to take the offensive.

I push her back toward the center of the arena, and even though she meets every one of my strikes, beads of sweat prickle her forehead.

Moving faster with my sword, I strike with the techniques Ryden taught me. I can feel his eyes watching me from the edge of the arena, where a crowd of competitors have gathered to watch our fight. Not that I fully notice all of the people. I'm focused on Sabrina, the unlucky target of my rage.

I slip past her guard in a backhanded move, and my sword slashes through the air. Sabrina throws up a palm, her eyes wide in panic. Inches from her neck, my blade hovers in midair. I don't waste time trying to fight the control she has over the metal. Instead, I drop into a crouch while swinging out my foot to catch her leg.

She stumbles and hits the floor, but before I have the chance to celebrate, she's rolled back onto her feet. This time her lips curl into a snarl, and her face flushes red with exertion.

I snarl right back and leap toward her. Internally, I know I can't beat her with swordplay alone because she has years of experience on me. But the rage and terror and frustration are giving me energy.

Sure enough, her movements become slower, although not slow enough. With the next hit, she catches my sword with both of her daggers in such a way that, with a flick, the weapon flies out of my hand.

"You can't beat me. I've been working with the best trainers the palace has to offer since I was out of the womb. The same ones the prince and the princess have exclusive access to. You. Don't. Stand. A. Chance." She leans into my face now, spit flying from her mouth. "And from the looks of yesterday, neither does your poor brother. If it weren't because of pure luck, he'd be dead right now. He *should* be dead right now."

My face falls flat, wiped clean of emotion. This time, I can feel the pressure of ice pricking at my skin, begging to be released on Sabrina.

Almost. Almost.

Observing my clenched jaw and empty expression, Sabrina gives me a vicious smile.

"Poor Keith. He's barely made it through, and it's only been two Games. I can't imagine he'll make it through another ten. What a tragedy that day will be. You'll truly be alone, without any family left!"

I give her a moment to bask in her taunts. Even though I can reach my sword, I don't grab it. Instead, I stare right back at Sabrina, who snarls at me before attacking me again. This time, I don't have a weapon to block the knife flying for my throat, but I don't need one.

I duck with my whole body, throwing myself into a roll. As I push myself upright, I bring an elbow out and direct it straight into Sabrina's stomach. She loses her breath and stumbles again.

I don't hesitate before sweeping her legs out from underneath her, forcing her to fall onto her back. Before she can push herself up, I catch one of her wrists underneath my shoe. I put all my weight on her it, and she winces, struggling to free it. Using her free arm, she swipes at my face with her second blade. I'm too slow, and it brushes against my cheek. Hot blood begins to trickle down my face.

Forgetting all the strategies Ryden's been teaching me, I bring my fist to her face. My knuckles connect with her nose, and blood rushes down her face. Making a sound somewhere between a frustrated scream and an agitated growl, Sabrina slashes with her knife, but this time I knock it out of her hand. Crushing both her wrists to the floor and picking up her discarded knife, I lean over her. I place the edge of the blade to her neck and stare down at her. She stares right back, hatred sharp in her eyes.

"At least I'm not a cocky brat who can't follow through on her threats." I can't contain my smile at the rage simmering in Sabrina's eyes. I start to loosen the pressure on her wrists, but before I release her, I lean back in. "And keep my brother's name out of your mouth. If I hear it again, I will end you."

Then I stand up, releasing Sabrina. She straightens, dusting herself off. Her face is bright red in rage and my delight only deepens. All the Lords are staring directly at me, their eyes wide in horror. Prill watches with pure hatred in her eyes. My smile shifts into a smirk. Prince Jacob is looking at me with pride in his eyes, and he inclines his head as a sign of his respect.

Loudly, so the whole room can hear it, I say to the prince, "And I don't need your handouts."

Prince Jacob only bows his head further.

I turn to see Ryden's reaction. He shakes his head in suppressed laughter. I give him a quick wink, and he returns it.

Turning on my heels, I walk toward the exit, dropping Sabrina's knife as I go. The entire room is silent as I leave.

Chapter Twenty-Four
Keith

I'M GRATEFUL I HAVE a better sense of direction than my sister. Miles isn't waiting outside my door for breakfast like he normally does—although, I wasn't expecting him to be. Aubrey made it very clear that Amaia instructed me to be left in my room for the rest of the week until the healers could be sure I was perfectly fine.

I knew that was ridiculous. I didn't even have a scar on the newly formed skin tissue where Asher had burned me. So that's why, despite Amaia's commands of bedrest, I had gotten up like normal this morning, dressing in the simple training clothes from my closet.

If I were to go to breakfast, I'd probably run into someone who would make a big scene and send me back to my room in a fuss. Considering I'm trying to avoid that, I decide to walk straight to the training room. I figure there's less of a chance of running into Miles, or Aubrey, or even my sister if I go there.

Sure enough, when I make it into the room, it's practically empty. Only a handful of people are there, none of whom I recognize. Two girls with matching strawberry blonde haircuts are sparring with each other in one of the far rings. A tall and broadly-shouldered boy is stretching in the corner. Another girl is helping a younger boy throw knives. Other than the five of them—and myself—the room is empty and quiet.

Ignoring the scoreboard in the corner, which places my name in spot fourteen out of the seventeen boys left, I walk across the room to the bow and arrows. It's the best thing I can work on without Miles or Aubrey here to help. Plus, it is something I want to improve on.

I quickly settle into a routine, firing a quiver full of arrows at the target and walking to remove them from the various spots where they hit the board, none of which hit the center of the target.

I set my feet to begin again when a girl's voice interrupts me.

"You're Camille's brother, right?"

I turn to look behind me, and the girl who had been helping the boy with his knives is behind me. The boy stands off to the side, and now that I see him closer, he's not as young as I initially thought. He's shorter than me, but his face is more developed. He might even be older than me.

"Yeah," I answer skeptically. "Why?"

"No reason, I was just curious." She holds out a hand for me to shake. "My name's Nicole, and this is Axel. We're both from the Gulf, just like you guys."

I would have guessed both of them were from the Gulf. Their golden-tanned skin matches mine, giving away their origins.

"My name is Keith." I return her handshake, only because it seems rude not to.

"I know," Nicole says matter-of-factly. "I was just trying to make conversation. Your sister cares a lot about you."

I raise an eyebrow. "And how do you know that?" It doesn't feel like it. Not since our arguments. She also left my room with Ryden yesterday in a hurry.

Nicole puts her hands on her hips. "I sat next to her during the first Game. Let's just say I was very entertained by Sabrina's insults and your sister's unwillingness to let her come at you."

"Well, thanks I guess."

An awkward moment passes before Axel speaks up. "Do you want me to help you with that?" He points to the bow.

"Oh, um, sure."

He shows me how to stand, nitpicking the tiniest of incorrect movements, while Nicole observes us from the side. Surprisingly, the first shot I release brushes the outside line of the center. Unsurprisingly, that's as close as I get for the next hour. More people start filing in, and I don't want to be caught practicing.

"We think you're pretty awesome, by the way." Nicole stops me as I begin to set the bow and arrows down.

"Why?" I ask, restraining a surprised laugh.

"You're kind of a legend actually!" Axel grins at me. "The stunt you pulled at the first Game was like a sucker punch in the king's royal face."

I stare at them for a moment. But both of their faces are bright as they stare right back at me. I'm still confused as to what exactly makes me "awesome" or a "legend." The more heroic move would have been to stay in the arena and save Oliver.

"But why?"

Axel drops his mouth open in disbelief. "It's inspiring, and it reminded me why I'm here." I pause, waiting to see if he'll continue, which he does. "I'm fighting in my own way, you know. Maybe that's why I find you to be such an encouragement."

This time, his eyes go blank as he fixates on the targets. I glance at Nicole, whose brown eyes are full of sympathy. She gives me a sad little grimace. "Neither of us want to be here."

"Then why are you?"

"Why are you?" she challenges.

It's a fair question. Not everyone is here because they want to be. Most of the competitors seem to wear the title of competitor with pride. I guess I had assumed that me and Camille being forced to compete was a rare occurrence. "I'm stuck here, that's different."

"Well, I volunteered. Both of my parents died a few weeks before the Games, and I couldn't survive on my own. Officers came knocking looking for a girl from the Gulf around my age, so I agreed to come here for these stupid Crowning Games." Nicole mentions her parents' deaths so matter-of-factly, but her face hardens.

"How did they die?"

Nicole gives me an odd look. "How do you think? My father was only trying to feed us and my mom..." Her voice breaks. "With my mom's condition, we needed more food. It was only a bag of apples he took. The store owner didn't even care. He was a family friend and always let it slide. But an officer caught him. Beat him to death in the square while my mom and I watched. A couple of days later, my mom died giving birth to my little brother, who ended up being stillborn." Nicole's voice is gruff as she recites the story, but her eyes are sparkling with tears.

"I'm so sorry." I reach a hand to awkwardly pat her on the shoulder.

She shakes her head. "It's not your fault. I won't say it's okay though, because it's not."

"I know it's not."

"That's why we need more people like you, Keith." Axel joins back into the conversation. "You know that they need a boy and a girl from each sector, right? To keep the Lords happy and to provide the idea that this whole system resembles something close to fair." I didn't know that, but I stay silent. "I'm here because they chose me as their lucky target. I refused. My family needed me to work, so officers came and took my little brother away. It was the only way they could get me to compete. They promised to return him after the Games. I don't know why it couldn't be somebody else." Axel's face is expressionless as he meets my eyes. "Noah's only seven. I'm just trying to make sure he sees his eighth birthday."

With my jaw is clenched, I give him a sharp nod. "One of these days, the king will pay for this."

Axel and Nicole nod back, their mouths pressed into thin lines. Not knowing what else to do, I walk out of the training area, leaving the two of them by the targets. I'm so lost in my own thoughts as I exit the room that I almost walk straight into somebody.

Amaia is standing right outside the door, her arms folded tight over her chest. Her eyes narrow as she surveys me. Either whatever the healers did—or my conversation with Nicole and Axel—must make me loopy, because the sight of angry Amaia makes me want to laugh.

"Are you not capable of listening to a *thing* I tell you?"

"To which incident are you referring?"

She glares at me. "The one where you were very directly told to stay in your room for the rest of the week."

I shrug innocently, watching as annoyance flickers on Amaia's face. "I feel fine. Plus, you aren't my mother." I point a finger at her. "How did you even know I got out?"

"I went to check on you," she says quietly.

"Oh? Well, as you can see," I gesture to myself and then my arm. "All good now."

She looks at me with her lips slightly parted. "What has gotten into you?"

I roll my shoulders. "Nothing like a near-death experience to bring out the optimism in someone." And honestly, it's true. Today I'm feeling the most positive I've felt in a long time. Even hearing from Nicole and Axel only reinforces the feeling because maybe, just maybe, enough people are willing to make a difference.

Amaia frowns, her arms still crossed over her chest. Her clothes are simple today, a loose shirt and pants. Her hair is in a messy bun, with wavy strands falling down the edges of her face.

"Do you know Nicole and Axel?" I ask.

She just looks at me, but now she's curious instead of furious. "Of course. Why do you ask?"

"Do you know why they're here?"

Her eyes narrow, but this time it's in confusion. "Why?"

Now it's my turn to feel annoyed. "You know why, don't you?"

She scowls at me but doesn't deny it.

"Why haven't you done anything to help them?" I demand.

"Well, maybe if I didn't have to worry about you getting up, running off, and hurting yourself because you refuse to listen to me. Then I could get on that." Her voice echoes in the hallway, concerned.

"Well, maybe you should stop worrying about me."

A blanket of silence hangs over us. I wonder what's racing through her mind. A part of me wants to retract what I said. I don't want her to stop caring about me. But the other part of me knows she's going to be marrying someone else at the end of these Games if my abysmal score is reflective of anything. It would make that final Game much easier to face if I could know that Amaia doesn't care for me.

I push into the silence. "Why do you worry anyway?"

Amaia rolls her eyes and refolds her arms. "Don't flatter yourself."

Despite my hesitations about her feelings, her reaction makes me grin. "Well then, don't make me stay locked in my room."

She bites her lip, contemplating something.

After a moment of staring at the roof, she sighs. "Fine. If you're going to be out of bed, you might as well come with us."

"Wait, where?" I say, caught off guard. "Who's us?"

She gives me a mischievous smile. "You'll see."

CHAPTER TWENTY-FIVE
Keith

"NICE TO SEE YOU up and around, Keith!" Miles says from his plush chair in the corner.

I give him a wary smile before taking in the rest of the room. It's a simple space. The walls are bare except for a couple of hanging pieces of armor and weapons. There's a set of matching chairs—one on which Miles is currently sprawled—and a long white couch that looks just as comfortable as the chairs.

There are three other people in the room, all looking at me with a mixture of surprise and disdain. Two girls are studying me carefully, their silver hair pulled back into matching braids. The third person, a boy who looks to be about my age, glares at me with contempt.

He turns to Amaia without hesitation. "Why is he here? You know he could ruin everything, right?"

Amaia rolls her eyes at the boy. "Hunt, you really need to learn how to relax. Keith wants to help, and I trust him."

Hunt stares at Amaia, mumbling under his breath. The two girls, while not as hostile as Hunt, are unnerving as their gaze shifts from me to their princess.

One of them—the smaller girl with brown eyes—says, "Of course you trust him." She gives Amaia a pointed look, but Amaia looks away and shares a glance with Miles instead.

Miles stands from the chair and stretches his arms. "Listen, Keith isn't a problem. Who knows? Maybe he'll be able to help on the mission."

Hunt doesn't seem convinced, but the other two girls accept Miles's words and go back to adjusting the swords at their waists. That's when I realize that everyone, except Amaia, is dressed in a complete set of silver armor. It's very similar to an officer's armor but seems to allow for more flexibility rather than pure strength.

"Excuse me. Mission?" I repeat.

"He doesn't even know what we're doing!" Hunt throws up his hands in frustration. Amaia waves him off.

"Ignore him, he just doesn't like anybody new." Amaia sticks her tongue out at Hunt, and he scowls at her, although his eyes soften as he plops himself onto the couch. "King Edward has tasked us with a little bit of an issue that's striking the Lates sector. Don't worry, we'll be back before dinner."

"We better be," Miles says from his corner, shooting us both a grin. "I'm starving."

"Of course, that's what you're concerned about." Hunt rolls his eyes, but it's directed at Miles. The smaller girl laughs.

The taller girl speaks up. "I happen to agree with Miles. Let's get this show on the road so we don't miss dinner."

"Give me just a moment. I have to get my armor on." Amaia quickly exits the room through a door I hadn't noticed. A blanket of silence settles over the room, and I'm still confused as to why Amaia brought me here.

Some pieces are starting to make sense. The taller girl looks vaguely familiar. She was present when Amaia took Camille and me from the Gulf. So, these people must be the princess's unit. That would explain the ease with which they all communicate and interact. Which is great for them but leaves me feeling extremely out of place.

"I still don't understand what's going on."

The taller girl gives me a scrutinizing look. "You'll figure it out as you go. My name is Lydia, and this is my sister, Precious." The smaller girl gives me a shy smile, glancing up from her sword belt. Other than their silver hair, their features are very different, and I wouldn't have assumed they were sisters. Lydia is stout, with broad shoulders and sharp cheekbones. Her eyes are more golden, while her sister's are a soft brown. Precious also has a soft face and a willowy frame.

"We are the king's intimidation factor," Lydia explains. "We show up when the sectors aren't behaving or one of the neighboring countries is getting confident in their abilities to overpower Myria. Right now, some people in the Lates aren't meeting their responsibilities, and it's slowing down the production lines. We go in, create a healthy dose of fear, and then leave."

Seriously, this is Amaia's way of trying to prove she doesn't agree with her father? Bringing me along to watch them terrorize a bunch of innocent people?

"Why am I here?" I ask.

"That is exactly my question," Hunt says bitterly from the couch.

"I don't plan on helping you bully a bunch of people."

Everyone in the room looks at me. Even Miles. Lydia and Hunt appear incredulous, but Miles is grinning at me. Precious is suppressing a small smile as well.

I shrug, suddenly embarrassed. "What?"

Miles is the first to break the silence, moving toward me and playfully shoving my shoulder. "Told you guys. He's chill."

Before I can ask for clarification, Amaia walks back into the room, clearing her throat. Her armor is more complex than her unit's armor. Instead of being pure silver, it's lined in black and decorated with twisted black vines. It clings tightly to her skin, versus the others' armor, which is bulkier.

"Alright, we're ready. Let's move."

At Amaia's words, the four members of her unit snap into place. Their shoulders are squared, and their chests are held high. I don't belong with these people, and I'm also severely underprepared wearing my thin training clothes.

"Listen, I don't have a spare set of armor, and I'm not technically supposed to take you with me, so I can't ask for another set. Please just don't be stupid," Amaia says.

"Wow, thanks for that stunning vote of confidence."

Amaia raises an eyebrow. "Well, you *do* have a tendency to do stupid things."

I sigh and shake my head, following the group as they move closer to Miles. Everyone places a hand on his shoulder, and I do too.

"Ladies and gentlemen, get ready for a ride," Miles chimes.

With a jerk of motion, we zip through space and land in a dank room. The walls are brick and decorated with dark stains. Blood stains. My stomach flips. Before I have time to fully get my bearings, a deep voice welcomes us.

"Princess Amaia. It is wonderful to have you out here. Department 302 has been causing issues and is refusing to cooperate despite our creative punishments."

An immediate dislike for the man forms as the words leave his mouth. He's an officer—a high-ranked one if the medals on his chest indicate anything. His head is inclined in respect for Amaia, but his eyes laser into hers.

"Yes, my father has already informed me of the situation. Lead us to the department, and we'll take it from there."

I've never heard Amaia's voice so cold.

Miles gives me a soft elbow to the ribs, reminding me to follow them. The unit forms a practiced arc behind Amaia as they walk behind the officer and out of the room. I move behind Miles and next to Lydia. Precious and Hunt flank Amaia's other side as we all walk in silence through more brick hallways.

Officers line the walls, similar to those in the palace, except these officers seem more sinister. Even the officers in the Gulf never felt this hostile. I glance at one and peek through his helmet. The officer's gaze makes me want to run away as fast as possible—maybe even summon another hunting leopard or bring back my wolf.

The feeling only doubles as the hall opens up into a massive room. Dirty fabrics hang from the ceiling, all in varying states of disarray. Every wall is lined with loud machinery, each manned by a line of people, who are all arranged shoulder to shoulder. Some people are bent over wash basins, desperately scrubbing filthy pieces of clothing. Others work with nimble fingers and rusted needles, intricately threading pieces together. In the center of the room, there's a group of officers all holding long whips. I wince at the thought of what those might be used for.

Amaia stops, and her unit doesn't miss a beat. However, I almost stumble and run straight into Miles. Considering the odd looks from a couple of the officers, I know everyone is wondering what I'm doing here. Although no one audibly questions Amaia. Not that I blame them. She is the pure, regal, powerful Princess Amaia right now, and her facial expression alone stops anyone from commenting on me. Still, I silently curse myself for being so stupid.

"Thank you, Officer Floyd. My unit and I will take it from here. Remove those officers." She gestures to the main pool in the center holding the whips. "And leave the ones on the wall. When we are finished, we will find you."

Amaia doesn't even glance at Officer Floyd again as she strides to the center of the room, taking the place of the officers, who all obediently exit the factory building. As soon as they're gone, Amaia's shoulders relax, and from beside me, Lydia cracks a smile.

"Lydia, Precious, take that side." She points to the far left wall. "Hunt, take the back wall. And Miles, you take the front. Keith, you're with me over here."

The rest of her unit doesn't hesitate to obey her orders. However, I slowly follow her, hovering nervously next to her as she stops by the wall.

Getting a closer look at the people, I see that a lot of them are young. One little boy can't be older than five. They all move their little fingers as fast as they can, displaying the Nightrock cuffs covering their wrists. Their faces are gray with exertion. Amaia approaches a young girl who looks to be fourteen, and the girl begins to tremble. The back of her filthy shirt is torn to shreds and bright red lash marks peek through the gaps. Refusing to stand and watch her torture these people any further, I reach out a hand to hold Amaia's arm back.

"Yes?" she speaks coolly.

"Stop," I say, my voice surprisingly calm. "Don't hurt these people. They're putting in their best effort."

Amaia rears back, hurt flashing through her eyes. "You really think that low of me?" she hisses. Jerking her arm out from my hand, she takes a step closer to the girl and reaches for the pile of clothes she's folding. She starts to help the girl.

The girl slowly stops shaking and looks up at Amaia with wide eyes. "Thank you."

Amaia dips her head. "Of course."

I stand, watching her in silence for a moment.

"I'm not evil, you know."

"I know." And I mean it. I don't know why I expected her to harm these people. She's shown over and over that she disagrees with her father and his methods. "I didn't mean to jump to conclusions."

Amaia sighs while handing me more shirts to fold. "They come in every morning, receive their cuffs, and are sent to complete ridiculously impossible quotas." She pauses, shifting down the line to help another man with hanging more clothes on a rack. He silently acknowledges her but doesn't say anything. "Then, they're allowed to leave. Their cuffs are removed, and their daily payment is given to them in the form of barely enough food to feed them and their family. Then they have to come back and do it all over again the next day."

The thought of this environment being these people's daily lives makes me want to vomit. The treatment is disgusting. I almost feel ashamed for doubting my father when he told me and Camille that the Lates had it worse than us.

What shocks me the most is that before Amaia sent the officers with whips away, there were ten total officers in the room. There has to be at least one hundred people in here, easily outnumbering the officers.

"Why do people put up with this?" I whisper. "How are the officers even able to watch this happen?"

"Myria and its ruler's abusive tendencies are ingrained very deeply in this country. It doesn't bother the people in command because they don't have to deal with it. The Lates is where all our manufacturing and resourcing happens, including gathering Nightrock. The mining process leaves people incapacitated, but it means the Lates sector has the easiest and most abundant access to it. They use the Nightrock to keep the workers weak, so even if they wanted to, they're not strong enough to fight back. There are some decent officers out there, though." She gestures her head to one of them standing by Hunt's wall. "The ones that are still in here. They'll turn a blind eye to us. They won't do anything more, nor do I expect them to. They have families of their own."

I shake my head in disbelief. "But why don't they rise up or attack the other officers?"

"Maybe all of them could manage something." Amaia stops folding to turn her sad eyes to me. "But nobody wants to be the first one to do anything. The fear of punishment for them and their family is too strong."

Methodically, I fold more clothes from the seemingly endless piles, trading between a handful of younger children. Every time I approach them, their faces brighten, if only a little bit, and they eagerly shift to make space for me. It gives me a sense of overwhelming sadness to see how little I have to do in order to make these kids' day. Amaia's words keep playing back through my head.

Of course, nobody wants to make the first move. They're scared no one else will join them. And what happens after they overtake the room? Do more officers get sent in?

A sudden thought occurs to me. I catch Amaia's gaze over a little girl's head. "How many of these factories are there?"

Amaia gives me a sad smile. "Easily over a thousand."

The number blows my mind. But if there's over a thousand factories like this, that means there's more than a hundred thousand workers. Certainly Central doesn't have enough officers to handle every single factory?

"Keith." Amaia's smile shifts into something different as she catches the look in my eye. Gently, she reaches a hand to my arm. "You're going to have to make a choice. The people of Myria need hope, and you get to pick a side. My unit knows what the price will be when we inevitably get caught, but we do it anyway. Even small things like this offer hope in impossible ways. But now that you've seen it for yourself, you're going to have to decide whether you want to fight with us or not."

I eye her carefully.

"Trust me, Keith, we aren't the bad guys. Don't forget that."

CHAPTER TWENTY-SIX
Camille

THIS GAME HAS TO be my least favorite so far.

I didn't see much of anybody all month. I stuck to myself, spending most of my time in the training room. I avoided Keith, even when I could tell he was purposefully trying to track me down or wait for me after meals. The only person I talked to was Ryden. And even those conversations consisted of me asking him to show me the way to the security room. What little time I spent out of the training room, I spent watching my father waste away in his cell, denying every opportunity to free himself and save Keith and me from the prison of the palace.

He could have saved me from having to dangle like an idiot from this cliff, which I can currently feel my fingers slipping from, knowing it's only a matter of time before I lose my grip. I desperately try to find a piece of rock to which I can lodge my feet on to relieve pressure off of my poor phalanges.

The crowd's thunderous cheers and terrified screams don't help to ease the pounding in my heart. I grit my teeth and adjust my grip, stretching my leg as far as I can in order to find purchase against the edge of the rock.

I don't understand how the competitors ahead of me made it across this climbing wall so easily. Thinking back to Keith and his near-flawless run, I can't understand how he did it either. He had finished his competition in eighth and easily could have placed higher had he not stopped to try to help a few of the boys cross. At the time, I had cursed him for his kindness, but now I had a whole new sense of pity for those who had needed help.

Wincing, I think about the boy who had fallen at this exact same spot long after Keith had moved on from the rock wall. Axel, I think his name was. I refuse to look down at his broken body, which still lies beneath me. They didn't clear away the dead before beginning the girl's round.

My heart only races faster as I hear the wall creak behind me. Somebody else has caught up to me, and all I can hope is that it's not Sabrina or somebody who wants me dead. All it would take would be a little nudge of my fingers, and my body would be joining Axel's. Although, as my fingers slip another inch off the rock, I think I might be joining him either way.

Trying to ignore the sounds of someone getting closer, I push myself up to readjust my hold on the rock. Chewing on my lip, I look ahead of me, trying to plan out my path, but I can't find another step within plausible reach. When I had initially started the wall, I thought I had picked the easiest route, but apparently not.

"Do you need a hand?"

The girl's voice would have made me jump if I hadn't been fifty feet in the air barely holding on. Instead, it makes me shift away from her, loosening my grip on the wall again. I feel myself start to slip.

Before I accept my death, I feel a hand wrap itself around my own and hold me up against the wall. Nicole's face is focused, and her lips are pressed together in exertion. Yet, she expertly holds on, with two feet steadily in place. The hand that's not holding onto mine is firmly attached to one of the protruding rocks. I scramble onto the wall and grab another crevice of rock, desperately trying to relieve the pressure off of Nicole's strained arms.

"Grab the spot directly beneath our hands," Nicole gasps out, breathing hard.

I nod, obeying. I adjust myself to hold on to the wall on my own and Nicole relaxes.

"Thank you," I mutter, my face tinged pink.

Nicole brushes it off. "It's not a big deal. Some of us would prefer you to not die, Camille."

Her nonchalant tone surprises me, and my eyes furrow in confusion.

"Don't worry, I'll explain it later." She gestures with her head. "Now put your foot there."

Wordlessly, I follow her guidance across the rest of the rock wall, finally reaching the end. From her own place on the wall, Nicole helps me regain my footing on the flat ground and then joins me on the platform in between the rock wall and the next obstacle.

Brushing away the sweat from my forehead, I say, "Thank you, again."

Nicole rolls her eyes. "It's fine, you'd do the same for me."

She leaps for the next obstacle, leaving me stunned in silence. The truth is, I probably wouldn't have done what she just did. I would have left her dangling instead of risking my own life for hers.

Shaking myself out of my stupor, I follow Nicole and leap across the shifting platforms that make up the next obstacle. Ahead of me, there's a crowd of other competitors, each having gained an extreme lead on me because of my slow progress on the rock wall. Setting my shoulders, I resolve to at least catch up to Nicole, who is already nearly to the end of the platform obstacle.

However, I'm only halfway through the moving platforms when a sharp laugh catches me off guard. I swivel around, holding myself steady and trying to ignore the drop underneath me.

Garden leers at me. "I don't understand why Sabrina finds you to be such a threat."

I grit my teeth, determined to ignore her. I step across to the next platform, but Garden brushes past me, almost sending me tumbling off the side. I crouch low, desperately reaching for a piece of the floor to hold onto.

"What are you doing?" I growl at her. "Why do you have it out for me?"

She cocks her head at me. "I don't know. Didn't you hear what I just said?" She waggles her fingers at me and rushes ahead.

I roll my eyes, but I'm grateful that she's gone. I finish leaping across the platforms and prepare myself for the next section. This obstacle is downhill and covered in rolling spiked logs. Beneath me, a machine pushes them out at various intervals. Some drop faster than others.

Trying to guess, I wait at the edge, counting the seconds between the rolling logs.

4 seconds.

6 seconds.

2 seconds.

15 seconds.

4 seconds.

The crowd cheers for the girls who are crossing the finish line. I have to hurry, or I'll have no chance of placing. But I've already waited too long, because from behind me, somebody shoves me forward, and I tumble right in front of one of the sharp logs.

I scramble to my feet and barely dodge it. Standing upright, Prill lands next to me. She'd been the one to push me off. Snarling, I shove back at her, and she almost falls onto the metal protruding from the logs. I want to stay and finish her off, but it'll waste precious seconds I don't have. Not if I want to place well. Hoping I can put enough distance between myself and Prill before she regains her footing, I sprint as fast as I can, urging myself to keep pace with the log in front of me.

It's not enough though because Prill tackles me. Instinctively, I reach for my gift, but it's not there. Not this time. The Nightrock bracelets they gave us before this Game snuff it out.

So I bring myself to my feet again, elbowing Prill as I go. She groans, still able to drag herself upward. Both of us are too out of breath to exchange verbal blows.

The next log comes rolling out.

"Shoot!" Prill mutters, sprinting in the opposite direction and abandoning me.

I'm right behind her, resisting the urge to look back at the pounding log that shakes the floor with every bounce.

Barely skimming the log, I sprint past the one in front of us, pushing myself to make it to the end of the obstacle faster.

I want to collapse on the floor and gulp in fresh air. Instead, I force myself to follow behind Prill, who begins to climb over a thin glass bridge. Underneath are five-inch spikes that have been buried into the floor.

I grimace at the thought of my body being pierced by one—a definite death. Trying to look on the bright side, it's probably a good thing that I'm so far behind. Otherwise, the bridge would be crowded and everyone would be pushing past each other to get to the finish line. By myself, I'm able to focus on balancing and not worry about anyone shoving me off. But when I reach about halfway through, I almost trip and throw myself off anyway.

Directly beneath me is Nicole Idomet's bleeding body.

Her blank eyes are looking right at me, and blood from her wounds coat her dark hair. For the first time since seeing death, I'm overcome with the urge to lose all the contents of my stomach. Shaking my swimming head, I make myself walk, doing my best to keep my wobbly feet on the glass platform.

I think back to when I almost fell at the rock wall. I'm grateful it's not my body down there. Of course, that's only because Nicole caught me. She had been much too kind to survive in a place like this. Still, her death makes me sick. I need to step up my game if I want to avoid ending up like her.

I cross the finish line and the crowd erupts into more loud cheers. I know they're grateful I made it to the end. Ignoring the smug look on Sabrina's face as she looks between me and Nicole's body, I collapse.

And throw up all of my breakfast.

CHAPTER TWENTY-SEVEN
Keith

I DIDN'T GET ONE moment of sleep last night. Every time I shut my eyes, Axel or Nicole's face would flash through my mind. At some point, I must have fallen asleep—if only for a couple of minutes—because I wake up in a cold sweat.

The sun has only barely begun to glisten over the horizon. There isn't any hope of me being able to fall asleep again now. Instead, I go into my closet and pull out a simple cotton shirt and a pair of loose pants. I lace on my comfortable running shoes, provided by King Edward and his staff. I almost snarl at the thought.

I scribble down a quick note for Miles, who is sure to come popping in later this morning. When I walk out the door, I realize I don't know if I can get out of the palace alone. Of course, I've followed Miles and Amaia outside before, but the officers hadn't batted an eye. With me alone, however, it would probably be a different story.

They might consider me leaving unaccompanied at the crack of dawn as something questionable.

Deciding I'll face the guards when I get there, I head for the gate that leads out to the stables. It doesn't take me long to get there. But sure enough, when I reach the gate, an officer stops me.

"What are you doing?" His voice is rough, and his eyes glint at me. I stifle a groan. Of course, the officer would be some dude who actually enjoys his job.

"I'm just trying to pass through. I'm not trying to cause any trouble," I say, but I can tell the officer doesn't believe me.

"You don't have clearance to leave, Atwood."

For a split second, my face displays shock. I know the competitors are well known, but for him to have so easily recognized me is a little unnerving. Quickly, I get over my surprise and try another approach.

"Well, I'm not leaving. I'm just going for a quick run on the grounds. If you'd like, you could always come along and supervise me. Make sure I don't attempt an escape."

The officer glares at me.

Getting slightly desperate, I take a step toward him with my hands held wide. "Listen, please. I promise I'm not going anywhere. I just seriously need to get some fresh air."

"No." The officer's response is blunt. "You may go back to your room."

I shake my head. He jerks a finger in my direction, and another officer comes forward to place a rough hand on my arm.

I clench my jaw in frustration, but I don't see a way of changing his mind. I think about running through the palace's hallways, but that seems like a sure way to attract unwanted attention. Before I seriously consider my other options, a forceful voice cuts through the air.

"Let him go."

The officer holding me immediately releases his grip and glares past my shoulder.

"We have direct orders from the king that Mr. Atwood must remain in the palace."

"And now you have direct orders from me." Princess Amaia glares at him. "Let Atwood go. If you must insist on ensuring he doesn't escape the palace, feel free to watch him."

I look at her curiously, and she slides her eyes to mine for a brief second.

How long had she been here?

The grumpy officer sighs and rolls his eyes. "It's your head the king will have. Not mine."

Amaia smiles. "Absolutely."

The officer steps aside to let me pass. Before I walk through the gate, I look back at Amaia, who gives me a sad smile. She dips her head in a regal nod, and I incline mine in gratitude. She watches me as I go.

Finally. A taste of actual freedom. I charge forward.

As soon as the smell of fresh grass and the crisp scent of clean air fills my lungs, the pounding in my head goes away. I can still feel the grumpy officer's watchful gaze on me as I run, but I don't mind it. If I focus on each of my individual steps hitting the spongy earth, everything starts to slip away.

The image of Axel's body falling from the climbing board only seconds after I had decided to move on, and another boy I might have been able to save if I had made a different decision both leave my mind. The picture of Sabrina pushing Nicole off instead of turning around and simply finishing the race leaves too.

Nicole had been too kind to die like that.

No. Push it away.

All of the people being forced to work in factories in the Lates. The hopelessness in the adult's eyes as we left... Only the children had a small spark of optimism.

Push it away.

Even thoughts of my father... I wonder if he's being tortured and starved? I don't doubt that he's scared and alone. Or who knows, maybe he's already dead.

If only he was here with me. He'd share in my anger. Considering the fact that he did try and execute the man, I'm positive he would happily join me in ripping the king's throat out.

Push it away.

I miss my mother more. She was always down to run with me whenever I needed to. If she were here, we'd stop by the little pond that I can see in the distance. I'd probably start to skip rocks while she watches with a gentle smile. We'd be there all day until I finally put words to what's bothering me. And then she'd wrap me up in one of her warm hugs and tell me that everything would be okay, and somehow, it would be.

Except, she's not with me today, and I don't know if it's possible to be okay.

I'm not sure how long I run through the grounds. But when the sun completely peeks over the horizon and fills the sky, I figure that's as good a time as any to come inside.

I walk back through the gate, ignoring the glare from the grumpy officer, and head back toward my room. My stomach is growling, and I desperately need to shower

and change before making my way down to the breakfast hall. The slight inconvenience of a hungry stomach
doesn't bother me much, though. Not when neither Axel
or Nicole will be eating another meal.

I try to take a deep breath and calm myself down, but
now, back inside the cramped hallways of King Edward's
palace, my frustrations and bitterness have nowhere to
go. My eyes are downcast to the floor as I turn the corner and run straight into someone. Upon contact, my
body retracts from the searing heat bubble surrounding
Camille.

"Ow!" I yelp.

Camille's eyes widen. It appears she had also been in
her own thoughts. "Keith! Are you okay?" She winces.
"Sorry, it's just kind of become a habit to keep my heat
up, you know?"

Her words strike a nerve, and my pain is forgotten.
"Why?"

Her brows furrow in confusion. "What do you mean?"

"Why has it become a habit for you to always be ready
for an attack? Why is it that we have to depend on gifts
we didn't even have before coming here? Why is this how
we have to live now?"

Shockingly, Camille doesn't look angry. She looks
thoughtful—and maybe a little uncomfortable. "Keith,

listen. The world we live in now requires us to always be on edge. Living in this palace is a lot different than living at home."

"You don't have to tell me that. Obviously, it's different. The worst thing you had to worry about was your crush on Micheal! I hadn't been forced to watch people I recognize die every month. Did you know Axel had a brother that he was protecting by being here? What's going to happen to him now? I could have stopped and saved him, Cam. He was only a couple of people behind me when I moved on. All because there was this idea that, in order to survive—as you put it—we have to win. But Axel's death doesn't feel like a win."

Camille only frowns at me. "You can't blame yourself for Axel's death. The same way Nicole's death isn't my fault."

I shake my head and sigh. "Fine, maybe it's not. But it is King Edward's."

"Stop!" Camille hisses. Her eyes dance around the hallway, surveying the walls and the ceiling.

"No, Camille, you need to understand that something is wrong, and it's bigger than me and you." I'm talking with my hands now, my agitation visible. "Amaia took me to the Lates sector a couple of weeks ago."

Camille's first expression of rage breaks her face. "Excuse me!" She's yelling now. "And you didn't tell me! You know you could have been killed there, right? And you didn't think it would be important to tell me? If you had died, I wouldn't have even known, and if the princess had an inkling of common sense, she wouldn't have put you in such a dangerous situation either!"

I brush off her words, trying to get to my point. "It was kind of a last-minute trip. Either way, do you know what I saw there?"

Camille glares at me. "I take it you're going to tell me?"

I glare right back. "I was inside one of their factories, and it's a terrible place, Camille. Kids are in there breaking their backs, slaving away at menial labor. They're all cuffed and stuffed into a tight line and forced to stand and work all day, only getting off for a couple of hours of rest before having to do it all over again. Amaia explained it all to me. Their wages are set in a way that is dependent on if they meet the expectations or not. It's this sick and evil way of getting the workers—adults and young kids alike—to come back every single day. Tell me, how am I supposed to see that and not want to do something about it?"

"Stop." Camille's voice is hard and sharp, but I still start to open my mouth again. She interrupts me. "Stop it, Keith. I get it. The world's messed up, but what are you going to do? Single-handedly take down King Edward and everyone who agrees with him? Do you really have the strength to destroy the entire Kingdom of Myria from the inside out?"

I open my mouth. She holds a hand up to stop me.

"No, listen. I already know what you're going to say. You get this attitude from both of our parents, but look where it's gotten them. One's dead and the other is practically dead. They didn't accomplish anything. So maybe, instead of being so willing to die for the world, we should be focused on surviving." She looks at me with a steely gaze. "Listen, Keith, all you can do is *survive*."

Her tone makes me pause. She's lecturing me.

"Cam, that can't be right." I shake my head. "There has to be more that I can do! I don't want to just survive. Cam, I want to fight. I owe it little Oliver, to Axel, to Nicole." My voice chokes. "To Father and Mother. Because, if I don't fight, all of their pain and suffering, their deaths, would be in vain. And I can't let that happen. I don't think we should ever be so focused on survival that we become content living like this."

"I don't want to lose you." This time, Camille's voice is small and timid. "I don't want you to die."

I peer at her in anguish. "But I'm not living."

Chapter Twenty-Eight
Camille

BUT I'M NOT LIVING.

Keith's words pound inside my head. It would be stupid and ignorant of me to pretend that nothing he said held some amount of truth. Compared to life in the Gulf, this was far from simply living. But we can't live if we're dead. That's why I have to survive. That's why Keith and I have to survive *together*.

The steely glint he had in his eye for our entire conversation scares me. I know Keith, and when he decides he's going to do something, there's no chance of changing his mind. The idea that, this time, what he decides to do could very well end up getting him killed, makes me want to run back, find him, and refuse to let him do anything rash.

Instead, I find myself outside a door.

And it isn't Keith's door.

No. For whatever reason, after standing in the hall where Keith had run into me, I hadn't continued to breakfast, and I hadn't gone back to my room—or even to the training room. Instead, I stare warily at Ryden's nameplate on the wall.

I've lost track of how long I've stood out here or how many times I've raised my hand to knock before dropping it. Although my gut tells me to trust him, the rest of my brain can't help but whisper doubts.

What if he's not trustworthy?

What if he runs to the king and turns my brother in for treason?

What if he's not really who he seems to be?

Finally realizing how stupid this is, I turn away from the door. But before I can walk away, it slowly swings open.

Ryden's face appears, and he smiles when he sees me.

"Sorry, I hope it's not too much, but I sensed your static out here and just thought I'd check on you." He pauses, taking in my distraught face. "What's wrong?"

I look up at the concern in his green eyes. I open my mouth to respond. Before any words can come out, my face crumples. Silent tears begin to streak down my face, and Ryden's face softens.

"Come here." He reaches out to me and wraps me in a hug. I'm not sobbing, but the tears are flowing quickly now, staining Ryden's dark green shirt.

I let him draw me into his room, releasing me only to shut the door behind him. He guides me to a plush couch pushed into the corner, keeping one hand firmly on the small of my back. I'm shivering, and I know I must be freezing his hand, but he doesn't move it.

"Here, sit down. I'll grab you a blanket."

I sit as he suggests, wrapping my knees up to my chest.

Ryden rummages in a small wooden chest at the foot of his bed before grabbing a thick woolen blanket. He lays it across me, and I give him a grateful smile through my tears.

He smiles back as he sits beside me. "Would you like some tea? I can have some brewed and brought up."

I shake my head, not wanting to be any more trouble than I already am.

But he just eyes me knowingly. "Chamomile or lavender?"

"Chamomile, please." My voice sounds so small.

"Only acceptable answer."

After he's rung for a servant and received two steaming cups of chamomile tea, he sits back down, handing me a cup.

We sit in silence for quite some time, sipping on our tea, and eventually, my tears come to a stop.

"Thank you," I whisper, breaking the silence.

Ryden nods. "There's no need to thank me. I'm only doing what any decent person would."

"I don't think I would have let some crying girl into my room." I mean it as a joke, but it falls flat.

"I disagree." Ryden leans back into the cushions, stretching his feet out on the carpet. "I think you have a huge heart and would gladly welcome somebody who needed your help."

"What makes you say that?"

He shrugs. "Call it my intuition. I'm pretty good at reading people."

I side-eye him, fighting a grin at his joke. "That was a bad one."

"I thought it was pretty good."

I huff, amused.

Another beat of quiet passes between us before Ryden speaks again.

"Do you need to talk about it?"

I like how he said that. He isn't asking if I want to, he's asking if I need to. Maybe that's why I find myself spilling everything to him so easily.

"I think Keith is going to get himself killed."

Ryden raises an eyebrow, but waves his hands, encouraging me to elaborate.

"I don't know. I guess Amaia took him to see the Lates. Keith, having the natural hero complex he does, wants to save all the people who are suffering. Now he's all pressed about making a difference in the world, and I think he wants to kill King Edward. Which, don't get me wrong, I don't think the king is doing anything right for anyone outside of Central and the Gust, but I don't think killing him is the right answer."

I pause and take a deep breath as everything that's been building up inside me spills out.

"The thing is, I know Keith means it. I've never seen him like this, determined to right some wrong he believes needs to be addressed. But, that doesn't make it right, does it? Or am I being extremely selfish? Should I be right beside Keith, fighting for those who can't fight for themselves?"

Ryden doesn't say anything, and for a minute I consider getting up and leaving. I've obviously said too much, but before I can move, he says, "I agree with you. Keith is probably going to get himself killed. Especially if he keeps talking like that around here. Does he not realize the cameras that watch your father watch the palace too?"

I had thought about that—the idea that someone could have been observing our conversations—but something in Ryden's tone makes me wince. He takes a deep breath.

"You still haven't told him about your father, have you?"

"It would only make things worse."

Ryden's eyes aren't judgmental like I was expecting them to be. Instead, he simply sighs. "I still agree. But, either way, to answer another one of your questions, no, I don't think you're being selfish. I think you see a messed-up country in dire need of change, but you also see that dying for it isn't worth it. You can't do anything dead."

His words strike a chord in me, and I stand up, flinging the blanket onto his lap. I pace in front of him as he stares at him.

I pause. "What? Why are you looking at me like that?"

He only smiles. "Nothing."

I give him a look that says I don't believe him, but I carry on anyway.

"That's exactly what I've been trying to tell Keith, and he just doesn't get it. He thinks I'm falling into line, which I suppose is true enough, but what else am I supposed to do? King Edward has an obvious curiosity for the two of us if that sparring fiasco proved anything. I feel like Keith is already drawing too much negative attention to himself, and if he hadn't been a part of the Games, I'm sure he would be in a cell next to my father."

I can hear my own voice rising, but Ryden doesn't seem to mind. He's leaning forward, resting his chin in his cupped hands. A loose strand of red hair falls across his face, brushing against his eye. My cheeks flush red as I take him in. I try to duck my head and return to pacing, hoping he didn't notice, but something about his silence and the light smile playing across his face tells me he knows what I was thinking.

Clearing my throat, I say, "Maybe there's more to be done from the inside. Maybe, if I can play along and survive long enough to gain more influence, they'll eventually let their guard down. Then I can do something like Keith thinks we should. Imagine what I could do as the Queen of Myria."

I hadn't thought about it like that before. Keith wants to do something now, but what power does he have to make a change? If I wait and take my time, I can do more once I have inside control.

Ryden's expression has shifted to amused. I sit back down on the couch, folding my arms against my chest.

"I don't know, maybe that's just silly of me." Tears burn behind my eyes, but I blink them away. "I mean, not to mention all the lies I've been telling him. My gift, our father…"

"He doesn't know that you had your gift before coming here?"

I shake my head miserably. "No. My mother always told me it was safer that no one knew."

Ryden nods. "She was right. With the strength of your gift—especially if it was *this* strong when you were younger—officers probably would have spirited you away to the Gust. Away from your family. That's what they do to everyone who has your kind of power. The king doesn't like to allow people like you to flourish outside of his control. In the Gust, you would have had one-on-one training under the direct supervision of His Majesty's best trainers. Who knows what would have happened to you there."

A part of me wonders if that would have been such a terrible thing. His fingers reach forward to brush my tears away. My stupid, persistent tears.

"Sometimes secrets are the only way to keep people safe." For a moment, he sounds like he's reassuring himself. "We both know Keith wouldn't be able to hold himself together. But you… you can keep quiet, keep yourself safe. Then, you're free to make more impactful decisions. Not to mention you're the most powerful person I've ever met. It would be amazing to see what you could do from the inside."

I snort and start to turn away, but Ryden grabs my hand, forcing me to face him.

"I'm serious. Your gift is stronger than mine, and you never even had an actual trainer to help you learn. How old were you when you first started using it?"

Rolling my tongue over my teeth, I debate telling him the truth. My mother's old warnings flash through my head, but they're quick to leave.

What does it matter? She's gone anyway.

"Three."

Ryden's mouth drops open. "That's the youngest I've ever heard of someone developing a gift. You have serious power, Camille."

I search his eyes, looking for proof that he believes what he's saying. It certainly doesn't feel like I'm very powerful. My gift has more control over me than I do over it.

Reading the doubt in my eyes, not my mind, Ryden wraps me in a hug. I allow myself to believe him. For now. I'm powerful. And one day I'll be strong enough to do something like Keith wants me to.

In between stroking my hair, Ryden whispers, "Just remember, you can't do anything dead."

Chapter Twenty-Nine
Keith

This morning, we all eat breakfast together. Aubrey suggested it, explaining that we hadn't been together since that day in the woods. It feels like ages ago and only yesterday at the same time. Yet, so much has changed.

Even though they never sat with us, Axel and Nicole's absence is stark. The corner they used to occupy is now a pair of empty chairs and a clear table. Seeing it nearly makes me combust with anger. Instead, I just feel overwhelming sadness. Aubrey seems to feel the same way, positioning her chair so she can't see the corner.

Ryden and Miles talk like normal, laughing and cracking jokes. Camille sits in between Ryden and Aubrey, occasionally smiling at something one of the boys says. She hasn't even looked in my direction since we all sat down, and I'm torn between feeling guilty and feeling grief.

Ever since we got here, it feels like all we've done is argue. Normally, at home, this isn't our routine. Sure, we've always bickered like siblings, but it's never felt as real as it has lately. I'm resolved to try to start repairing our relationship. However, she doesn't seem interested in talking to me today, so I leave her be. Maybe we both need more cool-down time.

I pick at my food, attracting the concern of Miles who breaks away from Ryden, Camille, and Aubrey's conversation about the Hedbauren estate.

"What's wrong, man?"

I look at him oddly. It's such a broad question for a place in which so many things are wrong. But instead of broaching the subject, I lower my head.

"Later."

Miles looks concerned, like he might have something else to say, but before he can, the doors swing open and the entire room goes silent.

King Edward enters followed by the queen and his two children. All of them are flanked by a multitude of officers.

"Good morning competitors."

Nobody responds as we all eye the king warily—even Sabrina and Asher. He's never visited us at breakfast before. Only dinner.

The officers move away from the royal family, lining the walls and leaving the four of them to occupy the center of the room.

"The last Game was a lovely competition, and I've enjoyed getting to see each of you fight so determinedly for the chance to best serve Myria."

Some people shift uncomfortably in their seats while others, like Sabrina, grin in excitement. I simply stare at the king, my gaze unflinching.

"But now, the Crowning Games can truly begin. We are reaching the final stretch, with only sixteen girls and fifteen boys left!"

The glee with which he speaks makes me want to shout at him. Nearly twenty kids have died for his entertainment. Amaia's quick warning glance stops me, though, and I fold my arms in disgust instead.

"Naturally, the Kingdom of Myria wants to get to know you since the pool of competitors has decreased. After you all finish eating, promptly make your way to your room where you will be assisted with getting dressed. There, you will also be joined by a journalist who is in charge of asking you questions which will be broadcast to every sector this week."

I have to fight the urge to roll my eyes as I think of home, with the rickety screens in Salcoast's main square.

They are always full of royal propaganda that people rarely even glance at. Even the workers from the Lates flash through my mind. How much say would they have in the Crowning Game's final vote? I doubt they would be getting easy access to the broadcasts.

Miles and Aubrey had briefly mentioned them before though. As the pool of competitors gets smaller, the king would arrange more public events and spectacles.

Apparently, enough of us have died now.

"From there, you will be escorted to another hall where we will capture lovely portraits of all of you together, and each of you separately. Enjoy the rest of your meal."

And in the same fashion they entered, the royal family exits without another word, still flanked by officers. Amaia looks at me before she turns away, but it's too brief for me to catch the meaning behind it.

As soon as the doors shut, Aubrey shoves her half-empty plate to the middle of the table and stands. "I wasn't hungry anyway." She blows loose red strands from her ponytail away from her face before turning to Camille. "You ready to go back to our rooms? I can take you that way."

Unless I'm imagining it, Aubrey gives me an understanding look. She must know my sister and I aren't getting along. I nod my head in gratitude as she and Camille leave, the latter without a backward glance at me.

Miles playfully shoves my shoulder. "Are you ready for some propaganda?" I sigh, but follow them both out of the breakfast room, our dirty plates left behind.

It doesn't take long before we've reached our hallway and part ways into our separate rooms. As my door swings open, a young maid jumps in front of my face.

"Hi, Mr. Atwood!" Her bright smile is contagious. She's a small girl—maybe seven or eight—with dark hair like Camille's. However, her eyes are light brown instead of green. "I have your clothes set aside for you in the bathroom. I thought you'd like to tidy up in there before I let Mrs. Slince in."

"Thank you."

Her smile, although I would have thought it impossible, only widens under the praise. "It's my pleasure, Mr. Atwood."

"You can call me Keith. What may I call you?"

It may have been a trick of the light, but her eyes seem to glisten. "My name is Willow, sir." She bows her head and bounces to the couch in the corner.

I swiftly change into the clothes Willow left for me in the bathroom. They're the most expensive pair of pants I have ever worn. They're dark black and silk. The shirt is a loose, silver material with long sleeves that brush my wrists. I look at myself in the mirror and have to hold in my laughter. I look much too fancy. When I stride back into my room, Willow has a similar reaction.

"Those don't fit you very well." As soon as she says it, she clamps a hand over her mouth and looks at me in terror. "I'm so sorry, sir."

I shake my head quickly to reassure her. "It's okay. I'm not offended." I quirk an eyebrow. "In fact, I quite agree." I pick at my shirt for emphasis. "Silver is definitely not my color."

Willow's grin has resurfaced. "Momma was right. You *are* cool."

There's awe in her voice, and I'm taken aback by the compliment. Before I can ask about her mother, she's skipping to the door to let in an old, wrinkled woman who I assume to be Mrs. Slince.

She introduces herself as such and doesn't pause before jumping into the interview questions. They aren't incredibly personal, nor do they directly ask about my father, which I'm grateful for.

"Have you made any friends at the palace yet?"

This is the only question I stumble over. Of course, Aubrey, Miles, and Ryden come to mind, but so do Nicole and Axel. And right beside them is Amaia.

Deciding to keep my answer vague, I respond with, "Yes, I've met some very extraordinary people here. And, of course, some not so extraordinary people. That's to be expected I suppose."

Mrs. Slince gives me a sharp handshake before rising from her spot on the couch and showing herself out of the room.

Then, Willow is right next to me again. "Do you know where you're supposed to go for pictures?"

"Pictures?" I say, suddenly filled with dread. "No, but would you be able to show me?"

Her face lights up again, and I'm not sure if it makes me happy or sad—happy because of the joy written across her face or sad because of how little it takes to make this girl's day.

I'm glad I asked, because without her, I would have gotten lost. Willow leads me to a section of the palace I've never been to before. The designs on the wall shift into something even more elegant, and the amount of officers increases tenfold.

Willow talks the entire time, mainly about her mother. Her mother works in the kitchens and gave birth to Willow at the palace. The little girl doesn't mention a father, so I don't ask. Mainly, I listen as she speaks about some of her friends and how jealous they were when she got assigned to me.

"Poor Shelly. She got Sabrina." Willow's voice shudders, and she gives me such a nasty look that I almost laugh. I also feel bad for poor Shelly. "I'm just glad Momma could pull some strings and get me with you. Do you know I've been assigned to you for the rest of the Games? Now that there are not as many of you, the king wants more personal care. At least, that's what Momma says."

She must sense my unspoken desire to not talk about the king because she quickly starts talking about her favorite hide-and-seek spots.

When we reach the room, Willow leaves me with a small curtsy, and I walk in by myself. The room is already crowded with the other competitors, people with cameras, and the prince and princess. I find Ryden and Camille and stand with them both as we wait for everyone to file in. I stand in silence, not wanting to interrupt their engrossing conversation. Plus, I don't think Camille wants to talk to me still.

When Miles arrives, he looks almost as silly as I do in his dress clothes, but at least we share a laugh before they begin taking pictures. The photographers move fast, adjusting us all into group photos and individual photos with ease.

After those are finished, each competitor waits to be called to get a picture with the prince or princess. While I'm waiting, I get my first real look at Amaia since entering the room.

Beautiful. That's the only word I can use to describe her. Her blonde curls fall down her back and over her shoulders. Bits of her hair are intricately weaved into a crown that circles her head. Her blue eyes appear even brighter than normal, brought to life by her dress.

Amaia and her brother must've been allowed to escape from Myria's colors: silver and black. Jacob's suit is green while Amaia's dress is blue. Although, blue isn't the best word to describe it. It's more of a dusty blue or bluish-gray. It hugs her torso before hitting her waist in cascading layers. The sleeves fall off her shoulders, resting on her upper arms. A silver necklace in the shape of a wolf rests in the hollow of her throat. I feel the heat rising in my cheeks as I wonder why she might have chosen that animal.

As always, she seems to know what I'm thinking. She glances away from the camera, which is currently snapping away at her and Ryden. She meets my eyes with a sneaky smile before flashing a stunning one for the camera.

Then it's my turn. I lightly placing a hand on Amaia's bare shoulder, as instructed by the photographer.

Aware of all the possible eyes and ears around us, I murmur as quietly as I can. "You look nice."

Amaia doesn't look away from the cameras. "Thank you." I can feel her shoulder rise in hesitation. "You look nice as well."

I try to bite back a chuckle, but it comes out anyway. "No, I don't, and we both know that. I look goofy, and I've already accepted it."

Amaia turns away from the camera this time, ignoring the photographer's protests. Her bright blue eyes are intense. "You do look goofy." But her voice isn't mean. Instead, it's light and gets even softer as she whispers, "But I still think you look nice."

The photographer clears his throat, and we turn to look at the camera. He speeds through the next couple of shots, and when he dismisses me, I remember what I wanted to tell her.

"I've made my decision."

Amaia looks at me with surprise, and something else in her eyes.

I speak so only she can hear me. "What can I do to help fight?"

CHAPTER THIRTY
Camille

THERE'S SOMETHING DIFFERENT ABOUT the Game this morning. It feels like there's more pressure than ever to succeed. My performances since the first Game have been abysmal. Between the public polls posted in Central's magazines, which Aubrey's been showing me, and the scores on the board in the training room, I've become a laughing stock. I have to do better today. Last night, I brought up how I was feeling about the next Game to Ryden. He brushed off my placement concerns. Instead, he suggested I talk to Keith before I start.

"You don't feel right because something's off between you two. I think you should try to fix it." I eagerly switched the topic and hadn't spoken to Ryden since.

I know it's stupid of me, but I don't want to talk to Keith. He's giving me space, but I can tell he wants to check up on me. Walking to the Games by myself this morning felt extra stupid. Keith is my brother, and I know he cares about me. I care about him too. Like every other competition, this could easily be the last day either of us are alive, and I didn't reach out to him. In fact, I've avoided talking to him for the last two weeks.

But now, as I watch the boys compete, I'm beginning to regret my stubbornness. This month's Game is less of a competition and more about survival. This arena is the largest yet, with swaying towers and weak framed buildings all scattered about. In different sections of the arena, unique weather phenomenons are happening. In Keith's corner, chunks of ice are zipping to the ground, tearing holes in roofs and even denting the floor. Both Miles and Keith are hurriedly dodging, trying to escape to a different section of the arena. Although the rest of them aren't any better.

Ryden is currently battling a windstorm, trying to keep his footing upright as the rain starts to pool on the floor. With the help of some officer's gift, I'm sure, the rainwater is pooling extra quickly. Already, the first floors of the houses have been completely submerged.

The other sections are just as bad. I try to memorize all of them; natural fires, floods, hurricanes, tornados, but they all keep randomly switching around, making it hard to track.

The crowd gasps and screams, and I try to locate what has them in a frenzy. Immediately, I check for Keith, but he's still with Miles, crouched underneath a half fallen piece of roof as even more hail pelts from the sky. The boards above them creak, but I know Miles will teleport both of them somewhere safe if it gets deadly.

Next, I go back to Ryden, who at first glance, I think is alright. He's reached the top of one of the towers, and although it's leaning quite precariously, he doesn't seem to be in any immediate danger.

"Watch out!" Aubrey shrieks. The terror in her words makes the hair along my arms stand on end.

Ryden looks around too, as if he heard his sister's cries. Even from here, I can see his face pale. A hurricane is working its way through a section, leaving destroyed buildings and even a boy's body behind. And now it's headed straight for Ryden, who is barely hanging on as it is. The water beneath him is too shallow to jump into, and if the weakest hurricane winds hit him, he will fall and have little chance of surviving.

I take a deep breath with Aubrey, who sits on the edge of her chair, leaning forward anxiously.

"He's going to make it." I don't know if I say it for her reassurance or for mine.

Either way, neither of us get a chance to see how he fares against the hurricane. Carter Prancis decides to take it into his own hands.

In a matter of seconds, he's shot up, making himself taller than the building Ryden is clinging to. With a swipe of his enlarged hand, he grabs Ryden in his fist. His bright red hair disappears under Carter's thumb. I want to scream because it doesn't look like Carter is letting go.

The crowd is on their feet, yelling in outrage. Ryden and Aubrey are rightfully favorites with the people, each respectively placing first in the public polls that had been released with the pictures and interview questions. The king and his son, however, look on with their normal expressions of glee. The king can't even extend sympathy for one of his advisor's children?

I turn to Aubrey's sheet white face, about to ask what we can do to save him when the crowd's cries of despair swoop into cheers of joy.

I snap my gaze back to Carter. He is scowling at his now open hand. Miles is balancing on Carter's wrist, with his pair of swords drawn, tiny in comparison to the other boy. He's bouncing around, piercing whatever bit of skin he can, jumping between Carter's shoulder, arms, and head. Huge drops of blood are falling, mixing in with the water pooling on the floor.

Desperately, I look for Ryden's red hair, and I almost cry when I see it. He's back on the building, but this time, he's hanging on by a couple of fingers as he dangles over the deathly drop above the shallow water.

The rain now pouring from the sky only makes his grip worse, and in seconds, his hand slips from the structure. A scream echoes through my body as I watch him fall. Aubrey's hand grips mine so tightly my fingertips turn white.

Then, with a screech, a huge pair of eagles swoop down, ignoring the persistent drops of rain hitting their backs. They grab Ryden's arms and jerk him up and away from death.

Ryden's arms are both bleeding from the birds' talons, but despite everything, he's crowing with joy. Aubrey and I both share looks of relief as Ryden is gently placed on the ground next to Keith, who is now in the wildfire section, with trees crashing down next to him. Ryden grins at Keith, who nods and jerks his head in Carter and Miles's direction. The two birds follow orders perfectly, attacking Carter's face with vicious talons and clicking beaks. Miles jumps off of Carter's back and zips over to where Keith and Ryden are running from flaming trees.

A sharp whistle rings out across the stadium, and in a flash, the entire arena is cleared, including the bodies of two boys I don't recognize. Time is up.

I ready myself.

Now it's my turn.

CHAPTER THIRTY-ONE

Camille

WATCHING THE GAMES IS much different than being in them. Just a few minutes ago, I was leaning out of my chair in anticipation as I watched Ryden nearly fall to his death. However, now that it's me fighting to survive these natural disasters, it's on a whole other level. Aubrey and I have been forced to enter from opposite ends of the arena, so I'm currently stranded in the middle of a hailstorm by myself. At least the buildings have been reset and are still standing tall. For now.

From watching Ryden, I know the buildings can be a double-edged sword, so I hug the edge of the one I'm next to, keeping the awning over my head and gripping the hilt of my sword carefully. I can see another girl through the hail, battling her way to shelter. However, her distant outline is all I can make out through the storm. I don't like being this blind. Deciding to use my gift and take a risk, I charge for the girl, calling on all my strength to melt the cubes of water before they strike my head. I still end up drenched, and because my gift is focused on melting the chunks of ice, I'm also shivering.

The girl doesn't see me until I'm a couple feet away, and as soon as she turns to me, I recognize Sabrina's cold face. I sprint away, and Sabrina races after me, so I urge my feet as fast as they will go. Something tells me she isn't going to let me live if she catches me. It was a stupid risk, hoping the girl would be a friendly face or an easy foe.

I make it to the edge of the section and almost run straight into a wall of flaming trees. I shoot a glare in the direction of the royal booth because there's no way that was there seconds ago. At least the hail is gone. If only they could have taken Sabrina away with it.

Without the hail slowing her down, she's much faster than I am. Knives fly through the air past me as she uses her gift to guide them. Using my gift, I turn toward her with a sweep of my hand. I send a flaming blast of scorching air at her face, and she grimaces, but it doesn't slow her down like I hoped it would.

Instead, it only enrages her, and she snatches my ponytail in her fist. My head jerks back as she tosses me to the ground. I curse my clumsiness as my sword clatters out of my hand, but I still manage to roll out from underneath Sabrina's blade.

Throwing myself up, I reach out with my gift. This time Sabrina hisses at the sharp pinpricks of ice I send up her spine. I move quickly before she can regain her composure, swiping up with my sword as I run past her. The arena shifts again, and this time a building spawns around me. Sabrina flings the door open, and regretfully, I look at the one staircase in the room.

It's my only option, so I climb fast, using all my concentration to turn the air around the stairs scalding hot. Sabrina runs straight into the burning wall, and she lets out a cry—either in pain or surprise, I can't be sure.

The staircase curves up the entire tower, offering no end until I reach the top. It opens up to the outside, where I get a good view of the arena. A couple of girls are trying to escape a landslide while a handful are dodging flying boulders and seeping lava from a mountain slowly emerging from the ground.

I can't make out Aubrey's bright hair. I'm going to have to take Sabrina on my own. I hope time will be up soon. Of course, that would mean I have some semblance of luck on my side, which I've clearly been lacking for quite a while now.

The stairs creak with Sabrina's footsteps. In my distraction, I had let my gift slip away. I curse my mistake and desperately search for a way off this tower. The ground beneath us is hard rock and a fall would equal my death. So, I steady my sword and prepare to fight.

Last time I'd fought her, I'd beaten her. But that had been in a practice ring under the supervision of Prince Jacob. Now, Sabrina has free reign to kill me if she desires.

Sabrina emerges with teeth bared, and immediately she charges for an attack. She definitely wants to kill me. She's quick, but not as quick as I thought she'd be. Miles, whom I practiced with occasionally, is much faster than her. But her speed doesn't matter. Her real strength is her gift as a metal manipulator.

My own sword fights against my every stroke, and my breath quickens. She's playing with me. She could end me in a blink of an eye, and I would be helpless to stop it. At the thought, my gift roars inside of me. Without thinking, I let it go. It surges out, as if desperate to prove me wrong. I feel it wrap its engulfing heat and piercing cold in sharp cords around Sabrina.

It's the first time I've ever heard her *really* scream. My sword arm falls with exhaustion, and my body goes weak.

"You'll die for this!" she snarls, and I don't doubt her.

The effort to keep Sabrina in place is taking a swift toll on my body. Black dots dance around my vision, and that's before the ground starts trembling.

I want to scream at King Edward and his band of gifted individuals who seem intent on making this as difficult as possible. The wooden towers creak and shake beneath us. To steady myself, I release Sabrina from my gift's hold. It is either that or tumble off the edge. Although, falling seems like it's going to happen either way because as soon as my hold on her releases, Sabrina kicks a leg out, tripping me and sending me flying.

Distantly, the crowd screams and in a wild moment. It's good to know some of them actually care about my well-being. Although, it could only be because it's exciting for them to watch me fall to my death.

Similar to the post that Ryden had held onto, my hands wrap around a beam before I plunge. This time, Keith and his eagles are not here. Just a sneering, injured Sabrina. She leaps to stab me with her sword, but it clangs sharply against another blade.

In a blink of an eye, a girl with long, braided, strawberry blonde hair appears, sword in hand. She glares at Sabrina with such hatred that even I shrink away. She's one of the Workinsire twins, Kiley. Her twin sister, Niley, died in the last Game. They both shared the power of invisibility, so that explained her sudden appearance.

"This is for Niley!" Kiley's words are venomous.

Sabrina, shocked by the girl's materialization, doesn't have the reaction time to stop the hilt of Kiley's blade from banging against her temple. She collapses on the floor in a heap, unconscious. Her chest still rises and falls in shallow breaths. The girl stands over her for a second, as if contemplating running Sabrina through with her sword.

But another girl emerges from the top of the stairs. If I hadn't been so focused on maintaining my grip, I would have looked into the sky and cursed my luck. Prill Prancis's hair is braided back and her sword is at the ready.

"If anyone gets to kill Atwood, it'll be me!" Prill snarls.

I want to correct her. I don't think Kiley's after me. Either way, Prill leaps at Kiley with teeth bared. Kiley must be tired from maintaining her invisibility earlier, because she doesn't disappear.

The wood beneath me creaks, and I hiss as two more of my fingers slip off. Focusing my concentration back on my own predicament, I try to swing my body. My grip loosens. I can almost reach the edge of the tower with my toes. Gritting my teeth, I throw myself to the side with all of my weight. My fingers fly off of the beam, and my body crashes against the building. The crowd's screams get louder, and the sounds of Prill and Kiley's blades clanging echo above me.

Desperately, I reach for the wooden edge of the shaking tower. For a split second, I think I'm going to fall. My right hand barely grabs onto the ledge, and the rest of my body screams in pain. Stealing myself for one final push, I throw my leg up and drag myself over the edge.

I land facing Kiley, who stands over both Prill and Sabrina's limp bodies. From the lack of wounds, I don't think she's eliminated either of them. Although, if she has, that takes care of my biggest competition.

"Did you kill them?" I breathe.

She stops and turns to me, her brown eyes wild. "I'm thinking about it."

Before I can react, a sharp whistle cuts through the air, and I'm swiftly jerked back to my original seat in the bleachers. I still struggle to wrap my mind around the immense strength of the people the king has at his disposal, but for the moment, my mind is preoccupied with Kiley. She doesn't address me, even at our seats. Instead, she turns away from everyone else and disappears.

I only wonder about her for a minute more before a pair of strong arms scoop me against a broad chest. Ryden's face is buried in my hair, and he's pulling me against him so tightly I can barely breathe. The crowd's presence and the sharp eyes of the royal family make me suddenly aware of the fact that a boy who is not my brother is hugging me in front of the man I'm supposed to be fighting to marry.

I gently tap his shoulder, and he pulls back just enough to look at me. Brushing my hair down with his fingers, he says. "I thought you were gone."

His voice catches, and I feel my eyes cloud with tears. "So did I." As quickly as the self-consciousness appears, it fades.

Before I let Ryden pull me in for another hug, I see Keith and Miles standing off to the side with Aubrey. I catch Keith watching me. His eyes are full of concern and fear.

He mouths "Are you okay," and I give him a small nod in return.

He gives me a tentative smile, and I return it. Maybe this will help him understand what I've been saying. Death is very real for us. And if we make a singular mistake, for even one second, we will end up dead.

CHAPTER THIRTY-TWO
Keith

KING EDWARD DECIDES TO grace us with his presence again this morning. This time, however, he's waiting for us in the training room, accompanied by both of his children. Jacob stands to the king's right and Amaia is to his left. Annoyance prickles my skin. I've seen enough of the king.

"What is he doing here?" I ask Aubrey.

From beside me, she shrugs. "I don't know, but I don't want to see his face," she grumbles.

King Edward's presence always sparks a flame in me, but today, I focus my attention on Amaia.

The last time I had spoken with her was when we had taken the pictures. Her last word had been "Okay," accompanied by a look of pride.

Now, she's standing in simple training clothes, eying me carefully. Tentatively, I smile at her, and she gives a quick smile back. My grin only grows but quickly fades into embarrassment as Aubrey snorts at the exchange.

"Yes?" I mutter.

Aubrey shakes her head, exasperated. "You two are ridiculous."

I ignore Aubrey and glance back at Amaia. She's still watching me, her blue eyes sparkling.

"Well, are you going to answer my question?" Aubrey tilts her head.

"Sorry, what? Can you repeat that?" I lean in closer. "I missed it the first time."

Aubrey shoves me away, laughing. "I asked, have you seen the pictures they took of us yet?"

"No, and I really don't care about seeing them. It's all just a publicity stunt anyway."

Aubrey smiles mischievously. "You're not wrong, but I think you should look at them when you get the chance."

I give her a questioning look, but I can't ask anything else because King Edward begins to speak.

"As you come in, please feel welcome to practice. I will be giving an announcement for the next Game once everyone has gathered inside."

Aubrey and I walk to the throwing board, and eventually, we are joined by Miles, Ryden, and Camille. We each take turns throwing until Sabrina and Garden saunter in.

Of course, they're the last ones to arrive. Sabrina shoots all of us a deadly stare and sneers at Camille. Camille sneers back as Garden lazily picks at her fingernails.

King Edward then begins his speech. "Thank you all for joining us.'"

As if I had a choice...

"The next Crowning Game will be a little bit different. As our group continues to shrink, the public wants to become more invested in the competitors. After all, two of you in this room are the future Crown Princess and Prince of Myria."

I look around and take in those of us who have almost made it halfway through the Games. Kiley Workensire catches my eye. She stands against the wall by herself, arms folded with a sour expression on her face. She looks like she wants to lodge the blade at her hip into somebody's throat.

"So, to give the people of Myria a little insight into who you are, we will be pairing you into teams to design a wagon. Cameras will capture you and your partner working together to create something capable of beating your competitors and winning a race. My children will reveal the group partners. Good luck."

He exits the room, officers swarming behind him. I watch him leave, curious as to what could have him in such a hurry. Not only was his explanation brief, but it lacked the usual harsh sneers and buried threats.

Amaia steps forward first and begins listing off the pairs. Miles and Ryden fist bump as they are announced. Aubrey rolls her eyes at both of them and mutters, "Unfair."

My partner ends up being Liam Adler. He's a taller boy, roughly my height. He's built more narrowly than I am though, with wiry strands of golden hair. Miles's words come back to me, reminding me that this is the son of Lord Adler of the Lates sector. I think back to the condition of the working environment in the Lates. I wonder if this boy knows, and if he does, does his family support it? After all, Lord Adler certainly isn't the one suffering.

As Amaia continues to read off the list of partners, Liam makes his way over to me.

Holding out a hand, he introduces himself. "Hello, my name is Liam. Although, I suppose that information is obvious."

I return his handshake, smiling. "My name is Keith, if you didn't already know."

"Ah, yes, thank you for sharing." Liam smiles too, and I find myself thinking that maybe this will be alright. Liam seems as though he doesn't hate my guts, which is a step in the right direction.

"Do you happen to have any experience building a wagon?"

Liam shrugs. "I have a little bit. My dad and I used to mess around with designing stuff together. His gift is similar to constructing illusions, so it was how we spent time with each other."

I don't know what to say to that, and nobody else chimes in. Aubrey and Camille are too busy paying attention to Jacob, who has started announcing the girls' pairings.

"How about you?" Liam continues. "Do you have any experience building anything?"

I laugh. "Nope, this project is probably about to be all yours. Although, I'll help however I can."

Camille hisses at me to quiet down. Jacob is only halfway through naming the partners, and Camille's name hasn't been said yet. Neither has Sabrina's or Prill's. Camille nervously chews on the edge of her fingernails. Aubrey's already been partnered with a small girl named Whisper, who I've never paid much attention to.

For the next pair, Jacob pauses before reading it. He looks up at the rest of the competitors, and Amaia rolls her eyes at his dramatics.

"Camille Atwood and Garden Burrow."

At least it isn't Sabrina or Prill. Although, from the look on Camille's face, this isn't much better. Garden doesn't even glance up from her nails before striding out of the room. Miles whistles softly.

"Yikes, good luck with that one."

Camille smacks him on the arm.

CHAPTER THIRTY-THREE

Keith

LIAM IS ACTUALLY REALLY cool. He, Miles, Ryden, and I are in my room, gathered over large sheets of paper. Miles and I have very limited knowledge of designing things—although he definitely knows more than I do. Part of me feels bad that Liam is doing so much of the work, but he insists that it will all even out.

"Listen, I'm not much of a fighter. I've really only survived this long because of luck, so when we're in the actual Games, you can make up for it by watching my back."

I don't have the heart to tell him we're in the same boat with that one. Or I guess the same wagon. I'm only alive by strokes of luck, not skill. So I respond with a simple, "I hope so."

Liam rolls his eyes, missing the morbid truth of my words. I could only hope to save Liam's life in the Games next week. I glance away from him for a moment, getting

297

hit by a surge of emotion. I had barely known Axel and spoke to him only once.

What will it be like if Liam dies on our wagon next week?

Or if Ryden and Miles hit a wrong turn and both end up gone?

Miles calls me and Liam over to look at Ryden's drawing, tearing my thoughts away from death. "Look at that," he says, gesturing to the paper. "Tell me what you think that looks like."

I frown at the picture. Sure, it looks a little skinnier than Liam's drawing, and it has more rounded edges, but I don't know what Miles is trying to get at. Liam, however, breaks out laughing.

"What's with the banana look?"

Ryden rolls his eyes and flings his pencil down. "It does *not* look like a banana!"

Miles laughs even harder. "Yes, yes it does." Then his face deadpans. "You're going to make me ride in a banana!"

Ryden scowls. "No, I'm not! I know it's a bit different of a shape than normal, but I wanted to go for something unique."

"Well, you did that, alright."

Ryden looks to Liam and me for support, and I shrug.

Liam is fighting a grin. "Sorry, Ryden, I'm with Miles here. I wouldn't want to ride in a banana either."

Ryden desperately looks at me, but I only shake my head. "I don't know what you guys are talking about. What's a banana?"

Miles and Ryden don't seem surprised, but Liam looks at me incredulously.

"You've never seen a banana?"

"Never heard of them."

Liam's mouth drops open.

Miles laughs. "It's alright Keith, you aren't missing much. Plus, if you really want to know what they look like, just look at Ryden's drawing."

A pencil flies through the air, and Miles ducks his head right in time.

A knock echoes throughout the room before Miles can retaliate. I jump to my feet, and Willow's bright face is beaming at me as I open the door.

"Hi, Mr. Atwood!"

The three other boys glance over at her. Willow sees the company and squeals in excitement. "Miles!"

She rushes to my friend and wraps her arms around him. Miles doesn't hesitate to hug her back, even playfully rubbing the top of her head.

"Hey, you! I didn't know you got moved to Keith."

Willow's face is glowing with pride. "Momma moved me up!"

"Well, congrats, kiddo."

Extracting himself from Willow's grasp, he cocks his head at her. "Did you need to tell Keith something?"

Willow looks back at me. "Oh! Yes. Mr. Atwood, reporters are here and they're coming to take pictures of you guys working. Momma told me to come give you all a fair warning."

"Thank you, Willow." Under my praise, the happy girl's smile only widens. "And how come you don't call Miles by his last name?"

She blushes a little before glancing shyly at the floor. "I can't pronounce it. Report. Respirt. Repsort." She purses her lips in concentration while the other three boys try to contain their amusement.

"Okay, okay, don't hurt yourself," I say

"Goodbye, Mr. Atwood!" She trots out of the room with a bounce in her step.

"Gosh, I love that kid," Miles murmurs as he watches the door.

"How do you know her?" I ask.

"She was born here. I was one of the first ones to hold her."

"Is she your sister then?"

Miles and Ryden exchange a long glance. "No, I just know her mom."

I nod and turn back to our sketch. I can tell when somebody doesn't want to talk about something, and right now, I assume Miles wants to change the subject.

Soon enough, it doesn't matter either way, because as Willow had warned us, a flood of photographers barge into my room. They chatter and insist we go back to working on our projects like normal.

So, we do, and surprisingly, I fall right back into our banter quite normally. It's almost easy to pretend that the cameras and their operators aren't in the room. Of course, there's still something slightly off. Miles doesn't make any more jeers at Ryden's banana technique, and Liam seems less engaged than usual. But Ryden still makes suggestions for our wagon, and I help adjust their papers as needed.

Eventually, the press filters out of my room, but as the last one leaves with a quick "Thank you" for our time, I still feel watched.

Even before I look, I know it's her.

Amaia's leaning against the doorframe, arms folded with a soft gaze. I wonder how long she's been there. She meets my eyes first before looking past me at Miles. They share some silent exchange, and then Ryden speaks.

"Are you just going to ogle at us or what?" He gives Amaia a pointed look. At Ryden's words, Liam looks up and almost draws a line straight through his blueprint.

"It's rude to enter uninvited." She replies with a shrug.

"So, you decided to stalk us from the doorway?" I raise an eyebrow.

She opens her mouth before considering the question. "I guess that really isn't much better, is it?"

Before I can invite her in, Miles rises from his place on the floor. "What do you need me for? I didn't think we had another trip until tomorrow."

Amaia quickly shakes her head. "You're all good. I'm here to speak with Keith."

The three other boys all swivel their heads to look at me, and I feel my cheeks burn red.

Awkwardly, I stand up, and Amaia gives me a small nod before turning down the hallway. Ryden, Miles, and Liam all look just as bewildered as I feel.

Ryden simply rolls his eyes, but Liam looks mischievous. And Miles almost looks disappointed. What in the world? Is this about me wanting to join their band of rebels?

I hurry down the hallway, trying to catch up to Amaia.

"Where are we going?" I can't hide the excitement in my voice, and I know she hears it.

Grinning at me like a maniac, she says, "Well, you decided you wanted to fight the system. I'm going to show you how."

Chapter Thirty-Four
Keith

AMAIA LEADS ME DOWN hallways I've never seen before, and eventually, they fade into more elegant designs than the rest of the palace. I figure this is the part of the palace reserved for royalty and important guests.

We stop outside a pair of grand double doors, and instinctively, I know this is her room. However, shockingly, there are practically no officers around. More maids scurry about than normal, but the lack of security seems unusual.

Sensing my question, Amaia says, "My father places more of his men closer to his quarters. In this part of the wing, I get to avoid all of that."

Amaia reaches for the doorknob but hesitates as her fingers brush the handle.

"If I didn't know better, I'd say you were nervous," I tease.

She viciously shakes her head. "No, why would you say that?" She pushes open the door as if to prove her point.

I wasn't sure what I was expecting from Princess Amaia's room, but this was not it. From the doorway, I can already tell that I could fit about four of my rooms inside this one—maybe even more than that. The walls are painted a beautiful deep red, and the curtains, which drape over the windows, are a thin white material. The far wall is completely covered by bookshelves, each one crammed with various novels and textbooks. A large navy blue couch takes up another corner, facing a huge empty screen. Her bed is about three times my bed's size and brimming with stuffed bright white pillows. Not a single piece is out of line.

At least until I look past the bed at an elevated alcove. Here, stacks of papers and worn maps are strewn across a large table that takes up the far corner. The walls are decorated with various weapons. This must be Amaia's personal collection. A gorgeous marbled silver and black sword hangs over the table, bathing in the spotlight.

I turn to poke fun at Amaia for the mess of papers, but when I look back at her, I pause. She's nervously chewing on her bottom lip, watching me carefully. Her fingertips are tapping against each other and the sight fills me with a mix of fear and giddiness. I'm making the Princess of Myria nervous?

Amaia clears her throat. "So, what do you think?"

"It's not what I expected."

Amaia blinks. "What were you expecting? A bright pink princess room?"

"No, but I was expecting you to be more messy." I point to the untidy alcove. "Like that but the entire room."

Amaia gasps, raising a hand of false offense to her chest. "Excuse me! I am *not* a slob."

I dodge the playful shove she tries to give me.

"How is your wagon coming along? Let me guess, Liam is doing all of the work, isn't he?"

I shoot her a glare before walking further into her room. She shuts the door behind us, and suddenly the air becomes thick with something I can't quite put my finger on.

"That's not fair." The words come out hoarser than I intend. "I have no idea what I'm doing!"

Amaia chuckles. "And how is that any different than normal?"

I scoop up a pillow from her couch and aim at her. She holds up her hands in surrender.

"Okay, I'm sorry. I didn't mean that. I don't think there's anything wrong with letting Liam construct your wagon. He's always been good at that kind of stuff. You have your own talents."

I eye her curiously. "Like what?"

She suddenly becomes fascinated with the floor, like she wants to avoid answering. "Oh, I mean, you have your gift now. And you are getting better with a sword. And you have this way of just... inspiring people."

"You think I'm inspiring?"

Amaia suddenly turns away from me. "Yes, but that's beside the point. I didn't bring you here to boost your self-confidence."

"Then why did you bring me here?" I ask.

"Come here."

She leads me into the elevated alcove full of her mess of maps, papers, and various weapons. From the doorway, this area appeared a lot smaller, but now that I'm standing inside of it, I realize the alcove goes farther back than I originally thought. Amaia strides to the back corner and opens a chest full of more papers, leaving me to observe what she already has laid out.

The largest map is a complete picture of Myria. Central is labeled directly in the center, and each sector is outlined as it splits from Central. The Gulf hugs the Myradian Sea in the South and the Marshes sector to the East. My finger brushes over the letters of my city, Salcoast.

It's nestled down in the Southwest, almost touching the border where the Gulf ends and the large forest begins. Except the forest is labeled with a name I've never heard before.

Everyone in the Gulf has their own name for the forest. My mother always called it the Forest of Hope, speaking about it as a place that offered an escape. Despite her mentions of disappearing into the forest, she never suggested we act on them. Others called it the Mystic Woods or the Distant Forest. But on Amaia's map, in big black bold lettering, it's labeled Rebel's Forest.

"Rebels?"

Amaia briefly pauses her search in the chest of papers and glances at me. "What do you mean?"

"What do *you* mean?" I counter. "You've labeled this forest the Rebel's Forest. Does that mean there are actual rebels?"

Amaia laughs. "Is it really that shocking that there are people who disagree with how this country is run? Of course, there are actual rebels. In fact, there's even different groups of them."

"Groups?" I repeat. "But that makes them sound organized. Sure, officers would put rebels to death all of the time or send them in for Combatant Day, but it isn't like there was ever a group of them."

Amaia walks over to me, depositing a pile of papers next to me. "Keith, do you think my father would inform the public that there are organized groups of people trying to undermine him? There's too much power in unity, it's better for him to make it look like random acts of insubordination rather than calculated moves."

"Like my father?" It's one of the first times I've addressed my father's actions to someone other than Camille.

Amaia eyes me curiously. "Potentially."

"Do you know what happened to him?" It's been a question I've considered asking but never had the opportunity.

Amaia's expression becomes guarded and hesitant. "I'm not sure. I've tried doing a little digging, but all my reports have come up empty. My father must be hiding him from me."

Something tells me there's more to this than what she's saying, but I decide not to press. Showing me these maps is already a step toward more information. I don't want her to revoke any of my privileges by prying.

She unfolds one of the papers, handing it to me. It's a report of missing officers. I skim through the paper as she continues. "Anyway, this is why I really brought you here." She gestures towards the pile. "If you didn't already know, Jacob and I have very split responsibilities. He's in charge of more diplomatic missions and interactions. I'm in charge of our internal forces. That means my father has placed me in charge of our soldiers—our officers. Despite his more recent attempts to separate me from them, I've gotten a hold of some newer reports."

She pauses for a moment, her eyes focusing on the table. I wonder about the king's recent behaviors. It seems risky for Amaia to be digging around. Certainly, her father could easily discover her.

Shaking herself from her thoughts, Amaia continues. "There's been a huge increase in missing soldiers right on the outskirts of the forest you were just asking about. Even more specifically, in your hometown, Salcoast. I've been trying to let my father clear my team for a mission, but he refuses to let me go. Jacob, oddly enough, has even tried backing me up, but the king insists it's unnecessary."

"What does this have to do with me fighting? From what I'm hearing, this sounds like you're helping King Edward."

Amaia smiles. "Do you trust me?"

I answer immediately. "Not completely. Not yet."

"That's a smart answer." She looks over the maps again, and something in her demeanor shifts. "However, I need to know if you noticed anything unusual about officer activity when you were there. Before Combatant Day, were there more or less than normal?"

I try to think back. "I don't remember."

Amaia frowns as if hoping for more. She gnaws on her lip while studying another paper. Mumbling to herself, she says, "What is he planning?"

"Who's planning something? The king?" The idea of King Edward, the same man who endorses the horrific treatment of the workers in the Lates, planning something concerning my hometown has me worried. Lizzy and Micheal still live there as far as I know, and I would hate for something to happen to them. Not to mention the other citizens who haven't done anything wrong.

Amaia doesn't even look up from her work. "I can't tell you."

I set down the paper and stare at her. My nerves get the best of me. "Are you kidding me? You take me up here after I said I could help, you ask me if I know anything, and then you want to leave me out of the loop on information that's clearly important?"

Amaia looks up at me, and immediately, I regret my words. Her face appears tired, like it's aged ten years in a matter of seconds. "Listen, I don't think you understand how much I've already included you in that I'm not supposed to. I'm trying, Keith. You have to give me time, and you have to trust me."

"Okay," I say. "But you should know, trust works both ways. I can't work with something you're also unwilling to give."

She releases a deep breath. "I know."

Chapter Thirty-Five
Camille

THE PAST TWENTY MINUTES of silence have been killing me. I should've ignored the maid who summoned me to Garden's room. However, tomorrow is a Game, and even though avoiding people is something I'm getting surprisingly good at, I have to work with this girl one way or another.

"Can you pass me that pencil?" These are the first words Garden has spoken to me since we were partnered together.

"Sure." I hold the pencil out, but don't let her grab it. "But first, tell me why you and Sabrina have it out for me."

Garden's eyes glint in annoyance. "You're awfully brave, Camille, which normally I might admire, but right now it's flat-out inconvenient." For a second, I think she might attack me by snatching the pencil and driving it straight into my heart.

However, I never find out because the door crashes open and a flock of photographers and journalists flood the room.

"Can you hand me that pencil please?" Garden smiles kindly at me, every hint of malice gone. She's perfectly poised for the cameras.

I fight the urge to roll my eyes as I hand over the writing tool. "Of course." I smile falsely at her, and the cameras catch it. It seems pointless to act like we get along, but I guess Myria's future queen must be able to appear diplomatic.

A journalist floats next to us, placing herself right in the middle of our work. "You two girls seem to be getting along so well! You always seem so against each other in the Games. Is that just for show?"

This time I smile brightly, showing Garden up in our silent competition. "Yes, ma'am."

Garden nods along with me. "What everyone should realize is that outside of the Games, we aren't competitors. We aren't all trying to win the title and honor of becoming Queen of Myria. Outside of the Games, we're all just people."

I bite my tongue to keep from snorting. Behind the reporter's back, I let my face fall flat and glare in her direction. She gives me a wink.

Fine, I'll give her that win.

"Would you agree, Miss Atwood? Is this also the case between you and Miss Pelos? I could only imagine the tension between the two of you after the last Game!" The reporter laughs, and I laugh along with her.

"Like Garden was saying, when we're in the Games it's different. There are no friends or enemies, just yourself fighting to win. So no, nothing Sabrina did to me in the last Game was personal." The lie tastes bitter in my mouth, but hopefully it'll win me some support from the more gentle-hearted viewers. The thought has me silently laughing. Nobody willingly watching these things can be considered "gentle."

"Well, that's so nice to hear!"

I think they're all going to leave, but instead another reporter—this time a male—jumps in.

"Everyone else already has their wagon sketches turned in. What's the strategy for leaving your blueprint to the last possible minute?"

Garden answers his question with an uncharacteristic giggle. "Well, if I told you, the other girls might find out."

The reporters laugh along with her, but I raise my eyebrows at her. She smirks back. I wonder if she thinks there's an actual strategy behind our delay. To me, there isn't. I actively avoided her.

The questions continue, and so do our fake smiles and laughter. Finally, the last photo is taken, and they exit the room. I slump down, letting my shoulders fall from their stiff, upright position. Another blanket of silence settles between us, and I'm grateful for it.

Garden, however, seems to squirm under the quiet. She's chewing on her pencil, staring intently at her sketch. Deciding it would be best to simply leave her alone, I stand up to leave.

"Wait." Garden's voice stops me. It isn't cruel and harsh like it normally is. "Listen. I brought you here to talk."

I stare at her incredulously. This is not how I imagined this going.

"I know. It's out of character."

"What happened to me being annoying?"

Garden curls her lip. "Don't get me wrong. You are." Her eyes drop, studying the floor. "But I was going to apologize."

My jaw drops, and she throws her head back to squint at the ceiling.

"You're making this impossible," she mutters bitterly.

I shut my mouth, fighting a grin.

She glares at me, but there's no heat behind it. "Whatever. Anyway, yes, I'm sorry for siding with Sabrina against you. You should understand that I've been her best friend since we were born—even though I wouldn't really call it a friendship. I'm the daughter of a Lord, but she gets superiority as a member of the Prince's Unit. And she takes that responsibility very seriously."

"What made you change your mind about me?"

Garden shrugs. "You asked me why I was always after you."

"That was enough to make you not want to kill me?"

"No, not really." She smiles. "But it made me think about how you're actually someone I've come to respect. You've got grit, and you don't put up with the other girls and their shenanigans. You also don't play into the king's every whim, and from somebody who has lived in the palace her entire life, that's pretty inspiring." She blows out a deep breath. "So, I guess what I'm just trying to say is... you're brave and talented, and I know when I'm on the losing side."

I give her a curious look. "You know I'm not acting against the king, right?"

Garden snorts into the back of her hand. "I would hope not. That wouldn't be the winning side at all."

"Good. I needed to make that clear." The tension in my shoulders releases. "There isn't a chance Sabrina feels the same way you do is there?"

Garden barks a laugh. "That is most definitely a no. It's for the same reason I'm picking your team that she'll never be friendly with you. You're her number one competition. She fears you even more than Prill."

Surprisingly, the thought doesn't make me mad or scared. Instead, it makes me happy. However, it doesn't make me as happy as the knock at the door does. Ryden is here.

He glances between Garden and me. "I'm glad to see the two of you getting along."

Garden rolls her eyes and folds her arms. "What do you want Ryden?"

I forget that she's known him longer than I have. The tinge of annoyance in her words gives her away.

"Sorry, Garden," he says with equal sarcasm. "I'm not here for you." He turns back to me with a grin, and I can't contain my mounting excitement.

Garden raises an eyebrow at me questioningly.

As nonchalantly as I can, I respond. "What do you need me for?"

"To see if you wanted to train."

I gesture to the paper on the floor. "Garden and I are a little busy."

Garden shakes her head. "I've got the rest Camille. Don't worry." She gives me a conspiratorial wink and pushes me toward the door. "Have a good time *training*." I don't like the emphasis she put on that last word. It makes me flush bright red.

"Well, send your maid to find me if you need any help."

Garden dismisses me with a hand before going back to the drawing.

Ryden holds out a hand, and I take it. He guides me down the hallway. It feels odd for my life to be dangling in the balance tomorrow, and yet, I'm holding hands with a boy.

"Are we allowed to be like this?" I hold up our intertwined hands.

Ryden doesn't stop walking as he looks at me. "I don't remember there being a rule against holding hands with anybody." At the cautious glint still in my eyes, Ryden playfully leans into my shoulder. "It's okay, relax. Everyone here, including King Edward, knows the reason for the Crowning Games isn't because of love."

My cheeks grow warm.

When he turns right instead of left at the end of the hallway, I pause.

"Where are we going?"

Ryden laughs. "Oh, so now you have a sense of direction."

I scowl at him. "I know the first turn."

"We aren't training. I have a surprise for you."

CHAPTER THIRTY-SIX
Camille

MY JAW DROPS FOR the second time today as I take in the scene Ryden has arranged.

We're on the rooftops, overlooking a twinkling sky of bright stars highlighted by the crescent moon. The grounds below us glitter with floating lamps, lighting up the fountains and gardens splayed across the ground. Although the view is enough to make me gasp, the decorations on the roof almost draw me to tears.

Lilies are delicately placed in a twisting line leading to a large red blanket that's sprawled out. Dancing candles dimly illuminate the basket of food Ryden laid out. A plate of sandwiches is accompanied by an overwhelming amount of fruit. Eagerly, I sit down on the blanket and grab a bright green grape.

Ryden laughs. "I knew I would be able to win you over with the food."

"You're missing the omelets," I tease.

"Actually," —He reaches into a basket across from him— "I'm not missing anything." He pulls out two aluminum-wrapped omelets, heat still drifting in tendrils from the foil.

Excitedly, I snatch them from his hand and begin nibbling on one. He grabs a sandwich and does the same. For a moment, that's all it is. Just the two of us sitting in peaceful quiet, both looking up at the stars, our fingers brushing just slightly.

"How did you find this place?" I ask as I finish the final bite of my omelet.

"Whenever our father would visit the palace, he'd bring us with him. Aubrey and I came up with things to keep ourselves busy. Our favorite game was hide and seek. It was one of the few games we would just play by ourselves. Including Miles and Amaia made things unfair—with Miles's transportation and Amaia's heightened sense of pretty much whatever she wants." Realizing what he said and my already open mouth, he holds up a finger. "Can we not talk about Amaia tonight? I don't want either of us to have to think about anything other than right here, right now."

I softly smile. "Okay. I'll try."

"Thank you." He leans closer so our shoulders brush. "Anyway, this was a spot an officer pointed out to me one time. I'd come out here, and Aubrey would never find me. The officer always had to come get me before it was time to go, but he never gave my spot away. Even though we stopped playing games, I still come up here whenever I need a moment."

Acting instinctively, I rest my head on his shoulder. "Why would you and Aubrey come with your father? I would've thought he'd leave you home, especially when you were younger."

Ryden fidgets, and for a moment, I consider changing the topic, but then he says, "It was always technically an option. When we were about four, we started coming with our father." He pauses, staring off at the stars. I feel him struggling with what to say next, so I let him sit in silence. "Our mother died. Aubrey and I were so little, I barely remember her. But I do remember my dad becoming someone filled with so much rage all of the time. He was constantly lashing out at servants, blaming them for our mother's inability to recover from her illness. In a weird way, I think he took us with him to protect us. He didn't trust any of them anymore with anything of value.

"Of course, that didn't mean we escaped his wrath either. I tried to save Aubrey from what I could, but he was equally rough with both of us. I was never the son he needed me to be, and King Edward would never allow me to take my father's place as Lord. Aubrey, as the oldest female in the Hedbauren line, automatically became Lady Hedbauren, and my father's expectations of her rose drastically. Except, Aubrey isn't really the type to sit down and pay attention during a tea party if you haven't already noticed."

I laugh at the thought of Aubrey sitting at a round table with a group of older women, clinking tiny teacups together. Ryden joins in, his laugh deep and warm. I feel it roll through his whole body, and I shift even closer to him. He wraps a hand around my shoulders, hugging me close.

"I know my family situation is nothing compared to yours. It's why I've never felt right bringing it up."

I look up at him. "I always want to hear what you have to say. And don't worry about your family being less problematic than mine. I *do* have a hard case to beat."

"That's true." Ryden sighs deeply as his chuckle fades and his shoulders relax. "Thank you."

"Of course." Words hang unsaid in my throat.

Ryden says them instead. "I know that in all reality I haven't known you very long, especially not compared to the majority of people in this palace. But somehow... I feel like I've known you my whole life. I wasn't even nervous to bring you up here, and I've never even shown Aubrey this spot. Well, I mean, maybe I was a little nervous, but that was more about whether you would like it or not."

We lock eyes. We're so close. And my heart is pounding out of my chest.

"Well, I absolutely love it." The smile that bursts across his face encourages me to continue. "Since I've been thrown into this mess, I feel like I haven't been able to be fully and completely myself. Even Keith scowls at me for happily eating the food. But with you, something is different. I feel like when it's just you and me, I can be exactly who I am, even the cold-hearted individual Keith thinks I've become. You don't turn away from me."

He brings up a hand, his fingertips brushing my chin. "I don't think you're cold-hearted. I think you have the biggest heart of anyone I know. The fact that you haven't burned this whole place to the ground when you are more than capable of doing so says more about who you are than what you've had to do to survive."

His forest green eyes search mine, holding the promise that he believes what he's saying.

"What happens if an officer catches us up here?"

Ryden pretends to think it over. "I think I could convince him to forget about it. Plus," —He taps a finger to his head— "I can hear them coming."

"I hope you're right. And thank you for bringing me up here. I feel..." I search for the right word to describe being up here with only Ryden for company. It's as if the past couple of months have been erased. "Free."

"Free," Ryden repeats softly.

A gentle breeze skims my skin and brushes across his face. I reach to move his red strands of hair back into place. Before I can touch them, Ryden catches my hand and pulls me toward him.

His warm lips collide against my own. He tastes sweet, like the chocolate cake they sometimes serve at dinner. My eyes flutter close as I breathe in his relaxing scent of firewood and forest. Home.

The kiss is slow, both of us savoring it. The moment, far too brief, is interrupted by a sharp alarm screeching through the air.

I topple over, and Ryden falls with me, almost crushing me with the weight of his body.

My pulse skyrockets. What is happening?

He gets up in a panic, dragging me up with him, and without a word, he pulls me to the trapdoor. I follow him silently. His face is flushed, and I can feel my cheeks grow crimson too.

Once Ryden safely secures the trapdoor behind us, I whisper, "What's happening?"

His mouth is set in a firm line as he answers me. "Nothing. Hopefully."

I fold my arms across my chest. "What's the alarm for?"

Ryden's eyes strike mine. "Rebels."

CHAPTER THIRTY-SEVEN
Keith

SINCE GETTING TO THE palace, I haven't seen this many people panicking. The officers keep their cool like they have been trained to do, and the royal family sits in their cushioned seats at the far side of the safe room, looking unperturbed.

Everyone else, however, is a jumbled mess. Miles sits on the edge of one of the cots, drumming his fingers against the metal. Carter chatters nervously with his father in the corner, glancing at the still-open doors. Even Aubrey is bouncing on her toes, skimming the crowd of competitors and desperately searching for red hair. I share her sense of urgency, especially as someone announces that the doors will be closing in one minute. My only sense of comfort is knowing that Camille must be with Ryden. At least he'll keep her safe. I hope.

Immediately after the alarm bells had gone off, Miles had jumped into my room and grabbed me, zipping us right outside the safe house doors. Officers stood in the doorway, immediately ushering us inside. The royal family had just arrived, and King Edward had been surrounded by a ring of higher-ranked officers, identifiable by their silver uniforms. As soon as I entered, I had felt Amaia's gaze fixed on me, but chose to ignore it.

Instead, I followed Miles to a corner, and we claimed a section of cots as our own. Aubrey hadn't been too far behind us, but Camille and Ryden still hadn't appeared. I had demanded that Miles go find them, but he had simply shook his head. "Once I'm in, I can't leave unless they let me."

"Ten seconds remaining."

Aubrey begins pushing against the crowd, fighting to get closer to the door. I trail directly behind her, catching a handful of elbows to the chest.

"Five seconds remaining."

The doors begin to creak closed, but through the gap, two figures are sprinting toward the room. I hope it's them, and that if it is, they get through the door in time. Aubrey, still craning to see over everybody's heads, lets out a frustrated shout as the doors shut with a resounding thud.

Urgently, I push more people out of the way, trying to make out either his bright red hair or her dark black waves. As the final crowd disperses, I see Camille. Her face is as white as a sheet as she clenches Ryden's hand tightly. I barrel toward her, ignoring her surprised squeal as I wrap her up in a tight hug. Aubrey does the same with Ryden.

Camille doesn't hesitate to hug me back.

"I'm okay. Don't worry about me." She smiles, her eyes bright from the adrenaline. "Ryden knew where to go."

"Why did it take you so long? Where were you?"

Camille glances over at Ryden before answering. "We were training, and then I got nervous, ran ahead, and naturally, I took a wrong turn."

Ryden's arm is thrown around Aubrey's shoulders. "Nearly got us both killed."

Camille blushes pink.

"Well, come on you two. Miles has a spot saved for us." Aubrey leads us back to our corner, sitting down next to Miles on a cot.

Miles's gaze dances between Camille and Ryden. "Ah, finally! The two love birds have decided to join us."

Ryden rolls his eyes, but I notice Camille's looking anywhere but at me.

"Don't worry about it. He's just jealous he's doomed to live a life alone," Aubrey mutters to Camille loud enough for all of us to hear.

Miles glares at her, and the rest of us begin to laugh, easing the tension. Aubrey breaks out a deck of cards from one of her jacket pockets and starts a game of what she calls Tack. Camille and I have never played, so during the first round we observe as Aubrey walks us through the steps.

The aim of the game is, at the end of seven rounds, to have the most cards in your hand. On each person's turn, they have the opportunity to simply grow their own deck or take a big risk by attempting to steal cards from other players. Camille and I easily pick up on the game.

The stress and panic of the room seems to simmer away as the night progresses. Some competitors have fallen asleep, while others whisper to each other in the dark. Eventually, Liam comes over and joins our card game, along with his friend, Flower. When Liam successfully steals almost all of Aubrey's hand, I expect her to leap up and strangle him. The rest of us laugh at the murderous expression on her face, loud enough to attract attention from the officers.

An older woman with a stern face scolds us for being so loud and confiscates our cards. "The Games are still tomorrow. Why don't you all get some rest?"

As she walks away, I internally groan. I'd forgotten about the Games. The fact that they aren't postponed is ridiculous given the circumstances. As it gets closer and closer, I'm starting to hate the idea that Liam is depending on me.

Our group disperses, each picking a cot and lying down. However, Camille stops at mine and sits down next to me. I shift to make room for her, and she gives me a nudge.

"Listen, I had a realization today."

"Okay." I raise an eyebrow. "Please, elaborate."

"I need to apologize to you."

I wait for her to continue, but she just sits there in silence.

"Okay, are you going to?" I prod.

She narrows her eyes. I know how difficult this is for her.

"Here, let me start," I say. "I'm also sorry. I've been a jerk to you lately, and I keep lashing out at you because, honestly, you're there. There's no one else here I can do that with and not face any consequences. But I know that's not fair to you. So, I'm sorry, and I'll try to be better about it."

Camille glares at me. "Now you've made it impossible for me not to say it."

"I know."

"Okay, well… I'm sorry too. I think I'm just scared of losing the only family I have left. I want to do everything I can to protect you. Although, I know you're stubborn and hate to have anyone help you, so every time I try, it just makes you more upset."

"I knew the insult was coming."

"Oh, whatever! You know it's true." She rolls her eyes. "Anyway, what I'm trying to say is… I'll try to let you go a little more and do what you think is best. And stop freaking out when you get yourself involved in dangerous things."

"Yeah, because being dragged out of a prison cell to come fight to the death as a guest in King Edward's palace is definitely not the place for dangerous things to happen."

Camille turns serious. "What was the alarm about? Did anyone tell you?"

"No, not really. Neither Miles nor Aubrey really seemed stressed until you guys were taking so long to get here."

Camille chews her lip. "Ryden said the alarms mean rebels. I didn't think they had organized attacks."

"Amaia said there are actual rebel groups, so maybe it's one of them?"

Camille looks like she wants to say something but then thinks better of it. "Maybe. Maybe it's just a drill."

"Maybe." I pause, confirming we've reached the end of our conversation. "We're good right?"

Camille smiles. "Yeah, we're good."

"I love you, Cam."

"I love you too, Keith."

Before she gets up, I ask the question that's been on my mind all evening. "So... you and Ryden?"

Camille swings the pillow from the cot into my face.

Whack.

CHAPTER THIRTY-EIGHT
Keith

"YOU'RE NOT GOING TO fall asleep on me during the Game, are you?" Liam eyes me.

I stifle another yawn before shaking my head. "No, of course not."

Between the quiet chatter of everyone and not knowing what was happening outside the safe room, I had barely gotten any rest last night. When the doors had opened, everyone rose and continued on like normal. Nobody has even spoken about it, which I find strange.

Liam raises his eyebrows. "Okay. Remember, I'm the one driving this thing. You better have my back."

"Actually," I say. "I had an idea about that."

I turn to look at our gorgeous wagon. Liam had done an excellent job designing it within the parameters we had been given. Certain factors had to be included, and only a certain number of materials could be used. The entire contraption was built from wood and lined with steel.

This was to prevent Asher from being able to completely burn up our wagon with a mere thought. Even if he set the wood on fire, hypothetically, there is enough steel to keep us up. The sides were built to cover our legs, leaving our torsos enough space to defend our wagon from attackers.

However, our only downfall is how we plan on going forward. Liam is going to use his super speed to run, give us momentum, and then he will jump back in to steer until he needs to run again.

I don't know why it hadn't occurred to me before now, but my gift offers a much simpler solution. With the crowd roaring from the stands, the girls eagerly watching from underneath the royals, and the male competitors making final adjustments to their wagons, I put all my thought into my gift.

Two large horses appear, perfectly aligned at the front of our wagon. Their golden coats shimmer under the sun, and their stunning white manes dance in the breeze. The crowd gets louder, filled with oohs and ahhs. Liam laughs and pumps his fist in the air.

"Dude, why didn't you tell me you could do this before?"

"I didn't think about it."

Liam looks at me in awe. "Well, that makes life a whole lot easier." Liam hurries to adjust the front of the wagon to accommodate the horses. A deep laugh comes from behind me.

"Well, that's certainly impressive."

Annoyance prickles underneath my skin as I turn to face Asher. He's twirling his sword menacingly. Quentin, Asher's partner, stands behind him, looking just as intimidating.

"Thank you," I say through gritted teeth.

Asher rolls his eyes and walks back to his wagon, which appears to be constructed similarly to ours. However, their framework is made of less metal, which could instead be found in a machine at the center of the cart. It must be how they plan to make their cart move.

"Competitors, to your carts!" The king's voice rings out through the closed arena. Liam hurries with the final straps and leaps into our cart. We both draw our weapons—my sword and his bow—and I reach out to my horses. I can feel them both eagerly awaiting the start. One of them tosses its head in anticipation.

As soon as the rest of the competitors climb into their specified carts, the bar separating us from the track begins to lower.

"Today's Game is different. Each group has been working together to construct their strategy and design their cart. However, rankings in the Game will still be individual. They do not need their partner to finish. As each competitor crosses the finish line, they place in the Game. And as always, each kill results in a higher ranking." King Edward smiles.

I glance at Liam. I hadn't even considered the fact that I might be able to win without my partner. Sure, Liam and I have gotten along, but how far would he be willing to go to win? If it came down to it, would he push me off to get a higher placing? I really hope not.

Before I have the chance to fully consider it, a horn echoes, and the rail separating us from the track clangs to the floor with a thud. Without much prompting, the horses charge forward, tossing their manes as they propel our cart into the race.

Liam notches an arrow into his bow, and I ready my sword. Miles and Ryden pull forward, leading the crowd of competitors. From the looks of it, Miles lost the banana argument, but to Ryden's credit, the cart moves with incredible speed. I can't tell how they're getting it to move, but my gaze is torn from their cart as an arrow flies by my face.

Swinging around to confront my attacker, I come face to face with Carter. His partner, Giler Rose, the son of Lord Rose, is leading their cart directly into ours. Horses pull their cart as well, but they look pitiful compared to mine. Using my mind, I urge my horses to move faster, and the sound of their hooves hitting the dirt track quickens. But it's not quite fast enough.

Carter and Giler thud against us, splinters from both of our carts flying through the air. I tumble to the floor from the impact, and my shoulder aches from crashing against the metal framework.

Liam jumps to my defense, blocking Carter's sword with his bow. Shards fly from the bow, leaving Liam with a damaged weapon. I hope it's intact enough for him to still use it.

Keeping my energy focused on channeling more strength into the pair of horses, I scramble to my feet, dodging an arrow from Giler as I rise. I grab my sword's handle and swing to block Carter's next blow. I only barely match his strike, and the force sends me backward again. The horses stumble due to my lack of concentration, and Carter's cart pulls ahead. I grit my teeth and send a new wave of energy spiraling toward the horses. They throw their heads up and gallop forward, gaining enough momentum to charge ahead of Carter and Giler's cart.

Before I can celebrate, Liam cries out as a flaming arrow strikes his shoulder. Hurriedly, he pats out the flame on his shirt but not before the smell of burnt skin penetrates the air.

"Asher!" Liam snarls. Blood drips from his wound, staining his silver shirt.

Sure enough, Asher is passing Quinten back his bow and unsheathing a glinting red sword.

With another burst of strength, I spur the horses even faster, but it's not enough to outrun Asher's machine. At its center, there's a sparkling flame, and I realize that must be what's powering their cart. With a loud crash, Asher's cart rams into ours, knocking our horses off their stride. Carter and Giler flash us matching grins as they rush past us, leaving us at the mercy of Asher and Quinten.

Quinten fires an arrow, which I narrowly dodge. I can feel my horses slowing down, fading from existence as my energy wanes. With flames dancing in his palms and licking down his sword, Asher makes an impressive leap into our cart. Liam nocks an arrow with incredible speed, despite his shoulder injury, and lets it fly into Asher's arm. Taking advantage of Asher's momentary distraction, I press forward with my sword, but I'm no match for Asher—even though he's injured.

He knows it too, but instead of ending me quickly, he plays it out. He flicks his sword to block my blows as we dance around in our cart. We've drastically dropped in speed, and one of the horses flickers in and out for a moment, leaving our cart tilting to one side. I consider signaling to Liam that we should go back to our original plan. I'd be able to focus on fighting Asher while Liam pulls the cart. But I quickly dismiss the idea. Too many arrows are flying, and if Liam were to leave the cart, he would probably die.

Instead, I urgently call the horse back, using the last of my strength. To my dismay, this drains me of everything I have left, and my gaze flickers black.

From the crowd, I hear a cacophony of ear-deafening noise, but in one glance, I immediately find my gaze clashing with Amaia's. She's staring at me, a small smile dancing on her lips. I shove back against Asher in frustration. So much for being able to rely on her. All she can do is laugh at my imminent death because that's clearly Asher's goal. If it had been to simply win the Game, Asher and Quinten could have already been across the finish line instead of keeping pace with my winded horses.

Asher falls backward, tumbling into Liam, whose head bangs against the metal bar. His eyes go out of focus, and his body falls limp. I feel a surge of panic for him and desperately hope he's not dead. I can't check on him though because Asher crouches, snarling in my direction. He pounces, flames wrapping his entire body. I jump—more like stumble—backward, trying to avoid the heat coursing from his flames and the blade flying toward my neck.

This time, I don't know where it comes from, but another surge of energy flies through me. It feels different—stronger —and more stable than what I had before. I roll myself out of Asher's way, sending him tumbling back onto his cart. With coordination I didn't even know I had, I leap up, scooping up Liam's splintered bow from the floor. It's got barely enough strength for another shot. Liam, still alive, but extremely dazed, hands me an arrow.

The arrow pierces Quinten's chest and with a silent cry, he crashes to the floor, his mouth wide open in shock. Asher looks at me, as bewildered as I am. Using his hands, Asher shoves his cart away from ours and pulls forward.

I focus the rest of my energy on our horses, pushing Liam and I through the finish line.

As soon as I ensure Liam is okay, I look up. Like always, Amaia's watchful blue eyes are on me.

Camille

"SNAP OUT OF IT!" Garden hisses at me as we stand ready in our cart.

I shake my head, trying to focus on the last handful of knots Garden told me to tie. But the image of Keith firing an arrow into Quinten's chest won't stop replaying in my head. I hadn't been able to tell if it was a fatal shot, and we had been ushered to the starting line before I could see if Quinten would rise.

Garden's concern for my concentration is legitimate. She somehow configured a machine designed to move our cart solely with the energy produced by the heat of my gift. For the entire race, a part of my mind must be focused on using my gift to keep the machine running. If the flashes of Keith nocking an arrow and Quinten collapsing don't stop before the Game begins, the distraction could easily place me and Garden in severe danger.

As I continue to fumble with the knot, Garden grabs me by my shoulders and pulls me up.

She looks me dead in the eye, brown hair flying viscously around her face. "Listen, I didn't decide to like you for you to get hung up on death. I get it. Keith just killed Quinten. But would you prefer he died instead?"

I set my jaw. "Of course not. I just had hoped one of us could have escaped these Games without losing ourselves."

Garden rolls her eyes. "I'd prefer losing a bit of my mind over losing my life." She grips my shoulders tighter. "Now, are you with me or not?"

I jerk my head in a nod. "I'm with you."

"Good, now start warming up the machine. The round is about to start."

Sure enough, the rail separating us from the track clangs down with a crash and releases our carts. Reaching for the metal cog, I throw the tendrils of my heat into the cold machine, propelling us forward. Garden grins, brandishing her sword. I reach for my bow, nocking an arrow.

Beforehand, we had decided to focus on getting to the end as fast as we could. Still, I can't resist brushing a strand of ice-cold air across Sabrina's face. Immediately, she focuses on me and snarls.

"Watch this," Garden says. Her eyes flutter shut for a moment, and I realize I'm watching her use her gift of creating illusions.

Sabrina immediately falls to the floor, swinging her sword at some imaginary foe. Her partner, Kimberly, jumps away from the reins in a panic, forcing their horses to pull back.

Garden opens her eyes, still smiling, and Sabrina continues to react to whatever "thing" Garden is throwing at her. Their cart jostles back and forth while Kimberly attempts to urge the horses forward again. A laugh bursts from my lips as Sabrina chops off the bottom half of Kimberly's braid.

"Watch out!" Garden barks out.

Instinctively, I drop to a crouch as Garden arcs her sword to deflect an arrow that'd been aimed at my heart. I don't have a chance to see who fired it because another cart bangs into the side of ours.

I spin around on my toes, drawing an arrow back as I go. Before I release the string, I make eye contact with Aubrey. She holds a hand up to her chest, fronting a look of offense. Then she winks at me and pushes past our cart, flicking the reins attached to two golden stallions.

Instead, I swivel my arrow to face toward a cart directly behind us. Prill is already aiming another arrow directly at me. I fire first, but she dodges while releasing her own. While I shift out of the way, Garden engages with Jay, Prill's partner, attacking over the edge of our cart. Prill fires another arrow, but this time, I'm ready. With a burst of energy, I melt the arrow in midair, and it dissolves in a pile of goop.

I smile at the surprise and anger in Prill's face as she drops her scalding bow. Silently understanding, Garden turns away from Jay, expertly spinning her sword as she moves. She hits Prill across the face with the flat of her blade, sending her tumbling backward. I grin while I fire a handful of arrows at Jay, defending Garden's back. Together, we're untouchable.

Feeling the adrenaline pulse through my body, I use more of my gift to push us farther ahead, only barely behind Aubrey and her partner, Whisper.

"On the left!" Garden yells, pointing to Sabrina's face of rage racing toward us. Acting instinctively, I reach out with my gift, targeting the gears spinning Sabrina's wheels. I grip the edge of our cart to keep myself steady as I release my gift of ice. Their wheels come to a stop, and their horses struggle to pull forward against the frozen spokes.

"Nice one!" Garden playfully punches my shoulder. "You have incredible control."

"Thanks," I say.

We charge across the finish line, leaving Sabrina's cart behind us. The crowd is roaring, and Garden is grinning. I grin back, actually feeling the thrill of the Game.

Garden reaches for my hand, holding it up for the crowd to see, and their cheers get even louder. The final carts cross the line, and King Edward gathers everyone's attention. While he gives his normal ending speech full of false niceties, a drawling voice whispers in my ear.

"Congratulations."

I jump forward, and Garden gives me a wary look. Behind me is Prince Jacob, his blue eyes dancing mischievously.

Curious as to why he is down here instead of with the king, I survey the rest of the finish line. The male competitors are still here, and when my eyes find Keith, I see him staring intently down at the floor. Ryden and Miles are standing next to him. Ryden gives me a brief wink, and this helps to release the tension coiled in my gut. I turn my attention to Prince Jacob.

"Thank you," I say, lowering myself into a quick curtsy. "Your Highness."

Jacob smiles. "You did quite an excellent job today. The stamina you have is admirable. I hope to see you again soon."

My eyebrows furrow in confusion, but before I can ask what he means, he's already walking away.

Garden slides up next to me. "That's different. I didn't think Jacob was capable of complimenting somebody."

The way she says this makes it seem like his compliment is a good thing, but dread settles in my stomach instead.

CHAPTER FORTY

Keith

I DIDN'T KNOW WHICH is stranger: the fact that the royal family has joined us for breakfast without a fancy announcement, or the fact that Camille and Garden are purposefully sitting next to each other laughing.

Miles seems just as intrigued by Garden's addition to our table.

"What are you looking at Repsport?" Garden snaps.

"I'm looking at you, Burrow," Miles says. "Is that a crime?"

Garden rolls her eyes at him and resumes chatting with Camille. I search the room, looking for Quentin. The king's healers fixed him right up, mending the injury that had missed his heart. It had been enough to knock him out of the Game, but not enough to kill him.

I was relieved to see Quentin stand up yesterday, grateful that my arrow hadn't killed the boy. However, I still wasn't sure exactly how I had managed to fire the arrow so quickly and accurately in the first place. It's for that reason that I avoid looking up at the table at the front of the room.

"He looks like he's doing much better." Miles jerks his head toward Quentin, catching my concerned glance.

"I'm just relieved he's alright," Camille says, her voice quieter than normal.

I look at her with a small smile.

"You guys are all so dramatic. It was an arrow to the chest, not some deathly wound he was never going to recover from," Garden says.

I stare at Garden, unsure of whether she's being serious.

Then Ryden speaks up. "Actually, I'm really impressed with you, Keith. It's never an easy shot to incapacitate someone without also killing them."

Aubrey nods thoughtfully. "How did you do that?"

I shrug, staring down at the scrambled eggs on my plate. That same question had kept me up all last night. Everyone sitting at our table knows how unskilled I am with a bow—or really any weapon—so of course they would be wondering the same thing. How had I managed to hit Quentin so perfectly? Not to mention the rush of energy that had surged through me, giving me the strength to finish the fight.

As if hearing the conversation, a pair of blue eyes pierce through the back of my head. So, when Miles stands up to clear his plate, I jump up to follow him, eager to escape Amaia's gaze. I'm not ready to confront her with my pile of questions, and I'm not sure she's ready for it either. Her amusement at my downfall still replays in my mind.

Miles and I exit the breakfast room together, followed by Aubrey and Ryden. Camille stays with Garden, another event that blows my mind. Miles is taking us to the palace's lake today, and Camille politely denied the invitation, even when Ryden had asked her again right before leaving.

The four of us spend the whole afternoon swimming in the lake and basking in the warm sunlight. It's the first time in a long time that I've gotten to simply enjoy my day.

The five of us trudge back inside, deciding to change before getting something to eat. My damp hair flops annoyingly against my forehead as I push open my door. Immediately, the hairs on the back of my neck stiffen, and I feel her presence before I see her.

Amaia is in the corner of my room, lounging lazily on my chair. She's glaring at me from across the room, arms folded. "You've been ignoring me."

I roll my eyes at her dramatics. "If you're talking about this morning, then yes, I was."

Amaia sits up in the chair, leaning forward on her elbows. "I want to take you somewhere, but if you'd rather not talk to me, that's fine too."

I stare at the ceiling as if pondering my options. But whatever annoyance I had with her is already fading. I know my response. From her small smile, she knows it too.

"Alright, fine. Where are we going?"

Princess Amaia loves her surprises. As we walk, I pelt her with questions, but she simply deflects each one with a mischievous smile. Eventually, I give up on discovering where she's leading me, settling for a question I've been dying to ask.

"So, what did you think about the Game yesterday?"

Sure enough, Amaia looks at me with a glint in her eye. "I think you had an awesome shot."

"Quite out of character for me, don't you think?"

Amaia's face is completely serious as she answers. "Not at all actually."

I scoff. "Can't you just give me a straight answer for once?"

Amaia flinches, and I know I hit a sore spot.

"I will one day. Hopefully soon." Amaia makes a sudden left, and I almost trip over my own feet to keep up with her. "This is so much bigger than you or me. We can't risk losing years of progress just to make sure you know everything."

"We?" I raise an eyebrow, and Amaia frowns at her slip up.

"Why did you ignore me this morning?"

"Way to change the subject," I mutter.

Amaia waits for me to answer.

"It all comes back to the Game yesterday. But you're still refusing to tell me what really happened." I roll my eyes. "Shocker."

"Soon, Keith. Soon," Amaia says.

We walk the rest of the way in silence, keeping perfect pace with each other. For a brief moment, I let myself watch her hands sway back and forth in time with her steps. I imagine reaching out and brushing my fingers against her hand. But I swiftly dismiss the idea, unsure of where it came from in the first place.

Amaia leads me into an empty room—even the walls are completely blank. Miles leans against one of the cream-colored walls, his arms folded.

"You knew about this?" I ask.

Miles grins at me, causally rolling his shoulders. "Of course I did. Aubrey and Ryden did too if that makes you feel any worse."

I shake my head, struggling to be surprised at this point. I refocus on Amaia. "Can I know where we're going now?"

Amaia shakes her head. "Not yet. You'll just have to see."

"I'm getting really fed up with the amount of surprises."

Miles pushes himself off the wall and strides to stand next to me and Amaia. "What's life without a little surprise?"

"Enjoyable," I mumble.

A grin splits across Miles's face. "You don't mean that." Miles holds out his hands, clearly wanting me to take one of them. Instead, I fold my arms, refusing to grab on until one of them decides to speak. With her hand already holding onto Miles, Amaia chews her lip, clearly thinking.

I stare right back at her, unwilling to be the first to give in.

"You know how I was asking my father for clearance to check out the Gulf?"

I suppress my smile at winning the standoff, and Miles rolls his eyes with an exasperated grin. "We're going to the Gulf?"

Amaia puts a hand to her chin. "Technically, no. Miles and I are going to perform a routine check up on one of the centers in the Shadows, which is normal enough. It just so happens that the Shadows border the Gulf."

I nod, picking up on their plan. "So, if Miles is a little off on his teleportation and lands us in the Gulf, there's nothing wrong with that. It's an easy mistake to make."

Miles holds a hand to chest, feigning offense. "Excuse me. How dare you accuse me of making a mistake! I could never."

Amaia and I share a grin, and any frustration at her previous silence fades.

"How are we explaining my presence?" I ask.

Amaia shrugs. "What do you mean? As far as I know, you're not with us."

I grab Miles's hand, grinning as we zip out of the palace.

CHAPTER FORTY-ONE
Camille

AFTER GARDEN AND I finish sparring in the training room, I leave to search for Keith. According to the plans we discussed this morning, I expect him to be eating lunch with Miles, Ryden, and Aubrey. But when I walk up to Aubrey's room, only she and Ryden are inside, eating sandwiches alone together.

With a light knock on the doorframe, I ask, "Have either of you seen Keith?"

Ryden's the first one to look at me, and our eyes clash against each other for the first time since the rooftop. Unwilling to touch the emotions swirling through me, I shift my gaze to Aubrey.

Aubrey only shrugs. "I think he and Miles are doing something." With the casual way she says it, I might have dismissed it. But Ryden's slightly narrowed eyes give her away.

"Doing what?" I fold my arms against my chest.

"Don't worry about it."

I plant my feet, clearly communicating that I'm not giving up. "Where is he?"

"With Amaia," Ryden says, keeping his eyes focused on the sandwich in his hands.

Aubrey dismisses my glare. "He's fine. Like I said, don't worry about it."

I turn my fiery gaze to Ryden, who has the courtesy to look ashamed. Spinning on my heels, I stride back out into the hallway. I don't get far before footsteps echo behind me. Instinctively, I slow my pace to allow Ryden to catch up.

"I'm sorry. I would have told you this morning, but I only just found out. I swear!"

I nod, unable to make eye contact with his green eyes.

"Are you mad at me?" he asks.

This jolts my attention, and I face him. "Why would I be mad at you?"

Ryden's face flushes as red as his hair. "Well, I didn't tell you about Keith. I haven't talked to you since... the..." He nervously runs a hand through his hair. "You know... the night the alarm went off."

Forgetting about all my previous hesitations, I lean forward and gently press my lips against Ryden's cheek. His mouth abruptly shuts, and his eyes widen in surprise.

"No, I'm not angry at you." I continue walking, gesturing for Ryden to follow me down the hall. "I just don't know how to handle all of this." I move my hands in a motion encompassing the air in front of me.

Ryden smiles, the worry disappearing from his face. "I understand. I'll wait until you figure out all of this." He copies my hand motion.

We walk side by side, and I feel rather happy.

"Would you be able to take me to see my father?" I ask.

Ryden looks taken aback by the request, but quickly regains his composure, glancing at a nonexistent wristwatch. "I can drop you off, but my father has a meeting with the king, and he's asked me to be there."

I grimace. "Oh, scary."

"You're telling me." Ryden scoffs before leading me to the left toward the security rooms. It doesn't take long before Ryden drops a light kiss on the back of my hand, creating a flurry of butterflies in my stomach. He then leaves me to walk into the room by myself.

The door clangs shut behind me as I survey the screens on the wall. The one that typically displays my father has changed, depicting only an empty cell, scrubbed clean of any old blood stains.

Confused, I search the rest of the screens, looking for any other signs of my father. Deciding that someone must have taken him to another room to force information from him, I sit on one of the soft rolling chairs in the center of the room. Time seems to slowly tick by, and each second doesn't offer any change to my father's cell.

"How long do you plan on staying here?"

I immediately shoot up from my chair, heat dancing along the back of my neck. I swivel to find the source of the voice and nearly stumble. Prince Jacob stands at the door, leaning against the frame with his arms loosely folded across his chest.

"How long have you been watching me?" I shoot back. It's unnerving that I didn't hear him enter the room.

Jacob raises his eyebrows. "How long do you think you'll grieve for him?" From the smug look on the prince's face, I know he sees right through my attempt at hiding my shock and confusion. "See, two can play at that game."

"What do you mean?"

Jacob cocks his head at me. "Your father served his usefulness at the end of last week. His body is nothing but ash now."

I fight to keep my face blank. My father is gone. King Edward has had him killed. I will never see him again.

"Oh." I clear my throat. "Did you find what you were looking for?"

Jacob shakes his head, eyebrows still raised, like he's trying to taunt me.

Flinching, I give in. "Why didn't you tell me?" I hate the desperation that seeps into my embarrassingly high-pitched voice.

"You didn't ask."

I simply stare at Jacob, awaiting the tears I know are supposed to come. But they simply don't. My eyes remain completely dry as I observe the prince's face. His own blue eyes are dark and thoughtful as he stares back at me, curious.

"You remind me of me."

I bark out a laugh. "And how is that?"

Jacob crosses the room in three long strides, leaning over me as I trip backward into the chair. Reaching a hand to my face, he caresses my cheek while running a thumb against my jaw. His closeness has every inch of me screaming for space.

"You know how to prioritize what's important over those silly emotions that render others incapable and incompetent."

"Call it an instinct."

Jacob grins. "Exactly."

Before I can react, he leans down, closes the gap between us, and presses his lips to mine. It's different from

Ryden's kiss. There's no passion there. Instead, it feels like a disguised threat. It's brief—more a brush of lips rather than a full kiss—and then he pulls away as quickly as he had leaned forward.

"You're quite the intriguing one, Camille." Jacob puts his arm on my shoulder. "I respect you—and trust me when I say that my respect is not something easily gained."

"I'm not sure if that's an insult or a compliment." My brain is whirling at twenty miles an hour as I try to process what just happened.

"I think you're a smart one. You'll figure it out." Jacob walks backward, reaching behind him for the door handle.

"How did you know I was in here?" The words burst from my lips before I can stop them.

Jacob rolls his shoulders in feigned boredom. "I don't think you need to know that quite yet."

Then he walks out of the room and leaves me with my mouth parted. I'm torn between saying something or letting him go.

Before he fully disappears into the hallway, he turns his head to look back at me. I sit in my chair, chin resting on my hands, awaiting his final words.

"Don't forget you owe me a favor for all of this." He gestures to the screens. Then he leaves me alone.

I grimace, staring at the bare cell still displayed on the wall. My father is gone. I owe Prince Jacob a favor. Keith is with Amaia... somewhere.

"All of this," I murmur to myself.

CHAPTER FORTY-TWO

Keith

THE SCENT OF SALTWATER dancing in the air hits my nose in a rush. I keep my eyes shut as the sound of waves crashing against the shore mingles with the distant call of birds. If I focus enough, I can almost feel my mom's arms wrapped around me, the way they always would be when we took breaks during our morning runs. But the pair of hands that touch my elbows reminds me that I'm not in that world anymore.

My eyes spring open, and Miles and Amaia are watching me with matching somber expressions. Their sympathy feels odd.

Amaia moves her hand from my elbow to my shoulder. "Are you alright?"

I nod absentmindedly, taking in the rest of the scene. We're in a small cove, nestled behind the side of a cliff. The Myradian Sea crashes against the rock, soaking our feet. I didn't think I'd see this place again.

"We should hurry before King Edward starts to wonder where we went," Miles says, leading us out of the cove and onto the shore.

Amaia and I follow close behind, winding our way around the cliff, revealing the rickety town of Salcoast.

Home. I take another deep breath before stepping out of the shadow of the cliff and onto the warmer sand of the beach. It's eerily quiet, with not even a single fisherman out on the docks.

"Is it normally this empty?" Amaia whispers.

I shake my head. "I wonder where everyone's at."

We walk through the streets, and even though I grew up here, every step feels foreign. There are enough people out and about that the three of us blend in, but the lack of cheerful children and smiles is apparent. Shutters are drawn, and the amount of officers striding up and down the paved roads is almost triple the number that had patrolled when Camille and I lived here.

Amaia pulls at her cloak, wrapping it closer to her body. I brush her fingers away, encouraging her to let the cloak fall naturally.

"It'll look like you're hiding something," I say.

"It feels so empty here," she murmurs.

Miles nods in agreement. Even the people who are outside keep their eyes downcast and walk quickly to their destination.

"What are we here for again?" I ask, ignoring the pit growing in my stomach.

"I wanted to see if it was true." Amaia's bright blue eyes look contemplative. "Something is happening. It wasn't like this on Combatant Day."

Unsure of how to take her words, I try to take a different approach. "Why don't we try the bakery? It's on the main road only a couple of blocks down."

Miles nods vigorously. "Cookies sound good."

As I had hoped, when the three of us turn down the main street, the mood shifts. A couple sits outside a store, both looking cheerful. A handful of children grip their parent's hands—not quite as boisterous as normal, but better than the darker streets.

I lead them into the bright bakery, greeting Patty, the old lady who owns the shop, with a big smile. The room floods with the warm smell of bread and freshly baked cookies. Using a handful of coins borrowed from Amaia, I pick out a couple cookies for myself while Miles and Amaia choose their own baked goods.

We sit outside on the covered porch at a wooden table. Miles excuses himself to use the bathroom, leaving Amaia and me alone.

Despite my warning to act normal, Amaia's shoulders are stiff as she takes small bites of her blueberry muffin, and her eyes scour her surroundings relentlessly.

"Relax. You don't want anyone to know who you are, right? Acting like a fighter isn't going to help your case."

Amaia opens her mouth to retort, but she shakes her head in defeat. Slowly lowering her shoulders, she says. "Is this better?"

"Better."

Amaia smiles as she takes another bite of her muffin. However, her eyes don't stop skimming over the crowd, settling on each officer positioned down the street.

Trying to distract her thoughts, I gesture to the muffin. "It's good, isn't it?"

Amaia nods. "Yes, I'll admit this might be the best blueberry muffin I've ever had. Is this the lady you were talking about that day in the woods?"

Immediately, I recall the day she had taken me out to discover how to use my gift. Memories of her closeness flood back in a rush. I break eye contact, feeling my cheeks flush. "Yeah, her name's Patty. I've known her since I was a little kid."

Amaia's eyes soften, if only for a moment. Then they sharpen back on the street, watching as a young couple walks past us. Trying a second time to encourage her to relax, I remember a question I've been meaning to ask.

"What's a banana?"

The question takes Amaia off guard, and she looks at me with a light laugh. "It's a type of fruit. We import it directly to Central from an Eastern country. They're yellow and curved. Pretty good actually. Why?"

"Well Miles, Ryden, and Liam mentioned it while we were designing our wagons…" My voice trails off as I realize she's only half listening. She's crowd watching again, her eyes focusing on everyone who passes us.

"Why are you so on edge?" I ask, giving up.

"I work closely with the officers in Central, but…" She shifts uncomfortably. "I don't know if the officers here would fully recognize my authority."

I'm about to point out that being the princess is all the authority she needs, when suddenly, she sits up straight again.

"Keith!"

Commotion breaks out farther down the street.

A teenage boy, not much older than me, bumps into one of the officers and falls. Instead of the officer helping the boy up, he gruffly says, "Excuse me, boy, where are your manners?"

For a second, nobody moves. The boy glares at the cobblestone, clearly trying to restrain himself from responding. He manages to choke out a "Sorry."

The officer isn't satisfied. He roughly grabs the boy by the arm. "You don't sound like you're sorry."

The boy turns his stormy gaze to the officer, and fear for the boy curls in my stomach. "I'm not."

Within moments, three officers surround the boy, and the rest of the crowd silently presses themselves against the nearest shops.

Already halfway out of my chair, my teeth grind together. Amaia urgently tugs on my arm, trying to force me to sit back down, but I only shoot her a dark glare. She sees the rage in my eyes, and her own anger plays across her face.

"Keith, look!" she hisses, pointing down the street. "Has that always been there?"

She's pointing to a thick black pole stained with spots of crimson. It's tucked away at the end of the street, and I hadn't noticed it before now. The stand has thick metal cuffs that look like Nightrock. Two of the officers drag the teenage boy by his stick-thin arms, while the third begins to unravel a rope from his belt.

My lip curls upward in disgust as I realize they plan on beating the boy. Before I have time to think, I push away Amaia's fingers and sprint across the street. In a blink, the people left on the street disappear into the shops. I tackle the officer holding the rope, landing a solid fist on the man's jaw. The boy is released by the other two officers, and he collapses to the ground, trembling. My victory is short-lived as a group of officers surround me. Despite my resistance, they easily shove my face into the cobblestone. One twists my arm so far backward that my shoulder pops, and I cry out in pain as it's yanked out of place.

"Who do you think you are?" one of the officers drawls, but I spit in the man's face. It thuds against his cheek, and the man's fist connects with my temple. Sharp pain rebounds through my head.

Another officer draws a gun from his waistband, leveling it to my forehead, and my heart thuds wildly in my chest. I look past the officer at the teenage boy, who looks back at me with the terror he'd been trying to disguise. There are worse ways to go, I remind myself.

In the next moment, the man is thrown backward by a flash of movement. Landing elegantly on both her feet, Amaia snarls at the group of officers surrounding me. The gun falls from the now-unconscious officer's hand.

"Let him go!"

The officers laugh, and despite the pain aching through my shoulder and head, I smile. Amaia does too. With the movement of a furious lioness, she leaps into the fray, knocking away the officers restraining me with ease.

More begin to flood the street, and Amaia grips me by the shirt, dragging me upward. With a sharp yank, she pulls me away from the nearest officer's charge, preparing herself to fight off the next pair.

"We have to go."

"What about Miles?" My words come out slurred as I feel my body sway. The pain in my head is now making my vision swim.

"We'll find him later. He knows how to take care of himself."

I attempt to nod, but the movement is jarring and my vision flickers to black for a moment. Amaia wraps an arm under my shoulder and holds me upright.

"Where should we go?" she asks.

My tongue feels heavy in my mouth. "I know a place."

"Is it safe?"

I look into Amaia's face, and her eyes sparkle with concern. I feel an odd sort of affection for her. She's worried about me. It's nice to see that she cares. Not to mention the sparkle makes her eyes look like a more brilliant shade of blue.

"You're beautiful. Do you know that?"

Amaia rolls her eyes, dragging me with her as she rushes away from the crowd of officers pursuing us. "Just get me to where you'll be safe, please."

CHAPTER FORTY-THREE
Keith

EITHER BECAUSE OF HOW long I've been away from my town or the head injury currently distorting my thoughts, I lead us directly to a dead end.

"I don't think you understand the concept of somewhere safe." Amaia gently shifts me off from her shoulders, steadying me so I can stand on my own.

I wince as the buildings surrounding us start to sway. "Listen, I know their house is around here somewhere. I just wish thinking didn't hurt my head so much."

Amaia hands me a dagger from the inside of her boot. My hold on it is clumsy. "Well, I hope you have enough in you to fight off a couple of officers."

Later, I would have to explain to Amaia that she should redefine her definition of "a couple." The alleyway floods with at least ten officers, but Amaia doesn't back down. Instead, she snarls at the incoming enemies. Before she charges them, she pushes me down behind a metal cylinder commonly used for trash. If I couldn't trust my mind at this point, I would've sworn I caught a glimpse of sharp canines flashing in her smile.

I'm frustrated that I've been rendered useless and forced to hide behind a trash can. At the same time, I grip my knife uneasily, knowing it won't do much good against the officers' guns. I peek around the barrel to see if I should jump into the fray.

Somehow, Amaia makes it work without a weapon. She moves with inhuman speed, throwing the officers around as if they are nothing more than bags of flour. Bullets are firing, rebounding against the walls of the alleyway, but she expertly moves to avoid contact and uses the butt of a stolen gun to render officers unconscious. Even though she's fighting with such grace and precision, an officer slips past her guard, forcing me to act.

Adjusting my grip on the knife as best as I can, I lunge out from behind the trash can, calling on my wolf as I do so. With a snarl, the wolf leaps on the officer, but the act drains me of what little strength I have left. The wolf fades, gone as quickly as it had appeared. Leaving me kneeling on the ground, the officer turns to an unaware Amaia. Her back is turned, and she is focused on keeping the other officers from reaching me. He steadies his gun, taking his time to carefully aim.

With a shout, I leap from the ground, propelling myself forward and arching the dagger blade to strike the officer directly in the back. The effort it takes makes me collapse right next to the bloody body of the officer.

My vision flickers, but in sudden desperation, I feel for the man's pulse. I let myself fall back when I feel a distant drumming, signifying the officer's life. I didn't kill him. Relief crashes through me, running away the last of my adrenaline.

I'm still awake enough to see the last officer drop to the floor, but it's not from Amaia's gun. It's from a new one. The stranger's face is familiar—even blood-spattered.

"Lizzy?"

"Gosh, Keith, you've definitely looked better."

I groan, and my vision fades completely.

"I can't believe you're actually her." Lizzy's voice sounds far away.

"Yes." Amaia's voice is closer but more tentative. "And?"

"You have no idea how much we look up to you!" This time it's a boy's voice. Micheal.

Their words don't make sense. Why would they look up to Princess Amaia? I'd barely known anything about her before being sent to Central. Micheal and Lizzy don't know her well enough to speak with such familiarity.

I peek my eyes open and immediately recognize the bed I'm lying in. Amaia is sitting at the edge, her hand resting gently on my leg, almost absentmindedly.

"I don't think anybody could look up to her. She's fairly short," I say. My throat feels rough and craggy. Lizzy's freckled face appears in front of me, her eyes full of concern. Amaia shifts her body ever so slightly—almost unnoticeably—so she's angled in between me and Lizzy.

"You're awake."

I laugh, the pain echoing in my chest. "Thanks for stating the obvious."

Amaia rolls her eyes, but Lizzy giggles. "I'm glad to see the royals haven't taken your sarcasm."

"I don't think anyone's capable of that," Micheal says, chiming in.

Propping myself onto my elbow, I get a better look at the rest of the room. This is Micheal and Lizzy's bedroom, identifiable by the standard pile of dirty clothes stacked in the corner and the bright shade of pink plastered on the walls. Painting this room was one of the last things Lizzy's father did for her before he died.

Catching the look on my face, Lizzy answers the question before I can ask it. "Mom died right after you guys left. Before everything started going sideways."

"Sideways?" Amaia asks.

Lizzy sits down on her bed. "I mean, ever since Mr. Atwood tried to kill King Edward, people have been inspired. Officers have been killed, and in return, people have been beaten to death for all of us to watch. It's given everyone a little courage to stand up against the cruelty, I think."

"So that's why security has been increased here. Why didn't he tell me?" Amaia mutters, mainly to herself.

"So, it doesn't have anything to do with the forest?" I ask Lizzy.

Lizzy's expression tightens, and her gaze swivels to the single boarded window. "What have you heard about the forest?"

I frown. "Nothing. Amaia doesn't tell me anything."

Micheal and Lizzy both raise an eyebrow at the informality in my tone. Micheal gives me a knowing grin, which I blatantly ignore.

Amaia waves away the comment. "You're on a need-to-know basis."

Lizzy's gaze darts back and forth between us before she continues. "Anyway, there's been rumors of people disappearing into the woods at night. Like Mrs. Sarah and her two kids. They were gone yesterday morning, and a neighbor swore she saw them sneaking around the alleyways in the middle of the night."

I try to sit up, eagerly engaging in the conversation. However, my vision immediately swirls, and a groan of pain escapes my lips. Lizzy jumps forward, placing a hand gently on my shoulder and urging me to lie back down. Amaia gives her a sharp look, but doesn't comment.

"Keith, what makes you think you can get up already?" Lizzy chides. "I may have been able to patch up your shoulder, but the hit to your head is more complicated. I'm not sure how to fix it yet."

"Wait, you got your gift?"

Lizzy smiles, twirling her fingers. "I'm a healer. Although not a very strong one. I do what I can. People come here after their punishments to ease their pain." Lizzy turns to Micheal. "Can you get a glass of water?" With a mischievous glint in her eye, she stands, shooting me a wink. "Actually, Michael, come with me. I'll show you where the clean dishes are."

She drags a confused Micheal behind her, leaving Amaia and me alone.

Surprisingly, Amaia is the first one to speak. "How do you know them?"

There's an edge to her tone.

"Old friends."

Amaia raises his eyebrows in question.

"Why? Are you jealous?" I tease.

"No." Amaia's curt response makes my eyes brighten in amusement. She gives me a gentle push on the shoulder and mutters, "You wish."

But her eyes are averted, and a blush is creeping its way along her face. My stomach does a somersault as Amaia becomes fixated on the pink wall.

Then switches the topic. "We need to find Miles and get back to Central. It won't be long before the officers trace us back here, and I don't want to risk another encounter with them. It's already likely that my father realizes I'm not where I'm supposed to be."

Right on cue, Lizzy crashes through the door, and a small girl, who's breathing heavily, trails behind her. "You guys have to get out of here! Officers have filled the streets, and they're searching houses."

I stand with help from Amaia, but I'm still a little shaky on my feet. "Thank you for your help."

I wrap Lizzy in a warm hug, ignoring the ache that courses through my body.

"Watch out for Camille, and tell her we said hello."

I nod. "Thank you."

Then Amaia is pulling me backward, urging me toward the window. Lithely, like a cat, Amaia slides out of the gap, and I follow behind, far less gracefully than her. I grimace as my head spins and my shoulders bump against the window frame. I almost topple out the window and land flat on the dirt, but Amaia catches me with a steady hand, gently lowering both of us to the ground. Leading us away from the thunderous sounds of officer footsteps, Amaia guides me down roads in a blur, keeping her hand in mine.

Unfortunately, she leads us down another dead end, and the footsteps are only getting louder.

"Who led us to our death now?"

Amaia doesn't answer, face furrowed in concentration.

Four officers round the corner. With a shout, they charge us, and Amaia steps in front of me. I frown and push myself so we're standing evenly. I don't want to be stuck hiding this time. Amaia rolls her eyes but draws another two daggers from her boot, handing me one. But before the officers can reach Amaia, a figure zips in front of them, grinning.

"Bring it on boys!" Miles brandishes two long daggers, both the length of his forearm. He advances toward the nearest officer. With a cry, Amaia charges next to him. However, they don't account for the officer in the back with a gun aimed directly at my chest. I don't have time to roll out of the way...

Bang.

With a gasp, I collapse to the ground, hot pain shooting through my body in fresh waves. Amaia growls, viciously tearing through the closest officer in an attempt to reach me. For the second time today, my vision goes black.

Chapter Forty-Four
Camille

I WISH RYDEN HADN'T left me in here. I certainly don't want to stay in this security room staring at my father's empty jail cell. So, I get up and leave, acting on instinct to get back to my room. Except, as always, my instinctive sense of direction is incapable of working.

Giving up on finding my room, I decide to wander the halls, hoping to stumble across something or someone helpful. Per usual, I ignore the watchful eyes of the officers in the hallways.

"Camille!" Ryden's shout echoes against the walls.

"How do you always manage to know when I'm lost?" I ask, turning to face him. The rest of my words die in my throat as I take in Ryden's face. Sweat beads on his face, and his breathing is labored. My face pales, and my heart rushes into my throat. With a sinking feeling, I ask a question I'm certain I already know the answer to.

"What is it?"

"Keith." That's the only confirmation I need to hear to have my feet propelling me toward Ryden. I grab his hand to drag him with me. Ryden is quick to pull ahead of me, rushing through the halls.

Ryden doesn't take us to the hallway containing the boys' rooms. Instead, he leads us down a section of stair-cases to a dimly lit hallway. The number of officers drops to zero. Miles lingers outside an open door, his arms folded as he contemplates the floor. Without a second glance at either of the two boys, I drop Ryden's hand and storm into the room.

Aubrey, who is pacing back and forth, abruptly stops, cautiously eying me. As she should. If she or her princess has managed to hurt my brother, I won't hesitate to burn her from the inside out.

My deadly gaze swivels around the room, looking for my brother. A cot is in the corner, and a pair of girls with silver hair block the person laying on it. Not to my surprise, Princess Amaia is standing by the foot of the cot, peering anxiously at the unmoving boy there.

I stride across the room, ignoring Aubrey's noise of protest or Ryden's hand trying to slow me. I push my way in between Amaia and the cot. Amaia's exclamation of surprise doesn't faze me. My entire focus is on Keith's pale face. His chest is moving up and down with shallow breaths. The front of his shirt is torn and blood-stained. The two girls with silver hair have their hands on his arms. Keith's hair sticks to his forehead with sweat, and his body jerks as the girl on the right hisses in exertion.

"He's going to be alright." Amaia's voice is unusually small. My lip begins to curl upward.

Twirling around to face her, I snarl, "You sound like you're trying to reassure *yourself*, princess!"

Amaia narrows her eyes. "Lydia and Precious know what they're doing."

My patience snaps, and I can feel the heat in the room begin to rise. "Where did you take him? How could you let him get hurt?" With each question, I stalk toward the princess.

Surprisingly, Amaia takes matching steps backward. Fear crosses Amaia's face, but its quickly replaced by determination as her jaw stiffens. She doesn't speak though, and this enrages me.

"You!" I shout. "*You* have been the one to put these ideas of danger and stupidity in his brain. If he dies right now, it's on you!"

Still, Amaia doesn't say anything. I snap, slamming my hands into her shoulders. She stumbles back.

"Are you hearing me?" I demand.

Amaia's face darkens, but not before my gift wraps around her, suffocating the princess in a blanket of heat. Amaia falls to the floor, her breathing rapid as her body begins to break out in a sweat. She trembles near my feet, entirely at my mercy. The two girls healing Keith look over, their gazes concerned. Still, they keep their hands steady on Keith.

Before my gift can go any further, Ryden wraps his arms around me from behind and picks me up. As soon as his arms encase me, I sag against his body, suddenly exhausted. The rage that had consumed me fades to numbness as Amaia rises from the floor.

For a moment, everyone in the room is still, and I can feel the tension ratcheting up. Aubrey is nervously chewing on her fingernails. Miles is in the doorway, carefully observing me. I ignore both of them, and instead, gently nudge against Ryden's arms, asking for freedom. Ryden loosens his grip but slightly shakes his head.

No. You need to calm down first. That's what his eyes say.

Amaia moves to step back toward Keith, and I shout at her. "Don't you dare!"

"Stop!" Ryden hisses in my ear, but Amaia doesn't lash out. She simply glances once at Keith, her eyes full of despair, before stalking out of the room. One of the healer girls stares hard in my direction, mimicking the reproachful look on Miles's face. The other girl jerks her head in Aubrey's direction.

"Go make sure she doesn't do anything stupid."

Aubrey obeys with a nod.

Miles steps farther into the room as Ryden removes his hands from around my waist.

Then Miles folds his arms and stares me down. His face is full of disappointment as he says, "I'd start making more friends if I were you."

Knowing he's trying to enrage me, I still rise to his bait. "I have friends, thank you very much. And currently, my *best* friend is lying on that bed dying thanks to your princess." I sneer at him.

Miles shakes his head and looks over my head at Ryden. "Keep an eye on her." He turns to follow Aubrey, before glancing back with a pointed look at me. "You should know, Keith knew there was a risk coming with us. It's no one's fault but his own for deciding that it's worth it." He pauses, frowning at my blank face. "And watch out. An angry Amaia is not somebody you want to be fighting against."

Then he's gone, leaving Ryden and me with the two girls leaning over Keith's limp body. I take Amaia's place at the foot of the cot. Ryden moves to stand behind me, and the room settles into an eerie quiet. The only sound is Keith's shallow breathing.

I'm not sure how much time passes before the two girls sink backward, shadows dancing underneath both of their eyes.

The shorter girl gives me a small smile. "He's going to be okay."

"Thank you," I whisper, my exhaustion layering my voice.

The healer gives me an acknowledging nod before walking out. The taller girl only gives me a deep glare before exiting.

I move to Keith's side, reaching for his hand. His breathing has evened out, and he looks almost peaceful in his sleep now.

"Why didn't he bring me with him?" I ask.

Ryden shrugs, resting his chin on my shoulder. "Have you considered that maybe Amaia has a point?" Ryden immediately raises his hands in defense against my sharp gaze. "Hey, I'm just saying. I think Keith would find a way to be doing things like this on his own regardless of what you would have to say."

I roll my eyes, but the words strike a chord. However, it's not one I feel like addressing right now. So instead, still holding onto my brother's hand, I lean my head against Ryden's chest, letting out a deep exhale.

"He's such an idiot."

Chapter Forty-Five
Camille

MILES COMES TO TELEPORT Keith back to his room, and Ryden goes to his own room, his eyes drooping with exhaustion. I walk back with him, stopping at the hallway leading to my room. However, I don't sleep. Instead, I ring the little bell beside my bed and wait for a servant to come in.

It's not the old lady from before. Instead, it's a tall girl who looks to be around sixteen, and she doesn't hold herself warily as some of the other servants do.

"What can I do for you, ma'am?" She dips her head in respect.

"Can you take me to Prince Jacob's room?"

The girl raises her eyebrows curiously. "I'm not sure if I'm allowed to take you there without His Highness's permission."

I expected this response, but it would have been convenient if the girl didn't put up an argument. "Don't worry, he's given me permission to visit him as frequently as I'd like." The lie rolls easily off my tongue.

The girl's eyes narrow, but after a moment of consideration, she shrugs. "Okay, I'll take you then." She holds up a warning finger. "But it's your head if you're wrong."

I smile. "I wouldn't expect anything less."

The two of us walk through the halls, and as we do, I notice an increase in the number of officers. Confident that we're nearing the prince's room, nerves dance through my stomach.

I try to push them away as the maid stops in front of a door a few turns later. Two officers flank the entrance. They wear uniforms laced with silver etchings, designating them as members of Jacob's unit. They don't look twice at me or the maid, who is quick to turn back down the hallway, leaving me with only Jacob's door and two guards for company.

I clear my throat. "Excuse me, I'm here to see Prince Jacob."

The one on the left looks at me with stone-gray eyes. "And who are you?"

"Camille Atwood." My voice is surprisingly strong.

"And the reason for visiting?"

"I have something important to discuss with him." Half-truths, I remind myself.

The young man on the right chuckles. "He's giving you a hard time. We've already been told to let you in."

"Oh, um… Thank you."

The guard opens the door, and the prince is already standing there, watching me patiently.

"Thank you, Flint, you may close the door behind her." The prince's tone is gentle as if he's talking to somebody he cares about.

Without another word, the door shuts behind me, and all my previous bravado disappears. The guards may not have known I was lying, but Jacob certainly does. I play with a thread on the edge of my shirt, hoping he will be the one to break the silence.

"Are you going to share with me why you decided to show up in my room at two in the morning?"

Dropping the thread, I start, "Sorry, I didn't realize it was that late. I have some questions."

Jacob gestures for me to continue, lowering himself down onto a deep red sofa.

"Why is Amaia so obsessed with my brother?" I ask.

Jacob barks out a laugh. "I believe she may fancy the boy."

I shake my head. That much is obvious. "No, it has to be something more than that. She nearly got him killed today, and I need to know why she even left."

Jacob's smirk slides away, replaced by a serious stare. "Amaia left the palace today with your brother?"

I hesitate, suddenly wondering if this is a bad idea.

What does it matter if he knows?

"I'm not sure. All I know is that she took my brother somewhere, and he came back shot."

Jacob's expression furrows. "She had a mission in the Shadows today, but it was supposed to be a routine checkup with some of her unit. It should have been relatively safe—even if, for some reason, she took your brother."

"She did," I reiterate.

"Interesting." Jacob rubs a hand against his chin.

He studies me for a minute before I lose my patience.

"What is going on and why is my brother in the middle of it?"

At the seriousness in my tone, Jacob scoffs. "And why would I answer you? Last I recall, you are the one who owes me something. Not the other way around."

"Consider it two favors."

Jacob smiles but shakes his head. He gestures for me to sit next to him on the couch, and I do. "I'm sorry, but that's not how it's going to work." He leans closer to me, and I can feel his warm breath brushing against my neck. My brain is screaming at me to get away from him. But I need answers. "That information will have to cost more than a favor."

I lean away from him, and he watches me intently. "And what would that cost be?"

Jacob stretches a hand lazily across the back of the sofa. "Something you're not ready for yet."

I fight the urge to roll my eyes, instead settling for clenching my jaw. "That's the most ridiculous thing I've heard." Jacob shrugs. Getting desperate, I make a reach. "What about making sure Keith and I survive? If I die, you can't even get the first favor from me."

Jacob grins. "I don't think you're likely to die before I cash it in."

I huff. "That's not true. I think you and I both realize that if Keith and I don't win, the only option for us afterward is death. I know the king won't let us return to our old lives. All I'm asking is that you make sure that neither of us die."

Jacob's grin only widens. "Keeping you alive is to my benefit, but what about your brother? What do I gain from keeping him alive?"

Ignoring the teasing undertone in Jacob's voice, I continue. "A second favor?"

"Sounds promising." Laughing, Jacob holds out a hand. "How about these terms? I do what I can to keep you and your brother alive, and in return, you do a couple of things for me in the future."

Searching through the agreement Jacob laid out, I ask, "Exactly how many is a couple?"

His blue eyes glint mischievously. "I guess you'll have to find out."

Warily, I watch Jacob's hand. He's offering me exactly what I've been looking for. A way to ensure Keith and I stay alive, but what will the cost be? What things could the Crown Prince of Myria want me to do for him? His hesitancy to give me a straight answer only adds to my uncertainty. A part of me wants to wait for Keith to wake up and ask for my older brother's opinion. But I already know Keith would never approve. Jacob is tied to the king, so this would never be an acceptable option in his mind.

Staring back into Jacob's eyes, I slide my hand into his, giving it a firm shake of acceptance. My stomach squirms. I hope I didn't just make a terrible decision.

Chapter Forty-Six
Keith

I'VE GROWN TIRED OF being on bed rest, but when Precious and Lydia finally clear me to get up, it only becomes worse.

For an entire week, a rotating guard accompanies me everywhere I go. Aubrey visits me in the mornings and walks me to breakfast. Ryden usually stays with me throughout the day, and Camille joins us as we either practice in the training room or explore the halls. Camille insists on trying to learn the palace better, so it's good practice for her. Then, Miles meets us right before dinner and walks with the group, following along behind me until I retire to my room for the evening.

But the one person I really want to see never visits. As indirectly as I could, I asked Miles about Amaia the second day after I'd left my bed. Miles had gone unusually quiet and simply mumbled that she was fine. Which I had taken as a sign that she was, in fact, not fine.

Dinner tonight is eerily quiet. Even now, Amaia is absent, leaving the rest of her family to occupy the front table. An unspoken fear for tomorrow hangs in the air between all of the competitors. Tomorrow is the sixth Game, marking the halfway point. Whoever survives only has six more to live through.

And if we can make it through the sixth Games, the chances of us surviving the Games skyrockets. I recall something Amaia first said to me and Camille when this whole ordeal started. In the second half, the Games would become less murderous and more focused on training the competitors on how to rule Myria, including exposing their personal life and personality to the public. But that meant that tomorrow would be all about eliminating the most amount of people possible in order to narrow the pool down. That's what King Edward has reinforced at dinner tonight.

I play lazily with my food, threading the thin noodles around my fork before giving up on eating entirely. If I put anything in my mouth, I'm almost certain it will come back up. I push my plate away from me and rise out of my chair. Unsurprisingly, Miles rises to follow me, but I give him a curt shake of my head.

Either Miles is as tired of the babying as I am or he sees something sharp in my eyes, because, thankfully, he gives me an understanding smile and takes his place back at the table. I don't miss Camille's worried glance or Ryden's slight frown, I simply choose to ignore them both as I walk out of the dining room.

I keep my gaze focused on the floor, and this causes me to run straight into what feels like a brick wall. At first, I'm overcome with the urge to laugh at my complete lack of luck. Asher stands tall with his shoulders held high as he sneers at me. Except, Asher is at least half a foot shorter than me, so the intimidating effect is lost.

But my amusement is quick to disappear as Carter and Giler approach, taking their places on either side of Asher. Both of them wear matching evil grins, and instinctively, I take a handful of hurried steps backward.

"Hello, Atwood." Asher spits vehemently.

"Hello, Asher," I reply cautiously.

"Why do I feel like you're always out of commission?" he drawls.

I force a small laugh. "That's a great question that I've been asking myself lately." Carter and Giler's smiles widen, showing their gleaming white teeth.

Asher ignores my response. "And why is Princess Amaia somehow always in the middle of it?"

The question makes me freeze up. "What does she have to do with anything?"

Asher's laugh is cold. "Sometimes you're so oblivious, Atwood. She has to do with *everything* considering we're all killing each other to marry the girl. But what we don't like," —He gestures to his two cronies behind him— "is how she seems to have picked a favorite. And between all of us, you stand no chance of winning. So why would she pick you?"

"Is that so?" I fight to stay calm, even though my heart is racing. "Maybe you guys should try not being complete cold-hearted murderers and see where that gets you." With a shove, I push my way past Asher and slip between Giler and Carter. None of them follow me, but as I walk down the hallway, I feel all three sets of eyes trained on the back of my head.

Needing somewhere to clear my head, I walk to one of the training rooms that Camille, Ryden, and I recently discovered. It's further away from the dining room—and hopefully empty. But as I begin to push the door open, a blade strikes hard against cold concrete, echoing through the room. Slowly peeking around the doorframe, I spot a flash of golden hair.

My mouth hangs open in amazement as I watch Amaia move with powerful, yet graceful strikes. Dummies are set up across the back wall, and half of them are already torn to shreds with blades sticking out of them. Amaia arcs her sword in a wide motion, swiping clean through one of the figures. Her blade glances past the floor before sweeping to strike the next target.

All I can do is stare.

At least until my foot shifts against a loose tile on the floor, and Amaia's eyes shoot across the room. For a moment, we watch each other in an unbreakable staring contest. A part of me is embarrassed for being caught, but a larger part of me wishes she would teach me how to move like that.

Amaia slides her sword into the sheath at her waist and stalks toward a second set of doors from across the room, shattering our silent eye contact.

Moving on instinct, I run to her. "Amaia, wait."

Amaia hesitates, faltering in her steps, but that's all I need to reach her. I place a firm hand on her shoulder, and she swivels around to face me.

"What do you want?" Amaia's voice is dry and emotionless.

"Aubrey told me about what Camille said to you while I was out. I wanted to talk to you about it. I've been trying to find you, but they don't leave me alone for more than a bathroom break. And now that I'm thinking about it, you probably put them up to it."

"I did." Amaia shrugs my hand off her shoulder, but she doesn't leave. Progress. "And what could you possibly want to talk to me about?"

I stare, suddenly drawing a blank on everything I wanted to say to her. "I don't know, Amaia. I just want to talk."

Amaia sighs, her deep blue eyes sad. "Your sister is right."

I fold my arms. "Excuse me?"

"I can't keep putting your life at risk." She throws her hands up in frustration. "It's not worth it. You should focus on winning the Games and not on all these ideas of fighting back. I shouldn't have put them in your head."

"You're wrong," I say, angrily. "I'm deciding to fight on my own. And with or without you, I'd be trying to do the same thing. Don't you understand? It's about what I've seen in the Lates—and now in Salcoast. How could I not want to do something after that? It's my home. So quit taking credit for something that's not on you."

Amaia shakes her head. "But you don't understand. My very presence is making you enemies. The fact that I'm involved draws a lot of attention."

I think back to Asher, Carter, and Giler in the hall. It's true that without Amaia's involvement, they likely wouldn't care about what I was doing. Or maybe they would. Either way, I know I want to fight back—with or without Amaia's help. But the truth is, I don't mind being involved with her. In fact, I like the idea of fighting *with* her.

When she turns to leave again, I reach out a hand. My nimble fingers wrap around her wrist, gently pulling her back toward me. "I don't care about what the other competitors think. I don't care if they give me attention because of you."

I can feel her breath quicken as it brushes against my face. I notice my own breath freezing as my gaze stays evenly on her eyes. Rebellious strands of hair dance freely from her ponytail.

"Yeah, well I do," she says.

And then she's gone.

Chapter Forty-Seven

Camille

FOR THE FIFTH TIME in a row, I find myself lying on the floor trying to catch my breath. Garden leans over me with a frown, a powerful wooden staff hanging in her hand. She has struck me one too many times, and I can't breathe.

"You keep leaving your left side open."

"Thanks," I hiss as I push myself up into a sitting position.

Ryden is watching us from the edge of the small ring, and from here, I can't tell if he's grimacing or laughing. Probably a little bit of both.

Garden holds out a hand and pulls me to my feet. "What's got you distracted?"

It still surprises me every time Garden picks up something that's bothering me. She's surprisingly intuitive.

"I don't know." I shrug, not bothering to attempt a lie. Garden is also unnervingly good at ratting those out.

"Keith's going to be fine," Ryden says. "I think he's just a little wound up from having to relax so much." He ducks under the rope separating him from the arena.

"I suppose."

Since talking to Jacob, a weight has lifted off my chest. In an unexplainable way, I trust Jacob to stay true to his word. I'm confident enough that he needs my help for something and will uphold his end of the bargain to keep it that way.

"Well, no use practicing if you aren't focused," Garden says matter-of-factly.

She's right, but I still bite back the urge to argue. Tomorrow is supposed to be the deadliest Game, and I have to be ready for it. Then the competitors are supposed to get a break.

"Yeah, some sleep will probably be helpful," I mutter.

Garden nods. "Just snap out of it before tomorrow."

With a grateful look, I walk out of the training room alongside Ryden. We've settled into a pattern the past week. I'm getting better at finding my way through this place, but Ryden always walks with me regardless, and it brings me comfort.

I reach out my hand, and he takes it with a smile, giving it a small squeeze of reassurance. Tomorrow is going to be fine.

"Thank you, Ry," I say as we reach my door.

"Of course." Ryden reaches a hand to cup my cheek. "I like our little walks."

"Me too."

Courtesy of the adrenaline still rushing through my body, I lift myself onto my toes, pressing my lips against his for the first time since the night on the roof. He wraps his arms around me, engulfing me in his warmth. I run a hand through his soft hair, trying to keep him there as long as possible. Ryden moves away first, tucking my hair behind my ears as he goes.

"Goodnight Camille." His warm smile lingers on his face, and I can't help but mimic it.

"Goodnight Ryden."

I close the door behind me, eagerly heading to my closet to get out of my sweaty training clothes. I've just pulled a soft cotton shirt over my head when a soft knock sounds from the door.

Hesitantly, I walk over and crack it open. Keith is standing on the other side, wringing his hands nervously. I immediately let my brother in.

Without a word, he enters, pacing around the room with his eyes downcast and his eyebrows furrowed.

Unable to stand the quiet pacing, I press against the silence. "What is it?"

Keith draws in a deep breath before speaking. "I'm sorry for holding it against you for so long." At my confused look, he adds, "You treating Prill the way you did. And the way you've been handling everything. These Games. This place."

I freeze, torn between confusion and guilt. If I'm being honest with myself, the thought of that first Game hasn't crossed my mind in a while. Prill hasn't been able to follow through on her threats of ending me. Not to mention, it seems so insignificant compared to the numerous amount of times Keith and I have nearly died.

"What made you think of that?" I ask.

Keith stops pacing and looks at me. Tears spring to my eyes as I recognize the broken look on his face. He falls on the edge of my bed, face buried in his hands. "I don't know."

I sit next to him and wrap an arm around his shoulder, sending gentle waves of warmth to surround him. "Where did you go with Amaia?"

Keith glances up at me, and I can tell he doesn't want to share. Maybe he even thinks he can't. But with another deep sigh, he whispers, "The Gulf. And it's terrible Cam. They have whipping posts set up and the officers are far more cruel." His voice drifts off before returning, this time cold and distant. "They were going to beat a boy for simply bumping into an officer. Or maybe even kill him, I'm not sure. I tried to help, but I don't know if he got away or not."

My heart breaks for my brother. All these people—Oliver, Axel, and now this other boy—are living in his mind, reminding him of all the things he should've done. I wish I could erase it for him. I wish I could drive it into his brain that none of this is his fault. There's nothing more he could have done for any of them. For a second, he reminds me of Nicole—far too kind of a person to be living in a world like this.

A moment of silence establishes itself between us, two siblings who have been through too much, and silent tears flow down our cheeks.

"I saw Lizzy and Micheal," Keith says eventually.

My eyes widen at the mention of our old friends. "Are they okay?"

"I think so. Lizzy has her gift now. She's a healer."

I know Keith is just searching for something else to talk about, but I'm at a loss for words.

"Do you think dad and mom would be upset with us?" Keith asks.

My tears come to a sudden stop. My next words sound bitter. "Who cares? They're both dead." Immediately realizing my mistake, my stomach seizes.

"What do you mean, both?"

When I remain silent, Keith reaches over and forces me to meet his gaze. "Cam, what do you mean?"

I decide not to pretend. "Our father is dead."

Releasing my shoulders, he settles deeper into the bed's mattress. His whole body sags under the revelation. "When did you find out?"

"The day *you* came back practically dead."

"And you only just told me?" Before I can defend myself, he shakes his head. "Never mind. It doesn't matter. I guess you haven't really had the opportunity to tell me about him."

Guilt gnaws at me with his forgiving words. Plenty of opportunities have arisen. I should have told him about our father's death sooner, but I also should have told him that our father was alive in the first place. It probably would have been wise to let him know that I had my gift long before coming to the palace too. How have I grown so distant from him?

Still deep in his thoughts, Keith stares at my door. "What's happened to us?"It's my turn to sigh. "We've been left with only one option: survive."

Keith shakes his head. "I think it's become bigger than that. We're more invested than when we started."

I want to argue, to defend my point. Instead, I keep myself quiet, watching the sunset through the window. There's truth in his words though. For the same reason Keith feels the need to do something, I feel the need to win. I want us to be safe and out of harm's way. Keith shouldn't have to cry because of the things he's seen. I want to be able to have the power and authority to make changes.

I want to be Queen of Myria.

CHAPTER FORTY-EIGHT

Keith

THE CROWD'S SCREAMS SEEM extra vicious this morning. They know what today is: the final deadly Game intended to drastically narrow down the pool of competitors.

I can't wait to get this over with.

The arena is inside this time, and massive wooden walls have been built between the stadium's bleachers and the arena itself. All the competitors have been placed at the base of the walls—girls and boys alike. The mystery of what lies in the arena only adds to my nerves. I can't see inside, but the harsh crashing of waves against the walls gives away the presence of water. Maybe it's just a swimming contest. I can do that, I tell myself. I know how to swim. But I have a sinking feeling it's not going to be that simple.

The girls won't be able to see the boys compete, and a worried glance from Camille tells me that she doesn't like that part. I understand her fear because I don't know if they'll allow the boys to watch either, and the idea of her dying without me knowing skyrockets my heart rate.

A large group of officers push their way to the front of the competitors, and an officer with a handful of medals on his chest speaks loudly to all. "For this competition, the Game will be played a little differently. The Game is not on a timer and will only finish when seven of you are left alive. Once the bell chimes, it will begin, and you will be teleported inside."

All of us are quiet after the drop of information. That means seven boys and six girls will die today. Miles and I share worried glances, and I can't help but wonder if he and Ryden will be okay. Too quickly, the bell chimes, and my body is jerked away. I land unsteady on my feet next to Ryden, who lands perfectly. Immediately, I survey my surroundings.

I'm standing on the deck of a ship. Over the tall walls of the arena, there are large rows of bleachers, providing the crowd with a good view of the Game. The entire arena is filled over halfway with water. Harsh winds—no doubt the spawn of somebody's gift—send waves crashing against the wooden walls. The ship I'm on creaks back and forth, and it isn't long before my stomach lurches. Camille would always notoriously tease me for my inability to handle the small fishing boats from the Gulf. Just my luck...

Dark, polished, mahogany wood makes up the entire deck, with handrails separating me from the wicked waves below. Elevated at the front of the ship is a large wheel and a giant statue. I can't quite make out what the statue is supposed to be, but if I squint my eyes just right, it resembles King Edward. A towering mast juts out from the center of the deck, decorated with ropes meant for climbing. At the top is a simple crow's nest that overlooks the water.

In each corner of the arena, there are matching boats to the one I'm standing on. Before I can look any further, Ryden shoves me to the floor, taking my feet out from underneath me. As I peer up, I decide that my boat is the worst one. Asher, Carter, and Giler have all spawned next to us, and Asher already has flames dancing along his skin. Ryden dodges Carter's sword, but I'm too slow to roll out from underneath Giler's powerful mace.

A spike slices into my leg, and I grimace in pain. I pull on my gift, launching the black wolf at Giler's face. Quickly testing the durability of my leg, I push myself up, albeit slowly. Ryden duals both Carter and Asher at once, acting as a barrier between me and them.

I wince as I shift more weight onto my leg. Drawing the sword from my waist, I take a step forward to meet Carter. At least, I try to, but I stumble instead. With a humorous smile, Carter advances on me, laughing at my limp.

"Feeling brave, are we?"

"I guess so."

Carter strikes, and instead of countering with my weapon, I duck my head and send a screeching eagle flying at his face. Talons rip into his skin, and Carter's frantic screams make me want to clamp my hands over my ears. With a sweep of my hand, the eagle disappears, replaced by a giant cobra, who is quick to snake its way around Carter's legs. It wraps his legs so tightly that Carter tips over.

With a grunt, I rise to my full height again. My leg still throbs. However, before I can attempt to take another step, I'm teleported away again.

Now I'm on a different boat—this time with two boys I haven't ever talked to. Andrew and Tanner, I think. Both of them are locked in their own battle, and I feel myself start to relax. But it's not long before I'm tackled to the deck. Heat flashes across my vision, setting my exposed skin on fire. Dark burns begin to appear on my arms as Asher wrestles with me.

Clenching my teeth, I call on my wolf again, and it crashes down on Asher, sweeping him off of me with a swipe of its large paw. Gulping down deep breaths of air, I force myself to sit up. My head pounds with every crash of the waves, and nausea settles in. Stuffing down the unease in my stomach, I grapple for my sword. I had dropped it when Asher tackled me.

With a yelp and an ache in my chest, the wolf disappears in a flicker of flames. Asher's teeth are bared in frustration as he leaps for me again. But as he's in midair with the point of his blade hovering above my chest, Asher is blinked off to a different ship.

This leaves me, Andrew, and if the blood-stained deck is any tell, a dead Tanner. Andrew doesn't hesitate before coming toward me, and just in time, I send a bear charging across the wood at him. Andrew plants his feet and takes on the bear, giving me a brief moment to catch my breath.

Shutting my eyes against the pain in my head and leg, I grit my teeth. With the roar of a bear, my eyes spring back open. Andrew stands by himself, a knife in hand. From the sting in my chest, I know the bear is gone. Feeling entirely drained, I search for anything I have left, pulling on the little bit of gift I have left. I can't help but give a delusional chuckle at the sight of the little squirrel that sets itself between me and Andrew. I'd been trying for a rhino, but a squirrel will have to do.

But then I'm teleported away again onto another boat. Miles is on this one, and he immediately jumps to my side. But not in time to support me before I've fallen to my knees, head swaying.

"How do you do this all the time?" I ask, grimacing.

"You get used to it," he says with a pale look on his face. Miles grips me by the shirt and pulls me upright before Carter and Asher can regain their footing.

I groan at the sight of their snarling faces charging toward us. I decide there isn't much point in denying it anymore. Life hates me. Well, at least those who are running this Game hate me.

Neither Miles or I realize there's a fifth boy on the boat until it's too late. Giler charges into me, knocking me off my feet. Already unsteady on my injured leg, I tumble off the edge and into the storming waters.

Immediately, water floods into my mouth as I fight to stay above water. I can barely make out Miles above, hacking away at the three other boys, his gaze hyper focused on blocking their attacks. The crowd's screams rebound against the waves, and it pounds against my skull.

As another wave crashes against me, I inhale water. I sputter as I surface again, but only for a minute. *I'm not going to make it.* As the thought roots itself in my head, my movements slow. *I'm not going to make it.* Hating myself for giving up, I watch as my throbbing leg gives out and the rest of my body stops fighting the waves.

Shutting my eyes, I let myself fall deeper into the waters. Amaia's face is what shoots across my mind as I resign myself to my fate.

Except, Amaia isn't having it. Her arms are folded, staring me down.

"Get up! You don't get to give up here!"

I don't react.

"Get up!"

Something about this girl strikes at my nerves. *I'm trying.*

"Are you really though?"

Her words wake my brain up. She's right. I'm not actually trying. I've given up, and my body doesn't want to fight the waves anymore.

But far too many people have lost their lives to the king's system. Oliver. Nicole. Axel. My father. My mother. I can't let their lives go forgotten and unavenged. Someone has to fight for people like them, and if I die here, it's not going to be me.

I peek open an eye at Amaia's ghostly figure.

"Don't you *dare* give up." This time she says the words softer, like she already knows what I'm going to do.

Then she fades away, and I feel my body drift even farther away from the battling ships above.

Chapter Forty-Nine
Camille

SURPRISINGLY, I'VE MANAGED TO keep myself reasonably calm. I keep my gaze fixed on the royal seats angled perfectly over the arena. Sounds of metal clash against the air, but not once do the shouts of pain worry me. The princess's face of clear and resolute calm keeps me relaxed. Anytime Keith's been in desperate need of help, Amaia's been unable to control her reactions, always appearing on edge. From beside her, Jacob's face is intently focused.

Abruptly, a giant shout echoes across the stands. Even the king's eyes widen, however, it's in excitement rather than fear. My gut instinct warns me that Keith is in danger, so I keep my gaze fixed on the pair of royal siblings, certain that Amaia will react if Keith is in immediate danger. Jacob is leaning forward, his chin resting in his hands, his head bent sideways in curiosity. Amaia's eyes are fixed firmly in the arena, her gaze unwavering.

From beside my elbow, Aubrey whispers, "What's going on?"

"I think they're alright. The princess would be riled up if something was going badly." As soon as the words leave my mouth, Amaia slumps back in her chair. Her eyes slam shut, and her body goes limp. Prince Jacob gives her a sideways glance but says nothing. Only the queen looks concerned for her daughter.

My body goes stiff, and I look around, trying to gauge the officers' reactions. They aren't paying much attention to the female competitors, staying preoccupied with the screaming crowd. The cries are starting to sound more passionate and fearful. My heart races up into my throat, pounding uncontrollably.

Unwilling to sit and do nothing, I push through the other competitors and slip past an officer who is currently pushing back against a herd of sobbing girls. Aubrey's right behind me, following wordlessly. Garden only watches the two of us go, giving me a quick nod of acknowledgement. An unspoken agreement occurs between us, and I know that, if need be, Garden will distract the officers.

We climb against the flow of observers who are all standing from their seats and fighting to get a better look at what is happening in the arena. Thankfully, the crowd doesn't pay us much attention, fully focused on the Game.

As soon as we reach part way up the bleachers, Aubrey gasps. I follow her gaze and my jaw drops. The biggest shark I've ever seen—which is saying a lot considering I lived in the Gulf—is splashing through the waters that take up the entire arena.

The four boats drifting on the waves look so small from up here, especially compared to the shark. The shark heads straight for a boat, and from the flash of flame, I can tell that Asher's atop it. In a rush, I search for Ryden's red hair. Most likely sensing my brain's sudden attention, Ryden's gaze meets mine from across the arena. Thankfully, he's far from the shark.

Silently, I ask him the question I'm dreading the answer to. Ryden points a single finger at the shark, and I realize what he means. Keith isn't dead. The shark hasn't ripped him from limb to limb.

Keith *is* the shark.

And he is going straight for Asher. But as his huge jaws are about to clamp down and break the pitiful boat in half, a bell cuts through the air, signaling the end of the Game. The seven survivors, shark included, blink out of the arena disappearing to who knows where.

Relief sweeps me. Keith made it. And so did Ryden and Miles.

With a jolt, I realize that means it's my turn. Aubrey pulls me back down the bleachers, carving a much easier path as the crowd begins to sit down. A group of middle-aged women spot Aubrey and me and begin screaming and pointing. With a sharp glance from Aubrey, the women immediately stop, and their heads jerk unnaturally back to the arena.

"Did you just... control their minds?" I blink in shock.

In between laborious pants, Aubrey nods. "Yeah, they were going to give us away."

Thankfully, Garden is already standing close to the officer we must slip by. She has his back turned to Aubrey and me as we slink into the group of competitors. Garden gives a small wink in my direction before blinking out of existence.

My own body is torn away, and I'm standing on the deck of one of the ships. Without hesitation, I draw my sword to defend myself against a blow from a raven-haired girl. The girl winces as she gets too close to me and the bubble of scorching air I've surrounded myself with.

Behind me, Garden faces off with another girl. From her strawberry blonde hair, I recognize her as Kiley. In a blink, Kiley disappears, fading into nothingness. Garden is shoved by an invisible hand, and she swirls around sneering. Kiley's invisibility fades, bringing her back into sight as she screams. Her hands flap around her face, warding off some nasty vision from Garden.

I refocus on my fight, sharply striking the raven-haired girl in the temple with the hilt of my sword. She collapses to the deck. I don't even have time to see if she's dead or not before I'm sent toppling onto another boat.

Sabrina leers over me, immediately slicing with her sword. Swiftly, I pinpoint the atoms of her blade and send a rush of heat into each one. Sabrina's sword combusts, sending flickering gray ash through the air.

For once, Sabrina gapes at me in shock. Even I'm surprised by my power, and I nearly tip off the boat from the effort. Shaking myself off, I attempt to bring my sword crashing down on Sabrina's head. I wouldn't mind if Sabrina doesn't survive this. However, Sabrina is quick to react. Using her gift, she jolts my metal blade so it freezes, hovering inches from her neck.

With a curl of her lips, Sabrina pushes my sword out of the way, sending me crashing down with it. As my body hits the deck, the sword clangs out of my hands, and Sabrina swipes it up.

With a vile smile, she says, "That was a cool trick, but not cool enough to save you."

Fruitlessly, I throw my hands up to guard my face as the sword inevitably swings to sever my head. But the sound of metal against metal sends my eyes flying open.

Garden is standing over me, her sword blocking against Sabrina's strike.

"It's a good thing she has friends, isn't it?" Garden twirls her sword.

Sabrina steps back with a hiss. "Traitor!"

Garden growls, "I know how to pick the winning side, Sabrina!"

And then Garden lunges in my defense. Rolling up onto my feet, I stand, desperately searching for some weapon. Before I can find my sword, Prill appears on our deck. Immediately, she lazars onto me and charges, tackling me right back down to the deck.

The two of us wrestle, but I'm quick to throw Prill off me. Silently, I thank Ryden and Garden for insisting I practice every day.

Prill lands on the deck, crouched low. She draws a knife from her belt and sneers at me. "I can't wait to finally kill you."

I don't bother responding. Instead, I throw myself toward my sword. It lies in between Prill, Sabrina, and

Garden's fight. Nobody seems to have the upper hand, each matching all of the blows. Prill leaps for me, knife tight in her grip. My hand wraps around the hilt of my sword as Prill's blade slashes into my side.

My breath leaves my body as blood begins to rush from my wound. Prill laughs as she shoves me over, and my fingers slip away from the sword. My head pounds as I try to focus.

"You'll never embarrass me again!" The pride tinged in Prill's voice drives me off the edge. Reaching deep inside, I let my gift flow freely. It crows in joy as it wraps itself around Prill. I feel the increasing heat coursing through her body. This time when she screams, I decide it will be her last. Tears flicker in her eyes as she stumbles, mouth gaping open.

I push myself up, hoping that I can turn to help Garden. As I stand, I feel Prill's life wane away. I glance down at her, some kind of cruel satisfaction taking root as she draws her last breath.

I swipe up her discarded knife, loosely gripping the handle. Looking back toward Sabrina and Garden, I bring my arm up, ready to throw the knife. But Sabrina and Garden are locked so closely together, I can't throw the weapon without possibly hitting Garden.

I hiss in frustration.

Using my gift on Prill has drained me, and for the first time, my heat responds weakly, with only enough power to make Sabrina uncomfortably warm.

In my moment of hesitation, Sabrina moves faster than I can process. She ducks underneath Garden's arm and drives her blade directly into Garden's chest. My friend's mouth springs open in surprise as she looks down at the blade projecting from her body. She drops her weapon.

My head pounds as a guttural scream tears itself from my mouth. Launching the knife from my hand, I hit Sabrina's arm, but the golden flakes in her eyes only glitter menacingly. She leans down to Garden's ear. "Doesn't look like the winning side from here."

Garden's body collapses on the boat with a thud. Before I can act on the rage coursing through my veins, I feel my body being ripped away. Horns echo, signaling the end of the Game, as I'm torn away from Sabrina's sneering smile and Garden's dead body. It feels like the Game went by in a matter of seconds. Only a few moments ago, Garden had been covering for Aubrey and me. Only yesterday, we were laughing together in her room.

Now, I'm being teleported to my room. I ignore the immediate sharp knock on the door and the ache stemming from the wound in my side. Instead, I fall to my knees and bury my head in my hands. The tears don't come like

I expect them to. Instead, all I can feel is a mounting, burning rage inside of me.

Sabrina will burn for this.

CHAPTER FIFTY

Keith

I'M GETTING SICK OF waking up in bed with a pounding headache. This time feels different though. In the past, when I've woken up after going unconscious, my entire body ached. But this time, I feel like jumping out of bed and running a couple of laps around the palace.

Opening my eyes, I'm not surprised to find myself in my room with a plate of steaming warm food laid out next to me. The smell of roasted chicken and potatoes warms my insides. Distantly, I wonder if someone in the kitchen knows this meal is my favorite. But I forget all about the food when I catch sight of the figure lying in an armchair next to my bed.

Amaia looks peaceful in her sleep. Her golden hair falls in waves against her face, and her shoulders are slumped instead of held straight. Her mouth is slightly parted as she takes little breaths. Beautiful. It's the only word I can think of to describe her.

The longer I watch her, the more I feel like something's changed between us.

Don't you dare give up.

The words she had said, even if only as a figment of my imagination, hit me like a ton of bricks. If I focus, I can almost feel her heartbeat in time with mine. As if pulled by an invisible string, I stand up from the bed. I reach over to her face and gently move a strand of her hair away from her lips.

At my light touch, Amaia's eyes shoot open. Any serene part of her body disappears as her shoulders straighten and she eyes me curiously. Unsure of what to do, I watch her, my hand paused midair.

"What are you doing?" Amaia asks softly.

I shrug. "You were chewing on your hair. I thought I'd help."

Amaia blushes, but she's quick to regain her composure. She's also quick to shift in her seat, putting more distance between us. I return my hand to my side, fighting off the disappointment at her rejection.

"How are you feeling?" she asks.

"Like I've been thrown across a room fifty times, but somehow, I still want to run a marathon."

A small smile peaks across Amaia's face, making me grin. "I'm glad that you're doing alright." When she leans back against the chair and flutters her eyelids closed, I sit on my bed, simply observing her.

My knee bounces as I fight off the question which threatens to burst out of me. Amaia's ghost of a smile dances across her face, even as she keeps her eyes closed. "Go ahead and ask. I know that you want to."

"What happened? The last thing I remember is drowning." My voice breaks, and I quickly clear my throat. "I remember drowning and then... I remember you, and now I'm here."

Amaia sits up straight again, her eyes bright with curiosity. "You remember me?"

My face brightens, and I study a spot behind her head. I nod. "Yeah, you were talking to me or something." Amaia's puzzled face unnerves me. "It wasn't a big deal. Just like some pre-death image, I suppose."

"And that's all you remember?" Amaia fidgets with her fingers.

"Yes, that's what I said, isn't it?"

Amaia ignores the hint of sarcasm in my words. Instead, she rises from the chair and begins pacing in the middle of the room. I don't fail to notice that the action also effectively puts more space between the two of us.

"I'm going to do my best to explain what happened. There are still things I can't share with you yet." At my exasperated face, she holds up a finger. "I promise you'll know soon. It's just not entirely my story to tell."

"Then whose is it?"

My question is genuine. Any of my annoyance at her habit of withholding information hasn't resurfaced. Not yet. Slowly the adrenaline from waking up is sinking away and a part of me wants to lay back down. I don't feel like starting an argument with Amaia right now.

She looks at me, almost sadly. "Soon, Keith. But I can tell you that in the Game today, you transformed into a shark."

It's my turn to stand up. "What do you mean? I can't turn into a shark. I might be able to call one with my gift, but I can't transform into animals myself. That's not how it works." I look down at my hands, eyeing them in case they turn into flippers. "How do you know it was me?"

"I don't know. Maybe it's because after the Game everyone was teleported back to their rooms, and the officer who was in charge of transporting you sent a shark back here." The humor in her tone is clear.

I glance around my room in disbelief and almost start to laugh at the thought of a full-grown shark in my room. As I look around, nothing is shattered into pieces as I would imagine a shark flailing around would cause...

As if sensing my question, Amaia answers before I can ask. "My father wasn't too fond of you destroying things. He sent up an army of servants to fix your room with their gifts."

Something is still bothering me, so I ask my next question cautiously. "Is it possible for somebody to have two gifts?"

Amaia hesitates, looking anywhere but at me. "It's never been recorded."

"What does the king think about my newfound talent? Surely he's curious about how I could have two gifts, isn't he?"

Suppressing a proud smile, Amaia finally makes eye contact with me. "Well, he doesn't necessarily know. The officer in charge of you for the Game is loyal to *me*. He told me about how he sent you to your room, but that you were a shark, so I immediately came to check on you. But by the time I got to your room, you were knocked out on your bed, soaking wet. However, the room was a mess. My father heard about the destruction in your room and came in demanding to know what you had done. I told him you had gotten angry, and I had knocked you over the head as a way to subdue you. He thinks the shark he saw in the arena was a projection like your other animals... and not actually *you*."

"So, now he thinks I'm some crazy angry psychopath?"

"Better than knowing you have two gifts." Amaia's pointed look is unnecessary. I have an idea of what the king would do to me if he found out I was a new puzzle for him to attempt to work out. And it wouldn't be pleasant.

"What about you? What's your gift? What about the—"

I break off, my hand frozen in the act of gesturing between myself and Amaia. *What about the cord tying us together? Unless you don't feel it. Unless I'm making it up.* But no, even now, I can feel her nerves ratcheting higher—and not from any outwardly expressed signs. I just know it.

It's the same way I know she isn't going to answer my question. She looks at me, a pained expression in her eyes. She wants to tell me. That, I'm sure of.

"I can't. Not yet."

Instead of arguing like I might have on any other day, I fall back onto my bed. "Okay, fine." I fix my eyes on the ceiling in contemplation. At my silence, Amaia walks back to the chair and sits down. I close my eyes, but before I completely drift off again, I say, "You're going to have to tell me eventually."

"I promise you I will. Soon."

"I'm starting to hate that word."

Amaia's light chuckle is the last thing I hear before fading back asleep.

431

CHAPTER FIFTY-ONE
Camille

IT DOESN'T TAKE LONG for Ryden to come knocking on my door. As soon as I hear him, I throw it open.

"Where is he?"

Ryden's hands shoot up in an apology. "I can't take you to see him."

"Why?" I snarl.

Ryden winces and I force myself to take a deep breath. There's no need for me to take out my anger on him. Steadying my voice, I try again. "Why can't I see him?"

Ryden's eyes are fixed on a spot past my forehead, pointedly refusing to make eye contact with me. "He's in recovery. He needs his rest."

My hands land on my hips. Gratefully, the cut from Prill had been shallow and the healers made quick work of patching the wound up. "Who said that?" Letting my frustration get the best of me, I don't let Ryden answer. "Oh, wait! I bet I know. Princess Amaia!"

Ryden nods, his green eyes finally meeting mine. Momentarily, my anger fades, but it doesn't last long enough as the image of the giant shark flashes through my mind.

Exhausted, I step backward onto my bed, throwing my head into my hands. Ryden is quick to join me, his warm, strong hands wrapping around my cold ones. I lean my head into his shoulder, breathing in the comforting smell of pine and the woods.

"Is he okay at least?"

I feel Ryden's head nod against my temple. "Amaia's watching over him."

With that simple sentence, what little relaxation I had felt is vaporized. "What?" I feel my back go straight and my gift begins to coil in my stomach. "Why does she get to be there if he needs rest?"

Ryden closes his eyes in defeat. "I don't know Camille. Now, can you please calm down, or at least stop yelling at me? I can't take you to see him. I have direct orders. I'm sorry."

Guilt aches in my stomach at the pure exhaustion in his voice. Taking a good look at him, I notice his knuckles are bruised and many shallow cuts have been etched onto his arms. Resting my forehead on his temple and listening to his deep sigh, I whisper, "I'm sorry."

And before I stay there wrapped in Ryden's arms for the rest of the day, I get up and head for the door.

Ryden's voice is surprised as his eyes fling open. "Where are you going?"

"To find someone else to yell at."

Without anyone to guide me, it takes longer than I had hoped. But still, I manage to find my way. I walk down the boys' hallway, steam furling in my wake as I march toward Keith's door. However, moments before I can reach it, Miles is in front of me with a wicked grin on his face.

"Not surprised to see you here, princess."

"Move out of my way!" I growl, not interested in his antics.

"Yeah, you see... Can't do that."

I throw up my hands. Miles leans his face back to avoid the scorching heat dancing from my fingertips. "He's my brother! Let me through!"

Miles narrows his eyes. "And he's my friend." He folds his arms, thoroughly unimpressed by my snarl. "So, I'm sorry, princess, but the world doesn't revolve around you. If it did, I think I'd much rather be in a different one."

I open my mouth again to demand that he let me see Keith, but he puts a harsh finger to my lips, shocking me into silence. "Listen, I want to know how he's doing just as much as you do. But what you need to learn—and learn quickly—is that Amaia cares about him just the same. And she has his best interest at heart, so please just give her a little trust." With a curve of his lips, he adds, "It would really make my life a whole lot easier."

Deciding that brute force and anger isn't getting me anywhere, I switch tactics. "Or you could just—" I mimic walking past him with my fingers. "Let me through and nobody would be the wiser?"

Miles laughs. "Did you really think that would work?"

I frown. "Not really. But why can't I go in and see my own brother?"

Miles sighs, and I fight the urge to punch him in his condescending face. "There's things out there that are bigger than you. Unless you realize that, you're going to be spending your life trying to chase answers to things that don't matter."

It's my turn to laugh. "Wow, where did that come from?"

At Miles's glare, I intentionally smirk. *Maybe if I can annoy him enough, he'll let me pass.*

But he doesn't budge. Miles rolls his eyes. "You are exasperating."

Before I can try another angle of getting past him, a sharp ringing pierces the air. This alarm sounds different from last time, and I know Miles recognizes it too.

He's quick to react, grasping my elbow and jerking me toward him as he whisks us away. In the blink of an eye, I'm standing in front of a cot. It's the same one I'd claimed the last time we had to use this safe room. Instead, this time, I wasn't the one unlikely to get inside in time.

Without thinking, I hurl myself at Miles who catches my wrists with ease. "What's your problem now?" he hisses at me.

He forces me to sit down on the cot. Desperately, with my heart pounding outside of my chest, I fight to break out of his hold. His rough hands hold firm.

"Keith is out there!" I sound desperate. "How is Keith going to get down here? You left him!"

Miles's usual cheerfulness is gone. "He'll be fine." He points to the front of the room. The royal family has already flooded in—minus one blonde princess. "See? Amaia will get him here."

Still helplessly struggling against his hold, I yell at him. "Why did the alarm sound different?" From his flinch, I get my answer. "Last time it was a drill, wasn't it? This time it's real. People are in the palace, aren't they?"

Miles doesn't answer. Instead, he blows a strand of his messy hair from his eyes. He's not even looking at me. His face is intently fixed on the tense officers surrounding the king. "Stay here, will you?"

Before I can refuse to promise that, Miles lets go of my wrists and walks toward the front of the room. Immediately, I rise from the cot, but I'm intercepted by a pair of fiery red-haired twins.

Ryden wraps me into his arms for a quick embrace. His lips brush the top of my head so briefly I doubt anyone notices. Aubrey is right behind him, crushing me in between her arms and her chest. The act surprises me. I didn't know Aubrey was the hugging type.

"Did Miles get Keith?" Aubrey asks as she pulls away.

Fear flashes through me hot as a knife. Miles left him. I feel like I can't breathe.

"No! I don't know where Keith is. And I don't know what's going on here. Sure, Amaia's probably with him, but that doesn't comfort me at all. I don't trust her!"

Aubrey flinches away from the spit that flies from my mouth.

"Go find Miles and our father. See if they need help." Ryden smoothly intercedes, stepping between us. "Come on. Just sit down."

He gently takes my hand. I could tear away from him and sprint toward the exit to find my brother if I wanted. But there's something in Ryden's eyes that begs me not to. So, I don't.

I let him lead me back to the cot, and we both sit. Trying to remind myself to take long, deep breaths, I attempt to slow my racing heart.

He'll be okay.

He'll be okay.

Nothing's going to happen to him.

He'll be okay.

Not like Garden.

The thought has my whole body frozen over—almost literally. Ryden reaches for an extra blanket and wraps it around me, pulling me close to his body. Garden isn't okay. What if Keith isn't either?

My body starts shaking. With grief, terror, or the cold, I'm not sure.

Ryden murmurs into my ear, "Ask me any question, and I'll answer it completely honestly."

I know what he's doing. He's trying to distract me from the constant thoughts pulsing through my head. Keith dead in a hallway. Garden skewered by someone she used to call a friend. But I'm grateful for the attempt, so I try to play along.

"What's your favorite color?" I tease, fighting to keep my voice steady.

Ryden looks at me incredulously. "Seriously? You were just yelling at me for keeping things from you, and now that you have the chance to get answers, you go with, 'What's your favorite color?'"

His crooked grin has me smiling. "It's an important question."

"Green." His voice drops. "But not just any green. The color of my eyes is too light." The look on his face is too intense for us to be sitting in a bunker waiting for news that my brother is still alive. "But yours." A rush of heat floods my cheeks. "Perfect."

I clear my throat, still struggling to keep my voice even. "See, it's an important question. Along the same importance level of my other question. Who's attacking the palace?"

"I said only one question." But Ryden is already frowning as if deciding how to answer. "I can't be positive. But it's likely rebels."

"Rebels are this close?"

Ryden nods. "Yeah, we've been getting reports of them getting closer every day. That's why we had the drill."

I smack him on the arm.

"What was that for?" He demands.

"You knew it was a drill?"

"Oh..." Ryden rubs the back of his neck. "Yeah, I did. The different pitches in the alarm give out information. But that's beside the point. Plus, you look cute when you're frazzled."

I smack him again, this time more playfully.

Aubrey and Miles show up seconds later. Aubrey is breathless and Miles is looking pointedly at me. Ignoring Miles, I look at Aubrey. "What is it?"

"They made it in."

CHAPTER FIFTY-TWO
Keith

THE SCREAMING OF AN alarm bell is not a pleasant way to wake up. This one echoes at a louder pitch than the last, sounding more urgent. Before I can roll myself out of bed, Amaia's reaching for me. The blanket she had been using is tossed aside as she holds her hand out to steady me.

"You're going to have to stand up." I don't bother telling her that much is obvious.

"What's going on?"

"Rebels are at the palace's borders." She cocks her ear, listening carefully to the ringing. "They haven't gotten through yet, but we're not going to risk King Edward's officers failing."

Keeping a hand outstretched for me to maintain my balance on, she strides across the room to my closet. She doesn't hesitate to step inside. Her fingers move quickly against the wall. With a click of a button, a portion of the wall shifts, revealing a dark tunnel. Wrinkling my nose at the smell, I follow her into the passage.

Carefully, she slides the wall back into place before placing a sturdy dagger into my hand. "Don't lose it. I only have two of them."

The ringing is even louder in the tunnels, echoing off the stone walls. I curse my own feet for stumbling against the scattered loose rocks. I lose track of how many times I almost fall flat on my face. Determined to regain some of my strength, I gently push away Amaia's hand every time she tries to offer support.

"Why did you seem panicked when you said they were at the walls?" I ask in between labored breaths.

Even in the dim light of the tunnel, I can see Amaia look at me strangely. "I'm not panicking." But something in my gut tells me she is. Maybe she doesn't even realize it. "Let's just get to the safe room." Her words are clipped. Maybe she *does* realize it.

Giving up, I focus on taking deep breaths as my feet fight to keep pace with Amaia's long, powerful strides. A rock bigger than the loose pebbles I've been stepping on juts out of the floor. Instead of sidestepping it, my foot hits it, and this time, I do hit the ground. Pain rolls through my entire body, but Amaia doesn't let me stay down. She grabs me by my shirt and pulls me up as if I weigh nothing.

"Stop being stubborn and accept my help."

"Stop being stubborn and tell me what's really going on," I counter.

Amaia freezes and glares at me. "Hurry up!"

She pushes me to run almost full out. Dreading the embarrassment that is sure to happen if I fall on my face for a second time, I try to keep pace. My legs feel steadier than before, as if falling to the ground earlier had improved their stability. Shaking my head at the backwardness of the situation, I propel my feet even faster, matching Amaia's stride.

Something is nagging me, and it has to do with the strength I can feel in my legs compared to her heavy breathing.

And yet, still, even with my surefooted feet, when Amaia comes to a screeching halt, I run straight into her. Thankfully, I don't fall backward.

Amaia holds a finger against my lip, keeping me silent. But I don't need the warning. Blades clash above us through a grated gap in the tunnel's ceiling. Carefully, Amaia skirts to the edge of the tunnel, staying clear from the light flickering through the slats. I follow her steps carefully, avoiding the loose rocks.

The sounds of fighting don't pause as we cross and continue hurrying down the tunnel. The rebels are inside the palace.

A part of me wants to turn around and ask the rebels how I can help. Maybe they'd give me a sword, and I could fight off some of the king's officers.

"Stop!" Amaia hisses at me, although I don't need the vocal command. Since I've already ran into her once, I'm being careful about keeping my distance in case of any more sudden stops. "When I open this, you need to sprint as fast as you can for the far door. The doors will already be closing if they haven't been shut already. Don't stop until you're through."

Without giving me time to respond, Amaia hits one of the stones in the wall, and a compartment slides out. Directly across from us is the slowly shutting doors to the safe room. I obey Amaia's directions, sprinting as hard as my legs can carry me. People have already gathered in the room, although none look in my direction. With an extra burst of adrenaline and speed, I push myself through the doors. I look behind me for Amaia but she's barely jogging. She looks like she's too far behind me to catch up...

The doors shut.

"The princess is still out there!" I shout into the room.

Everyone looks at me, including the king and queen.

"You have to open the door!" I plead. "Just for a minute little longer."

The lack of a reaction from anyone makes me want to scream.

"Don't you get it! Your princess is out there, and you're going to leave her to die!" I'm speaking directly to the king, for once unafraid of his dark eyes. He meets my gaze, an amused smile playing on his face.

"Keith, you can calm down. I'm fine." Amaia's voice speaks softly from behind me. I jump around, relief crashing through me. Not caring who might threaten me for it later, I wrap my arms around her and bring her toward me. She lets me hug her, but she doesn't hug me back. I didn't expect her to, but some part of me still deflates at her sudden coldness.

I release her, and she leaves me with only a sharp nod. King Edward carefully watches us both, his wicked smile never changing. My eyes challenge his for a handful of seconds before another figure tackles me from the side.

"Thank goodness you're alive." Aubrey's voice is muffled against my shirt. Camille follows behind Aubrey, and when she turns to me, her eyes soften and sparkle with tears.

"Are you alright?" Camille asks.

I give her a nod, but I can tell she doesn't buy it. While certainly not shaky anymore, my legs feel like they're going to collapse under me. I swear the contents of my stomach are about to spill everywhere. Amaia's unusually cold eyes don't help.

Wrapping a helpful hand around my shoulders, Miles supports me as we walk back toward the cots they've chosen. Camille immediately takes her place beside me while Aubrey, Ryden, and Miles sit directly across from us.

Camille gives my hand a gentle squeeze and a look that says she has things to talk to me about. Raw emotion lingers in her eyes, and I can tell it's not just from my near-death. I notice Garden, who has become a consistent member of our group, is nowhere to be found. Her curt nod is all the confirmation I need.

I admire Camille for her restraint. I can tell from the way her gaze keeps flicking across the room to Sabrina that she's holding a tight rein on the emotions raging through her. Carter also stands off to the side, shooting daggers at my sister. Prill isn't at her usual place by his side.

"Anyone want to tell me what I missed?" I ask.

Camille's eyes go dark, but she nods. "Only if you tell us what happened to you."

CHAPTER FIFTY-THREE
Camille

I SPEND THE EVENING listening in silence to Aubrey and Miles catch Keith up on everything that had happened since the Game. Keith's transformation, Garden's death, and Amaia's state of unconsciousness...

At the last one, Keith develops a frown. "What happened to her?"

"I've been wondering the same thing," I say.

Aubrey and Miles shrug it off, but I swear they exchange a glance. I don't push it because they also leave out the part where I killed Prill. I'm not ready to see the disappointment in my brother's eyes.

The conversation peters out after that, and we all go to our separate cots. If I'm being honest, I desperately want to take a pause from the craziness of today and rest my eyes. It's easier to drift off than I expect, but flashes of Garden's pale face, Sabrina's rage, Prill's scream, and

Keith's dead body have me snapping awake in cold sweats throughout the night.

Hours later, when the doors finally open, I'm beyond grateful for the freedom they present. Aubrey, Keith, and Miles are quick to get up and head for the exit. Keith shoots me a quick glance as Ryden hangs back with me. He gives me a small smile and then faces forward again, tossing an arm around Miles and Aubrey's shoulders.

They talk in hushed whispers, and I wonder what they're talking about. Strangely, Keith hasn't spoken much about his side of the story or his journey to the safe room.

Everyone is as eager to get out of the bunker as I am, but even as Ryden reaches for my hand, I gently shake my head. "I'm going to hang back for a little bit. I have somebody I want to talk to."

Ryden raises an eyebrow as if he wants to protest. But I can see the tiredness battling in his brain, and I watch it win. With a small nod, he says, "Okay, be careful."

He leaves—albeit a bit hesitantly. I don't doubt Ryden knows exactly who I want to talk to.

King Edward and his queen have already exited, leaving Prince Jacob and his sister to ensure that everyone gets out of the room before the officers shut the door. The prince is the first one to see me approaching. He smiles, seemingly amused by my plan. With a tap on the shoulder, Jacob gets his sister's attention. He jerks his head in my direction, and immediately, her icy blue eyes find me.

With a sigh, Amaia leans over to whisper something to Jacob. He nods and waves his hand in dismissal, still watching me carefully. Ignoring him, I follow after Amaia as she walks from the room.

She doesn't look back at me once, but I know she's aware that I'm right behind her. Still, in case I'm wrong, I keep my footsteps as quiet as I can against the marble floor. As we clear the immediate hallway, Amaia's pace begins to quicken, and she lengthens her strides. I grit my teeth in frustration as I half-jog to keep up. Even if I knew where she was going, I wouldn't have any idea of how to get there.

She finally leads me into a new room that I've never been in before. Books cram up nearly every inch of space on the walls, and shelves line the floors, holding even more books. I don't try to hide my admiration for the library. At least, not until I tear my gaze away from the books and focus on Amaia.

She stands with her feet apart and her arms folded against her chest. A sword dangles from her waist and two smaller blades are strapped to her thigh. Her expression is unimpressed, and for a moment, I wonder if she's planning on gutting me with her blade. Nobody else is in the room. Nobody else would know.

Pushing the thought aside, I try to match her confidence. I hold my head up straight and stare her directly in the eyes.

"What do you want, Atwood?" Her voice is cool and composed.

"I want to know how you're connected to my brother," I say.

She cocks her head at me. I feel like I'm a bug and she's trying to decide whether she wants to squish me underneath her boot or let me scurry away. "It's none of your concern."

Her collected tone is what sets me off the edge. "He's my brother. Of course, it's my concern," I snarl. "And if you want something from him, you're going to have to go through me."

Amaia's eyes narrow. I wonder if she can also feel the temperature of the air rising with my voice. She takes a step toward me, pointing with her finger. "You have to get yourself under control. I think you've got heart, but not enough brain to use it."

Her words only enrage me. "What do you want with my brother? Why are you so interested in him? Why have you sent your cronies on him since the moment we got here?" I don't bother trying to keep my tone relaxed.

Something like rage flashes through her eyes. Unease pricks at me. She's going to murder me right here in this gorgeous library. But then... She leans away from me, looking at me curiously. "You ask all the wrong questions, Camille. I'm looking out for your brother, and I'm looking out for you too. It would be ideal if the two of you could just decide to trust me."

I pause, halted at the sudden exhaustion of her words. A part of me wants to comfort her somehow. Maybe give her a reassuring pat on the back and tell her everything is going to be okay. But it's only a small part of me. So instead, I say, "Your father is King Edward, so please understand me when I say I'm incapable of trusting you until you give me a reason to."

And with that, I stride toward the exit of the library.

Chapter Fifty-Four

Keith

IT'S ANOTHER HANDFUL OF days before I give up on waiting for Amaia to come to me. After breakfast, ignoring protests from Miles, I decide to go and find her myself. I have questions about the rebel attack, and this time, I'm going to get answers.

Aubrey and Miles have already both refused to take me to her.

"It's your skin, not mine," Miles says, raising his hands in defense. "I'll be deader than dead if she finds out I took you to her when she's asked me not to. Multiple times, I'll have you know."

Aubrey simply ignores my question, stuffing her mouth full of pancakes to avoid answering.

Leaving them both behind at the breakfast table, I rely on my vague memories of when she brought me to her room before. A maid scurries by me as I head through the hallways, her head ducked low. Reaching out a hand to

452

stop her, I ask gently, "Do you know where the princess is?"

The girl looks at me with timid eyes. She opens her mouth, but no words come out. I move my arm out of her way so she can continue about her business. She hurries down the hallway without a second glance.

I try to fight off my disappointment but still find my shoulders sagging. As quickly as it appears, my disappointment evaporates.

"Hi, Mr. Atwood!" Willow's cheerful voice echoes through the hallway. "I heard you ask Rianna where to find Amaia just now. I can show you the way to her room if you'd like." Proudly, she holds up a sealed envelope. "I have to deliver this to her anyway."

Smiling brightly at the young girl, I say, "Thank you so much. That would be greatly appreciated."

She beams at me before skipping ahead, leading the way. The two braids snaking their way down her back dance with every step.

The halls start to look familiar, and I recognize her door before Willow stops outside of it. "Here, you can take this." She hands me the letter, giving me a wink. "It'll give you an actual excuse to be here." Then she bounces away. I watch her go with a smile on my face. It's nice to see that her innocence has still managed to survive in this place.

Turning to face the door, my heart starts thudding against my chest. Nerves jolt through my body as I reach up and knock. I hear footsteps near the door even before it peeks open.

Amaia's eyes widen in surprise as she takes me in. "What are you doing here?"

I hold out the envelope Willow gave me. "Delivering this."

She rolls her eyes, reaching for the letter. I snatch it away from her. "You promised me answers."

Hesitantly, she glances behind her back in her room. "Right now?"

"Only if you want this right now," I say, waving the envelope.

Amaia looks at me with a mix of frustration, amusement, and maybe even some respect. Glancing behind her again, she reluctantly opens her door farther. "Fine, you can come in."

I step through the door, a proud smile on my face, but that immediately falls away as I take in the other person in the room.

She watches me nervously, her hands tapping rapidly against her legs. Her black hair, so similar to Camille's,

is tied behind her head into a loose bun. But her eyes...
Her eyes are like mine.

Amaia stands behind me, nervously looking between
the woman and me.

"Mom?" I whisper.

Tears spring to her eyes as she opens her arms. Without
a second thought, I fall into her embrace. She cradles a
hand to my head, hugging me close. Consciously aware of
Amaia carefully watching us with a guarded expression,
I only allow myself a brief moment to inhale my mother's
warmth before leaning back. "What...? How...? How are
you here?"

My mother just shakes her head, her eyes still sparkling
with tears. "I've been waiting for the right time to tell
you, but the king's been watching so carefully." She takes
my face in her hands. "I couldn't risk him finding me."

I'm still reeling from the fact that my mom is in front
of me. Alive and breathing. And not killed like the rest of
the ungifted. "How did you escape? How are you alive?"
A terrible thought forms in my head. "Did Dad know?"

Sharp sadness forms in my mother's eyes. "Yes, your
father knew. It's a very long story, but King Edward must
never know I'm here. I work in the kitchens as my cover,
but I meet with Amaia when I can." Tears glisten in her

eyes as she cups my face in her hands. "You've grown up so much. I'm so proud of you."

I fight back the tears that threaten to spill down my cheeks. "I don't know if you should be."

My mother's face hardens, but not in anger at me. "I was devastated that you and your sister were getting sent to compete in the Games, and it's one of the things I regret most about your father's plan. But I've watched every Game. And yes, I *am* proud of you."

"You knew about Father's plan? How?"

My mother bites her lip just like she always does when I ask a hard question. Her voice is just above a whisper. "I helped organize it."

Realization dawns on me, and things begin to click together. However, before I can ask any more about my mother's involvement with the rebels, Amaia gently clears her throat.

I turn to look at her, and my happiness at seeing my mother dies in my throat. The envelope I had given her hangs loosely in her hands, the seal torn. Her face is sheet white, and she's looking at my mother, terrified.

"What is it?" My mother's tone shifts to something more serious.

I move out of the way so she can reach for the letter. Amaia hands it over, her eyes unfocused. While my mom's eyes rapidly scan the paper, I approach Amaia.

"What is it?" I repeat.

She shakes her head. "I'm sorry. We shouldn't have gone. We shouldn't have risked it."

"Shouldn't have risked *what*?" I ask again, my voice rising in volume.

My mom's voice scares me. I've never heard her sound so lifeless. "They've murdered everyone in Salcoast. Dragged them out of all of their homes and killed them in the streets. They're burning the bodies tomorrow."

The words hit me like an avalanche. I imagine all the people I've grown up with. Patty at the bakery. The kind school teacher I had when I was five years old. The man who used to walk down the streets with his little daughter, always waving good morning when I saw him. Lizzy and Micheal.

My eyes shoot to Amaia's. I know she sees the fire in me. It matches the rage building in her.

I'm done settling for survival in this place. I'm ready to start fighting.

The Story
Continues In...

A Secret
To Kill

THE CROWNING GAMES
BOOK 2

Acknowledgments

First off, I want to say a huge thank you to all of you for taking the time to, not only get a copy of A Call For Blood, but also for reading all the way through it! You guys are awesome, and I can only hope you enjoyed reading Keith and Camille's story as I did while writing it!

To all of my beta readers, thank you for putting up with the early versions of this story and being my biggest cheerleaders throughout this process. You've seen this story from the very beginning and somehow still had good things to say about it!

Of course, shout out to my amazing line editor, Danielle Herrington! I loved getting to work with you and appreciate all the comments you sent me and the encouragement you provided throughout the entire process.

To everyone in the bookstagram community, thank you for all the support and love you've given this story before you've even read it! You guys remind me that there are people who want to read my writing and are who inspire me to keep writing stories.

Also, shout out to everyone in my Writing Buddies discord and to Emma Hill and Stephanie Crachiolo. Without those writing sprints, this book would only be partially through the first draft and definitely nowhere near the finished project it is today.

And I appreciate all of my ARC readers and those who read a copy of my book before release. Every time I received a message from any of you it absolutely made my day. You guys are awesome!

Thank you to my college friends: Meadow, Sabrina, and Caleb. You guys are awesome and I'm beyond grateful for the role you've played in my life and the encouragement you all always provide.

And thank you to my family! Mom, Dad, David, Joshua, Rachel. You have all taught me the importance of family and what it means to always have each other's backs. Never once have you ever told me something is impossible, and you've always been ready to support me no matter what my newest endeavor is.

I know they're about to have a page to themselves, but I also want to reiterate how grateful I am for my Kickstarter backers who made all of this even possible through their support.

But most importantly, I want to give a huge shout out to God. He deserves all the praise for placing me where I am at in life and shifting me in ways, that while may originally seem uncomfortable, are all for my own good. Without Him placing me where I'm at today, none of this would be possible. I wouldn't be writing anything, much less publishing a book.

Kickstarter Backers

These are the amazing people who believed so much in "A Call For Blood", they backed it through Kickstarter before it was released!

Abby Johansen	Jacqueline Villarreal
Adeline Franklin	Julie Colburn
Althea Balisi	Karen Bulgarelli
Amanda Balter	Kimberleigh Dixon
Amanda Bethard	Laurie Colburn
Amber Dilday	Lisa Clément-Guy
Angela Morse	Lucas C. Kascher
Cortney Babcock	Macey Keller
Danielle Harrington	Megan Astell
Dave & Terri	Meghan Duzrichko
David Holzborn	Melody F. Barney
Deborah Knackstedt	Nichole Heydenburg
Emma Hill	Olympe Challot
Eric Gorden	Samantha Newberry
Gaby Tabora	Sara Francis
Haleigh Collier	Stephanie Crachiolo
Holly Morgan	Susan Butts

Thank you all so much!!!

If you're interested in following along on Kickstarter for the rest of the series, check out the author's profile.

About the Author

Natalie Colburn is a young adult, Christian writer, who lives in Arizona. She spends her time reading any book she can get her hands on and writing about any idea that flows into her mind. While this is her first YA Fantasy novel, she's written a poetry book, Me Through Us, and has future plans including other fairytale retellings, romance, and dystopian novels.

When she's not writing, Natalie is most likely with her friends or her Australian Shephard, Marshall. She loves to play board games, listen to Taylor Swift, and swing dance. Her favorite food group is potatoes and if she had to choose to be friends with any character in A Call For Blood, she'd pick Miles or Princess Amaia!

Natalie hopes that her words can give the readers a place to dream and inspiration that they too can accomplish what they put their mind to. Her stories are to provide hope in a world that sometimes can seem so hopeless.

KEEP IN TOUCH!

NatalieColburnWrites

NatalieColburnWrites@gmail.com

Consider leaving a review on Goodreads and Amazon to help spread the word about A Call For Blood!

What Character From A Call For Blood Are You?

While you were reading, did you find yourself wondering what character you are? Well, here's a quick, fun quiz, made by the author, in order to find out!

Scan the QR code to find out which character from A Call For Blood you are!

Author Q & A

Is A Call For Blood a standalone or a series? If it's a series, how many books do I have planned for it?

Yes, A Call For Blood is the first book in the Crowning Games series. As of right now, the series will be four books long. Although, there could potentially be other stories told in the same world, with some of the same characters!

What part of the story came to me first when the idea of A Call For Blood came to be?

The first scene I ever imagined for this story was actually the first chapter. It orginated from a dream I had when I was much younger and began as Keith and Camille's father trying to kill the King during a parade.

What was the creation process like for A Call For Blood, in regard to the inspiration, brainstorming, outlining, etc?

I only began seriously writing this story in June of 2023. Before that, the entire book was simply different chunks of random scenes scattered throughout my Google Drive. When I started seriously writing, that is when I finally sat down and begun to write as much as I could before I hit a point where I needed an outline. Once I had an handwritten outline, I loosely followed it until I hit the final chapter.

What inspired me to write in general? And specifically, A Call For Blood?

Since I was little, I've always written stories. In the summer of 2023, I had just graduated high school and didn't have anything else planned for my break, before I went to college. I sat down and decided, why not? I created an Instagram account for my writing to hold myself accountable and fell in love with it. A Call For Blood was one of the story ideas that most often came back to me during my periods of wrting when I was a kid and it's the story that resurfaced again as I wanted to start getting serious about my writing.

How many years in the making has this story been?

My first document I ever created for anything A Call For Blood related was in November of 2019, almost exactly five years before its release. The story began under the title of "Tinder" than, once younger me realized that's the name of a dating app, it became "Kindling".

What inspired me to write a sibling relationship?

Since the beginning, Keith and Camille have always existed and so has the unbreakable bond between them. I have a great relationship with my family, especially my siblings and I think strong family bonds aren't written about enough. Hence, Keith and Camille, a pair of siblings who will do anything to protect each other.

What's my favorite scene in the book?

This is such a hard question! Chapter 42 and 43 were fun chapters to write and is where things really start to get wild. Chapter 36 makes the romantic in me happy (if you know, you know). Although, the end of Chapter 46 might have to take first place... again, if you know you know!

Who is my favorite character?

This question is like asking a mom to pick between her children. I love Keith and getting to watch him stand up for what he believes in. Amaia is probably most like myself and I feel like Miles and I would be best friends.

Who was the hardest character for me to write?

Hands down, it was Camille. She took forever for me to get a good feel for and she's such a complex and emotional character. Despite her being the most challenging, she's also probably my favorite character that I wrote. Her dynamic with everyone and the role she plays is irreplacable.

What was my go-to song while writing A Call For Blood?

Surprisingly, it was not anything Taylor Swift. (I'd start singing instead of writing). Despite my story having nothing to do with pirates or the ocean, the Pirates of the Carribean soundtrack is what I would consistently have playing as I wrote.

Would you like to see an animated version of this series once you're finished with the books?

This would be awesome! Along with hitting a bestseller list, seeing my stories made into any kind of film would be absolutely mind blowing. The day that happens will be like a dream come true!

How long have I been writing? Has it been something I've done since I was little?

I think in either Kindergarten or First Grade was when I began putting the stories in my mind on paper. Distinctly, I remember writing and illustrating a story about a frog and stapling the papers together. I have stories in my Google Drive dating back to 2013, when I would have been nine. But it wasn't until midway through high school that I started to wonder if I could ever publish one of my many story ideas.

Am I a plotter, pantser, or a little bit of both?

I consider myself a plotter who likes to consistently go off outline! I like having an idea of where the entire story is going but try not to hold myself to a strict, no wiggle room plotline. I've tried just writing and always end up needing some kind of outline.

What's my favorite part of the writing process?

Honestly, I think I love every step that goes into creating, fine tuning, and finishing a novel. Although, I think if I could eradicate some step, I'd choose outlining. I wish I could just envision the entire story without having to take the time to write down and visualize the entire plot.

Who's my biggest writing inspiration?

I think the author/book series that really kickstarted my "writing career" was the Percy Jackson series by Rick Riordan. The amount of old story ideas I have incorporating some kind of old mythology or made-up gods is outstanding. J.K. Rowling, Suzanne Collins, Veronica Roth, and Christopher Paolini are all people I inspire to be like, especially Paolini who was a successful writer at such a young age.

More recently, as I've begun my self-publishing journey, Amanda Auler and Kayla Ann have been my greatest inspirations.

What was my favorite and least favorite part of self-publishing my book?

For a while, I bounced between self-publishing or pursuing the traditional route. When I made the decision to self-publish, one of the things I was most sad about losing would be the likelihood of my physical copies being in bookstores. While it's not impossible, my book will likely never be in Target or Walmart. However, I did not want to lose my creative control.

For instance, I was able to design and format my own book, launch a Kickstarter with some awesome merch, and create my very own book cover. To me, that creative control is my favorite part about self-publishing and allows me to have the final say in every part of my book.

What advice would I give someone who is thinking about starting the process of writing a book and self-publishing?

First off, know that it's not going to be easy. It's not going to be quick. You can't rush it and you can't cut corners if you want your story to be the best that it can be. But every moment of work and effort that goes into it is entirely worth it.

So, if you're writing, keep doing it. Find a way to hold yourself accountable with other writers. Think about your story and fall in love with the plot and characters, no matter what anyone else thinks about it. Specifically in the world of self-publishing, connect with other authors and writers! We aren't doing this alone and the wealth of information from the incredible people I've met since writing has been vital for me getting from an idea to publication.